To LORETTA & TONY

WITH LoVE,

Kurt

LIFE OF A
HOLOCAUST SURVIVOR

AUTHORS & ARTISTS
PUBLISHERS OF NEW YORK

NEW YORK

Authors & Artists Publishers of New York
3 Kimberly Drive, Suite B
Dryden, New York 13053 USA
www.IthacaPress.com

Cover Design   Gary Hoffman
Book Design   Gary Hoffman

Manufactured in the United States of America

9   8   7   6   5   4   3   2   1

Library of Congress Cataloging-in-Data Available
Ladner/ Kurt   Holocaust, World War II, Second World War History

ISBN   978-0-9815116-8-9

First Edition   Printed in the United States of America

www.KurtLadner.com

LIFE OF A
HOLOCAUST SURVIVOR

Kurt Ladner

The United States Consitution

Amendment 1: Freedom of Religion, Press, Expression Ratified December, 15 1791

Congress shall make no law respecting an establishment of religion, or prohibiting the free exercise thereof; or abridging the freedom of speech, or of the press; or the right of the people peaceably to assemble, and to petition the Government for a redress of grievances.

Note to the reader:

This book is a personal, autobiographical account written by the author who lived it. It is his memory of the events as they happened to him. There has been historical discrepancy over events that should be irrefutable as reported and remembered by those who lived them, witnessed them, and recorded them.

You are a voluntary reader, and no facts or opinions are being forced upon you. If you do not agree with or are negatively affected by the contents in the book, you may close it. This book is a firsthand account of the experience of a Holocaust survivor, and it is published under the First Amendment Rights of the Constitution of the United States of America.

Please grant this author his right, as detailed in the first amendment to the U.S. Constitution.

I have known Kurt Ladner since I began my work as President Clinton's Special Representative on Holocaust Issues and learned about his remarkable courage and dramatic Holocaust story. In his book, he has movingly and compellingly told this story for the whole world to read. This should be required reading for everyone wishing to understand the personal trauma through which Holocaust victims went. Kurt Ladner is an inspiration to us all.

Stuart E. Eizenstat

former U.S. Ambassador to the European Union, Under Secretary of Commerce, Under Secretary of State, Deputy Secretary of the Treasury, and Special Representative of the President and Secretary of State on Holocaust-Era Issues (1993-2001)

I f you want to learn what life was like for a young Viennese Jew before, during, and after the Holocaust read this book. I have known Kurt Ladner since before Hitler took over Austria, I knew him in Theresienstadt, and after the war in Vienna and then in the US. I know first-hand about life in Auschwitz and in other concentrations camps, about what it was like coming back to Vienna from the camps and then starting a new life in the US. I can testify that Ladner's account of his experiences is both accurate and typical of the experiences of the small number of other young Viennese Jews who were fortunate enough to survive the Holocaust in Europe. A valuable and highly readable addition to the Holocaust literature.

Fred Sterzer, Ph. D.
President, MMTC Inc.
Princeton, NJ

This is a book about hope and resilience. Kurt Ladner lived through a time when more than six million Jews perished in Europe. Shipped out of his native Vienna in 1942 he spent the war years at Terazin, Dachau and Auschwitz. He entered the Holocaust as a strong teenager with job skills and athletic ability. He left a near skeleton. He survived because of his own skill, the goodwill of many people and either luck or Divine Providence. Perhaps his survival can be attributed to all that. For sixty years following World War II, Ladner has tried to heal and live.

As a child, Ladner was blessed with a loving, loyal, hardworking family. His love for that family survived the horror they lived. As a boy, Ladner was talented enough to earn money singing in his community's temple, and we learn that he was an agile soccer player whose athletic skill later becomes a negotiating point during his imprisonment. When the police pulled his family from their apartment, young Ladner was taken into a neighbor's home. He remembers her praying during the night. By morning his family was released. That night he escaped harm, but harm did come to his family eventually. Even when he heard neighbors whom he had long trusted screaming words in support if Hitler's war that scared and pained him, young Ladner did not realize the extent of the danger ahead.

The story offers slices of hope amidst the horrors of prejudice and oppression. Ladner says that writing the story of his life was "a cleansing of repressed feelings."

But while he wrote the story for himself and his family, he hopes others will see value in this story of hardship and survival. He balances the descriptions of loss with stories of valor. There are few other Holocaust survivors alive and willing to tell the story, but Ladner has written a book he hopes will make a difference.

His story doesn't stop with his liberation; the death camps were only a piece of his life. He wants people to understand that even in those camps, there was life. People lived and loved and found ways to survive. After the Holocaust, he moved to America, found work, married, and fathered two children. Today Ladner and his wife, Betty, live in New England.

Pat Desmond
The Milton Times

This book was written by my cousin, who is a great storyteller and a fine human being. Kurt's stories have filled the imaginations of us children in his family for more than 60 years. There have been so many afternoons and evenings when we have sat spellbound, transformed, terrified, and enraptured by Kurt's life and survival through three horrific years in Teriesenstadt, Aushcwitz, and then Dachau. Our reactions were very mixed, because Kurt's story is not simple.

In some cases Kurt's life was ravaged by Nazis. In some cases his life was saved by Nazis. My parents had a similar fate. After the Anschluss, my parents tried to enter Switzerland illegally. They had a visa to leave Austria, but no visa to enter Switzerland. When they arrived at the border, an SS officer approached them and asked them if they were Jews. They said yes, and he said, "You want to go to Switzerland." They lied and said "no, we're here for a vacation." He answered more firmly, "You must go to Switzerland!" and instructed them to meet two men that evening at a local bar. They were terrified, but they complied. They had no other choice. It turned out that the SS officer was in the underground and the two men led my parents to safety through a forest to Switzerland.

When I was studying for my Ph.D. degree in clinical psychology at the University of Wisconsin, we read Bruno Bettleheim's paper on how Jews had "identified with the aggressor," meaning that many fashioned their prisoner's clothes to resemble Nazi uniforms and became more fierce to their fellow prisoners than the Nazis were themselves. Bettleheim described how we Jews sank to the lowest moral levels and survived only by cunning and cruelty to their fellow prisoners. I called Kurt and told him about this paper. Kurt said, "spell his name for me," and went to a register he had. When he returned he said, "that man is a liar. He was never in Dachau." When I reported this to my professor he ordered me to be quiet and not challenge his authority or he would throw me out of his class. Years later I read an expose of Bettleheim that revealed a career of carefully constructed lies. Bettleheim had made it all up.

Kurt's story shows that we Jews, and also that we humans mostly rose to moral heights of self-sacrifice and care for our fellow prisoners. Some were not very good people, true. But Kurt survived through the care and kindness of others, through friendship and camaraderie. He also survived by caring for others.

Kurt Ladner is one of my great heroes. I am very proud of him, proud to have known him and to count him as friend, mentor, and family. His whole life has been about giving to others. As a salesman he helped organize the fiercely independent children's clothing salesmen into a guild, fine people who were being taken advantage of by manufacturers. His tireless efforts helped his fellow salesmen get a good deal, one with dignity. Kurt was a key player in seeing to it that Jews who were holocaust survivors got a good deal in compensation from Austria, who claimed maliciously that she had been Hitler's first victim. As Kurt's book shows, Austria welcomed Hitler with open arms, Nazi flags at the ready. Kurt is a diplomat. He worked with the Austrians and other members of the commission to ensure that thousands of survivors were compensated.

No one will ever forget the story that Kurt tells in this book. Every time I eat a fresh baguette I think of a starving Kurt having to transport a wheel barrel full of fresh bread to the Nazi guards, fighting his intense hunger and his teenage defiance. Eating that bread would have gotten Kurt shot. So he refrained. Every time I see a friend of mine in need I think of reassuring and being there for my friend, much as Kurt has always been there for everyone else in his magnificently triumphant life.

Read this book. It will change your views about the character of our tribe and of our species through one of the darkest times in all of history.

John M. Gottman, Ph.D.,
Author of The Seven Principles for Making Marriage Work

Preface

This is my story. I have written it as I recall having lived it. I have carried this memory silently with me, and only upon the urging of my cousin, Dr. John Gottman, and my children, Fern and John, have I consented to write my life story. This has been somewhat of a cleansing of repressed feelings. It was especially hard remembering my parents, brothers and sister, who so cruelly lost their lives to the Hitler regime and his murderous underlings.

As the sole survivor of my family and for my children and grandchildren to learn about my past, I have undertaken this difficult task. I suggested that many stories have been written about the Holocaust and the subsequent lives of survivors, and asked why another one? The answer came from my daughter and son, as well as John. Yes, stories have been written, but not yours. In retrospect, I would like to thank them for making me write and also thank my wife for her patience and putting up with my departure from the norm while writing this book.

CHAPTER ONE
1938

March 12th and 13th, 1938 were the saddest days in our house. My brother, Pepi, his wife, Berta, and some of their friends sat around the kitchen table engaged in deep conversation. They were trying to assess and comprehend what took place that day. I sat next to them stroking my dog, a Doberman that was trained by the Canine Corps of the Austrian Police, listening to their discussion. As an eleven-year-old, I could not grasp the seriousness of the situation.

Adolf Hitler and his German armed forces had entered Austria, not conquered mind you, just entered, to a tumultuous welcome. Streets were lined with thousands of people. Flowers were handed to the passing Germans, their hands raised high with the Hitler salute, screaming from the top of their lungs, "Heil Hitler."

I could not follow everything my brother said, but I did understand that they were planning to leave Austria. Neighbors came in asking for my parents, and my brother directed them into the bedroom. I followed them and saw my father almost glued to the radio, interpreting the events. The Chancellor of Austria had abdicated without ordering the Austrian Army and the Austrian people to resist the unlawful annexation of his country. My father said to anyone who could hear him, "This is the beginning of the end for Jews in Austria." He got up and walked past us into the kitchen to speak to my brother. He must have agreed with my brother's decision to leave, because he kept nodding his head in agreement to what was being said.

My brothers, Fritz and Hans, came home, telling us that gangs of Austrian Nazis, who had elevated themselves to positions of power, were roaming the streets, dressed in light brown shirts, matching caps and swastika arm bands. That evening, across from our apartment building at the headquarters of the Vaterlaendische Front, the party of the departed chancellor, huge signs and flags were being broken and ripped into pieces, then thrown crashing to the street. I stood at the window and watched it all happen. Our next door neighbor, who only a few months before let me raid his Christmas tree of chocolate and cookies, had opened his window next to mine, and in a high pitched scream called, "Heil Hitler! Heil Hitler! Sieg Heil! Kill the Jews! Kill all the Jews!" I ran to my mother, scared to my bones, telling her what Mr. Welleba was screaming. She said that she had heard and that I should not be afraid. I slowly returned to the window and saw swastika flags displayed everywhere. The Austrian people must have had these flags prepared in their homes for them to appear in their windows overnight.

My entire family was worrying about my married sister, Greta, and her husband, Abraham, who lived in the Second District. The word was spreading that Jews were being arrested and beaten and that it had started in the Second District and was spreading. It had gotten too dark outside for me to observe anymore so I sat down on my bed with my dog Tommy's head in my lap. My parents, brothers and neighbors were talking in muffled voices in the kitchen, when a banging on our door interrupted the conversation. Tommy started to growl. Another bang on the door and my dog started to bark. Men in Nazi uniforms entered our apartment, and one in a loud, commanding voice asked my father and the rest to follow them. By then, my dog and I had walked into the kitchen. I heard my father ask the leader, "For what purpose?" Then, in a threatening voice, the leader answered, "You'll find out, Jew," and grabbed my father's arm. At that moment, my dog jumped at the leader and bit him on the arm. With some effort, I restrained him and pulled him back, while my father ordered me to go back into the bedroom. Two other men entered, carrying rifles, and ordered everyone out. One by one, they all disappeared through the front door, and I was left alone in the apartment. I ran to the door, to the window, back to the door, but I saw no one. The commotion had subsided. I went to the window again hoping to see some hint of the whereabouts of my family, but there was no sign as to where they were taken.

I made a split-second decision to follow them. I slammed the door, left my dog behind, and ran down the steps. When I reached the second floor, I was intercepted by Mrs. Probst, who pulled me into her apartment. Mrs. Probst was a very religious Catholic and one who had not changed her values overnight. Once inside her apartment, she lit a miniature statue of Jesus in His mother's arms, surrounded by a Nativity scene and elevated on an altar. She kneeled and started to pray silently while holding my hand, glancing at me occasionally. Hours must have passed before we heard some commotion in the hallway. She went outside to investigate, and, when she returned, she told me that my family had returned and sent me upstairs. I ran up, taking two steps at a time, and into my family's apartment. Seeing my mother sitting on a chair, I jumped onto her lap and my dog jumped on both of us. Before I could inquire what the gang of Nazis did to my family, our next door neighbor again started to air his lungs by yelling, "Kill the Jews! Heil Hitler!" We listened to his ranting for quite a while. The screaming only subsided when his voice gave out, leaving him with only a hoarse roar. My mother, who also was very religious, said that I should not worry. "God will take care of our Nazi neighbor," she said. She then dismissed his existence.

Not until our Jewish neighbors came in did I learn what had happened that evening. All Jews were brought to an assembly station. Then, each group was assigned a certain street to scrape and scrub away the leftover campaign slogans of the various competing parties. My parents and three brothers scrubbed as a group on the corner of Wallenstein Platz and Wallenstein Strasse, diagonally across from where we lived. They had to especially remove the three-arrow logo of the Socialist Party. The soldiers watching over them screamed at them and ordered them around while they threw pails of water on my family. My brothers got kicked a couple of times by some hoods, who, under normal conditions, would not have dared to come near them. After a couple of hours of scraping and scrubbing, a uniformed German officer and a neighbor from another building passed my family while they were on their knees and soaking wet. The neighbor said to the German officer, "Not Mr. Ladner and his family." The officer then ordered my father to get up and to take his family home. My parents could not explain the reason for their good fortune while other families had to scrub until the wee hours of the morning. The neighbor who walked with the German officer turned out to be a big shot illegal Nazi under the previous government. He subsequently was awarded an earned drop of blood from Horst Wessel, an ardent early supporter of the Nazi party who was supposedly killed by the Communists and was later martyred by the Nazis.

They even wrote a song about him, and it became the anthem of the Nazi party during World War II.

The first day of the Annexation had passed in turmoil for all Jews and marked the start of an unknown future, while the adoring Austrian public went to sleep hoarse from screaming "Heil Hitler!" and "Kill the Jews!" My father kept repeating how easily the German-Austrian merger was accomplished. Not one dissenting voice could be heard. The transformation of Austria over the first weekend was astounding, from a country that tolerated Jews to a country of hatred and viciousness, all of it directed against Jews. Vienna, the city of wine, women, and song, turned their camouflage into the real color of anti-Semitic slogans, leadership and a model of how to persecute Jews. It was easy to see where Jews lived, for theirs were the only windows not decorated with swastika flags and other Nazi ornaments.

That Sunday, our small apartment was crowded with people. My brothers, my sister, my sister-in-law and several of their friends as well as my Uncle Pincus, who lived with us, had gathered to plan how best to leave Austria. I could overhear several escape propositions. Some said we should go to Switzerland, some said Holland, while others said Belgium. The conclusion was that one of Pepi's friends would attempt to smuggle himself into Belgium, create a route of escape, establish contacts, and, if successful, would send all the information to my brother. After two hours, the meeting broke up with everyone agreeing to the plan. That was the last time my family was all together in one place.

CHAPTER TWO
MY FAMILY

Less than four months before the Nazis came to Austria, I was eagerly awaiting my eleventh birthday. December 26, 1937 was a special birthday for me because I was expecting to get my own bike. I usually received nice presents from everyone, but my own bike – that was special. I also received most of my spending money on my birthday, which I carefully kept in one of my mother's stockings, along with my marbles.

The only good things about winter were that I would go sledding or have a snowball fight with my friends and, of course, my birthday. Winter was not my favorite season because I could not play soccer outdoors. I did play in hallways, any large room that was available, or in one of my friends' large apartments. Soccer is made to be played with many people, but during the winter months, the best I could do was play one against one, and many times I kicked the ball around by myself. Some of the money that I would receive for my birthday would definitely go for a new soccer ball, and the rest I'd save until the Prater reopened. The Prater was the greatest amusement park a kid could wish for.

It was 3:00 a.m. when I reasoned all this in my head. Thank God my sister got married because I inherited her bed. Until she left, I had to sleep across the bottom of my mother and father's bed. I usually woke up around this time, because that was when my mother got up to go to work. She would walk out into the kitchen in her thermal long johns to prepare breakfast for all of us. Between slicing bread and making coffee, she got dressed. She wore several layers of clothing: her boots, made of a leather and wool, a heavy wool coat that almost reached the floor, a hat-shawl that completely covered her head, neck and shoulders, and gloves that were cut off at the knuckles and then tucked into heavy mittens. Over all that she wore a gigantic blue apron with deep pockets that had loose change jingling in them.

After her chores in the house were done, she walked several miles to the warehouse where she worked. It was always cold and icy with a heavy snow blowing. My mother owned a poultry stand in a market, which had to be set up and broken down every day. At the warehouse, she met Jack, her all-around helper, and together they loaded a large hand-pulled wagon with wooden planks, bottom stands and neatly stacked crates of poultry. Even in mid-winter the geese, chickens and ducks were packed in ice, and to handle them was not fun, to say the least. Once they were loaded, Jack strapped himself into a harness to pull this heavy load, with my mother pushing the wagon from the rear. It was several blocks from the warehouse to the Karmelita Market. When they arrived, they would hurriedly set up the stand, and she was open for business before 6:00 a.m. She would cut poultry into halves or quarters for orders placed already and for what she hoped to sell that day. She stood and worked in the cold until mid-afternoon. Then she packed everything that was left into the crates, chopped ice to cover the poultry and, with her helper, broke down the stand, loaded the wagon and returned everything to the warehouse, only to be repeated again the next day.

On those wintery days, I usually met my mother halfway home. It was cold and windy. She swung her apron around and wrapped her huge coat partially around me to protect me from the harsh elements. We used to stop at the bakery, the butcher or the grocery, and she always bought something for me that I liked. Fru-Fru was my favorite. It was a fruit flavored drink, endorsed by my idol, the greatest soccer player in the world, Sindelar. He was who I wanted to become, and I used to copy every move he made on the soccer field. With every purchase of Fru-Fru, you received a picture of Sindelar, and I had hundreds of them. Whatever my mother purchased, I helped carry home.

I loved my mother. Whenever I felt like hugging or kissing her, I did it without giving it any thought, but so did she, grabbing me to sit on her lap, talking to me about everything from her tasks with her to where we would go the following Sunday, her only day off. Always near my birthday, our conversation would veer to the winter I was born. I learned that my mother worked until one week before I was born. She had told my father that the time had come for her to stay at home and for my father to take over her work at the market. The routine was familiar to him, for he had done it before. Still, my mother explained the procedures again and again. The week before Christmas was especially busy. It represented a major portion of her income. She kept explaining to my father which cases of poultry to open first, because all previous orders had to be filled. She named customers who had to pay cash and others he could give credit. My father mostly nodded his head in agreement and understanding. Should he need help, my mother went on, just ask Aunt Lina, whose stand was next to my mother's. My father told my mother to relax and not to worry, that he could handle everything. Outwardly, my father seemed calm, but he was very concerned about the impending birth, because my mother was past her thirty-ninth birthday, and, at that time, that was old for having a baby. I am sure that I was not planned, because it was eight years since my mother had been pregnant. On December 26, 1926, under the supervision of a doctor and midwife, I was born in our apartment. I was the fifth child of Isacher and Fani Ladner.

My father's family had moved from Krakau to Vienna when my father was a little boy. He had two brothers and two sisters. His younger brother, while still a very young boy, fell off a roof and became permanently deaf and dumb. His other brother was killed during the first World War after being shortly married to my Aunt Lina. He also had two sisters, who coincidentally married painters and lived very near us. I grew up a small kid in a very large family.

My father was brought up in the painting business, and was a painting contractor who, during the spring, summer and fall seasons, was always very busy painting houses, apartments, and businesses. During the winter months, it was rare for him to get an outdoor job, hence the second venture of the poultry stand, which was a perfect supplement to our family's income. I don't remember my paternal grandparents. They either died before I was born or shortly after.

My father was a widower and had two children, my sister Greta and my brother, Hans. Their mother died giving birth to my brother, Hans. My father had a tough time, having to work for a living and take care of a two-year-old and a baby. His whole family was concerned. Everyone took turns taking care of the kids, while my father hoped to marry someone with substance.

My mother's sister, Emma, and my uncle Joseph (Joschi) happened to know my father. Uncle Joschi was a door-to-door salesman and always searched for merchandise he could sell to his clients. Several commodities were not available in Austria, but could easily be obtained in Hungary. So, he asked his friend, my father, to become his partner, smuggling and dealing in the black market. Back and forth crossing the Austrian-Hungarian border illegally, skilled and shrewd, bartering, they brought this merchandise back to Vienna and sold it for a substantial profit. Whenever these two talked about this past venture, it was like remembering adventure and danger.

On the way to the Hungarian border, the two usually stopped at my maternal grandfather's house to eat or to sleep over. That is where my father met my mother. They saw each other almost weekly, and, with the urging of my aunt, Emma, my father proposed marriage to my mother. My mother did not jump at his proposal right away because she knew that marrying my father meant instantly becoming a mother of two little children and taking care of the family. She loved my father, but her hesitation was justified, and, after a while, she finally agreed to get married.

My grandfather was a wholesale and retail butcher, and each of his five children, one son and four daughters, had to take care of one branch of his stores. My mother's was several villages away, and she often had to walk or ride on an oxen cart to her branch. My mother was a good looking young woman, and she could butcher with the best of them. She thought nothing of lugging a quarter of a cow, slinging it onto her shoulder, carrying it from a wagon into her store, and leaving it on a huge overhead hook. She did it with ease. When she informed my grandfather of her decision to get married, he gave her his blessing and paid her a share of the inheritance in cash. The whole family and the entire village, who were all considered family, eagerly awaited the wedding. Some were related through marriage and some were two or three times removed, but they were as close as any family.

My grandfather was one of the leading citizens of his town, Kobersdorf. Therefore, a wedding in his house was an occasion to be planned and chartered to its last detail. It was a very religious ceremony followed by a big bash where food and drink were in abundance and a Gypsy band played most of the day and night. As a newly married couple, they returned to Vienna and got an apartment in the Twentieth District.

My father brought his two little children home, and my mother started her new life as a housewife and mother. My sister, Greta, was three years old and my brother, Hans, was barely one. With my mother's inheritance, my father opened his painting and contracting business. My mother helped to solicit jobs and in general helped my father to establish himself. My mother was married one-and-a-half years when in December 1912, my brother, Pepi, was born. The family was growing. My father's business started to get very busy. More and more jobs came through recommendations, and he was able to subcontract some of his jobs to my uncles. Their working together enabled my father to bid on bigger and bigger jobs. My father and my uncles had formed an excellent relationship.

Just as my father's business was taking off, World War I started, and he was drafted into the Austrian Army. He served on several fronts, and during this terrible war my father almost lost his eyesight. He was sent to Czechoslovakia to recover, and slowly some of his vision returned. He remained very nearsighted and wore very thick eyeglasses. He was discharged from the army as a disabled war veteran and was given a disability pension.

My mother had a tough time during my father's stint in the army. She supported the family on a meager income and some support from her father. During the school year, she remained in Vienna, but as soon as school was out, she took her three children and moved into my grandfather's house.

When my father returned, he resumed his painting business, while my mother was awaiting the birth of my brother, Fritz. After the war, painting jobs were slow in coming, and my parents began looking into a second venture opportunity. After the birth of my brother, Fritz, in May of 1918, it took quite a long time for my parents to decide to open the poultry stand. My mother's knowledge of running a butcher store came in handy, and, without any apprehension, she took over this venture and, to a small measure, succeeded. It did place a greater burden on my mother. My sister, Greta, had to help with the chores after school. For the major cleaning and washing, my mother hired a young woman, who remained with our family long after I was born. My parents had to survive many hardships in business as well as having to provide for an ever-growing family.

The political landscape changed after World War I and the demise of the emperor. Political parties were competing to attain power, and not always competing peacefully. Jobs were hard to come by, and the real anti-Semitic trend seemed to manifest itself. Jews were denied government positions. They could not hold any positions of power, or even work for the railroad. Jews were always mentioned in a demeaning and negative way during the many campaign speeches. But somehow Jews managed to earn a living by opening stores, even department stores. Some became doctors or lawyers, but most learned trades. My sister, Greta, learned her trade working on ladies' hats; my brother, Hans, eventually joined my father in the painting business; my brother, Pepi, became an electrician and plumber; while my brother, Fritz, became a leather worker. With the devaluation of the Austrian money and the oncoming depression, our family just barely managed to stay above water. Jews, of course, were blamed for everything, and the confrontations between the Right Wing Party, the Socialists and, to a smaller extent, the Underground Nazi Party, sometimes became violent.

As I've said, I was born December 26, 1926, eight years after my brother, Fritz, arrived in this world. My birth inconvenienced my mother at her busiest season.

My mother did not return to her place of business until my sister, Greta, was drafted to full-time household duties and to take care of me. My earliest recollection as a child was a time I was sick. My bed was pushed into the kitchen near the stove to keep me warm. My sister often came over to fuss with me and to kiss me, but I swung my little fist and hit her in the eye. I remember looking in bewilderment as tears ran down her cheek.

In my early childhood, I also remember my family coming home from work, but I never saw them leaving in the morning. Not until much later did I notice that everyone left at different times. My mother was the first to leave, then my father and my brother, Hans, and a bit later my other two brothers. This stagger system was almost a must, for we only had a three-room apartment. There was only one water faucet in the hallway, and we shared it with the other tenants on the floor. Two of the families shared the toilet, also located in the hallway. I believe that only one or two apartments had their own bathroom, and they were the richer tenants. We had to store water in cans for drinking and washing. The drinking water was in a white enamel bucket with a spout and a ladle. In the other buckets, we stored water for washing purposes. We had two wash basins, one for washing our hands and face and a very large one to wash everything else. Once or twice a week, we went to a bathhouse for a hot bath, which only cost a few Groschen.

My sister, Greta, who took care of me during the week from morning until my mother came home from work, was a softy – a pushover. Anything I wanted I could get from her. When it was possible, she took me to the park, watched me play soccer even as a toddler, took me to movies, for walks and occasionally for ice cream. I also left my apartment by myself to visit my friend one floor below us. I must have been three years old when my friend and I walked alone to the little Danube, which we had done before without any mishaps. From the bridge, we could watch little boats go by, watch people sun themselves, or we could hang around the fruit stands and watch them sell fruit and vegetables. We then decided to walk down to the water's edge. We slid down the embankment where little boats were anchored. I asked my friend to jump into one of the boats. While I was preparing to take the leap, unfortunately, the boat tilted. I lost my balance and fell into the water, which carried me a distance downstream. A ferryboat captain thought he saw something unusual floating in the water. He took a pole, which had a hook on the end, and caught me by my suspenders, pulling me into his boat. Surprised to see a young child and still breathing, he turned me over to the police. The officer wrapped his coat around me. Apparently, I must have told him who I was and where I lived, because he carried me in his arms to my building. The word must have spread about what had just happened, because the next thing I saw was a frantic woman, my mother, looking ready to beat me. The policeman stopped her and told her that I was all right, to put me to bed and keep me warm. If the captain had not seen me floating on the water, the little Danube would have deposited me into the big Danube and on to the Black Sea, and I would have been long gone. Thereafter, I became water shy. People were always talking about it. I had to promise never to go near the water again without supervision.

It was not easy to keep this promise, because we used to picnic at the old, (or "big"), Danube. My mother prepared enough food for the entire family and my brothers' friends – pieces of roast goose, cucumber salad, boiled eggs, bread and fruits and usually some kind of pastry. Sodas and pickles were sold by vendors, and, on these outings, my father was generous with money. I always looked forward to these outings. They were happy times for me. The hottest soccer games took place then. The big guys chose sides, and I was always left standing until my brothers said, "He is a little kid – give him to us as a throw-in." I was probably five or six years old then. But even at this early age, I was a very good soccer player and was a thorn to the opponents. As I got older, I was no longer considered a throw-in, but a chosen side player. Older soccer pros and future pros participated in these matches, and they preferred these games to the ones played in the stadium. I played, ate, and sunned myself, but I never went in or near the water until my brothers, Pepi and Fritz, took me. One grabbed my feet, the other my arms and they started to swing me in the air. Swoosh one, swoosh two, swoosh three and they let go of me, throwing me into the deep water. They were right near me, urging me on to swim, and I did. I swam my heart out. I think I knew all along how to swim, but was scared to go near the water because of what had happened before when I fell in. My brother gave me additional swimming lessons, and I became a water rat. I swam mostly in the little Danube. The big one was more of a challenge. It was against the law to swim in the little Danube, but a lot of people violated this law, especially in the summertime. We used to take our clothes off, storing them at a chosen place downstream, so that we could sun ourselves. We then walked a distance upstream, jumped into the water and swam until we reached our clothing. We repeated this several times. The current was not very swift, but it carried us downstream rather quickly, especially since we were young kids. So, our marches upstream got longer and longer. Boy, did we have a good time!

My father was a short, stocky man, and, despite his war injuries, he was a very busy and hard worker. He was so strong that he could lift a large barrel full of paint and not even breathe hard. Because of his poor eyesight, while painting, stenciling or rolling patterns, he often missed spots or misapplied them, and he often has to pay a second visit to his clients. He was a great father, a frustrated opera singer who possessed a beautiful tenor voice. A collector of recordings of great tenors and famous cantors, such as Caruso, Gili, Volpi, Schmidt and Tauber, and Cantors Rosenblatt and Kwartin, my father was the driving force behind me becoming an alto soloist in two different temple choirs. He always made me sing duets with him of chants that he taught me. He knew every opera, every aria and every chant that cantors perform. We sang in harmony, and he was so proud of me when I could hold my own, because I was barely six years old. He and I listened for hours to old and new recordings on a very old gramophone that he had to crank every couple of minutes. He was my father and pal until it interfered with my soccer playing. Then all bets were off. He was an enthusiastic soccer fan and took me to many Hakoah games. His interest in his wife, daughter and four sons was limitless. He was a patient parent, supportive of his children in their endeavors and free with pocket money, even when he had little for himself. It was easy for me to get extra money for an ice cream cone or a kokus kuppel (coconut layer tart). Movie money I had to earn by performing various chores. He was a great companion on outings; he carried me on his back, whether I was tired or not. My father was not a disciplinarian, except on rare occasions when he said, "I mean it," and we all knew when he meant it. He read two newspapers from front to back every day. Politically, he was an active social Democrat, working in the lower echelon of the Party performing the nitty gritty of necessary labor. He was an early alarmist about Adolf Hitler but did very little about it. He was a conversationalist at gatherings that took place weekly with relatives and friends. He was a hugger and a loud kisser. When he kissed my cheek it reverberated throughout the house. He had a shot of slivovitz every day and an occasional glass of wine or beer in his favorite Gasthaus. His relationship with my mother was both visible and private: he would openly hug and kiss her in front of everyone, but oftentimes they stood beside each other engaged in quiet conversation.

My mother was the youngest of the Hacker girls, born in Kobersdorf, Austria. She was a good looking, twenty-three-year-old when she married my father. As a businesswoman and mother of five children, she more than managed her time working six days a week in her business and the rest of her time engaged in chores concerning her family. She was a gentle mother, yet tough at the same time. If I did something wrong, she dished out the punishment, and if she could not handle or catch me, she ordered my brothers to discipline me. She handled the finances of the family, and she made everyone save some portion of their earnings. She was quite the opposite of my father. She loved current, popular music and operettas, and she also loved to sing contemporary hits. She was more than the matriarch. She held everything together and was a smart family guide without being bossy. My mother had sayings pertaining to every situation. When my father had to climb up three flights of stairs because he forgot something, she used to say, "If you haven't got it up here," pointing to her head, "then you better have strong legs." When my brothers went on dates, again pointing to her head, she said, "Let the big head do the thinking, not the other one." To my sister, an avid reader, she said, "Reading should not be all consuming, but if you must read, do it outdoors. At least you get fresh air, and I don't have to chase you from corner to corner." Her favorite activity was going on outings with the family, despite all the preparing she had to do for so many of us. She was a great cook, and when she was complimented, she would always refer to her sister, Aunt Adele, as the greatest and best cook in the world. She was the one everybody came to with their problems. Not just our own family, but also most relatives and friends. She was a problem solver, and when she could not solve it, she made it seem as if she had. She was a very religious person, saying she had a close and believing relationship with God. I had seen her pray silently by herself. She was unhappy that she had to work on Saturdays, but it was the busiest day of the week, and it represented half of her weekly income, which the family needed. When I was sick, she took care of me and eased the hurt; she could bring comfort to anyone is discomfort. She held, hugged and kissed me, and nothing else mattered except for me feeling better. She was like that with all her family and all of us felt better when she took care of us.

During the summer, the entire family would go to the Prater, the major amusement area in Vienna. I would go on a few rides and watch a few side shows with barkers encouraging us to go inside. We usually wound up in one of the three coffee houses along the Hauptallee, the main road through this area. We ate and drank, spending time waiting until the variety shows at Leicht's started. If there was a soccer game at the nearby stadium, I threw tantrums until someone took me to the match. It was usually one of my brothers who was chosen to take me, and he was not very happy to miss all the performances at Leicht's theater.

CHAPTER THREE
THE CHOIR AND SOCCER

When I was six or seven years old, my father took me to the Kaschel Temple for an interview with Cantor Kreitzstein. My father felt that I should be hired to join the sizable choir. Cantor Kreitzstein asked me to sing anything I knew. I sang some chants that my father had taught me, and I was hired on the spot. I was the youngest member. I had to rehearse for a long time. Finally, they gave me a robe and a hat, and I was told that as of the coming Friday, I would actually be part of and participate in the evening services. I also received a salary of a few shillings, and it was the start of my working life.

I sang in the Kaschel Temple as an alto for a while when a Mr. Riseman, the Choir Master of the large Klucki Temple, heard me sing and suggested that I see him the following week. When I told my father, he grabbed me, hugged and kissed me and asked me not to miss this appointment. I sat in the choir section above the main floor synagogue waiting for Mr. Riseman to appear. I thought that it would be a meeting of the two of us, but the entire choir and two cantors were present. They were to rehearse various changes in the repertoire. Mr. Riseman finally asked me to run through the scale, which he first played on a good sized organ. My tryout lasted only a few minutes, and he said that he would like me to join his choir. My father had already given me orders that if Mr. Riseman wanted me to join his choir, I must accept. I did, of course, and it would prove to be a very important event in my life.

I knew most of the younger boys in the choir, but I didn't really know the older boys or the adult singers. To go to rehearsal twice a week and to sing on Fridays, holidays and occasionally for Saturday and Sunday weddings was no easy task, especially at such a young age. Even though I earned more money, I did not look forward to going to the temple. The Christian kids in the neighborhood were always waiting for us as we came and left the temple, to chase and beat us up. We always had to fight and run and hide behind the grownups for protection. The gang's leader, a tough kid from the Hanover Gasse, and his cohorts used to hide in doorways of adjacent buildings, and as soon as we appeared they would jump us. Each time, more and more of them participated in beating up Jewish kids.

After a very scary episode, when one of the gang pulled a knife, I told my brothers that I did not want to sing in the choir anymore. Half talking and half crying, I explained what had been happening. The following week, I walked out from the synagogue, looking carefully in every direction. Seeing no one, I started to run toward the Wallenstein Strasse. Out of nowhere, gang members appeared and started the chase. I was almost in their clutches when my three brothers and two of their friends also appeared out of nowhere. They grabbed a couple of gang members, including their leader. My brother, Fritz, said to the gang leader, "Now look, this is my brother," putting his hand on my shoulder. "I am going to hold you responsible for the welfare of my kid brother. Should anything happen to him, we will come after you. So, spread the word to your gang buddies, not to get out of line." He made him repeat that he understood, and then we slowly walked home. I looked at my brothers starry-eyed, with so much pride. How did they manage to be here during the week? I was so happy I could have burst.

That single incident started my freedom. I walked right through the Christian boys' hostility as if the ocean was parting. It was a great feeling not to be chased and always fighting older boys or being harassed and called a dirty Jew. Some of my friends were not that lucky and some got hurt badly. The irony was that the leader of the gang and I played soccer on the same team, and we became, not friends, but friendly. Even in the early 1930's, it was no picnic being Jewish.

From the first grade on, there was competition between a kid and me as to who was the strongest kid in class. He and I were very good friends and never fought each other so we went through school as the co-strongest. One day, there was a scuffle and kids were pushing back and forth. Either by accident or design, some kids pushed my friend into my back. I turned around and pushed him back, and a fight started. I beat him up in no time flat. I vividly remember this fight. After I pushed him back, he grabbed me in a nelson and then a headlock. He squeezed my throat so hard that I could hardly breathe. I was able to pick him up and roll him over me until he was behind me on the floor. His hands relaxed, and I turned and put my knees on his chest and my fist near his face. He struggled for a short time, trying to get free, but by that time I had a tight grip on him, and he just gave up. We remained good friends and played soccer together almost every day, but I knew then that I was the strongest kid in class. It was empowering, after having been beaten up so often as a younger child.

My school work was done late at night or early in the morning and always under duress and the threat of my mother's hammer-like arm. If I did not do my homework, my mother whacked me until I realized that homework was not as bad as going to the dentist. If my mother could not chase me, she made my brothers catch and hold me. I did not have time for homework – it interfered with my soccer matches. But I always got good grades, so my parents were forgiving.

We called the four corners of the Karl Meisel Strasse and Karajan Gasse our stadium. The greatest soccer matches took place there. We either played two against two or four against four. My team was staffed by the four best players in the area, Uhlrich, Goldstein, Sterzer and the youngest, me. We had not lost a game for a very long time. Our nemeses were the police and a janitor of one of the buildings. They chased us and confiscated our ball. The janitor was a short, fat, roly-poly man. Every time the rubber ball landed near him, he attempted to pick it up, but had a hard time bending over and awkwardly kept kicking the ball a little further with his pudgy foot. We laughed watching him try to grab our ball. There was always time for one of us to kick it out of his reach and run away. The police told us to quit playing in the street and always gave us one warning. If we continued and got caught, we got a ticket. One of the policemen used to ride on a bike and in front on an attached platform sat a huge police dog, while another one was walking the beat. Between the three of them, two cops and one dog, they managed to catch one or two of us every time. But we just kept on playing and worried about the consequences later.

As we got a little older, eight or nine, we played against other neighborhood kids. We had regular teams, with uniforms and soccer shoes and a number five soccer ball. We rented a local soccer field, the B A.C. Platz, for a few schillings, and the hottest, most competitive games took place there. A lot of youngsters graduated from the street team into the youth teams of the major leagues.

Playing soccer totally consumed my free time. When I got caught playing in the streets, I was gently dragged to my house and either my father or mother had to pay two schillings as a penalty. The officer always said to them, "When your son is older, he'll pay you all the money back because he is the best young ball player I have ever seen." He must have been watching us play before he grabbed one of us. It was not always me. My best friend, Ernest Sterzer, whose father was a lawyer, had to pay. It became a routine, and even the cops took some pride in our skills.

We had a beautiful park called the Augarten right near us. My friends and I spent a good portion of our youth there. Every spring it burst with flowers and thick foliage and after a rain, you could smell the fresh, soft earth. I tracked through the bushes, mud and all, in search for a new place to erect our hideout, always totally camouflaged with fresh branches and leaves. Several caretakers guarded this beautiful park. If any of them saw us walking in the grass or through the bushes, the chase began. They huffed after us, wielding a cane, and we ran in several directions, hoping they would chase either Ernie or me, rather than one of the slower kids. There was also a swimming pool for children, which we frequented every other day, alternating with the girls. We had more fun and enjoyment than anyone can imagine. As you entered the pool grounds, you checked your clothing, and they gave you a dogtag on a string, which you put over your head to make sure that you did not lose the tag, or you had to wait until closing time after everyone left to get your clothes back. We swam and played water ball until we were completely waterlogged. When we finally emerged from the water, the big tournament began. On the cement beside the pool, we painted a soccer field with leaves or grass. The goal was carefully measured and a dry, clean cherry pit was the ball. With the string from our tag, we defended our goal by stretching the double string across it, while the attacker tried to flip the pit with his string over the defense and score. These games were hotly contested, until the lifeguard made us clean the green markings.

Everything we did had a soccer connotation to it. We lived in a hotbed area of soccer players. Kids before us grew up to become major league stars, and some became all-stars. My brother Fritz's best friend, Walter Probst, became an all-star. After Sindelar's early death by suicide, Walter Probst, who lived in our building, was the one I looked up to. He took me to many of his games, and I just knew that some day I would be on that field playing for Hakoah, the only Jewish team in Vienna.

By now, I had also become a proud soloist in my school choir. We sang songs ranging from Lieber Augustine to the most patriotic songs Austria had to offer. I sang these songs with the greatest conviction and belief in my fatherland.

Once, I was standing in front of my house when a truck loaded with supporters of Dolfuss rolled by rather fast, with men shooting their guns in the air. I could not imagine what was going on, so I attempted to follow the truck when my father's hand grabbed me and pulled me into the corridor of the building. He ordered me not to leave our apartment until he said so. Through bits and pieces of conversations, I learned that a civil war had started. Buildings in the Second District and projects in the Second and Twenty-first were under siege. My family had friends living in the war zone where the Right Wing Party of Dolfuss was engaged in the fighting against the Socialists for the future leadership of Austria. This revolution was short-lived, and my father was very unhappy when they announced that Dolfuss would be the new Chancellor. He was in power only a short time before he was assassinated.

CHAPTER FOUR
SUMMERS IN KOBERSDORF

O ver summer vacation from school, my parents used to send me for the entire summer to my Aunt Adele or my Aunt Resi in Kobersdorf. There usually was a debate about in whose house I would be staying. I was a hellion at this age, never on time for lunch or supper. Every other day, my shoes had to be fixed, because I tore them regularly playing soccer.

Kobersdorf was a vacation village, and kids from Vienna usually played against the kids from the village. However, when we played against another village, only the best players from both factions were selected. I was always on the team.

On one occasion, my Aunt Adele complained to my Uncle Bernard, her brother, about my shoe situation. He then went out and bought me a pair of brand new Bally's, and, even better, my first pair of real soccer shoes. His son, my cousin Oscar, was a top prospect to play for Hakoah Vienna, but, after several tryouts, he was rejected. I was absolutely sure that he would be the first professional soccer player from our family.

My Uncle Bernard, who took over my grandfather's business, was one of the leading citizens. A good person who, with his family, gave of themselves for charity, it was not unusual to see several strangers invited to eat at his house. He tried to interest me in his butcher business, and I watched when they took cows or calves to the slaughterhouse. Everything had to be according to the dictates of the Jewish religion; in other words, strictly Kosher. Once in the slaughterhouse, my cousins swiftly tied the cow's legs, and then the man who performed this religious execution approached the cow with a razor-sharp knife and cut its throat. The poor cow shook for at least a minute in its own blood and then just lied there. Before my cousins could continue with their work, they tested the cow to see if it could feel anything and was actually dead. They would step on the cow's tail and roll their booted feet over it several times. If there was no reaction from the cow, they started to skin and strip everything. I must confess that I was very interested in this gory work the first time, but soon after, I declined to watch, somewhat revolted.

I did have to perform a service for my Aunt Adele. I had to go to Sauerbrunn, the source of a naturally carbonated water well, carrying two big clay pitchers, fill them to the top, and carry them back to Kobersdorf. To do that, I had to walk through woods, starting at Lampleberg and follow a well-known route to Sauerbrunn. Kobersdorf had this same water, but my aunt insisted that the water from the source was fresher, colder and better tasting.

When I walked into my uncle's butcher shop, he would always ask me what I wanted to eat. I told him either beef or schnitzel, and he would ask my Aunt Resi to cook it for me. My poor aunt! She never got out of the kitchen, between her own big family, me and the many people she served for charity. I am sure she could not wait until Saturday, her only day off, to go to the temple with the rest of her family. I loved my summer vacations, and they always seemed too short.

Back in Vienna, I was told that my sister was getting married. The following weekend, I met my future brother-in-law. He was slightly built, good looking, with a very neat dresser. I remember his Clark Gable mustache. He was a first-class tailor and pattern maker and worked for one of the leading custom tailor houses in Vienna. He was born in Rumania and had lived in Vienna for a few years. He did part-time work for my cousin, who was also a custom tailor, and through him met my sister. I interviewed him by asking if he liked soccer, going on picnics and dogs. His answers were yes, yes, and yes. He then was okay in my book. He asked me what kind of dog I had. I said sadly, "At the moment I haven't got one.

But I will get one soon." That is when my father let the cat out of the bag. He told the family that by the next Friday, I would have my dog. My father was scheduled to paint a kitchen for a policeman who ran the Canine Corp. It was a trade: a small amount of money and an almost trained Doberman pup.

CHAPTER FIVE
TOMMY

I could hardly wait until Friday. I kept nagging my father with questions. What color? How old? Is it a boy or a girl? I went on and on. Apparently, my father could not stand my pestering and said, "Come with me. I'll show you the dog." We went to the policeman's house, and there was the most beautiful, black, Doberman puppy waiting for me. The policeman handed me a leash and said, "You can take him home today." I bent down to hug the dog, and he licked my face and forehead. From that moment on, the dog seldom left my side. The policeman explained and showed us how obedient the dog was and the various commands. He suggested that I visit him over the next few weeks to finish the dog's police training. He was such a good dog. I wondered why did the police not keep him.

I named him Tommy. He obeyed every command, gesture and understood nearly every word I said to him, except when it came to food. At meal time he could not see, hear or feel. He only had eyes for his bowl. My mother brought home chopped beef she bought for the entire family's supper. A short time later, she wanted to prepare the beef but could not find the package. She sent me to the butcher store to inquire if my mother had forgotten to take the package home. The butcher said, "No. Your mother put the beef into the big straw bag." I returned home, and Tommy came to the door to meet me. The wrapping from the beef was still visible, hanging from his mouth. It took quite a while to calm my mother down, with her all the while threatening to give the dog away, but the rest of the family found the incident amusing. With everyone laughing, my mother slowly started to smile. My poor dog did not know what was she was saying; all he knew was that he had some supper.

When my sister opened the apartment door, Tommy would run out to meet me at school. He used to wait for a long time until I came out. The kids were afraid to pet my dog, but once I told Tommy it was okay, he let the kids touch him. I guess that was his police training. In order to meet me at school, Tommy had to cross major and minor traffic, and one day he was limping very badly. My father took him to a veterinarian who said that he must have been hit by a large object. For four weeks he wore a brace until his health was fully restored. Not even in fun could anyone wrestle or fight with me when Tommy was around. Once, my friend got his pants torn from his rear because Tommy was very protective of me. He even growled when one of my family members yelled at me.

The day my cousin Gretel got married, my entire family walked to the temple in the Second District. I walked ahead with my father, and a distance behind was the rest of the family. My father walked in very long strides, and for me to keep up with him, I had to make two strides and one skip. I was considering whether I should walk with my mother in normal steps, or if I should continue to skip. I turned to see how far back they were, while I kept on skipping forward, and as I turned my head back, BANG! Right into a steel lamppost. I fell to the ground, screaming my head off, and wouldn't let anyone look at my eye, until my mother sat me up and talked to me. It ended up not being a serious injury, but I would have a shiner for a few weeks.

The young ones had the honor of standing under the Torah's arc during the wedding ceremony. Standing there, my eye got more and more swollen with less and less vision. After the bride and groom kissed and walked out of the sanctuary, my Aunt Emma put cold towels on my eye and forehead, and the pain was reduced to an unbearable throbbing. However, I participated in all the kids' activities, not wanting to miss anything.

When my cousin, Lina, got married, I repaid my Aunt Emma's kindness. She was standing up making a speech of well wishes. She then attempted to sit back on her chair, except I had pulled the chair to the other side and my poor aunt fell to the floor, hurting herself. I made a flying leap through the open window to avoid being killed. After a short chase, my brother, Hans, cornered me. A few smacks and a stern lecture were my punishment.

My brother, Hans, was a very quiet man, unlike my other brothers and sister. The only reason for his quietness, I figured, was that he had to share his room with my deaf and dumb uncle. He seldom spent even his free time with the family. He visited various aunts and uncles on his own and never went to dances with my other brothers. He only went to waltzes. He danced the waltz like no other, but never danced or learned to dance the modern dances. His circle of friends was a bit older. Few came to visit us, and the only one I knew well was Walter Beyer. Sometimes I saw Hans with a very pretty woman in the Prater. He worked diligently with my father and never complained. He laughed out loud as if he were gasping for air. He was not an athlete, but he watched me play soccer when his time allowed. When I was short on movie money, he was always good for ten Groschen. I used to call him my silent brother, and whenever I did, he would burst out laughing.

My other two brothers were just the opposite. Pepi was a bike racer and an excellent skier. He was tall and good looking, with big shoulders from weight lifting and always in condition to race. He very seldom won, but biking and skiing were his passions. His girlfriend was a bit older, and, after an argument, she left Vienna and married someone else. He then dated her younger sister, whom he eventually married.

It was a cold winter night when my brother, Pepi, went dancing. After the dance, he found out that his winter coat had been stolen. Instead of taking the streetcar, he walked the long distance home, as usual. He was all sweaty from dancing, and it was a bitter cold night. Pepi became gravely ill. The cold had settled in his kidneys, and he was in the hospital for more than nine months. At times he was motionless and could not see. He lost a lot of weight and between my mother, father and Aunt Emma, an around-the-clock vigil was held at his bedside. The diagnosis was that his kidneys were shrinking. Then, one of his doctors tried a new cure. My brother had to drink a mixture of iodine and sulfur, if I remember correctly. Somehow, between the medicine, my father's prayers, my mother fasting every Monday and Thursday, and several visits to a wonder-Rabbi, Pepi got better. His vision returned, and he finally came home. He never returned to his trade as an electrician and plumber. Instead, he obtained a route delivering bread, rolls and pastries to various establishments such as grocers and restaurants. Before any one of us got up in the morning, my brother had brought home fresh rolls and bread, had his breakfast and then continued his work.

Pepi was always surrounded by friends. He and others had joined the Jewish Defense Front, a paramilitary organization whose members wore dark brown uniforms and carried rifles. Their main job was to guard synagogues during the high holidays. Before they took over these guarding duties, jousting and harassment, as well as vandalism, took place daily.

Once he began going steady with my future sister-in-law, Berta, my bike rides with my brother became less frequent. I then started to rent bikes and rode mostly with my friends. Our bike rides were an adventure. Rental time was between thirty minutes and two hours. Bikes had to be returned punctually. My buddies and I always tried to stretch the distance we covered and still be on time. It did not work all the time. When we returned our bikes a bit late, we argued with the owner of the bike shop until he gave in and did not charge us for the extra time. Excuses we gave were that the chains came off, or one of the kids fell and could not keep up so we had to slow down.

After the bike ride, we played marbles. With our shoe heels, we dug a small hole in the earth and made it as smooth as possible. We dug into our one stocking, a silk stocking from our mother, and then asked our opponent how many. We started slowly, six against six. One guy would hand me six marbles, and I would ask him odds or even. I then threw the marbles into the hole with some force (that was the rule). If two remained in the hole and the call was odd, I would start to push the rest of the marbles into the hole with my finger. If I could accomplish that without missing, all the marbles were mine. Should I miss, he proceeded to roll the marbles into the cup. Whoever rolled the last marble usually threw the marbles first for the next game. My middle finger was callous from pushing marbles. Sometimes, my mother's stocking was filled to the brim with these colorful clay marbles, and sometimes it was only half full, depending on my luck or skill.

We played a game called "Look at the Stars." We took a jacket from an unsuspecting kid and held one sleeve into the air, pointing to the stars. We told the kid that if he narrowed his focus, he would see several stars close up. While he looked through the sleeve, one of us got a pitcher of water and poured it through the sleeve onto the kid's face. Most of the kids it happened to, including me, laughed at the joke, but some babies started to cry.

We also played hide and seek. In Vienna, apartment buildings were locked after 9 or 10:00 p.m. Every family had keys to enter, but if you forgot your keys, you had to ring the superintendent's bell, which rang in his apartment. He then dragged himself to the front door and let you enter, for a couple of schillings, of course. During the day, we asked a kid to hide his eyes and count to 100 very slowly. We stood near the bell and asked, "Are your eyes shut?" If yes, we ordered him to start counting. Before he could reach two, we had rung the bell and ran away as far as our legs would take us. This poor kid was still counting when a raging janitor came after him. On rainy days, we stayed home trying to conjure up various ways to make mischief. My friend lived one floor below me and across the yard. He would often open his window. This particular afternoon, I launched a potato. My arm was less than perfect and the potato veered to the right and broke another neighbor's window. Once again, I was punished. My parents paid for a new window, but had I learned my lesson? Maybe...

My parents would ask me, "Where and who teaches you to do such outrageous things?" My standard answer was, "My brother, Fritz." They always laughed when I said it, so I kept repeating it. My brother, Fritz, found out about my saying, so he was after me. But I took a hook slide under the bed and by the time he could pull me out, my brother, Pepi, or sister, Greta, would come to rescue me.

Fritz and I were very close. The eight years difference in our age was of no consequence. I spent more time with him than with anyone else. First and foremost, he was a soccer player – not as good as his buddy, Walter Probst, but a pretty fair player. He had dropped out of high school to become a leather worker, first as an apprentice, then a journeyman and soon after a master leather craftsman. My brother, Fritz, was the best looking, the best dancer and the heartthrob of women. Girls were his first and last interest. He used me often as bait in the park or at the Danube. If he liked the looks of a girl, he would send me, a little kid, over to start a conversation. He then would come over to get me and rescue the girl from my bothering her. In the meantime, he took over with his smooth talk and would invite her to go dancing.

When my services were no longer needed, he would say, "Scram, kid." Fritz was a bit shorter than Pepi and taller than Hans. His hair was his crowning glory, and he took care of it, always perfectly cut and groomed. His dark hair and eyes were a striking contrast to his fair skin. Once at a dance, there was danger that a fight would break out because one of the local girls was cozying up to him while dancing. Her so-called boyfriend and his buddies were waiting for Fritz outside. My brother was lucky. At the same dance were two cousins, four of his best friends, and my brother, Pepi. The girl had warned him to be careful when he left. The dance was over and the first guy to emerge from the hall was Pepi, followed by the rest of the fellows surrounding Fritz. Pepi walked over to the girl's boyfriend and asked him if he had any problems, then he and his friends meekly backed off.

My mother used to say that Fritz gave her the most problems, until I arrived. When Fritz was about three or four years old, he walked with my mother and Aunt Lina along Wallenstein Strasse. When they reached the corner, my aunt said goodbye to my mother and kissed my brother, then proceeded to cross the street. She was almost across, when my brother pulled his hand from my mother's and ran across after my aunt, just as a streetcar was approaching. The streetcar driver had the presence of mind to apply the brakes and to drop the safety shield, so that Fritz would not be touched by the rolling steel wheels. The streetcar rode a distance, until it could come to a full stop, while my brother was rolling along the cobblestones, in front of the safety shield. After a long hospital stay and a long recovery period at home, skin started to grow again on my brother's raw body. My brother would point to a tiny spot on his little finger and say, "See this piece of skin? That is the only original piece that was left on my body." But he grew up to be a handsome devil.

When he was short of money, he could always con me into giving him whatever money I had. But when I needed extra money for a soccer ball or a movie, he would never let me down. I could always count on him. Once, I had saved my birthday money for my fling in the spring, the greatest amusement park in the world, the Prater. From the giant Ferris wheel to the rides and the side shows with clowns and magicians, it was a great park. I went on one of the rides and lost my wallet, with several schillings in it – a lot of money for a little kid. My friend and I looked all over. When it stopped, we looked on top of the ride, underneath it, and all around it. We retraced our steps but my money was gone. When the realization set in that I was in the Prater and broke, I started to cry. My tears were streaming down my cheeks like a waterfall. People stopped and asked me what was wrong, but I could not talk. I was crying and sighing and sniffing. Just then my brother and his friends appeared, and the first thing he asked was if I was hurt or had anyone hit me and what had happened. I then told him my sad story, still crying, trying to talk and catch my breath at the same time. I said, "And it was only my first ride, and I can't go to the movies." He put his arms around me to calm me down. Once he succeeded in doing that, he and his friends huddled together; everyone chipped in some money. My brother gave me more money than I originally had. I spent most of the money riding the Riesenrad, the giant Ferris wheel. I loved that ride. Fritz always looked out for me.

Going to the Sunday movies was my real passion. Mostly, they showed cowboy pictures. Buck Jones, Tom Mix and George O'Brien were the cowboys I liked. When I was short of money for the movies, I was able to obtain some money. In the movie house was a gambling machine. You put ten groschen into the slot that fell down to a flipper. By pushing down on the flipper, you could flip the coin into slots that could give you twice, three, or five times your investment. But, if you missed, you lost your ten groschen. When the coast was clear, I pulled a piece of shaven wood out of my pocket. When I put it under the flipper, the coin always landed in the center, and I won five times ten groschen. I usually could do it twice without being noticed. Once the other kids did the same thing, the machine was removed.

I absorbed all of Fritz's techniques with the girls. As little as I was, my friends and I often had girl visitors in our hideout in the Augarten. We did nothing naughty – just kissed and giggled. My education on girls started at a very young age from just listening to my brother and his friends talk.

After waiting almost one year since I had met my future brother-in-law, Abraham, my sister's wedding finally took place. After the ceremony, there was a lively reception with a band in the cafe next to my house. Everyone came: family, relatives and friends. I was told several times to behave. I was as well behaved as I could be. Besides chasing my cousins over and under the table and dropping cake into my mother's lap, I was an angel. My parents furnished an apartment for the newlyweds, and when my sister hugged and kissed me and tearfully said goodbye, you would have thought that they were moving to China or Africa. They only moved to the Second District, and I spent a good part of my little free time at her house. In Vienna, I was never far from home or family and friends. It was the kind of upbringing where home was whatever house I landed in that day.

My soccer playing became more organized, singing in the choir more enjoyable, homework was done on time, and, since my sister was married, I had my own bed. I could not wait for my eleventh birthday. I was promised a bike, and, if there was no snow on the ground, I could ride it all day. Pepi, then engaged to my future sister-in-law, Berta, bought matching touring bikes, and for my birthday, I received Berta's old girl's bike. I was somewhat disappointed. I had hoped for a racing bike. It did not have to be new – just a racing bike. The seat on Berta's bike was still a little too high for me to sit on, so I had to stand on the pedals and ride the bike uncomfortably at first. But I got used to maneuvering it, and it was great to have my own bike. My friends envied the bike, so I often let them borrow it. In addition to the bike, I received money from my aunts and uncles and some from my own family. The money went right into the marble stocking, and it would stay there until the Prater opened in the spring.

CHAPTER SIX
THE ANSCHLUSS

My family was not oblivious as to what was going on in Germany, the rise of Adolf Hitler and the persecution of Jews. I remember the joy my brothers and father felt when Joe Louis defeated Max Schmeling for the heavyweight boxing championship. I, myself, was awake early in the morning when my family listened to an old Eumig radio. The newsreels in the movies showed the Olympics in Germany and the fantastic achievement of Jesse Owens. All the Jewish kids celebrated his victory by hugging and jumping up and down.

Party candidates were politicking with nighttime marches through the city. Torch lights were everywhere. Each party had their own insignias. The Vaterlandische Front, the party of Kurt Schuschnik, had a TEED cross.

The Socialists had three arrows. There were swastikas and many more.

The 1938 New Year was only one day away. Everyone in the family planned Silvester (New Year's Eve). On occasions like these, I was left out with the excuse that I was too young. I did stay up until my brother, Hans, poured lead, which formed into all kinds of shapes when dropped into cold water. The result and interpretations of what these shapes were (everyone had a different opinion) was hilarious.

Like every year, I was invited by our Christian neighbors' to help them raid the Christmas tree. That week I had chocolate in abundance, not like a few weeks before, when Krampus and St. Nicholas scared the daylights out of me. Krampus was dressed like the devil with chains and switches, only to be rescued by St. Nicholas. My shoes were always polished for Krampus Day, awaiting glorious gifts. I did get some gifts in my shoes, but not many. The rest was filled with coals. I, therefore, looked forward to receiving chocolates and candy after Christmas.

I was eleven years and one week old. My holiday vacation was over. I attended school on Jaeger Strasse and was chosen to be a soloist in the school choir. Amazingly, my dog walked me to school and picked me up. I wondered what he was doing during school hours. I could not wait for it to be spring and to be able to play soccer again. My parents were talking about my brother Pepi's marriage to Berta, raving about my brother, Fritz's, fine leatherwork on behalf of Austria at a world's fair, and that they would enroll me into a gymnasium at the high school, but at no time did they speak of the possibility of Hitler occupying Austria, nor did anyone else. The days of January and February went by quickly, and, on March 13, 1938, our world caved in.

The word came from Pepi's friend, of how, where and with whom he crossed the German border into Belgium. Shortly thereafter Greta, Abraham, Pepi and Berta left Vienna for Germany to take the prescribed route to Belgium. I was told that they had to pay money to various men who guided them to and over an unpatrolled border crossing. A few days later, we received word that they were in Antwerp, and they urged us to attempt the same route. Hans and Fritz wanted to follow, but two of Pepi's friends got caught near the border and were thrown into jail. The Germans thereafter plugged all the holes crossing into the bordering countries.

From then on, the bulk of my family's activity was to explore ways to leave Austria. They went to the United States Embassy and looked through many area phone books in the United States for names like Ladner or Hacker. My family wrote many letters asking for help, for them to sponsor all or any of us. My brother, Fritz, did receive a letter from a man named Ladner, stating that an affidavit for him would arrive shortly. A couple of weeks later it came, but he was thrown into the quota system and had to wait until his number came up. He was told that it could take weeks, months, or years.

As the weeks passed, the situation looked grim for us. The confrontations against Jews started to escalate. My own friends started to avoid me at first. Then, there was a slow progression toward confrontation, and eventually fist fights. Most, if not all, became members of the Hitler Youth, who in their uniforms looked like miniature S.A. men.

Out of fear of retaliation against my dog for biting that obnoxious loudmouth in the arm on the day the Nazis came to our house, we were advised to give the dog away. My parents gave my dog to a butcher they knew who lived in the countryside and would give him a good home. Now, my pal and best friend, my chief protector, was gone. Some of my Jewish friends either moved or immigrated. The choir at the temple was disbanded, and I felt that my young life was entering very critical times.

The order was that Jews could no longer frequent the Augarten, among many other parks in Vienna. My mother's stand at the market was taken away. Jews were no longer allowed to conduct their business. Juden Frei (Free of Jews) was the motto of all Aryans. Jewish businesses and apartment buildings owned by Jews had to be relinquished, and all were taken over by Aryans. My father's business had dropped to nothing, but he was able to obtain jobs working for the Jewish community. This went from bad to worse. Fritz lost his job in the leather factory and he also got a job working for the Jewish community, retraining men and women as leather workers. He was an excellent teacher, and many doctors, lawyers and business people took his courses. Most of the students hoped to immigrate to somewhere and the leather trade would make them employable.

I no longer played soccer. All I did was go with my mother, who registered me with every foreign country delegate, hoping that I could leave Austria on a children's transport, either to England, Sweden, Switzerland or Belgium. England looked promising, but every time we went to inquire about the next departure, we spent the entire day standing in line. That's how many people were there with their kids.

The only constant thing in my life was my family. With everything out of control, the prospect of leaving them was not a comforting thought. It was very difficult to go to school. Hitler Youth gangs were constantly after Jewish kids. Earlier we could have asked for protection from our teachers, but they too abandoned us. Then the official order came from the Nazi Party that all Jews must attend a designated school, which was miles from my house. When this school became known to the Hitler Youth, we became their focal point. They made a sport of harassment and beatings. They waited for us before and after school, isolating one or two kids and beating them until a merciful rescue arrived. I belonged to a clique of boys who lived in the Twentieth District, and we usually walked in groups to and from school. We protected each other from attacks, and we also included the girls who attended separate classes. We did not always succeed in protecting ourselves. Some of us came home with swollen lips or a black eye, but we also dished it out, and the ones who we were able to fight seldom returned. More and more kids dropped out of school, and fewer and fewer remained in our group; therefore, we became very vulnerable. It became too dangerous and difficult to attend school.

This situation was short-lived because our next-door Nazi neighbor demanded our apartment, and we were ordered to move. Besides having to look forward to moving, there was no chance to leave Austria in the near future. My poor brother, Fritz, almost lived in the U.S. Embassy, constantly begging and asking for information about his chances for a visa. But wheels were turning very slowly at the U.S. Consulate.

I went alone to see Rabbi Murmelstein from the Klucki Temple who now was a leader in the Jewish community, but getting in to see him was impossible. I managed to reach the outer office just as Dr. Murmelstein was about to enter his office. In a raised voice, I called to him, saying, "Can I see you for a minute?" Either he recognized me or he saw a kid alone and waved his hand for me to come along. His secretary and guard let me go through, and, once inside his office, I told him who I was, that I sang in the choir of his synagogue, that I was registered to leave for England, but that my parents had no response. He assured me that day that a children's transport to England was being arranged and that he would try to include me. A short time later the transport left, but I was not on it. We were planning to move into my sister's old apartment when November 10, 1938 arrived.

CHAPTER SEVEN
KRISTAL NACHT

Kristal Nacht, my father and brother left for work early in the morning. Fritz and I left together to go to our schools. I was in class only one hour when school was dismissed, and we were told to go home and to stay home and not to loiter in the streets. On my way home, I saw a lot of activity. S.A. men, Hitler Youth and the police were scrambling and assembling on all major street corners.

When I got home, my mother explained to me what and how serious the situation for Jews was at that time. She explained that a Jewish man named Greenspan assassinated a German diplomat in France. Reprisals against Jews had already started in Germany and were about to begin in Austria. Just then, we heard a band of S.A. men marching and singing about drowning the Jews in the ocean. My neighbor and friend, Sigi Hudes, came running to tell me that the windows in the Klucki Temple were being shattered and that Jews were being arrested in the streets. My mother went pale worrying about my father and brothers. She looked at me, then pulled me close to her and kissed me, for she had made up her mind to send me to warn my father and brother, Hans. I am sure she did not make this decision lightly, but she figured a little boy dressed in lederhosen and a Tyrolian jacket might be safe and worth the risk. She told me where to go and to tell my father to take the shortest route home, or go to the nearest aunt. I was just about to run out of the apartment, when she said to me, "You come home by yourself, not with your father."

As I jogged up Wallenstein Strasse, I looked toward the Klucki Temple and saw Jews being herded and hit with night sticks. I also saw smoke near the temple (we found out later that they burned all the Jewish scrolls, or Torahs, and later the building inside). I ran by the Klucki street rather fast. What I saw was very limited but enough to make me very scared. Also, I was hoping that nobody would recognize me on the street. I saw people assembled, so I crossed the street and the Friedens Bruecke into the Ninth District to my father's job. When I got there, I was told that my father and brother had left about twenty minutes ago. I then went to the house where my two aunts lived, but my father was not there. I warned them not to leave their apartment, and, at full speed, I ran home.

I reported to my mother what I had seen in the Klucki Gasse and that my father and brother had left before I got there. My mother walked up and down, from the kitchen to the bedroom window, back and forth. She finally asked me if I had any problems in the street or if anyone attempted to stop me. I replied, "No. I ran almost all the way, and when I saw a few people standing, I crossed the street." She nodded with a faint smile and said, "Could you run to Fritz's school and tell him to come home?" I said, "I'll run the other way, so I won't pass the Klucki Temple."

I put my jacket back on and ran down the stairs. His school was known as a Jewish retraining place by the Nazis. It would have been easy for them to grab a whole bunch of Jews in one swoop. I had just reached the first floor, when I saw my brother, Fritz, coming up. He grabbed me around my waist and picked me up, demanding to know where I was going. On the way up, I told him that I was on the way to warn him to come home. I also said that our father and brother were still not at home. When we both walked in, my mother hugged us, and Fritz said to my mother, "It is very risky to walk in the street." The only thing we could do then was wait and hope that my father and brother would be home soon.

We sat around and waited and waited, and, for the first time, I listened to my mother thinking out loud, and I got really scared. She painted the worst scenario of what could have happened to my father. Our neighbors, the Hudes, came over and told us that they jailed the Jews and held them in the Karajan Gasse School. They also told us of cruelty and beatings. Many things we heard we hoped were only rumors. But everything turned out to be true.

It was not until late in the afternoon when my father and brother walked in. My mother immediately started to scold them and ask questions. Why had they not come home earlier? As my mother was talking, you could see what tension she was under and how relieved she looked when they walked in. My father said that they went to another job in the Second District. They were dressed in dirty painting clothing, carrying ladders and bags of brushes. They actually passed the S.S. and S.A. men and groups of Austrians who assisted the S.S. in capturing Jews, but no one ever looked at them or stopped them. On their way home, they saw the Leopolds Temple being destroyed and Jewish men being herded together. "But," my father said, "We kept on walking and thankfully got home."

It was a frightful day. We were sitting around, afraid to go near the window, wondering if the Nazis would come into homes and apartments to arrest Jews. We were up most of the night not knowing if relatives and friends had been arrested. None of us had telephones, and our communication with our relatives was through visits.

It took a few days for this episode to calm down, and Jews slowly started to emerge from their houses. We learned that two of my cousins and several friends of my parents and brothers had been arrested. It took weeks before we heard from my cousins, Karl and Hans. One sent a postcard from Dachau and the other from Buchenwald. The entire extended family was scrambling to obtain exit visas for our cousins. At that time, if you could show the authorities that an exit visa to any foreign country existed, the prisoners would be released and ordered to leave the country within the shortest period of time. For a great sum of money, their families were able to acquire visas to Shanghai, China and Yugoslavia. After a few weeks, they were released from their imprisonment. Once at home, they were depressed and totally silent. If they should reveal what took place in these concentrations camps, they would be arrested again. In fear of that threat, they did not speak at all. They left Austria just in the nick of time because, a short time later, all releases were canceled.

My parents and Fritz went into high gear searching for visas to anywhere, especially the United States or England. After many denials, you could not even buy visas for any amount of money. Everything was closed for Jews. The only chances people had were the ones waiting for their quotas to open. Fritz was told by the U.S. Consulate that his number should be coming up shortly. One of the secretaries said that he would try to move him ahead because his sponsor's affidavit was substantial. In the meantime, my parents inquired on a regular basis about the next children's transport, but to no avail.

We finally moved into my sister's apartment in the Second District. On one hand, I was sad to leave our apartment, and on the other, I was glad to get away from our hateful, dangerous, neighbor. I attended school for Jewish kids in the Second District, but very little changed. Different Hitler Youth were waiting for us after school. I used to walk with one teacher hoping that he would protect me, but these gangs just ignored him. I told my parents that I did not want to attend school any longer, and I gave them plenty of reasons why I should not. They agreed that I could get a tutor from the Jewish Community Center, who came to our apartment three times a week.

A narrow strip of park along the little Danube was designated as Juden Park, for Jews only. I used to go there almost every day to meet new Jewish kids, boys and girls, until it became too dangerous to go there. Nazis, old and young, used to come to the park to beat us for their entertainment. From then on, kids used to meet in each other's apartments. Even at our age, the conversations always led to how awful it was for us in Vienna.

CHAPTER EIGHT
BELGIUM

Some time had passed when my parents were notified that the next children's transport would be leaving in one week and that I would be on it, not to England, but to Belgium. My parents made the decision for me and wrote to my brother and sister in Antwerp that I would soon be coming.

I will never forget that week. I still can recall my parents' extreme sadness and how quiet my brothers were then. That entire week, I saw my mother crying and always wiping her tears when I came near her. She spoke to my father and brothers in whispers, and I was choked up and felt like crying myself. But how must parents have felt sending a kid, not twelve years old, to a foreign country, not knowing if they would ever see him again?

I spent most of my time saying goodbye to my aunts and uncles and to the Probst family, who told me that my dog was seen near the house and probably was still around. My dog had run away. I ran toward my former school and, sure enough, sitting on a grassy spot in front of a church was a very skinny, disheveled, unclean Doberman. I had to call several times, "Tommy, Tommy." He then came running in short spurts. He finally calmed down. I took him back to our new apartment, and my parents could not believe that the dog had come back. I fed him potatoes, which he had never eaten before, and he devoured a whole bunch of them. I then had to clean him, and he constantly kept coming over to me, and finally settled down next to me. My father immediately said that we could not keep him. We would have to find a better place for him. I was leaving in a few days, and I did not put up any resistance to my father's emphatic decision. My father returned my dog to the policeman who originally gave him to us.

The day of my departure arrived. I said goodbye to Hans, who had to leave for work, and I wanted to say goodbye to Fritz, but he said that he would come to the train station before I left. My parents and I arrived at the station. Jewish workers with arm bands were directing parents and kids. They gave me papers that I had to put into my coat pocket and warned me not to lose them. I was assigned a compartment and a seat. Once the luggage was stored, I jumped off the train and waited with my parents until we had to re-board. I received my instructions from my parents for the hundredth time, to write, to take care of myself, and how to take care of myself. I was told not to leave the railroad station in Brussels until Pepi's arrival. My mother kept on talking out of nervousness and to keep from crying. I kept looking around for my brother, Fritz, but he was nowhere in sight. Whistles started to blow, and there was a lot of shuffling of people. Some departing kids were preparing to climb back on to the train, and at the last minute, my brother arrived. I ran toward him. We walked silently for a short distance, and then he turned to me and said, "You are too young to understand the entire situation, but you must always remember what I am telling you now. No matter where you or I may be, it is our responsibility to save and to take care of our parents." He then grabbed and kissed me and left very abruptly without seeing me board the train. I returned to my parents and we said our tearful goodbye. My father put his hands on my head and said a prayer. We hugged, kissed, and cried, and I left my parents standing on the platform crying as the train pulled out of the station. I didn't know if I would ever see any of them again.

The train ride was uneventful. I kept looking out the window and saw beautiful scenery passing by, occasionally interrupted by swastika-flagged houses, which brought me back to reality. My thoughts went back to my parents. By listening to adult discussions, I knew that the Jews of Austria hoped that the Catholic Church would intervene on their behalf. I heard my father say,

"Cardinal Innizer will not lift one finger for us, and I believe that he is collaborating with the Nazis against the Jews." I heard him speak very often about his disappointment with the Catholic Church's tolerance of Adolf Hitler. I thought of Fritz telling me that I didn't understand, that I was too young. I understood that all Jews were in danger, that my Christian childhood friends were waiting to beat me up. Why? I was an Austrian; I sang the National Anthem in the choir and many other patriotic songs such as Andreas Hofer. I played soccer with them. I kicked the winning goal many times. I was a good friend. But I was a Jew.

We crossed the Austrian-German border, and once in Germany, we stopped for a short time. Occasionally, railroad personnel checked our compartment, while the train continued toward Belgium. At the Belgian border, we came to a complete stop and railroad personnel again checked the train, followed by the border patrol, who checked our papers. I had my papers prepared, but they never asked to see them. The last check was made by the S.S. They took a long time looking into compartments and finally the train crossed the border into Belgium. Again, we stopped, and Belgium border guards repeated the inspections and shortly thereafter, we were on our way to Brussels.

The train rolled slowly into the station, and I was already searching the platform for Pepi. I then scrambled for my suitcase and backpack, ready to get off the train. I jumped off with my backpack and someone handed me my suitcase from the train. My brother spotted me and ran toward me and I toward him, completely neglecting my baggage. I jumped into his arms and he swung me around and up into the air. He kissed my forehead, and, still carrying me, we went to retrieve my baggage. We walked to another platform to wait for the train that would take us to Antwerp. He asked me how our parents and brothers were. I assured him that they were all fine and that we survived Kristal Nacht without any mishaps. I asked about my sister, and Pepi said that I would see her later. My brother wanted to know if my parents sent any messages or if I had a letter. I then gave him all my papers from my coat for safekeeping. Pepi wanted to know everything and about everybody left in Vienna. I told him what I knew, about the 10th of November, about my cousins, and what Fritz had said on my departure. I then asked him where I was going to live. He explained that, for the time being, I would stay with him until I obtained a British visa, and then I would continue on to England. The train to Antwerp arrived, and Pepi said that within an hour we would be home. He did mention that he had to wait several hours for my train to arrive.

We pulled into Antwerp after a short ride and walked from the station to my brother's place, which was not too far away. They had one room in the attic on Van Larius Street. The room had a low ceiling and very sparse furnishings, consisting of a bed, a chest, one closet and a small table with chairs. A folding bed stood in the corner for me to sleep on. The floor below them had three rooms. Another refugee lived in one of them. There was a co-op kitchen and one other room, the diamond-cutting room. The owner and his brother lived on the first floor in a beautiful apartment, and their business was diamonds.

A few minutes after we got home, my sister-in-law, Berta, walked in. We repeated the hugging, kissing and questions, and she asked me if I was hungry. I had very little food since I left Vienna, and I said, "Yes, I am starved." She left to go downstairs, just as my sister and brother-in-law were walking up. I ran down a few steps into my sister's arms. She was crying and held onto me for a long time. I repeated everything that I told my brother, that the rest of the family were okay, and none of us were hurt by the destruction that took place Kristal Nacht. We all ate, and my sister and brother discussed how best to take care of me. I could not stay with my sister because my brother-in-law was a Rumanian citizen and therefore not considered a refugee. They had to live illegally in Antwerp, in a very small room, unregistered. My brother was an Austrian, and he was considered a legal refugee, legally registered and allowed to work, while my sister and her husband had to work secretly and were always afraid they would be discovered. I, of course, arrived in Belgium with a legal visa, which entitled me to go to school and receive support from the Jewish community for food and rent subsidy, among other things. My brother told me that the support I would get would be meager, but that we would manage. I received instructions as to what I could and could not do. If I visited my sister in her place, I had to be very careful that nobody saw me entering or leaving her house, or reveal the existence of my sister in Belgium. I was also told to be respectful to our landlord.

The next day, Berta took me to the Kaiserlei and to a movie. I was very impressed with the beautiful avenue and the upholstered seats and furnishings in the movie house. This country seemed solid and safe. After the movie, we joined my brother for a walk through the park, which was only a couple of blocks from where we lived. We walked around the pond and Berta said, "I'm chilly. Let's get back to the house." While walking at the edge of the pond, Berta pointed to some bushes near the water saying, "Don't ever go in or near the water." Still pointing to the bushes where a bunch of rats were running around, Berta said, "These rats give me the shivers," and she told me to be careful. We returned to our room, had something to eat and went to sleep.

The next day my brother registered me in school and at the Jewish Community Center. At school, a teacher took me to a room. He had my report cards that I had brought with me from Vienna. I was tested in a couple of subjects, and he assigned me to a class to which I had to go immediately. As I walked into the classroom, the kids looked at me as if I came from Mars. I looked different to them, dressed in lederhosen, a loden jacket with heart patches on my elbows, white socks with tassels, and shoes to match my clothing. The teacher said something to the kids, directed me to a seat, and continued to teach. I sat there like a dodo. The teacher and pupils spoke only in Flemish. I sat there not understanding one word they said. I felt totally useless. Then, the math teacher came to teach. At least I could participate. Fortunately, I had learned most of the math in Vienna. I did okay with the homework the teacher assigned. French lessons were even more difficult. I had to translate everything into German and then try to match the Flemish word. It was very hard, and it took a long time for me to comprehend. As time went on, it got easier, and I was able to converse in broken Flemish, because many words sound alike in German, but my head was swimming in foreign languages. In Vienna, I took French and English. Now, with Flemish, at times it got confusing.

I was able to make some friends who took me to the park where, for the first time, I met kids from Austria and Germany. They were playing soccer on a large asphalt corner along a fence. These refugee kids were playing against the Belgian kids, against each other or against other area kids. This corner in the park was what I called "the stadium" in Vienna – it was very busy, very congested and a fun way to play in the park. The kids asked me if I knew how to play soccer. I said, "Of course," and started to play with them. They soon found out how good a player I was, and I was immediately installed as a permanent player on the refugee team. I was the youngest among them, but I was as good a player as most of them and better than some. These soccer games became my passion, just like the games I used to play in Vienna. I hardly ate because, right after school, I took the shortest route to the park. Occasionally, we walked to a soccer field to play against other teams, but my time was spent mostly in the park.

One day, my brother asked me if I would like to sing in a choir again. I felt like saying no. Then, my brother took me to see Cantor Kreitzstein, with whom I sang in Vienna. He was glad to see me, but said that his small congregation was not the place for me to sing. He said that he would introduce me to the choir director of the largest synagogue in Antwerp. My brother and I went to see him, and he asked us to wait. When he called us in, he tested my vocals by having me follow the scale. I had to repeat, note for note, what he played on the piano. I could hardly read music, although I had to sing from a book in Vienna. I acquired a feeling of difference, how much higher or lower I had to sing, depending on which line or in between lines the note appeared. I knew what full, half and quarter notes were, but I could not read music from a sheet. What was very much in my favor was that I sang in a choir for six years and knew most of the chants. I was hired and the choir master, Mr. Gantman, told my brother how much I would be earning. My brother was pleased, and I started rehearsals the very next day. I became the alto soloist, and had many solos and several duets with Cantor Dim. It was a large choir with several sopranos, altos, tenors, baritones and bassos. The congregation liked me, and I really enjoyed singing in Antwerp.

Just as everything was going great, trying times began again. It was very difficult for me to understand. My sister-in-law, Berta, became pregnant and she turned into a very, very complicated person. She made my life impossible. When I was quiet, she would say that I was sneaking around, that I scared her. When I walked in a normal way I got on her nerves. When I walked or ran upstairs, she would say that I interfered with her rest. I moved my stuff to my sister's, just as they were preparing to move to a refugee camp (Marneff). My sister told my brother that she would be gone from Antwerp within two weeks. Her departure made it even harder for me. Walking to school or choir was a much longer distance, but I had no choice. After my sister left Antwerp, I slept in a different place every night. One night, I slept on a tailor's cutting table, which had to be vacated very early in the morning. Another night, I would sleep on the temple's caretaker's porch, or an elder's back room, the basso's apartment, or the choirmaster's ante room. I would alternate sleeping in four or five different places. I ate in a different home every day. I could not understand why I could not stay with my brother. He checked with me almost every day, and I would meet him in the park, but I very seldom went to his house because of my sister-in-law.

Between school, choir, homework and going from place to place, I had no time to play soccer. In order to play, I started to skip rehearsals and occasional classes. My excuse was that I had to move my belongings for that night's lodging and that I had to do my homework. Both were true, but I left out the important afternoon soccer games.

Instead of things getting more organized, they were getting worse. My choirmaster was not pleased with my lack of supervision and persuaded the basso of my choir to make me move into his apartment permanently. The basso, who was married and had a little baby boy, talked to me, and I accepted. That arrangement lasted only a few weeks. I learned that he had taken me into his house for the sake of his and his wife's personal freedom; I had to baby-sit all the time, before I went to school, after school, after choir, and most evenings. One evening, it was very warm in the apartment. The baby was lying uncovered and unclad in the bassinet when he started to cry. I walked over to pick the baby up, as I was told to do, and the baby peed all over my shirt and pants, and it smelled. The bassinet was soaking wet; I did my best to cover the sheet. Then, I put the baby back to go to sleep. When the parents came home they screamed at me for letting the baby sleep on a semi-wet sheet. I started to yell back, complaining about my shirt and pants and the smell. I think they had made up their minds even earlier that having me stay with them permanently was not a good idea after all. I am sure that I contributed to the situation by ranting and yelling. I was the busiest twelve-year-old in the world, absorbed with schoolwork, choir, and baby-sitting. In addition, I had to study for my Bar Mitzvah. Since I was the soloist in the choir, the congregation had planned a big shindig for that day. All this and not being able to see my friends or play soccer got to me. The confrontation with the basso that evening was a frustration I could no longer hold in. The basso took my belongings, put them into my suitcase, carried my suitcase down and asked me to leave. He closed the door behind me. It was past 10:00 p.m., and the night was very still. I stood there for a while, confused and hurt. I picked up my suitcase and walked to my brother's house. I stood there for a few minutes, tempted to ring the bell, but I just sat down and waited on the front stoop until morning.

The landlord opened the door. I walked up to my brother and told him the whole story. My brother sat erect while listening then said, "We'll have to change the way you live." My brother went with me to the Jewish Community Center and re-applied for additional financial help for me, and they granted it. He then asked my choirmaster for a raise on my behalf, explaining my situation, which was also granted. With the additional support money and my increase from singing, my brother rented a room for me that included breakfast. Now, I was totally on my own: my own room, my own responsibilities. All I had to worry about was food. I continued to eat every day in someone else's house. Sometimes I did not know whose house I was supposed to eat at or on what day.

Now, I could arrange my time much better. Right after school I went for my Bar Mitzvah lessons. Twice a week I had choir rehearsals, played soccer all afternoon, then went back to my room to wash and change for supper, came home and did my homework and I was done by 9:00 p.m. The lady I rented the room from did my wash, and very often I had lunch with her. I adjusted to my new situation and environment very well. Twice a week, I wrote to my parents, and I received three and sometimes four letters in return. In one of these letters to Pepi, my mother revealed that Fritz was sent to a Polish concentration camp, but she did not know where. My sister-in-law was awaiting the imminent birth of their child, and I was getting very well prepared for my Bar Mitzvah.

We were playing soccer one afternoon when two men approached my friend, (a terrific soccer player), and me, and asked us to try out for the youth team of a first division major league team. The youth team manager said that I was good enough to play for the team, but that they had an age limit, and I was too young. He expected me to return in one year and told me that I would not have to try out again. I was a strong and well-developed kid, and it was terrific to hear from the manger that I was good enough. That evening, I ate at my brother's house, and as I informed him of my progress, he interrupted me to tell me that he had heard from my sister. He said that transports to Central America and the United States were contemplating leaving from the refugee camp, Marneff, and that it would be a good idea for us to join them. My brother said that he would send me, and that he, his wife and their child would follow at a later date.

CHAPTER NINE
MARNEFF

Within two days I was relocated to Marneff. My brother put me on a train, and, when I arrived, my sister was waiting. Within minutes I told my sister about my tough escapades in Antwerp, especially about my sister-in-law, my short stay with the basso family and then, finally, about having my own room. I told her that I had very little time to say good-bye to all the people who helped me. I managed to see Mr. Gantman, my choirmaster, and Mr. Dim, our Cantor, and everyone in whose house I ate and slept. It was hard to say so long to my soccer playing friends, who urged me not to leave, but I told them that I had no choice. I had to do what my brother and sister thought was best for me. My sister had assured me that Marneff was a wonderful place for the time being and that our ultimate goal was to immigrate to the United

States or Santo Domingo. She further explained to me that if we could make it to either place, it would then be much easier to help our parents.

Marneff was a camp of mostly German and Austrian Jews. The place itself looked like a castle, or at least a very large estate, with ample grounds. A married couple received a room along the main corridors, and it was furnished to satisfaction. Boys had separate quarters in large dorms, individual beds and storage for clothes. Girls had exactly the same accommodations on the other side of the building. All of us ate in a large dining room, which was staffed by selected refugees. The camp was run by the Belgium government and the director in charge was a Belgian. There was a civilian security guard, also from Belgium, who made sure that we went to sleep on time. Kids had curfews, and more than once he had to raise his voice to quiet us down. He had a rough looking exterior, but was the nicest and softest enforcer in the world. He liked kids, and he liked his job. I don't know how he spelled his name, but he was addressed as Mr. Pisk. The director of the camp was a tall, lanky man who resembled Dolfuss, the assassinated Chancellor of Austria. When he walked through the building to check various items, he was all business. I never saw him smile or even just stand around. He was a very serious man.

The refugees performed all services in the camp. Teachers, doctors and dentists attended school, medical and dental stations. There was a carpenter and plumber's workshop, cooks and laundry attendants, and each person took care of his or her expertise. Under the director was a group of men and women assigned to running the camp. There were many talented people who made our stay very pleasant. We had shows every week, movies once or twice a week, serious plays and one operetta. Saturday nights there were variety performances, and I was always asked to sing, which was great because I could stay up beyond curfew and watch the rest of the performances. I acted in a play called Joseph and His Brethren. I played the role of Judah. I studied my lines, which I goofed up in rehearsal but recited perfectly at show time.

What I considered the most important place in this camp was the adjacent soccer field. The sports director was a former major league soccer player in Germany, to whom I gravitated during every free moment I had. He was an excellent teacher, and I learned from him a much higher plateau of soccer than I ever learned before. I did play with the kids, Austrians against Germans, but I mostly played with the grownups. One day a Belgian Army team came to us for a challenge match, and I was the only youngster installed in the starting line up. We lost, but I kicked two goals and the entire Belgian team came over to me after the game. They patted my back and rubbed my hair, (which I hated), congratulating me for the good game I played. Boy, was I proud. I enjoyed playing with better soccer players than me. They seemed to understand my passing the ball and, most of the time, were in the right place to receive my passes. Even at that time, I was told that I was a well-schooled technical player.

It seemed that I was finally in a place that I loved. I made many friends, boys and girls. We had parties. I had everything that I wanted in Marneff. A couple of months had passed, and my confirmation was approaching, but there were no transports to America or any place else. The older people became restless and in constant pursuit of exit visas. There was no country that wanted us. My sister and brother-in-law received legal residency to stay in Belgium, in any place they chose, and they decided to move back to Antwerp.

I was left alone again. A young couple, Rosita and Gustav Kohn, took it upon themselves to take care of me. They made sure that I attended all my classes, ate my meals and had clean clothes. They generally took over most parental functions. I liked them very much and never once violated their orders.

Shortly after my sister had left, I received a letter from her saying that our brother, Pepi, was very ill and was in the hospital. Enclosed in the letter was train fare for me to come to Antwerp. I immediately took the train. My sister met me and took me directly to the hospital. I entered Pepi's room and he looked pale and thin. I walked to the bed, took his hand, and he turned his face to me. With a faint smile, he asked me how I was doing and said he would not be able to come to my Bar Mitzvah. I told him that I would be okay, as long as he got better. I spoke to him about school, soccer and the real possibility that the children from Marneff would be going to Central America. I just kept talking and talking, but he had slowly turned his head and closed his eyes. He may have been listening, but I did not think so. My sister came over to me, put her hands around my shoulders and slowly pushed me away from my brother. Outside his room, she explained to me the seriousness of his kidney ailment and said that the doctors could only hope that he would respond to the treatments he was receiving.

We slowly walked to my sister's new apartment, and waited a short time for my brother-in-law to come home. We had something to eat, and they walked me back to the train station. My sister said to me emphatically that if there were no children's transports within the next couple of months, which was heavily rumored, that I was to move back to Antwerp and live with her.

I returned to Marneff, and a few days later I learned that Pepi had died. He left a wife and a new baby son behind. I was in correspondence with my parents in Vienna every week. My sister had written to them about Pepi, and I knew how my parents felt about his loss. Therefore, my letters to them were filled with cheerful drivel about my life in Marneff, and their replies to me were loving and hopeful. I learned nothing about the Ratzias and hoarding of Jews and the decaying conditions in Vienna from my parents. The real news, that transports were continuing to Poland and various concentration camps, I learned from my sister and the people in Marneff.

From my sister I learned that my brother, Fritz, was sent to a concentration camp in Poland. His expected visa from the United States Consul never came. All other countries and borders were closed. One day, while working, he was arrested. My parents heard nothing from him for several months, until one day they received a letter from him from Russia with a detailed horrifying story of his escape from a concentration camp. He had written about dangerous crossings of rivers, circumventing German Army patrols, walking and crawling only during nighttime and in constant fear of being recaptured. It took over one week for him to reach safety in Russia. I received his address from my mother, and we exchanged, in total, two letters. In one of his letters he wrote that he would try everything to get my parents and brother, Hans, to Russia, but also that my sister should try to explore every avenue to get them out of Austria. Then correspondence with Fritz broke up. I never heard from him again.

We were now into the New Year, 1940. I had my Bar Mitzvah in Marneff. My sister sent me a watch, baked goods, and a lot of other trears, but she could not attend. The Kohns ran the party, and all the kids got special attention, like cookies and hot chocolate. It was a joyous day, but it was also a very sad day – my parents and brother, Hans, were in Vienna and in danger; my brother, Fritz, was in Russia; my sister was in Antwerp; my brother, Pepi, was dead; and I was in Marneff without any of them.

I befriended many people in Marneff. From a Mr. Gottlieb I learned about photography, from a Mr. Deutsch, art and acting, from Rosie Kohn, Spanish and French. The days passed in this beautiful, secluded place, not too far from the German border. Besides having a good time, we also had serious air raid drills. We had to assemble in the halls and march down into a designated area in the cellar.

CHAPTER TEN
GERMANY ATTACKS

O n the morning of May 10, 1940, we were scheduled to have an air raid drill. A bell rang, and we assembled in the hall, but at that very instant, German bombers were flying over our place. We heard anti-aircraft guns shooting and distant bombs exploding, and what was supposed to be a drill became a scary reality. There was confusion in the camp. People came running down into the cellar from all directions, and within three minutes the entire camp was ordered to evacuate.

The Kohns and I packed just what we could carry, and, with a group of about thirty people, we started our march toward France. I was told that Germany had attacked and that French and Belgian soldiers had repelled the initial attack. We explored every railroad station we passed in the hope that we could catch a train but there were no trains running. Buses, trucks and even horse-drawn wagons were stuck in traffic. People by the thousand were walking by them, all in the direction of France. Belgian soldiers with rifles and equipment on their backs were walking alongside us and in the same direction. We asked them about the German invasion. Had the Germans crossed the Belgium border? Where were they fighting? Who was winning or losing? We could not get any answers from anyone. We asked the soldiers about trains. They said that the fastest way to get anywhere was to walk; to walk fast and to walk many hours. Every so often we heard planes. Some flew over us, and we heard the explosions of near and distant bombs. Just at the sound of a plane, we jumped into the ditches alongside the road. We always anticipated being bombed. We were walking, running and lying in ditches from very early in the morning until very late at night.

We walked from Marneff through Namur and Charleroi. Days were passing, the roads were impossible. We were always searching for food and water. There were many days when we had nothing to eat. We passed beautiful landscapes that looked so peaceful, and all along my mind was wandering, searching for happy thoughts. We heard planes flying over us, so we jumped into a ditch. Mr. Kohn said, "I see a German bomber." I looked and searched the sky, and all I could see was one plane. At that moment, not more than fifteen yards from us, hidden in thick foliage, an anti-aircraft cannon started to fire at the plane. The sound of that cannon was the loudest, most ear-piercing and frightening sound I had ever heard. My eardrums were in pain, and the earth under me was shaking and vibrating, while other planes appeared and began mingling in the sky. The cannon had stopped flaring and was watching the planes fly around. I could not distinguish one from the other. The cannon intermittently started to blast again, when suddenly I saw smoke from one plane that was rotating and diving down directly at us. At that time, in that ditch, is where my true relationship with God really started, for I prayed every prayer I could remember or repeat in the short time before the plane hit the ground. In what seemed to me a short distance from us, suddenly the plane swerved, rolled in a circle, and fell in another direction, away from us, with a loud crash. I heard no explosion, but an even whining sound came from the fallen plane's direction. We got up and ran into a thickly wooded area away from the road and waited until the whining siren-like sound had stopped and everything was seemingly quiet.

We then continued to walk, always walking. Some people joined us while others left us, but the group from Marneff was more or less still intact. Some people told us that a train would pick up people in a little town that sounded like Loab. When we arrived at this tiny railroad station, other people were already waiting. We walked into the station hoping that someone could give us some information about trains to France. We had just set foot inside the station when, out of nowhere, German dive bombers appeared and bombed the tracks and the little station. The Kohns jumped and rolled under benches and dragged me with them. Glass and rocks were flying and even hit us under the benches. We were fortunate to have had some protection from the falling debris. Bombs were exploding what seemed like only yards away from us, and the short duration of this attack seemed like hours. I cannot explain how scared I was; only people who have been in similar situations can really understand that kind of terror.

When we finally walked outside, I saw bodies lying on the ground, a woman walking on stumps, and, on top of telephone wires, there were articles of clothing. Mr. Kohn covered my head with his jacket, and I could no longer see the consequences of this bombing. Mr. Kohn guided me, walking away from this little station, and did not let me look at the surroundings until we had reached a grassy, open field. We walked alongside the tracks for a distance, and sure enough, we heard a train's slow rumble. The train soon passed us with people hanging from everywhere, on the roof, between cars, hanging from the rear and sides, but it only went by us for a very short distance because the tracks were not in a passing condition. Apparently, the tracks were bombed and the train could not proceed. Therefore, hundreds of people joined us on the march until the Marneff group decided to seek a less crowded road to continue.

We walked until it was pitch dark. We slept mostly in barns, and it was time to look for the night's lodging. Most of the farms were abandoned. Cows were dragging their full udders, constantly mooing, and some were actually following us. We had one brave guy among us. He put a small basin under a cow, bent down and pulled on the cow's teats, and we had warm, fresh milk. There were warning notices not to drink the water. Dead people and animals were supposedly lying in the waters and therefore contamination was suspected. To get liquid, we would suck on raw rhubarb. It was sour, but it was refreshing and thirst quenching. I went into a large, abandoned, stone farmhouse, and I walked down into the cellar where I found a large quantity of biscuits and half-churned butter. What we could not consume on the spot, we carried with us.

After days and days of walking and carrying baggage that got heavier with every step, we started to throw things away and consequently traveled a lot lighter than when we started. I was left with one backpack. By then, there were only fourteen of the original group members left. We stuck together because we decided that we should try to reach the Channel or the French coastline. So, we walked through Moberge, San Quentain to Rouin and hoped to go either to Calais or Le Havre and maybe to England after that. We walked for hours before sunrise and were still walking until way after sunset. Food was hard to come by. We read no papers and did not have a radio. The only news we heard were rumors from people who passed us in either direction.

We got halfway toward the Channel when masses of people came toward us telling us that the coast was very dangerous. It was being shelled and patrolled by German ships, and there were no English ships in sight. All of the people had turned around and were now walking to Paris. We also turned around and joined the many walking now in the other direction. It did not take too long when people coming from Paris told us not to go there, for Paris would be bombed. The word "bomb" was enough for us to decide to circumvent Paris.

In the evening, we found a barn with some comforts: it was empty, had fresh straw, and was very large. We were able to go to sleep spread apart. Usually, we slept very crowded together. We were always tired, and I am convinced that I walked many miles fast asleep. All of us had blisters on our feet. I had less than most because I was wearing mountain climbing shoes. Somehow they did not hurt my feet as much, and I was able to walk with less friction.

I fell asleep immediately, and when I woke up early in the morning, I was all alone in the barn. I jumped up and ran toward the barn door, which was ajar, and saw Mr. Kohn coming toward me while the rest of the crowd stood near the road. When he saw me standing in the door, all of them came running, put their arms around me and began to tell me a horror story. They said that a bunch of rats were in the barn and were jumping and running all over me and some others. One of the men was able to obtain a broom made out of tree branches to chase the rats away from me when one or two of the rats bit him. The people emptied the barn, while telling me to wake up and continued to yell from the outside, but I remained fast asleep. I don't know how long they waited to re-enter the barn, to wake me or to drag me out. Mr. Kohn said, as I met him, how lucky I and the rest of them were to leave the barn with only one casualty. The poor man who tried to get near me received severe bites on his face and a bite on his arm. Our relief lasted only a couple of minutes because we had to continue walking.

The next goal we tried to achieve was to reach Spain and Portugal. I cannot remember the exact town in which the barn was where we slept two days later. It must have been somewhere near Vernon. Like every morning, we got up very early when we heard heavy trucks and motorcycles all mashed into a rumbling roar. We all thought that the counter offensive by the French Army, which was rumored every hour on the hour, had started. Mr. Kohn sent me out to investigate. It was a misty twilight, and I had to be much closer to the main road in order to be able to see anything. I saw gray outlines of vehicles passing by when someone yelled halt. I stopped in my tracks. A German soldier approached me. He held a rifle loosely in his hands and asked me where I was going and who I was, all in German, of course. Before I could answer, a motorcycle with an attached sidecar pulled up, while the soldier repeated the question, pushing me a little closer to the German officer sitting in the sidecar. When I answered them in German with a well-rehearsed story: I had visited my sick brother in Belgium, and he had died. The war started, and I could not get back to Vienna. They started to smile, to my great relief, and asked me if I was alone. I answered, "No, friends of my brother are still sleeping in the barn." They then advised me that the fighting and the front were only a few kilometers from us, and that I should not go in that direction, pointing west. The officer said, "The best thing for you to do is get back to Belgium, which is in our hands." From there, trains would run, and I would be able to get back to Vienna. The solider sitting in the cycle sat very quietly. They then wished me well and took off to join the column of trucks. I ran back to the barn and reported what I saw, what the Germans said and that we should not continue in this direction. That was where the shooting was. The women started to cry and the men looked devastated. They all got very quiet and concluded that we must separate. By staying together the Germans would know that we were Jews. The Kohns and I slowly said goodbye to everyone, and we staggered our departure from the barn.

The Kohns decided to return to Brussels, so we began our return march. As we walked on, we encountered more and more German troops pouring into France. Soon thereafter, we joined a group of returning Belgians and somehow felt safer walking with them. Not until we reached San Quentain did we see the first S.S. man. A distance later, we were able to hop on a train that took us across the Belgian border, where we had to get off and continue walking. Soon thereafter, we were able to get on a train that took us to Brussels.

Once there, we went to the Red Cross, and they assigned us to a German occupied Red Cross building in the Avenue Paul Heger. I shared a room with the Kohns. We sat and thought through our next options. The building next to us was totally occupied by German soldiers, and as I looked out of my window, I could see a beautiful soccer field with German soldiers kicking the ball around. Even though my heart was up in my throat, I walked down to the field. I told them the same story about waiting for transportation back to Vienna. They, not knowing that I was Jewish, treated me like I was one of them. I started to kick the ball around and more soldiers joined us until we had two full teams. When other soldiers arrived and wanted to play, they exchanged with the other guys and not with me. I played the full game, and, when the match was over, they said, "In a couple of years you will be playing for the Austrian all-star team." When I came upstairs, Rosita Kohn said she had heart palpitations, worrying about me playing with the Germans.

This situation lasted a few days, then the Kohns and I went to the Jewish Community Center in Brussels looking for help. There we met some people from Marneff, who had just arrived from Antwerp. They told us that my sister and brother-in-law were there. Somehow Rosita got in touch with my sister and between them arranged for me to go to Antwerp. The Kohns took me to the train station. We had to wait awhile, and we said our goodbyes. Rosita Kohn held me in her arms for the longest time, all the time crying and finally saying, "I hope to see you soon," as the train pulled in. The Kohns were the kindest and best human beings I have ever known. They took care of me as if I was their own son. That was the last time I saw them.

When I arrived in Antwerp, my sister was waiting for me, and after our usual greetings, I noticed that I was taller than her. She commented right away on how much I had grown. We exchanged experiences about various close calls of bombings and shellings we had endured. I asked about Abraham, and my sister said that he was back tailoring and was very busy making uniforms for the German officers. That evening, when Abraham walked in, I realized that he was only as tall as I was. I must have had a growth spurt when I was in Marneff and on the march back and forth from France. My brother-in-law smiled when he saw me. We patted each other's backs and during dinner, we repeated stories of our flight from the Germans, only to be under their control again.

The following day we went to the Jewish Community Center, what was left of it, and they were able to get me some clothing, for I had almost nothing to wear. Either I had thrown some of it away with my suitcase while walking in France, or it was too small for me. My sister-in-law, Berta, and her baby never left Antwerp, and my sister and I stopped off to visit her. I spent some time with my baby nephew, and Berta urged me to move to her place, that she had room for me, but I thankfully declined, remembering her past behavior. I assured her that I would visit her and the baby. My sister immediately wrote to my parents that I was safe and with her in Antwerp. We hoped that Antwerp's Jews would be included in any future transports to the West, now that we were under German occupation, only to be disappointed again that no exit visas would be granted to any country.

School was closed for the summer, the temple's congregation dispersed, and my soccer playing friends were no longer in Antwerp. I walked the streets during the day, avoiding every German in sight, or I slept, for we had air raids every night. British and Allied planes flew over Antwerp on their way to Germany, and I could hear the distant wailing of sirens, with the eerie sounds coming closer. Soon thereafter, you could hear the murmuring sound of planes. I would say, "I hear them," and we would rush down the stairs and run for one block to an air raid shelter, which we had to share with horses. No one died from bombs at that time, but there were many casualties from anti-aircraft shrapnel. I used to collect shrapnel fragments. Every piece had a different shape, and I could imagine all kinds of sculptures. Some of these iron pieces were as big as baseballs with an occasional football-sized piece, but most were rather small. Some were so close to the explosion that you could not pick them up because they were burning hot. We repeated exercise nightly, and many nights we could not leave this shelter because the "all clear" siren did not go off until early in the morning. Eventually, we just stayed in the apartment and ignored the sirens.

The German occupation forces were now intermingled with the S.S. and some S.A. sections. Jews were being arrested, and all Jews had to register. The correspondence between my parents and us became even more frequent. In every letter, they urged my sister to send me back to Vienna if possible. My sister wanted to know what my chances would be to immigrate to another country if I were to return. In the next letter that we received from my parents, they wrote that children's transports were leaving from Vienna to Sweden. My mother further wrote that even if I could not immigrate to another country, at least I would be with them, reunited. We had a consultation with the leaders of the Jewish Community Center, who told us that it did not matter whether we were under German control there in Antwerp or in Vienna. Neither place would be good for Jews. A few more letters from my mother persuaded my sister to let me return.

My sister and I went to Brussels, and I marched alone into the German military headquarters requesting permission for my return to Vienna. I always told the same story about why I came to Belgium. Within fifteen minutes, I received military permission and an I.D. card and was told to have it approved by the Austrian Embassy because their permission was also needed. I showed them my military I.D. card, but those bastards stamped a big red "J" for Jew on my I.D. With my re-entry permit in my pocket, my sister and I returned to Antwerp.

The next day, we visited the Jewish Community Center again, and we were told that they would make all the arrangements for me to return to Vienna. They provided me with a railroad ticket from Antwerp to Cologne, and I was informed that a girl would also return to Germany at the same time. The instructions were that upon arrival in Cologne around 4:00 p.m., the girl and I would be met by two members of the Jewish Community of Cologne, who then would purchase tickets for me to go to Vienna and for her to go to Meinz.

My sister made supper the night before my departure, and my sister-in-law, with the baby, came over to be with us. Later, we said our farewells, and I had to promise that I would write and keep them informed.

CHAPTER ELEVEN
RETURN TO VIENNA

The next day I was approaching the train to Cologne with a twelve-year-old girl in my care. I hugged my sister one more time and jumped onto the train and joined the girl in the compartment. That was the last time I ever saw my sister, brother-in-law, sister-in-law and the baby.

The train ride was interrupted several times by flights of English planes and repair crews working on the tracks. We did not arrive in Cologne until 11:45 p.m. The train station was deserted, and the two of us stood alone on the platform. No one met us. We walked up and down the train station, and there was not a soul in sight. I remembered the name of a hotel, Hotel Tils, where my sister stayed for a few days before her illegal crossing into Belgium. I was finally able to ask someone for directions to the hotel. At the hotel, I had to ring a bell, and an elderly lady came to the door. I had to explain who I was, mentioning my sister, our dilemma, that the train was late and no one came to pick us up. I then asked for a room and told her that the Jewish Community would pay her in the morning. She eventually let us in and gave us a room. I told the girl to go to sleep while I gave the lady all the information she requested. By the time I went upstairs, the girl was fast asleep, and soon after I too fell into bed.

In the morning, the lady called the Jewish Community Center, informing them of our arrival and asked for someone to pick us up. A short time later, a man came and took us back to the train station and purchased tickets for us. The girl left the same day, but I had to sleep one more night at the Center. The train ride from Cologne to Vienna was uninterrupted and arrived on time. I jumped onto the platform looking for my parents. When they saw me, they came running toward me while I was running to them. The hugging and kissing went on and on until my father asked me for my luggage. I pointed to my backpack and said that was all I had and that I would explain later about my lack of clothing.

It was a long walk from the railroad station to the apartment and I alternately walked with my father and mother, telling them about my life in Belgium. The moment Pepi's name was mentioned my mother started to cry. My father, who was carrying my backpack in one hand, put the other on my mother's shoulder, trying to stop her from crying. Not until I changed the subject and quickly directed my story in another direction did my mother stop crying.

While I was gone, my parents and brother had moved again, this time across the street from where I had lived. We had to share this apartment with three other families. We occupied the living room, converted to a bedroom for the four of us. The inconvenient part of having the largest room was that two families had to walk through our room to get to theirs. To the left was a small bedroom where a husband and wife lived. To the right was a larger bedroom, which an older lady with her daughter and two grandsons had to share. On the other side of the entrance was another bedroom, where an older couple and their cousins lived, and one tiny kitchen that made up the total of our new apartment. The people in the last bedroom were distant cousins of my mother and we considered them family.

Only Jewish people lived in this apartment building, with the exception of the superintendent and her family, who were Christians. One tenant in the building was the only living Jewish general of the Austrian-German Army. General Sommer was retired and he and his wife had an apartment all to themselves. That alone indicated the preferred status he enjoyed with the German and Austrian Nazis, who still addressed him as "General." He and I spoke occasionally about the German Blitz Krieg and the efficient execution of the war. He questioned me about my experiences in Belgium and France, and we struck up a mini friendship. He was a very serious man and never expressed his opinion to me. We listened to the radio's constant bulletins, and he used to say that many of the reports were not newsworthy.

I attended school for a short time. Then the Nazis closed all the schools to Jews. A couple of teachers held classes in someone's apartment and I attended them for awhile. In the meantime, transports of Jews went to Poland daily. The only reason we were not included was because my father and brother worked as painters for the Jewish Community Center and were mostly assigned remodeling projects for German housing. Then a decree came down that every Jewish person fourteen years of age or older must register with the Austrian Arbeits Amt (Department of Labor), to perform meaningful work for the Third Reich. I delayed my registration because I was promised to be on the third transport to Sweden. One transport had left Vienna, then the second was canceled, and all further transports were stopped. Even if someone had a legitimate visa, their departure was delayed or canceled. I, too, had to register for work, as I was just past my fourteenth birthday. My father kept working for the Jewish Community Center, but my brother, Hans, was assigned work in a dump, sorting useful commodities for the war effort.

I was waiting for my assignment when my father met a painter he knew and asked him to give me a job. He was a tall Aryan, well connected with the Austrian or German leadership. He went to the labor department and requested for me to work for him, which was granted. His work was mostly for the German armed forces, the Gestapo as well as private jobs. He was a pretty good guy. He was always nice to me, paid me a fair wage and occasionally gave me some food products to take home. I was supposed to do only menial jobs, but he taught me the painting business, from mixing paint correctly, coloring, consistency, the proper way to prepare walls, first and second coats, and how to spray paint. In addition, I learned to paint straight lines with and without shadows, paint and roll patterns and apply stencils of figurines and flowers. If anyone from the authorities came to check, I was told to say that I worked in the warehouse, carried ladders and scraped the walls. I had good and bad jobs. The good ones were mostly in private homes or private businesses. The owners usually fed me and gave me a tip at the end.

In the beginning, I had problems learning to walk on a ladder. The taller the ladder, the more difficult it was for me to lift the ladder with one leg to the right or left and drag the other half over. I had to paint a very large restaurant in the Prater. The ceiling was very high and I had to walk on the tallest ladder we had. I was a very difficult job, but when I finished, I walked home with two bottles of wine and a very good tip. The wine I gave to my father and the money to my mother. I had no use for money. I could not buy anything or use it for entertainment. My mother usually bought food on the black market and had to pay very high prices.

The worst job I had to do was scrape walls in the Gestapo Headquarters in Vienna. It was a former hotel in the First District and the ceilings had intricate plaster designs, which had to be washed and the uneven walls had to be plastered. None of the work bothered me except my boss told me not to wear the Jewish Star as long as I worked there and that I should not worry about it. Mind you, every Jew in the whole of Germany and occupied countries (under severe penalties) had to wear a yellow star with the word, "Jude" on it. Here I was working in the Gestapo Headquarters without the Jewish star. I was nervous and scared all the time. Many times I was left alone and Gestapo, S.S. and S.A. men were rapidly passing me. I felt that sooner or later they would find out that I was a Jew. I often asked my boss to relieve me from this torture, but he would always smile and repeat his three words, "Not to worry." Every day I brought this nervousness home with me, and my mother asked me what was bothering me because I was so quiet. I just babbled and told her about my work at the Gestapo Headquarters. Talking about it must have helped me, but now I had my family worried.

As it was, I found my parents much more serious and sad since my return. My mother used to be a happy and energetic woman, who easily laughed, told funny stories and used to sing. Instead, she seemed older and cried silently, sitting in a chair. The only time she seemed to return to her old self was when I consciously jumped on her lap, like in the old days, and talked to her. When my father came home from work, he seemed to be more tired and his shoulders drooped as if he carried the entire world's problems. My parents understood the consequences of being a Jew much more than I did.

I still had a few friends and a steady girlfriend, but it did not take long for me to grasp the seriousness of the situation. That week, the Nazis rounded up Jews from everywhere for transports to Poland. They blocked off streets in various neighborhoods, herded the Jews onto trucks and drove away. In some cases, some people were given one or two hours to pack their belongings and ordered to report to a designated area. Some were notified by mail to report to a school, now a collection camp, which I had attended for a short while. The Gestapo and their Jewish Police helpers came searching for Jews from house to house and then took them away. They also came to our apartment house, but our superintendent told them that all of the people living in the building were working for the war effort and that General Sommer was also a tenant. I was only nine or ten yards away from this conversation. As two S.S. men approached, I retreated inside the building and saw the two turn and walk away. Somehow the word spread about our building, and they never returned. The three families who lived in our apartment were notified by mail to report. All were sent to Poland. None survived.

Between the years of 1940 and 1942, Jews in Vienna were limited to a meager existence. Ration cards for food were totally inadequate. Whatever money we had

we spent for extra food on the black market. Our superintendent was the go-between for obtaining extra food,
and I visited Mrs. Probst many times, who helped us out.
Jews were forbidden to ride in streetcars with few exceptions and then only on the rear platform. Our entertainment was limited to visiting each other after work or on
Sundays. I spent most of my time at my girlfriend's apartment, listening to recordings and teaching each other to
dance. There was a curfew, and my time spent with her
was all too short. The small section of park along the
little Danube where Jews were allowed to congregate was
eventually abandoned because of the many raids and fist
fights with gangs of Hitler Youth.

Friends and neighbors were being sent to concentration camps almost daily, including my girlfriend
and her parents. There were now fewer and fewer Jews
in Vienna, and I began to spend most of my free time
at home. I was being trained by military personnel to
become an air raid warden. At certain hours during the
night, I had to stand on the roof and watch for fires and
report air raid attacks. They taught me to handle incen-
diary bombs in case they happened to be dropped. Vienna was totally blacked out, and I read all of the Karl
May and Jack London I could find by a flickering kero-
sene lamp. In the morning, my eyes still saw the printed
flickering words that I had read until the wee hours. My
mother reminded me frequently during the night to put
the books down because I had to go to work in the morning.

So my life became solitary, with an occasional visit to two girls who I knew from Marneff, Belgium, who had also returned to Vienna after the German occupation. When I was at their house, we seemed to suppress what was happening to Jews. We only talked about the good times in Marneff. Then, my father came home earlier than usual and told us that we had less than one week to report for resettlement.

CHAPTER TWELVE
TERESIENSTADT (TEREZIN)

In 1942, my father was past his sixty-second year, my mother was fifty-five, my brother, Hans, was thirty-two, and I was fifteen. The morning after we received the notice for resettlement, I told my boss about it. He got very quiet, walked out of the room and returned ten minutes later. He told me that he could take care of me, so that I would not have to leave Vienna and could continue working for him. However, he could not do anything on behalf of my family. He urged me to accept his offer for reasons he was unable to explain. When I got home and told my parents what my boss had offered me, my father said that we were only going to a ghetto called Theresienstadt and not to a concentration camp. My parents decided that we would stay together under any circumstances. That day, General Sommer was also ordered to go to Theresienstadt. Well, I thought, if he goes to Theresienstadt, then it would not be that bad. Over the next few days, I learned that every Jew who was still left in Vienna would be sent there, and Vienna and all of Austria would be free of Jews at last.

We spent the last few days giving or trading our household items for things we thought would be of value to us. I had extra money, which I received from my boss when I said goodbye, in addition to my paycheck. I added some linens my mother gave me, and I bought a pair of German Air Force boots. They were a perfect size, if worn with an extra pair of socks, and they were fur lined. Even though the weather was warm, I planned to wear them, because I knew that even in the coldest weather, my feet would be warm. A friendly shoemaker waterproofed the leather for me. But he warned me to wear my pants over the boots so that they would not be recognized by anyone. He thought that possession of these boots, especially by a Jew, was illegal. I had nothing of value to worry about, but I would make sure that no one touched my boots.

We prepared for our departure. My father received permission for us to report directly to the train station. The following morning, we left Vienna with only our luggage. We could carry nothing more. We arrived at the train station and were directed to a particular compartment, which was already partially occupied. Representatives from the Jewish Community Center and railroad attendants were pushing people onto a train that was already overcrowded, while the S.S. and the Austrian police stood by smiling. By now, leaving Vienna at that time meant absolutely nothing to me. My girlfriend, family and friends had left months ago, and my only bond to Vienna was that I was born there.

The train ride to Theresienstadt was very uncomfortable, so it seemed very long. On the train, I met two guys about my age, Herbert Heimerling and his family, and Max Witrofsky and his parents. The three of us struck up a friendship and promised to stick together once we arrived in the ghetto. The train stopped and it took a while to get off. People were climbing down and suitcases of all sizes and shapes were thrown to the ground. My father and brother stood guard over our luggage while I helped my mother to get organized and climb off the train. S.S. guards and Czech gendarmes ordered us to move along, following others into the actual ghetto. Along the road, people working on roadbeds using picks and shovels immediately engaged us in conversation. They asked us where we came from. I answered, "Vienna." Then I asked in return where they were from. Most answered Prague. I wanted to ask more questions, especially about the ghetto, but the gendarmes moved us along. A bit further down the road, I recognized a young woman, Eva Weiss, who was married to a good friend of my brother, Fritz, Herman Weiss. I stopped and told her who I was. She got excited and wanted to talk to me, but with the guards around, all she could say was that she would look us up in the ghetto after work, half yelling after me, "I'll promise to see you later." All I knew about her was that she and her husband escaped from Vienna to Czechoslovakia about two weeks after Hitler entered Vienna. I know now that her husband wound up in Russia, but I never found out how they became separated.

As we neared the ghetto, it looked like a walled-in city. I could only see it from our approach, but it seemed to curve to the right. We entered through a large opening, guarded by two gendarmes and one S.S. man. All conversation seemed to stop. All we did was follow the crowd in front of us. We were then directed into a large room. Several tables stood end to end in the center of the room, and men were behind them. We had to put our suitcases on the table, open them one at a time, and the men rummaged through them. They confiscated items indiscriminately and left us only with our clothing. An S.S. guard walked up and down among the men, looking over their shoulders and occasionally gave them some orders. The entire work took maybe thirty minutes.

Once outside again, we had to wait for further instructions. We then were led in groups to our quarters. We learned that we arrived in the Hamburger Kasserne quarters that previously housed soldiers. We entered a large room where an orderly showed us a section of the floor and said that it would be the temporary area for the four of us. No beds, no cots, no blankets, just a little square on the floor. We leaned our suitcases against the wall, sat down and looked at each other in bewilderment. Other people, who also were in a state of semi-shock, joined us to the left and right. The orderly had long since left us, without any further explanations. The huge room kept filling up with more and more people who kept asking the previous arrivals what this was all about and none of us could answer any questions. I got up from the floor and started to look for familiar faces, but there were none in my room. I walked out into the open air corridor that circled the entire floor and leaned over a stone wall that almost reached my chest and looked down into the huge center courtyard, which was crowded with many more new arrivals. I returned to my parents, sat down and waited. Two men entered our room and announced that we would receive temporary coupons for food, informing us where the kitchen was located and that they would assign permanent quarters for us as soon as possible. We were free to roam around in the Kasserne. We stood in line to receive our coupons and were advised that pots and utensils could be obtained in the front room. As we had brought nothing along to eat out of, I rushed toward the designated room, followed by my brother and father, only to learn that quite a few people had beaten us to the door. We waited our turn, and we received several pots with covers and four metal dishes that were rather large. Spoons, forks and knives were located in boxes, and we could help ourselves. That evening we received a piece of bread, which was distributed in our room, and for our soup we had to stand in line in front of the kitchen window where cooks stood behind and dished out one portion per person.

I spent an uncomfortable night dozing off and on until early morning, when two men with a huge bucket came and dished out black coffee. We were told not to go too far from our room until we were assigned permanent quarters. After I was able to get a spot in the washroom, I changed my clothes and set out to find my new friends, Herbert Heimerling and Max Witrofsky. I found Herbert within five minutes, which was not too hard to do. Herbert was about six feet ten inches tall, and you could find him from any elevated spot, provided he was standing. He was rather proud of his height, because when asked how tall he was, he always added an inch, but never said that he was shorter. We both set out to find Max, asking people if they had seen anyone who looked like him. We found him and his parents on the very top of the Kasserne in a room that looked like an unfinished attic.

The three of us began to explore the entire place. When we reached the front gate, to our surprise, a ghetto policeman stood guard. The ghetto police were staffed by mostly Czech Jews, under the control of Czech gendarmes and, of course, the S.S. We approached him to engage in some kind of informational conversation. He was a very nice guy and told us that we could leave the Kaserne and explore the entire ghetto, but we must be back before 11:00 a.m. We walked out and found a very busy place. People were walking and working on various endeavors. We were stopped several times and asked mostly where we were from. Our walk was short. I searched my pocket for my wristwatch, and it showed almost 11:00 a.m. I always carried my wristwatch in my pocket. It was an old watch, but it worked very well. When I used to play soccer, which seemed a long, long time ago, I formed this habit of taking my watch off to store in my pocket.

Herbert, Max and I arranged a meeting place after we received our ration of food. I ran up to my parents and found them all packed and ready to be moved. I was told to remain for I would be quartered with fellows my own age. My parents and my brother were moved across the street from the Hamburger Kasserne into a two-story structure. My mother was placed with thirty or so other women in one large room, while my father and brother had to share quarters with the same amount of men on the second floor. They were assigned bunk beds, which were their entire living domain. My mother received the first bunk on top of double deckers and therefore had only one person to her right. My father and brother had bunks against a wall and also had only one person next to them. The rest of the prisoners had to sleep side by side in narrow, uncomfortable bunks. They stored their belongings near the head of the bunk, and the rest was placed under the bottom bunk. I walked into my mother's place. It was so very, very crowded, but my mother was more concerned with our separation, even though my father was only one flight up. She repeatedly questioned me where I would be quartered. I told her not to worry. The entire ghetto was not that big for us to be too far apart.

I returned to the Hamburger where a young fellow was watching my luggage. He was a redhead with freckles, and his name was Peter Neuschiller. Herbert and Max had brought their luggage to my room, and we stuck together until we knew where our permanent quarters would be. The next day, I started to explore the ghetto thoroughly on my own. I spoke to people and inquired about the life in the ghetto, Terezin. I was anxious to learn everything as soon as possible. I was told that everyone worked in their expertise, if possible. The ghetto was self-governed, but under the rules and regulations of the German S.S. The best jobs went to the cooks, bakers, butchers, or people working in the clothing chambers. I asked, "Why just these jobs?" The reason they gave was that the food rations given were little, too much to die and barely enough to live. The older people could not adjust to the meager existence and therefore were much worse off than the younger people. Unfortunately, when we entered the ghetto, my father gave painters as his and our profession, which I was sure would be our work.

The first Jews who arrived in Terezin came from Prague and other Czech cities. They had the choice jobs and even in lesser work details, they were the heads and foremen. The ghetto elder was a Czech Jew by the name of Edelstein and all his major offices were headed by the first arrivals. The layered guarding system in the ghetto was headed by the S.S., Czech gendarmes recruited by the S.S., and last by the ghetto police. The head S.S. man, or camp commander, was an Austrian S.S. man named Seidl, followed by another Austrian named Rahm. They commanded a sizable contingency of S.S. men. All entrances and exits were guarded by gendarmes and, in order to pass in either direction, you had to have iron clad permission. Should an S.S. man or German soldier pass you on the street, you were obliged to remove your cap or hat in recognition. Beware the poor soul who did not offer this respect.

In my search for Eva Weiss, the woman I recognized entering the camp, agencies and people who could have known her address told me that she probably left on the same train I arrived in Terezin on. I asked, "Where did she go?" and the answer was, "Poland."

My stay in the Hamburger was also short lived. They transferred all men and young men to the Dresdner Kasserne. Separation of the sexes was the order of business. A husband and wife and their son and daughter could possibly live in four different quarters. There were also children's buildings, boys' and girls', separated, but within the complex. The good part was that you could visit each other freely and without supervision after work. We received our food rationing card at the Dresdner, but nothing had changed. You still had to stand in line to receive your portions. As you reached the kitchen window, a person clipped our ration card and relayed to the cook how many portions to give and, in full sight of the cook, put the clipping into a box. The person could say two portions and only deposit one clipping. What the cook put in your pot was your only source of food, which was meager, quantitatively and nutritionally. The food tasted so-so and looked puny, no matter how the cooks tried to camouflage it. In the morning, we received fake coffee – it was really just black liquid. For lunch there was soup and one other dish, sometimes hash, sometimes knoedel (dumplings) with imitation sauce on it. For us, this was a delicacy. For supper, we had only soup. During the day we received a portion of bread, and once in a while a slice of what they called honey. Most soups were thin liquid with nothing in them. Once a week we received a potato soup, which was thick and probably the most nourishing food we got. Everyone's wish was to become a cook. It would free the ration card, and cooks had substantially more to eat. I myself started to fantasize about becoming a cook.

As I was walking down the corridor in the Dresdner I saw a familiar face. After a moment of recognition, we hugged and at the same time called each other names. It was my boyhood best friend, Ernie Sterzer, whom I had not seen since before I left for Belgium. I did not realize that he had remained in Vienna and was on the same transport to Terezin as I. We talked and exchanged information about where we lived and planned to see each other as often as possible.

As anticipated, my father, brother and I had to report to the painters' station for work assignments. Working with my father and brother was a first. My working with my boss in Vienna on diversified jobs with new and advanced methods of painting made it only half painful to be a painter. But the apparatus that was available in the ghetto was antiquated and old fashioned; painting with a brush and pail, up and down ladders, was all that we could do. My father and brother did not mind painting former stables and huge barracks for conversion for German use and no other reason, but I hated it with a passion.

A few days later, Herbert, Maxie, Peter and I were transferred again, this time to a building for young men up to the age of nineteen. As we entered the two-story building with our belongings, a man asked us to wait for a room to be assigned. The surprising first question that we were asked was whether we were Zionists. I replied, "No," without consulting my friends. My negative reply to the question was for good reasons. In Austria before Hitler, most Jewish kids belonged to one so-called Zionist Club. I had joined such a club because some of my friends belonged, and they had the best Ping-Pong tables. Just one block away from our club was a competing club called Betar. Their members wore uniforms, not unlike Hitler Youth, brown shirts, leather straps from shoulder to belt. The only thing that was missing was the swastika. Fist fights were common between these two clubs. I, again, was saved from combat because the other club knew that my three brothers would not have tolerated any harm done to me. My brother, Fritz, whom I looked up to the most, asked me to quit the club, for he could not understand why Jewish kids should fight against each other. Whenever there were Zionist elections, even the grownups argued and fought with each other. He believed that Zionism was not uniting the Jews, but was dividing a common cause. He carefully, but with some authority, explained the downside of being a Zionist. I then quit my club and became an anti-club, anti-Zionist believer. Hence, the quick "no" answer to the question, "Are you Zionists?" The man smiled and said, "That's all right, you and your friends can join the fellows on the first floor, first door to the left."

We entered this large room. Its walls were covered with bunk beds, left and right, from the front entrance to the one rear window, which was the end of the ghetto. The fellows in the room were all from Austria and had just arrived minutes before us. I knew no one, but Herbert and Max knew most of them. One fellow was Kurt Reich and I said, "Being that you was here first, you can be Kurt Number one, and I will be Kurt Number Two." We all laughed. We got acquainted for a couple of hours. Among the guys I met were Walter Wolfgang and Walter Fantl. Two Kurts and two Walters. The unusual part of the room was that from the ceiling a window partition existed as if to divide the front one-third from the rear two-thirds. Herbert said that we would take the front one-third, meaning himself, Maxie, and me, but the division had to be occupied by six people. We included Kurt Reich and Walter Fantl. Peter wanted to remain in the large part near the window. The last three fellows came into the room and Herbert and Kurt knew one of them, Heinz Schafer, who became the sixth to join us in the front part. I liked Heinz from the moment I met him. He was older than us, and I believe he just got into the youth quarters under the wire of the age limit. My friends immediately put their heads together to plan the layout of our room. Herbert, Maxie and Walter Fantl were the master builders while the rest of us did very little. Eventually, our one-third was completely partitioned into a separate room. Four of us slept on top, barely below the ceiling and two slept on the bottom, while the rest of the room was the so-called living quarters. We had a table, a couple of chairs and a makeshift bookshelf. Attached to it were the spokes for us to climb up to our bunks. The entire room was only, maybe, ten by ten feet, but it was our room, private and separate.

We had hardly settled in when Ernie Sterzer came to inform me that people played soccer in the ghetto and that we should immediately form a team. To be more specific, a youth team, in order to compete on top of the elevated area called The Bastei. He also informed me that a major league existed, and they played in the Dresdner Kasserne. Ernie was my best friend. We had played soccer together on one team since I was three years old, and he was four-and-a-half. We understood each other's playing and got along on and off the field.

Between working as a painter and forming a soccer team, I was a busy guy. Through various tryouts and several practice sessions, we finally fielded our first soccer team and joined the Youth League as Vienna. Our goalie was Jackie Hacker, the two backs were Gotesman and Kolb. I played center half; Ernie played center forward; Pepi Goldstein was our right wing and Josefsberg was our left wing. There were a few other kids who substituted for one another, for the field was small and only seven men could play. There were several teams, but it was always the Vienna and Czech all-stars who wound up in the play-offs. I especially remember the final game between us in November of 1942, our first year. They kicked two goals before the first half of the game was over. During the intermission, Ernie and I talked things over and decided to switch some players. I would play center forward, Ernie would play center half, and we put put the two fastest guys on the wings. Behind by two goals, we adjusted to a totally offense-minded game. Right at the beginning of the second half, they committed a foul on me, right in front of their goal. A penalty was awarded and Ernie converted it. Now it was two to one. A few minutes later, they scored a goal. It was three to one. We hardly had centered the ball when they scored another goal. Now the game was four to one. At this point, the game seemed out of hand. We then decided to play two-two-two. We narrowed our offense but told the fullback to run into the wing position at every offensive play. They were pooped, but it worked. They did not cover our defensive players as they moved up, so their defense was wide open, and I was able to score. The score was four to two. They kicked off and Ernie intercepted, passed through the hole to me, and I passed the ball to Pepi, my right wing, who, on a give and go, passed the ball immediately back to me. I kicked the ball from twenty or twenty-five meters into the left corner of the net. The score was four to three. We had less than two minutes left to play. Ernie ran into the net, picked up the ball and centered it for their kickoff. The whistle blew. They passed the ball backward, which I anticipated. I was just able to tip the ball to my left wing. He took the ball and ran with it almost to the left corner spot. He stopped, turned and centered the ball in front of the goal. I was able to kick the ball right from the air into the goal. The goalkeeper threw himself in the corner, but it was too late. The game ended in a four to four tie. The oldest kid who played for us was Ernie at seventeen. The Czech kids had some older players, and I learned that three of them played with teams in the majors.

After the game, a man approached me and said, "I am Mr. Fischer and the manager of the Viennese soccer team in the majors, and I would like you to play for us." He asked me to join him the next day in the Dresdner Kasserne. The next day, late afternoon, without my tryout or reserve status, I was installed as the starting center half for Vienna's major league team. This league was made up of many teams and various combinations. The teams were named mostly according to the jobs they performed, like the Cooks had a team, also Gardeners, Electricians, Ghetto Police, Clothes Chamber (Kleider Kammer), and Youth Agency (Jugend Fuersorge). There were many formidable Jewish soccer players who played for major league teams in their respective countries before Hitler. Therefore, the majors in the ghetto were very competitive.

Because of my age, I was able to play in the majors as well as youth soccer, and many times I played two games in one afternoon. Then, a rule was passed that anyone playing in the majors would no longer be permitted to play in the Youth League. When I explained to my friend, Ernie, that I had decided to play major league only, my understanding and forgiving friend, Ernie, was not a happy camper. I tried to talk to Mr. Fischer about Ernie playing with me in the majors but he said that Ernie was not a hard and resolute player, no matter how long we had played together.

I asked my manager and supporters of the team if they could get me a better job than a painter. I specifically requested to become a cook, because painting was a lousy job, dirty, with long hours, especially when we had to work outside the ghetto. It left little time to practice soccer, and, most of all, I was always hungry. I was promised that I would get a job in the kitchen, but promising does not make it so. Through playing soccer, I became better known, and when I stood in line to receive my ration of food, I usually got a little extra soup or something else. Every little bit of extra food helped, for food was not easy to obtain.

During the winter of 1942 / 1943, we had very few days when we could kick the ball around and keep in some kind of shape. That is when I joined a group of young men who took judo. Our teacher was a young Czech gymnast with world-class credentials. His name was Freddy Hirsch. His job was to work for the youth organization as a teacher, and a gymnastics and judo instructor. He was a good guy and a good teacher. I attended almost all of his classes in my free time. After one of his classes, I met a young Czech girl and we started to see each other, but ended up as good friends.

Freddy Hirsch bugged me about my playing soccer for Vienna. He felt that since I was living in the youth quarters that I should play for the organization that represented youth (Jugend Fuersorge). I said to him, "They promised me a job in the kitchen as a cook. I just have to wait a little longer." He said, "Promising and getting are two different things." He was sure that if I played for Jugend Fuersorge they could place me in a kitchen job directly. I took no further notice of this conversation, but a month later I was approached by a small delegation of three men: the manager of the soccer team, Jugend Fuersorge, the head of my youth quarters and a doctor, who cared for us as best he could. They outright asked me to switch my allegiances from the Viennese team and to join their team. I explained that I was waiting for a job as a cook, which they had promised, and that it may be happening soon. They said that this was only a maybe but they would give me a job as a cook right away. Driven by the need for food, my answer was automatic. "Get me the job first, and then I'll switch." Just as they promised,

I received a job transfer from painter to cook in the Dresdner Kasserne, and I switched from Vienna to the Jugend Fuersorge team. I did not feel that I deserted the Vienna Club because my friends and I had a greater allegiance to the fellows I lived with than a city that betrayed us. Besides, other known Viennese soccer players in the ghetto played for other teams, like Fischer for Kleider Kammer, Rummel for Butchers, Ehrlich for the Police and others. Now I was playing for Jugend Fuersorge.

I lived in L218, the last house on the street. Just beyond was the Czech and German headquarters, and looking out of our window, you could see every gendarme and S.S. man coming and going. Sometimes you could hear them talking. That's how close our room was to the bordering fence of the ghetto. Many times we saw men and women being dragged by our window into the German headquarters for whatever crimes they had committed. They were then sent to the Kleine Festung (Little Bastian), which was converted into a prison within a prison. Only the S.S. knew the reasons for being sent there. Trying to escape was one reason; smuggling information to the outside was another. Also, forgetting to remove your hat when an S.S. man approached, or taking vegetables while working the gardens were grounds for punishment. We heard all kinds of stories about why people were sent to the Kleine Festung. They became so redundant that we only listened to gruesome stories in the abstract because we all knew that we were only a tiny step away from experiencing it personally.

Just as I was about to begin my job as a cook, my friend, Ernie, got his job in the bakery, which meant that his and my family would have a little more to eat. Working in the kitchen was no picnic. In the beginning my job was to stir whatever was being cooked that day. I walked around with a huge scraper, between two or three gigantic kettles, constantly scraping the bottom of the kettles, mixing the soup or hash and making sure that nothing settled or burned. Most kettles were fired by coal and a fireman came constantly, checking if the coals were burning evenly while skillfully stacking coals in every corner of the oven. My scraping and churning was absolutely top priority and the head chef kept checking, taking the scraper out of my hands and testing the bottom of the kettle himself. This took hours of hard work, and the heat was sometimes intolerable. Yet, thousands would exchange their job for mine. The hardest and most exhausting work was to make a starchy thickening mix, which was mostly added to soups or gravies. We made this usually once a week, and, if I was in charge this particular day or night, I could not even go to the bathroom, for if you did not constantly scrape and mix, this substance could burn in a very, very short time.

My working in the kitchen made it a lot easier for my family and me. It freed my ration card, which I gave to my mother, and when I had to staff a window to dish out food, I was always able to give my mother, father or brother a little extra. The head chef usually poured some extra portions into my bucket whenever possible. The stations were constantly checked by either the chef or by a detail of private kitchen police, who made sure that no one was shortchanged or given more than the ration cards they possessed. If I was ever short of portions, it was not more than one or two, for portions were carefully measured. Portions were being ladled out of a huge wooden barrel that had two ears with holes. An iron bar was put through the holes, and two of us had to carry this humongous wooden barrel filled to the brim with soup or whatever. Sometimes, we had to carry it down two flights of stairs without spilling a drop. If my partner was taller than I was, its weight would shift toward me, and I had the major lifting to do. Therefore, I made sure that my partner was either smaller than or at least as tall as I was.

Once a day we had to pick up coals from a large bin in the cellar that was carefully watched by guards or gendarmes. Brown coal was plentiful, but black coal was like gold. We could only get one load; therefore, our wooden square trunk was longer and deeper, and it took six men to carry it up two flights. This trunk had four large handles. One man on each and two additional men in the rear helped to lift the huge and heavy wooden thing, filled to the very top with coal, up the stairs. Once we got to the kitchen, we had to lift it up high and dump it into our coal bin. My chef and foreman was Heine Horn, who was about five feet two inches tall and just as wide. He was the strongest man I had ever seen and known. He watched the four men trying to dump this coal. They picked the wooden square up all right, but it was too heavy to dump it over. Heine came over to make his standard comment that I learned from him and still constantly use: "When I was young, I could carry this thing on my watch chain." He did not disappoint us and added, "You guys are a bunch of weak girls." He said to me, "You grab the one end of that little thing, and when I say 'hooo-rook,' we dump it." In jest I walked over to one side and grabbed the handles. He took the other side and, in a commanding voice, yelled, "Hooo-rook!" and dumped this gigantic coal bucket into the bin, along with me. Heine and I were good friends. He was lenient and free when giving me food to dish out. I always got a good measure, and he was never cross with me when I fell short of rations. However, there was one thing he never forgave me for: leaving the Viennese team to play for Jugend Fuersorge.

I really loved playing for my new team. We were all young; we practiced and played well together. Our goalkeeper was Franta Klein; the fullbacks were Breda and Eisenberg. I played center half. Klauber was outside right. Burka was center forward and Greenfeld played outside left. We were mostly an offensive-minded team and played with a dedication to the game. We had good players. We meshed and worked well together. Burka was a tank, a bulldog and a goal scorer. For him to be at his best, I had to play him free, to draw his defender away and pass the ball to his far right, almost out of reach. He had to have room for his tank-like approach to soccer.

The opponents never defended him, and if I could not pass the ball to him as I described, he was less effective. That always left Klauber, Greenfeld or me to score. We usually wound up in the play-offs and played the finals against the Kleider Kammer, who were the best team in the ghetto because they were able to recruit players before they even entered the ghetto and before anyone else could talk to them. Therefore, they had former Czech league players and a couple of former Hakoah Vienna soccer players on their roster.

Every Jewish kid in Austria had a dream to be able to play for Hakoah in Vienna, the only Jewish team that could successfully compete against other teams that had a much larger pool of players to recruit from. I had cousins, excellent soccer players who played for their town, who were never able to make the first or second team of Hakoah. My friend, Ernie's father, was the lawyer for the sports club, Hakoah, and he made me promise that, should we survive, I would sign a contract with him to play for Hakoah Vienna. Other people approached me on behalf of their teams including the directors of Sparta and Schalke. One wanted to make sure that I would play for Rapid Austria after the war. Another man said that his family had an interest in Bratislava, a Czech team, and that he wanted me to play for them. All that was, of course, music to my ears because all I ever wanted to be was a professional soccer player. But I was not yet seventeen years old, and I was definitely not in the right place.

Then, I was transferred from the Dresdner kitchen to the Hamburger kitchen. This Kasserne was for women only. As a cook, I occasionally had to work night shifts. For this work, I had to obtain a pass that allowed me to walk the streets after curfew. Besides the meager rations of food, there was sickness, typhus, para-typhus, typhoid, sleeping sickness, meningitis and a severe outbreak of impetigo. Sickness took friends and acquaintances from our ranks. Because of the close quarters and irritable people, petty arguments often became catastrophic confrontations. So, if someone could find a few moments of happiness, they took full advantage of it. I found it playing soccer, having relationships and friends, and I still had my parents and brother with me and alive.

It became evident that the Germans had a master plan for Theresienstadt. They ordered a beautification program for the ghetto, and it became clear that something was going to happen. With this information, rumors started to spread. One rumor was a visit from Hitler. Another was that we were preparing the future quarters of the German Army. Another was that an international Red Cross inspection would take place. This was the rumor that was later confirmed. The Germans wanted to show the world the "fair treatment" the Jews were receiving in Terezin and wanted to document this visit in case the German Army was defeated. To further prove the case, they built a park with a gazebo in the center of the ghetto where orchestras and bands played every day. They enacted further improvements: stage plays, comedy acts, singers, even operettas were performed in preparation for the coming event. The Clothing Chamber gave out respectable clothes, and I was again drafted into the painting corps on behalf of the panicky process of suddenly beautifying the ghetto. We worked like dogs, painting only the fronts of houses, while in the rear the same old filth remained. House after house on street after street was painted, but still only the fronts. I did retain my status as a cook, so I could enter any kitchen and get my food without using my ration card. That was very helpful. I also had become some sort of a celebrity by playing soccer, even among some German S.S. men and Czech gendarmes. One night, I was on my way to report for the night shift when I was stopped after curfew in the street by an S.S. sergeant who roamed the ghetto only to cause pain. He was a short, stocky man. I removed my cap and attempted to reach into my pocket for my pass when he said, "Never mind, Ladner, go on."

The beautification program was progressing slowly and more and more men joined the project. While this historical charade was going on, transports to Poland went on uninterrupted. Then they stopped. None of us could interpret this good fortune, but we believed that it had something to do with the Red Cross visit. Our first ghetto eldest, Mr. Edelstein, was abruptly removed from his post and sent to Poland. Shortly thereafter, the second ghetto eldest, Mr. Epstein, followed. The story connected with both men was that they refused to cooperate with the Germans, to plan the liquidation of Theresienstadt and expedite the selection process for transports. Therefore, they were punished. People who had been sent to Poland previously had promised to write to their family and friends, but no one had written, and they were never heard from again. The word "Poland" meant fear and extreme anxiety. I did not know that Poland meant Auschwitz, Birkenau or Treblinka. I thought it was a place similar to Terezin and just another place to work. But rumors persisted in the ghetto that Poland meant death. I sat many evenings with my parents and brother, Hans, and spoke of what might happen to us, but my religious mother left our future in God's hands and somehow it more than softened the thought of being sent away and separated.

The next ghetto leader was, to my surprise, Rabbi Murmelstein from the Klucki Temple in Vienna, in whose choir I once sang. Once again, my past experience in the choir would come in useful. Rabbi Murmelstein took the helm with authority, and he must have done outstanding work to satisfy the Nazis' plan to exterminate the Jews in Terezin and Jews who had as yet not arrived.

I met Heine Horn and asked him if he could get me out of the beautification program and back into the kitchen. He suggested that I go and see Rabbi Murmelstein, who could change my status instantly. I did go to see him and was intercepted by his male secretary, who said that I could go back to work in the kitchen, provided I would play soccer for the Viennese team again. I got my reassignment and the following week I rejoined Team Vienna.

As it usually happens, my first game was against Jugend Fuersorge. It felt strange to stand opposite my old teammates. Vienna would normally have lost against Jugend Fuersorge, but that day I kicked two goals, and we wound up in a three to three tie. After the game my old buddies said that I should have let the game end three to two for old time's sake, exactly the same utterance of words I heard from my Viennese friends when I left them. By then, it was a well-known fact that a Red Cross inspection team was coming to Terezin. Would they report the truth to the international community about the persecution of Jews, or would this visit whitewash the Nazis?

Earlier while painting the quarters, or better said, the front of the girls' quarters, I met a young, cute Czech girl with long, blond hair and a beautiful figure. She was only past her fourteenth birthday while I was past my seventeenth when we became friends. Soon thereafter, we were going steady. I spent most of my free time with her. Maybe we were a bit young for such serious companionship, but we loved each other and we never knew what tomorrow would bring. People had disappeared from the ghetto, and my friends and I lived from moment to moment and extracted the best that was offered to us at that time. We went to the cabaret performances, jazz concerts, and comic reviews. We sat in front of the gazebo and listened to the orchestra, and we could not believe the drastic change of ghetto life and what was being offered for our entertainment. In addition, we had private parties and we could freely visit without interference by anyone.

My girlfriend was the child of a mixed marriage. Her father was Jewish and her mother was a Christian. Her mother lived free, while her father was imprisoned somewhere. Why my girlfriend was sent to the ghetto, no one could understand or explain. All she ever told me was that her mother was trying everything to get her released. She received an occasional postcard from her mother, and that kept her hopes alive that she would soon be freed. In the meantime, she was with me and my family. She liked my parents and my mother loved her. She saw them every day after school, and when I had to work the night shift she would usually spend the entire next day with me.

The days passed, waiting for the Red Cross inspection, hoping that they would be our Messiah. It was like a pause from all that was evil, and we gratefully accepted what was offered to us during this period. This international gathering of Jews in the ghetto told us that no Jew was safe in any country. They had arrived from Austria, Germany, Czechoslovakia, Holland, and Denmark. Then we learned that a train full of Jewish children from Poland had arrived, but were quartered outside the ghetto. Rumor had it that these kids would be sent to Palestine. Two youth leaders were chosen to accompany the children. One was my friend, Freddy Hirsch, and the other,

Aaron Menzer. Both were Zionist Youth leaders. I later found out that the transport was sent to Auschwitz and all the children were gassed. Aaron stood with the children to give them comfort and calmness, while Freddy Hirsch did not want to deliver the children to their death, so he committed suicide.

Terezin became a very active community. Among the ghetto-ites were famous musicians, actors, singers, and comedians, like Ernest Morgan, Hans Hofer and Bobby Jones. I attended a performance of the Three Penny Opera starring Kurt Gerron and Gisela Wurzel. I learned that the Germans were filming the activities for a documentary film that would include soccer games. For this purpose, Kurt Gerron and others were recruited, people who had extended experience from the stage to film. I remember seeing the German S.S. and others filming soccer games on the Bastei and in the Dresdner Kasserne. On the Bastei they stood nearby, but in the Dresdner they stood on or near the roof. Most of the German S.S. and gendarmes used to watch our soccer games from the roof of the Dresdner and filming was an added attraction.

The entire ghetto seemed to have changed; newly painted fronts on houses, music, children were stopped on the street by the S.S. and given chocolate and then taught to say, "Chocolate again, Uncle Rahm," or whoever gave them the chocolate. People seemed to be dressed nicer. We even prepared our kitchen in the Kasserne for a possible visit by the Red Cross. When I visited my parents, they seemed happy. My mother said that no one had died in her room for three whole days. When my friends and I got together with our girlfriends, we had a good time. It was all puzzling to me. The typhus epidemic continued, sleeping sickness was rampant, and people died every day by the hundreds. But somehow the younger ones did not see, or did not want to see, what was happening around the corner; the suffering of others and all the people who were sent to Poland by the train loads.

Then, one day, the Germans ordered the ghetto to be emptied. All the ghetto-ites were gathered in a large field outside the ghetto. One block after another we were ordered to leave and not to take any of our belongings with us. You could see the fear in peoples' faces, and I was no different. This order took us by complete surprise, and only negative rumors spread. Thousands of us stood in this field, surrounded by armed Czech and German guards, and we did not know the reason why we were standing in the cold and wet field. In whispering voices, the ghetto-ites were trying to guess the purpose for all this. One whisper suggested that they were searching for escapees, another that they were looking for weapons, that a census was being taken and that we would be counted one by one, and that the ghetto was being fumigated. The worst story was that we were all going to be shot. People were shivering and silently crying, even the younger ones were very quiet, anticipating that something terrible was going to happen. We could not find out what was going on in the ghetto.

After hours of standing in a cloudy, rainy field, we were ordered to return to our quarters. It was very late in the afternoon when I returned, and I ran to check on my family before curfew. I arrived at my parents' quarters just as they returned from the field, and my brother, Hans, came a few minutes later. My girlfriend also came running to check our return, and we were comforted that nothing of consequence happened. We all returned to our quarters hoping that this was the end of another fearful episode.

The beautification program continued. My father and brother were now at the forefront of a huge collection of painters. Occasionally, my father and brother were summoned to work outside the ghetto. At these times it was very favorable for my family. We would return into the ghetto with vegetables that were earmarked for horses. My genius mother always made something edible out of kale leaves, turnips and almost rotten carrots. I contributed to the feast by bringing items like dumplings that did not rise while cooking. They looked like twisted rocks and were just as heavy. I solidly packed them into my kidney-shaped pot. You could pack quite a few of those cement-like dumplings. Most of the cooks carried this kind of pot around. It was easily hidden in your jacket or pants, and, unless frisked, could not be detected. There were several kitchen detectives around. The two top cops were Viennese – a Mr. Hochman and his friend.

They inspected all kitchens, watched you dish out food, and, generally, kept an eagle eye on all kitchen workers to make sure nothing edible left the kitchen. There were several arrests, mostly warnings, but you lost your job in the kitchen. I knew Mr. Hochman and company well, but I did not take any chances. I once carried two portions of food in my pot, which I openly displayed. I walked straight to Mr. Hochman, lifted the lid and said, "That's my personal ration, please check with Heini Horn." They just said to go on and, from that day on, I was never asked, checked or frisked if I carried anything out of the kitchen. When I gave my mother these dumplings, I don't know what she did, but in the evening, she gave me some to eat, and they was so good. They were diced and seasoned and served with some kale. It would have been delicious even by regular standards.

I also exchanged food for bread with my friend, Ernie. He always had one-fourth of a piece of bread for me. I never asked Ernie if his bread was obtained illegally or if it was his extra ration, and he never asked me how I got extra portions of hash. At times, he told me that he could not give me any bread for he needed it to exchange for insulin. Ernie was a diabetic since childhood, and insulin was his life. The ghetto had little or no extra medicine. He had made a connection through a man with a Czech gendarme who provided him ample injection needles and insulin.

They were beautifying at a furious pace, but since the day the Germans emptied the ghetto, I had nothing but sobering thoughts. How easily they could have killed us all with a few machine guns, and all the people we knew who departed for Poland were never heard from again. My thoughts of possible harm to us were very real, and they were on my mind more than I liked. What was this little garrison city called Terezin, overstuffed with between sixty or seventy thousand Jews from all over Europe, with thousands coming and thousands leaving? Not enough food for the majority and uncontrollable sickness. Every planned entertainment or soccer game was being filmed, but for what purpose? Occasionally they filmed at night, and huge stands with lighting fixtures illuminated areas. Participants were ordered to take part in various scenes, pretending to sit at concerts or musical revues, and just pretend to be engaging in every day strolling.

The day came when the Red Cross Commission arrived. They were escorted at all times by the place where the S.S. Children were playing. The band performed at the gazebo, and the Red Cross visited various pre-selected quarters. Several prepared interviews took place, and as quickly as the Commission arrived, they left. What the Commission accomplished, I never knew, and I personally never saw them. All I ever learned was that the S.S. propaganda machine was served.

After the inspection, my fears came to a sudden realization. The beautification work stopped, friends and even members of the ghetto government were being sent to Poland with an accelerated urgency. The entire life and pace of the ghetto started to change for the worst. Entertainers who had kept us laughing and hopeful were now nowhere to be seen. People around us spoke of nothing but which person or friend must report for relocation to Poland. Even the continuing soccer games had a sad aura because so many of the players were now gone.

Herbert, Maxie, Ernie and I, with our girlfriends, formed a cocoon and spent most of our free time with each other. The quarters where my parents and brother lived all of a sudden had empty bunks. My mother's greatest fear was that we would be separated, and even though she was already a very religious woman, she became even more so. She prayed every day and even attempted her fasting routine, like when my brother, Pepi, was so very sick. My father explained to her that we had been fasting ever since we arrived in Terezin. I tried to reach Rabbi Murmelstein, hoping that maybe my family could remain in Terezin, but I could not even get into his outer office. After several attempts, the secretary told me that he could not help anyone and that he could or would not see anybody. It was then that the desperateness of the situation became very obvious.

It was between Rosh Hashanah and Yom Kippur, 1944, when I arrived in my quarters and was told that the entire staff and all of us living there were ordered to prepare for transportation to a labor camp because we were needed to work for the war effort. I ran into the office for information, just as Herbert was coming out and said, "It's the day before Yom Kippur," and later revised that it would be the day after Yom Kippur. I ran to my parents to bring them the sad news. My mother started to cry, and my father was very quiet. My brother, Hans, came into the room to inform us that he also had to report. The first words my mother spoke to us were that we all must fast on Yom Kippur in the hope that the Germans would rescind their order. We did as my mother asked us to do. That night, Herbert's and my girlfriends stayed with us all night. We tried to console each other for the next day's departure.

Early the next morning, Herbert, Maxie, Kurt, Heinz, Walter and I left our quarters to report. I carried a suitcase and a backpack, and we marched toward the Hamburger where we had to report. Before we even entered the building, we were told to return to our quarters because the transport had been canceled. We were jubilant, and we began to smile again, for all of us hoped we could survive Hitler in Terezin. Rumor had it that the war was lost for the Germans, and if we could hold on and nothing drastic happened to us, we could go home alive within a short period of time. My girlfriend came running, all excited, and jumped into my arms. We crossed the street to tell my parents the good news, but my brother had already told them. My mother told us that her prayers for the cancellation of all transports had accomplished it.

When we returned to our building and saw the rest of the guys coming back, everyone looked happy and relieved. That evening we got the bad news that we were to report the next morning to be transported. I again said my sad farewell to my girlfriend and parents. My brother had already reported and was in the Hamburger. I told everyone that I would write as soon as possible. I told them that if I wrote the word "rain", then it was very bad, but should I write the word "sun", then it was not bad wherever I was. I made them promise that they would not volunteer for any transports until they heard from me. We hugged again and kissed and said our good-byes. My father walked with me a short distance, then he stopped and put his hands on my head and said a prayer, just like the time I left for Belgium. He then gave me one more kiss on my forehead, and he turned and walked over to my mother. My girlfriend and I walked across to the Hamburger, and I told her to proclaim that she was of a mixed marriage and that she should remain in the ghetto until her mother could free her.

That day the train came into the ghetto for the first time. It was a long train, with many cattle cars. All my friends were in front of the Kasserne, with their baggage, waiting for everyone to arrive in order for us to be together. As we entered, I saw my brother among a group of men. We waved to each other while we lined up in front of tables. One by one we passed through and headed toward the cattle cars. After a long wait, the German S.S. guards sounded a shrill whistle, and Czech gendarmes started to load the train. Herbert and Maxie were the first two to climb onto the train. I threw my backpack and suitcase toward Herbert, who further relayed them to Maxie, and then I climbed aboard. More and more people joined us in our cattle wagon, and it became very crowded. Dr. Sterzer, Ernie's father, was the only one selected from his family for the transport. Ernie and his family remained in the ghetto, but only for another week. Besides Herbert and Maxie, there were the two Walters, Peter, Hardy and several other Czech friends with us in the box car. The S.S. were walking up and down the length of the train, making sure that the chain of guards was intact. My brother was several wagons behind ours. I tried earlier to have him join us, but the guards rejected my request. While we were still standing, I moved toward the open door. I saw only S.S. men and several guards. Some of them climbed onto the train in the front and rear. Then a couple of ghetto policemen, gendarmes, accompanied by the S.S., walked from one box car to the other, sliding the doors shut. How they locked them, I could not see, but when they came to our door, you could hear a loud clamp, and we knew that we were locked into this crowded cattle car. I sat on my suitcase next to Herbert, and said to him quietly, "I think we are in for very hard times." But Herbert, forever the optimist, shrugged his shoulders and said, "We'll manage. After all, how hard can they work us?" Maxi asked, "How sure are we that we are going to a labor camp?" But Herbert insisted that they needed us to work.

The train was crowded with people and baggage, and it started to move very slowly out of the ghetto. It started to pick up speed, and according to our Czech friends, we were heading in a northeast direction with a possible destination of Danzig. All chatter and even quiet conversations had stopped. Friends tried to look out of the few slats in the cattle car to give us information as to where the present position of the train might be. I got uncomfortable sitting. I stood up and meandered through people who were lying down, then hurdled over some baggage and sat next to Dr. Sterzer. He was very quiet and not really interested in small talk. I then sat down between Maxie and his father. Maxie had turned and was very optimistic about the future, while his father seemed very depressed. I opened the conversation by talking about Vienna, the various landmarks, soccer teams, and our favorite places in Austria. The conversations led to fatigue, and I returned to my place next to Herbert.

I must have fallen asleep, for when I woke up the light between the slats had disappeared, and all I heard was the monotonous sound of a rolling train. I was wide awake when the train came to a complete stop. Some of my friends tried to strain and focus their eyes, looking through the slats to see if they could distinguish something from the pitch darkness. There were no sounds. The eerie quiet was only interrupted by an occasional cough or sigh. We stood on this spot until early morning, and we still could not see anything resembling civilization. Soon the train started to move again at a very slow speed and fifteen minutes later came to an abrupt halt. We heard voices and dogs barking outside, and it seemed as if an entire city had come to life. Then the doors slid open, two men jumped onto our car and ordered everyone to jump off the train.

We were hardly able to move from being so crowded together, but we managed to throw our belongings out of the door and then jump out after them. We saw men dressed in striped pants and everyone wore a different jacket and a funny looking beret type of hat. As they came closer, we realized that they were prisoners. They spoke to us in Yiddish: Gaitz aroise. Aufgaine zo finef. (Everybody out and line up in rows of five.) People were pushing and shoving. The prison guards were trying to line us up, but as soon as everything was just right, another group of people from the train disrupted the orderly line-up. After a few minutes we stood like soldiers, five men in each row, and the loud shouting quieted down to a slight murmur. S.S. guards stood short distances apart to make sure that none of the new arrivals escaped. The Jewish prison guards in passing us by always said, Ihr seit gezint, Verstehst? Gezint, which meant, "You are all healthy. Understood? Healthy." My eyes wandered toward the S.S. guards. There were at least a dozen of them. Every so often one would yell some command to the Jewish guards, and they immediately obeyed and executed the order by pushing some of us into a more military line-up. Just then a bunch of S.S. officers appeared and stopped in front of the first line, which was a distance away. In my row was Maxie, his father, Herbert, Peter and myself. In the row directly in front of us were Dr. Sterzer, another elderly man and three friends from the youth quarters in Terezin. It got quiet, and the Jewish guards stepped away from the new arrivals. The lines started to move slowly forward, and we dragged our belongings with us. I still could not see what was going on in front of us. As our line came closer, we were ordered to remove our hats and a guard reminded us that we were strong. As we almost reached the front, I could see what was happening. Three S.S. officers looked everyone over, from head to toe, occasionally speaking to some of the men. One of them made the decision, whether you go to the left or the right, by pointing his finger. They were looking at the line in front of me. Dr. Sterzer was asked to go to the left (their right); the other four went to the right. Our line was next, four of us went to the right, while Maxi's father was asked if he was stark and gesundt (strong and healthy). Mr. Witrofsky answered in his Viennese accent, Ja wohl, sehr stark und sehr gesundt. (Yes, very strong and very healthy). The S.S. officer kept looking and looking at him and finally decided to send him to the right, and he immediately joined us. We were constantly asked to move further and further up, and then we started to march as best we could, still dragging our belongings.

Not much further down the road, barbed wire encircled areas to the left and right. Once we were past the selection ordeal, the prisoners who guarded us became more vocal and started to speak in short sentences to us, but out of the earshot of the very few remaining

S.S. guards who walked along the perimeter. One of the guards walking to the right of me said to drop everything valuable to the side of the road or throw things over the barbed wires. Before I could ask what he meant or ask why, he was already several yards ahead of me. I still did not know what he meant until we saw barracks to the left and right and an additional fence with a guard tower twenty or thirty yards from the fence. Inside the camp, we saw women lined up along the barracks. Some were yelling something at us, and most stretched out their arms as if to beg. In front, people were throwing things over the barbed wires. Something must have hit the wires and the item fell very close to the inner fence. One woman ran over to pick it up. I heard at least one gun shot and the woman fell to the ground. It was so shocking and unexpected that we started to trot in order to get away from the scene. The prison guard was next to me again, and I asked him, meaning to inquire about Dr. Sterzer, where all the people who went to the left were going. He looked at the sky and answered, Geneden (meaning, heaven or the Garden of Eden). That was my introduction to Auschwitz.

CHAPTER THIRTEEN
AUSCHWITZ

Shaken by what we had seen, we continued to walk toward a very large, open field. To our left were barracks and men walking around. The entire camp was surrounded by wires, and Herbert, the electrician, immediately said that the wires were electrically charged and pointed to several connectors to show us. We had stopped at this open field, and Maxie asked, "What kind of place is this? This place does not look like a labor camp." There was a foul smell in the air. The S.S. guards had disappeared. From then on, the prison guards, who sounded a lot like the German S.S., gave all orders.

Wooden structures that looked like barracks were in front of us. Further to the left, we could see additional barracks standing, one after another. The rows of five slowly disintegrated, and people were standing in groups discussing what had happened so far and what they had seen. My group's discussion was very subdued. We had to come from a ghetto to a... Mr. Witrofsky was the first to say the dreaded words—concentration camp. We all learned that we had landed in Auschwitz/Birkenau. I remembered my cousins' silence after they returned from Dachau and Buchenwald, and I remembered the fear in their eyes much more vividly now than before. Mr. Witrofsky said with a quiver in his voice that this was the end for all of us, and he grabbed his son, Maxie, holding onto him for a few minutes. The first sentence that I spoke was to Herbert, mentioning that the smell in the air was awful, and that I felt like throwing up. Herbert said, "It's the smoke in the air." I knew that, but why the terrible smell?

The orders came to line up by five again, and we started to move toward a large wooden structure. It took quite a while for us to reach the front entrance where, again, three S.S. officers looked at everyone from top to bottom. Some were ordered to remain on the side. All others entered a large room, were ordered to strip naked and to take only our shoes and belt with us. The rest of our belongings were to remain in the room. Several of our camp guards took our stuff and dragged it to an adjacent room. We were further told that we must go through a delousing procedure and a shower. I was carrying my German officer boots and my belt and slowly moved in the direction of another door. Just then, a capo (camp police or foreman) came over to me, looked at my boots and confiscated them, or, to use a better word, stole them from me. I, therefore, was one of the very few without shoes. As I entered the room I saw inmates with razors. One of them was shaving Herbert's head. Herbert, who was a very tall, tough kid, was yelling with every stroke of the blade. Not only was Herbert yelling, but everyone in the room who was being shaven was also yelling. It was my turn. Whatever hair I had, and I was very hairy, was shaven off. It would be more accurate to say that they ripped every hair off my body one by one, until I was bleeding from several cuts in many areas. This was only the beginning of pain. I then had to step down into a foot deep hole that was filled with a liquid that smelled like gasoline. A guy with rags wrapped around his hands washed me from top to bottom. The contact of this liquid with my bleeding open cuts burned like acid. It was so painful that it was difficult not to cry out loud; silently, I did cry. Past this station, we entered a shower room and had to wait until the room was filled with people for them to run the water. I just stood there aflame with pain, waiting for some relief. They finally turned on the water, and not until I was totally soaked did the burning subside. When they stopped the shower, the burning and the bleeding returned but with a lot less pain. While still soaking wet, we marched on and again had to stand in line; this time in long single rows, when two S.S. men walked along looking us over and staring at our naked bodies. One of them, a big, fat pig, carried a big kitchen knife and pressed the blade against one of my friend's side, who jumped about two feet. The S.S. man jokingly said, "Boy, are you ticklish." He moved further down the row, flinging his knife from right to left, approaching another friend. He lowered his knife toward my friend's penis as if to circumcise him again. The S.S. men were laughing; that was for their entertainment, but our fright was very real. Still wet, we walked out into the open air, and everyone started to shake from the sudden cold breeze. Along the right were tables lined up and behind them stood prisoners, eyeballing us for our approximate size. One gave out a pair of pants; another a shirt and jacket; another a hat, underwear and socks; and the last one a pair of shoes if you had none. I received a shirt, almost my size, underwear made out of talesem (Jewish prayer shawls), a much too long pair of pants, and a lister jacket, which is a silken black jacket that Orthodox Jews wear mostly on Saturday. The jacket was lightweight and two sizes too small. I could not button it. I then received a beret-type hat that was three times too large for me, but that was good because I could pull it way down over my ears. I got two pouches that were supposed to be socks, and last I received a pair of low-cut pointed shoes, without laces, at least one size too small. With all of this in my arms, I arrived at a large outdoor opening where everyone got dressed. Herbert's pants were much too short for him. My pants were a little longer, so we exchanged. Other than that, I wore what they gave me. We never saw our suitcases with our clothing again.

As more and more of my friends joined us, we looked at each other and could barely recognize one another. In this sad situation, we looked at each other and began to laugh. The transformation from ghetto to concentration camp inmate was so abrupt and so severe that some of the older men had crying spells that contributed to our shared depression and degradation. Maxie's father was very bad off. The first thing I had to do was to step heavily on the heel or rear of my shoes and bend the leather in order to be able to slip them on like slippers. Not only were the shoes too small, but the pointed front cramped my toes.

We stood at this open area for a while. The wind started to swirl around us, and it seemed to get colder by the minute, when we heard the familiar line up by five. We then marched slowly on a semi-muddied road toward the barracks. The further down the road we walked, the more pronounced the awful smell became. We reached our assigned barrack. As we walked in, a guy was assigning bunks. At that time, Herbert Heimerling, Max Witrofsky and his father, Peter Neuschiller, Hardie Fleischman, Walter Wolfgang and maybe five or six other friends were still with me. The barracks were large. To the left were all the bunks, triple deckers, and through the center of the barracks was a low wall. I could not figure out the purpose of this wall, but I spent most of my time sitting on it. When I climbed up to my bunk, which I shared with Herbert, I found a bowl and a spoon at the bottom near my feet and nothing else – no blankets or pillows, just a wooden bunk.

By then, we had learned a lot more about Auschwitz from other prisoners. All the people who went to the left side would be gassed and then cremated. The awful smell in the camp came from the crematoriums burning flesh, which burned people twenty-four hours a day, day in and day out. Just thinking back to those days, I still can recreate the terrible stench in my mind. Herbert, Maxie, Peter and I sat around lamenting and knowing that any one of us could be part of the burning odor. As hungry as I was, the first two days I could not eat the soup they gave us. It looked like muddy water with some poison ivy cooked in it. The combination of what the soup looked like and the unbearable smell in the camp took my appetite away. Eventually, hunger overcame the smell, and I began to eat the soup and small ration of bread.

To further complicate our existence, it started to rain. "Rain" is not really the accurate word for it – it poured for several days, and the mud, which was nominal at first, became at least one foot deep. The shoes I had to wear, whose rear leather part I eventually cut out for easier entrance, were definitely not suited for this kind of weather and accumulation of mud. Many times I stood on one leg, advanced one shoe by hand, placed it loosely in the mud, slipped my foot in it, and repeated the sequence with the other shoe. In this fashion, it took a while to go from one place to the other.

When people got sick in the barracks, they were taken away and never seen again. All that my friends and I could think of, talk about, and wish for was a way to get away from this horrible place. The more I thought about it, the more helpless and depressed I felt. Friends thought of suicide or escape, which actually meant the same thing. None of us could come up with an answer that made sense. We were also told that we would be given a number and tattoo on our forearm, which meant that we would remain in Auschwitz. Herbert said, "I am not going to get tattooed. I am not going to stay here."

I was sitting on the little wall talking to Maxie, when someone from the doorway yelled out my name. "Kurt Ladner. Is Kurt Ladner in this barrack?" I did not know if I should answer his call, so I just sat. Then someone in the front said, "Yes, he is in the back, probably in his bunk." I then raised my hand to identify myself, shouting, "Here I am." As this guy came closer, I recognized him as a soccer player from Terezin. He said that he needed me. The older prisoners of Auschwitz had challenged the new arrivals from Terezin to a soccer match. The game was not only sanctioned by the S.S., but they expected the match to take place. At that moment, all I could think of was the mud, the smell and my shoes. For the first time in my life, I had no desire to play soccer. I asked him, "Will they give us shoes to play?" His answer was no. We had to play with what we had. I then showed him the shoes I had received and asked him to say that he could not find me. But he insisted, saying that I could play, even without shoes, better than most. I begged him to forget about me playing. I assured him that he could find many other guys. He would not have a problem fielding a team without me. I removed one of my shoes and held it in my hand. He finally could see my dilemma and that I must have really felt bad if I was refusing to play. To this day, I don't know if that match took place.

I had been asking around to see if anyone knew where my brother, Hans, was. I was told that he was several blocks away with a large group of men from Terezin. We met that afternoon, and I saw a sad and dejected brother. We talked for a while, encouraged each other not to give up, no matter how bad, serious or dangerous our lives became. We hugged and had to go our separate ways. After that meeting, I never saw my brother in Auschwitz again.

Days passed. It kept on raining and the mud got deeper. We performed menial jobs, like latrine duty or transporting sick people, who lay coiled and intertwined, on a wagon to a barrack for the sick and other in camp jobs. Then all work assignments stopped. We were ordered to remain in our barracks and await further instructions. Some of us had to go to a neighboring barrack to have our number tattooed on our arm. Herbert said, "We've got to get out of this line. We don't want to remain in Auschwitz." We had already reached the upper steps and were about to enter when Herbert turned and asked us to follow him. We returned to our barracks, and five or six of our other friends followed us. Before we reached the door, a capo stopped us, asking us where we were going. Herbert said that we were asked to report there and that we were following orders. He let us pass. We entered our old barrack, which, in addition to the remaining people, had new prisoners who had taken our places. Another capo asked us how we got there. We repeated our story that we were ordered to report here, and we did not know why. Herbert lied like crazy. So did I. The capo asked no further questions, and he included us as his charges. Little did we know then what we had done.

An S.S. man came in and asked us to line up. As we slowly walked out of the barracks, the same three S.S. officers who we saw at the train arrived. We went through another selection process. By then we all knew who Dr. Mengele was. He was a man who could decide whether you lived or died by a motion of his finger. Luckily, most of us passed the selection and returned to the barrack.

After that, no one could leave, and no one could enter our premises. That very night, that very dark, dark night, where you could not see anything, the S.S. moved us into a different structure. We had to stand, body against body, as more and more people were pushed in. We had to stand in this pitch darkness. You could not see anyone, not even your own hand in front of your eyes. Maxie, his father and Hardie stood right next to me while Peter and Herbert stood behind me. It was still and eerie. All of a sudden someone in the rear started to scream: "Murderers. You killers. The Russians are outside the camp, and when they come in, they are going to kill every S.S. man." It was frightening. Someone must have gotten to this guy; maybe someone jumped him, for the sound of his voice became more and more muffled. Then it got quiet again, and I mean nearly silent. The fear of the unknown befell all of us. I could sense the anxiety in the pitch darkness. Herbert, who always talked a mile a minute, had not uttered one word for the last hour. Maxie, who was never afraid of anything, asked me in a quivering voice what I thought was going to happen to us. We all knew very well what could happen to us. The gas chambers were working overtime and the crematorium could convert us into the smoke and smell that we had to endure since our arrival in Auschwitz. To make the situation even more unbearable, Mr. Witrofsky's mind started to crack. He asked Maxie to hold him, to give him a last hug and kiss. He was absolutely certain that we were in the gas chamber. He started to cry and reached for everyone, to touch them. He kept up this intermittent crying for a long time. Maxie was finally able to talk to him quietly, to calm his nerves, but he sure scrambled mine.

We stood and stood; our legs started to hurt. I shifted my weight from one leg to the other, when I faintly saw strips of light showing through cracks near the top of the structure. I poked Maxie and pointed to the open spaces in the ceiling. "This is not the gas chamber," I said. "The gas could escape through the cracks." Maxie then showed it to his father, while I did the same to Herbert. Dawn broke, and we could see that we were in an empty barn. A short time later, we could see each other's pale faces while our fears started to subside.

In the morning, we exited through the rear and saw a place that was unbelievable. There were wagons full of dead people, waiting to be burned or buried. They looked like a scrambled mound of arms and legs with an occasional torso or face. The capo told us that they could not burn the people fast enough and would dump them into mass graves. We again reached a large open field to face the S.S. and maybe Dr. Mengele for one more selection process. We stood in rows of five and were slowly inching toward several S.S. men. This time, instead of pointing fingers, they yelled out numbers. As your number was called, you had to step out and walk toward the other side. My row was next, and I was number two. The S.S. looked us over. We had to drop our pants and lift our shirts to expose our entire body. The next voice I heard was an S.S. man calling number four. I knew that I was number two, but number four did not move at all. Instead he looked at me as if to say, "You are number four, not me." Then an S.S. man ran over, grabbed number four, beating him over the head with a billy club, and dragged him to the side. Our row then moved up and joined the others.

After an extended time standing, I felt cold in my scanty clothing, which got wet in the misty rain. We no longer stood like soldiers. We started to mingle amongst ourselves. My group of friends stood in a semi-circle, questioning each other. "What is in store for us next?" Maxie was very subdued and sad, for his father was taken out of the row. Maxie kept shaking his head trying to console himself, hoping that his father would join us shortly. We soon heard a command. "All line up!" We slowly formed lines and walked toward a waiting train. Before they loaded us into the cattle cars, we received a piece of bread, then they literally stuffed us into the box cars. The first few men formed a row against the wall, then had to sit down and spread their legs apart. Then the next row of men sat down in between their legs and so on, until the entire boxcar was filled without an extra inch of space. In my immediate area sat Maxie Witrofsky, Herbert Heimerling, Hardie Fleischman, Peter Neuschiller, Walter Wolfgang, and several other friends were further away. We sat and waited like that for at least two hours, and all we kept saying was, "When? When are we finally going to leave? When are we going to get out of this horrible place, Auschwitz Birkenau?"

We still did not know where we were going to end up. I just sat there, feeling so helpless, so totally in the hands of the German S.S. I sat slumped forward, my thoughts wandering back to Terezin, to my parents. How sad my father was when he laid his hands on my head and blessed me, how abruptly he walked toward my mother, how I had kissed my girlfriend goodbye. I thought of my brother, Hans, someplace on the train, all the dead people stacked on the wagons, the ever-deepening mud, and the awful smell of death in Auschwitz/

Birkenau. I was so angry, I grabbed Hardie's arm, and I really hurt him by squeezing it. His abrupt jerking away of his arm brought me back to my uncomfortable position of sitting on the floor. The door was still wide open, and I could see where S.S. men were walking and talking, occasionally pointing to the train. Then, a large bucket was thrown into our car that was put into the far corner. Then, a group of S.S. men came marching, carrying bayonets on very long rifles, and took their posts between each boxcar. S.S. officers took one more glance in our direction, and, a few minutes later, the doors were closed and locked.

It was very dark in the boxcar after the door closed. Whatever light we did get, came through a few air slats on the upper half of the cattle car. The piece of bread and the large bucket they gave us indicated to me an extended stay on the train. Since the day I had left my parents as a little kid to go to Belgium, I became very apprehensive of unknown destinations. However, to leave Auschwitz, that hellhole, eased my mind. Nothing worse could follow this place.

We stood in the locked train for a while longer, and when the train finally started to move, Herbert patted my back and shoulder as if to say, "We made it out of here." I immediately ate my whole piece of bread, and tried to settle in as comfortably as possible. We traveled at a slow speed into the night. At one point, the train came to a complete stop. We knew it was somewhere in Czechoslovakia, but did not know where. By early morning it was getting very gamey in the cattle car. Guys did not make it to the bucket and peed through a small opening between the sliding door and the wall.

My legs got stiff and painful and, in order to stretch them, I had to get up and take one or two steps. It was almost impossible not to step on someone because it was that crowded. The more the guys shifted around, the more uncomfortable it became. Herbert's legs reached a couple of rows, and the poor guy just sat motionless.

The next discovery we made was that there was no water on the train. We sat with nothing more to eat or drink on a crowded floor in a motionless train that smelled of urine, and everything else. As much as I tried to fall asleep, the thoughts that kept going through my head kept me wide awake. Being able to get out of Auschwitz alive, in my mind, was a major accomplishment. By stepping out from the line to be tattooed, we directed our future into an unknown destiny. However, I still asked myself, "Have we gone from bad to worse?" The answer always was, "Nothing can be as bad as Auschwitz."

It was early in the morning when the train started to roll again. We asked our Czech friends to look through the slats in hopes that they could recognize the surroundings. They saw some Czech markings. Hence, we were still in Czechoslovakia, but where? We had no idea. The train would speed up, slow down, and stop on occasion until we reached Austria.

The door to our cattle car was opened, and fresh air streamed in. Armed S.S. men stood guard in front of every car. I jumped up as best I could and reached the open door. I saw a group of guarded prisoners across the tracks disappear from view. A few minutes later, they returned carrying buckets of water, which they distributed to each prisoner. That was when I had my first drink of precious water in more than a day and a half. We were not allowed to leave our cattle car, and the pushing and shoving from the rear almost knocked the guys in the front off the train. I moved back to my place to make room for others. I yelled to Maxie that someone should dump the toilet bucket, which was filled to capacity, but some guys had wisely already done so. The S.S. locked the doors again, and after having had some water and fresh air, I almost felt good.

The train took off. I closed my eyes, and I got used to the drone of wheels turning on the tracks. For the first time in three days and nights, I fell fast asleep. When I woke up, I had no idea how long I had slept. The train had stopped. We heard voices outside, but it was impossible to make out a complete sentence. By linking together isolated words, which Hardie Fleischman relayed to us while he had his ear pressed against the wall, we learned that we were stuck for a while in order for them to repair some broken rails. There was still no hint as to where we were or where we were going.

We stood and waited. It started to smell again in our packed cattle car. Some of the guys did not bother to reach the bucket and again peed through the keyhole in the wall. Fights broke out, and it got very tense. What bothered us the most was that we could not stretch our legs. Mine felt like they belonged to someone else, and that someone else had pain, occasional cramps and the feeling of pins and needles. I got hungry and thirsty, but there was no food. Sometimes I was awake, and sometimes I slept. The train kept on rolling at a very slow speed and eventually came to a halt. As this was not unusual, we did not look through the slats above to orient ourselves, until Peter Neuschiller hoisted himself up to the slats and yelled, "We are in Vienna." I tried to get up, but my legs failed me. I pushed Herbert to make room for me to roll onto my stomach, and with some effort, I stood up. I looked through the slats just as we came to a full stop, right in front of the Riesenrad, the giant Ferris wheel in the Prater. Everyone from Vienna had spent many happy days in the Prater. It was pure enjoyment for children. I saw myself walking to the sports stadium to watch an international soccer game. This was an added torture perpetrated on us by the German S.S., showing us Vienna, as if to say, "Here, take a good look one more time because this is the last time you will ever see the Riesenrad." Hardie Fleischman headed over to look and see. He said that his mother lived only two blocks from where we were standing. I made room for him to get a better view. The train started to move; everyone sat down again except Hardie and me. A few minutes later, Hardie yelled, "That is my apartment. Look, look, I can look into my window. I see someone moving around." By the time I was able to concentrate, we were further down the track, and all the windows I saw were dark. There were many apartment buildings in this area that had a large Jewish clientele. One of the buildings was the former Jewish Theater where every major Jewish star performed. I don't know if Hardie saw his mother through the window, or if he just imagined that he saw her. Hardie had slumped to the floor and was sobbing and repeating, "I saw my mother. I saw my mother." I never knew that Hardie was of a mixed marriage, and his mother had remained in Vienna. In such cases, where the Christian got to stay in the apartment, it was necessary that the Christian parent divorce the Jewish parent. The Jewish parent then became "eligible" for transports to Poland. I never discussed these details with Hardie. He was punished enough sitting on the train with all of us.

It was strange that throughout this train ride we did not hear any sirens, or planes, especially Allied planes, and no bombings. What was happening in the war? Were the Allies winning? We knew nothing about the raging war. We all heard rumors while still in Terezin that the Russians in the east and the Western Allies in the west were advancing and beating the Germans on all fronts, but there was nothing to prove to me that it was so. I could not believe these hopeful rumors. Here I was on a crowded train, hungry, thirsty, and not knowing if there was a future for many of us. Even my ever-optimistic friends, Herbert and Maxie, were uncertain.

CHAPTER FOURTEEN
DACHAU AND SATELLITE CAMPS

The train was now traveling at a high speed, and when it stopped, the men crowded around the door in anticipation of food and drink and to be first in line, but the door never opened. The door did not open until around two or three the next morning. Sitting in such an uncomfortable position for this length of time created cramps and stiffness in our legs, and we were uncertain whether or not they could support our bodies. We had stopped. We heard German commands and dogs barking when the door of our cattle car slid open. Dogs were barking, and the S.S. were screaming, "Everybody out! Out! Out! Everybody out! One, two, three, out, out!" I could only see occasional silhouettes created by flashlights. Two S.S. men hopped onto our car and stood in the door with clubs in their hands, beating everyone out of the train. I had slowly crawled near the door. I grabbed Maxie, who stood in front of me complaining that he had no feeling in his legs, and I pulled myself up. I had absolutely no control over my legs. I just stood there watching how other fellows were clubbed out of the train. As Maxie and I reached the door, the S.S. man was yelling, Rrraus! (Out!) Maxie yelled back, Ja wohl, and jumped off the train without being clubbed. I also yelled, Ja wohl, but I got smashed in my back. The force of the blow catapulted me out, and I fell to the ground, twisting my ankle. Once we were off the train, other S.S. guards ordered us to run. Bear in mind that it was pitch dark. Only a little beam of a flashlight pointed the direction in which to run. We ran, barely feeling our legs, with dogs barking and snapping at anything they could reach. How I finally reached the assembly area, I don't know. It was a miracle that I was belted only once and was not bitten by dogs, as so many were, including Maxie. Commands came at me from all directions, clubs were flying, dogs were biting, and I could not see anything. Slowly my eyes adjusted to the darkness. Names of friends were called in the dark for identification, until we were ordered not to talk and to stand still.

We stood very quietly for a long time. It started to get a little light on the low horizon, when we were ordered to line up in rows of ten. We had to yell out our own number. The first guy yelled one, the next two, then three, and so on. As rows were assembled, still surrounded by guards and dogs, we started to march. I had no idea where we were going or into what kind of situation. Flashlights were still leading the way. They could have walked us into a river, a wall, or even into a gas chamber. We were totally at the mercy of the German S.S. We walked for at least forty-five minutes. My legs felt almost normal; my back was still hurting where that S.S. bastard had hit me with his club, and I limped, for my ankle had not returned to normal. My eyes had now fully adjusted, and I could see trees and bushes, when suddenly a camp appeared.

We walked through a big swinging barbed-wire gate with guards on either side. About six prisoners with arm bands counted us as we entered. I observed a few wooden structures and barracks, which seemed to be underground, with only the roof visible. We assembled in a large, open area within the camp and stood on one spot until it got light. Prisoners and a couple of S.S. men stood at a distance, engaged in conversation while I tried to reconnect with my friends. A whistle blew, and prisoners appeared from the barracks. They lined up on the other side from where we stood and had to count off in loud voices. They then marched in single file past a table, where coffee was dished out, which the prisoners drank as they marched out of the camp.

Then, all the attention was directed at us. S.S. men, capos, or prison big shots and about six men were blockaelteste (heads of barracks). Combined, they supervised all the prisoners. They walked among us and looked us over. Someone in the row behind me asked, "Are there any Viennese among you?" I turned around to look at this guy and said, "Hugo? Hugo Epstein?" He twirled around and came over to me, asking me who I was. I pulled off my cap and said, "Kurtie, Kurtie Ladner." He yelled out loud, "Kurt!" and hugged me, telling me to get all my friends together and have them line up in front of him to his right. I took everybody I knew and everyone who looked familiar and lined up. Hugo counted the men I selected and then took a few more, and we became the group in his charge.

Hugo marched us toward a barrack and asked us to wait until he returned. My friends mingled around me, asking me questions about Hugo. At this point, I could only tell them that he was a friend and a good guy. Hugo and another prisoner appeared, carrying a large pot with black coffee. Hugo asked us to enter the barrack one by one. We all still had a bowl hanging from our belts, which we received in Auschwitz, and were eagerly awaiting the hot black liquid. Hugo ladled the coffee into each bowl and asked us to find a place for ourselves inside, anywhere.

To enter the barracks, we had to duck, because the door was slightly lower than average height, and we had to step down four or five steps. The entire length of the barracks, left and right, was covered with straw, except the center walk. Every two men shared one blanket, and we eagerly consumed the coffee. This was our first liquid since the water we had received on the train.

Herbert Heimerling, Max Witrofsky, Walter Wolfgang, Peter Neuschiller and I took places on the left side of the barracks, while Hardie Fleischman, Jackie Hacker, Heinzi Stengel and others were opposite us. I shared my blanket with Herbert, which was not easy. He had to cover his almost seven foot body by pulling the blanket up or down, with me sliding in both directions to remain covered.

After the last guy had entered the barracks, Hugo and I had a chance to sit down and talk. Hugo Epstein was the fiancée of my sister-in-law, Berta's, best friend. But I knew Hugo from way before. He lived in my neighborhood, and, although he was much older, we did play ball together. He also had a terrific Turner bike on which he often took me for a ride. He took me on his bike to choir rehearsal, and to soccer matches on many occasions. My first question was, "Where are we and what kind of place is this?" He explained that we were in a satellite camp of Dachau, called Camp Number Seven, Landsberg/Kaufering. He knew of at least eight to ten such camps around Dachau. He also told me that this was a work camp, and we would be assigned to work for firms called Holtzman and Moll, construction firms, among other work commands that may arise. He was a blockaelteste, the third rank of leadership among prisoners. The first, other than the S.S., was the lageraelteste (camp leader), who took orders only from the S.S. The camp leader was responsible for the entire camp's performance, good or bad. The second echelon were two Ober Capos. They were the head foremen and also in charge with the lager and blockalteste for discipline and policing. There were also capos who actually led the work groups. The camp leader and the block leaders remained in camp to perform some camp duties, while the capos led the workers. Little by little, he explained to me the workings of Camp Number Seven and finished by saying, "This is the worst place I have been." I asked him how he got here. He told me his sad story. He was sent to Poland around the same time my brother Fritz was, in 1940. He was in several concentration camps and wound up in the Warsaw Ghetto. He was there when the uprising started. He, among others, escaped and wound up with the Polish partisans, only to be recaptured and sent to Auschwitz, and from Auschwitz to Dachau. He arrived with the first transport with other prisoners who built Camp Number Seven.

I asked him, "What are we being fed here?" He said that we would get coffee after appel around five in the morning. Appel meant standing at attention for hours exposed to the elements, sometimes for the purpose of being counted and sometimes for punishment. When and if the S.S. were satisfied with the count, we all marched to work. At some work commands, we would receive soup and at some we got nothing. After we returned to our barracks again, after appel, we would get soup or coffee and eight men would share one loaf of bread. (That was in the beginning. Later, sixteen men shared one loaf and toward the end, we received no bread at all). He also said that the lageraelteste, Peter, was a tough son of a bitch, who would beat you just for fun, and that the capos were just as vicious, with one exception: Ober Capo Michael. All the above had privileged status in the camp. All were criminal prisoners and almost all of them were homosexual. The green triangle they wore, indicating political/criminal prisoners, should have been only criminal, as well as pink triangles for homosexual. We saw very few red triangles in camp, for true political identification. All these men were long-time prisoners and none of them were Jewish.

Hugo asked me about my family, and I brought him up to date with everything I knew. I returned to my place next to Herbert, when the door to our barrack opened, and a tall, thin man walked down the steps and spoke to Hugo. He wore a Bavarian-type hat and had a cane over one arm. They were engaged in conversation, when Hugo called me over and introduced me to him. Hugo said that I was his good friend from way back and turning to me, said, "This is Ober Capo Michael." He said hello and that when we assembled the next day he would look for us. After Ober Capo Michael left, Hugo told me that he had been in prison since 1934 for killing some brown shirt (S.A. man) in a protest march in Munich. He may have done other things to wind up here. By transferring criminal or political prisoners to be in charge of the Jewish prisoners, you gave them power. Most of them used this uncontrolled power to torture, hurt, beat and even kill Jewish prisoners without having to justify their actions.

I asked Hugo if he could get me some clothing, especially shoes. He said he would try. He was able to get me a wool coat and only a pair of wooden shoes. We never had enough to eat. When Hugo dished out coffee or soup in camp, if possible, he would give me an extra portion and occasionally an extra piece of bread. Any additional food I was able to get was like a gift from heaven. I then lay down, trying to get some much needed sleep. My back was hurting, and my ankle was swollen, which lasted a few days.

Around noon, a whistle blew, and we were ordered to assemble on the Appelplatz. We lined up in several long rows and had to count off. Some lower level S.S. men supervised the counting. If the man next to you said forty-four, you had to say forty-five, and the next guy said forty-six. Once the entire row was counted, we had to take two steps forward, while the S.S. man walked along the next row behind us, continuing the count. If a man could not yell out his number or missed the count, he got beaten over the head by one of the capos with a wooden billy club. Some poor prisoners did not understand or speak German. They had come from Poland, Czechoslovakia or some other country. These prisoners had to learn fast or get beaten to a pulp every day. Once everyone understood what was expected from him, the count began to speed up. Some days we stood for hours until the German ego was satisfied.

When the last row was counted, and a bunch of S.S. men and capos assembled in front of us, the head S.S.

officer, the camp commander, accompanied by Peter, the lageralteste, appeared. The S.S. commander stepped up onto a little podium and started to speak to us. He said, "You are here to work and to obey. You must comply with every order given, or you will be punished. To escape from this camp is impossible, and every effort to try has been totally in vain. There is no chance to escape." Pointing to the barbed wire fence around the camp, he continued. "The wire fence is electrically charged. Touching it means instant death. Even if someone was successful escaping from work, he would be recaptured and executed." That was his whole speech. He stepped down from his podium, turned on his heels very abruptly, and walked off with the S.S. man following him. Then, Peter, the lageraelteste, stepped up and started to spread his venom. With a fisted hand he said, "Whatever the S.S. does not see, I will. If you do not obey or do wrong, I will punish you by beating the shit out of you. This is no idle threat." After a few more warnings and some more intimidation, he finally stopped talking.

Before we returned to our barracks, each of us received a number. From then on I was no longer Kurt Ladner. I was Number 115816. When your number was called, you had to report at once, and they never called a number the same way, so we had to be alert and always listening. If you did not report right away, a capo would beat you, or whack you with his billy club. We returned to our barracks, and Hugo told us that we were through for the day and we could rest. I asked him if I could walk outside and visit the other barracks. Hugo said that I could, but he would not advise it. The possibility existed that some capo would stop me and ask me to do some work in camp. Other than going to the latrine or washroom, we were better off remaining in the barrack.

The raised wooden structures I saw when I entered the camp were the kitchen, washroom and latrine, and the smaller structures were the quarters of the privileged. The latrine was nothing more than a board over a deep hole, which smelled of urine and of the white disinfectant powder they poured daily. The washroom consisted of a long basin with a pipe above it into which holes were drilled every two or three feet. When the water was turned on, a thin flow of water emerged through these tiny holes. To wash yourself was an art. There was nothing to hang your shirt or pants on. The floor was always muddy. I mostly tied my shirt around my waist, and vice versa with my pants, to wash myself. I spent a lot of time in the washroom in the hope that I would not get infested with lice, but I soon learned that it was impossible to prevent that from happening. Within days, we were loaded with those miserable pests.

That first night I remained in the barrack. Hugo went out to get our ration of soup and bread, and I followed his valuable instructions. He said, "Whatever food you receive, eat it right away. Also, guard your belongings because stealing is rampant in camps." Most men slept with their clothes on. I usually rolled some of my clothing and shoes into a ball and used them as a pillow, making sure that no one could take them from me.

I sat down with Herbert, Maxie, Peter, Walter and Hardie and told them everything I had learned from Hugo. Herbert said, "The amount of food we are receiving is not enough to live very long." From the happy guys I knew in Terezin, we had turned into a bunch of very worried guys. I lay down on the straw, grabbed half of my blanket and went to sleep. It seemed like I had just fallen asleep when a whistle blew. A capo opened our barrack door, banging his stick against it, while yelling, "Everybody up and out!" Hugo immediately repeated that command. We got up and dressed in seconds and assembled for appel. Hugo said, "It must be 4 a.m." I had no idea what time it was. None of us had a watch left. A sun dial would have been handy, but not that early. We lined up and this time we were counted by a capo. He walked up and down the lines. When Peter, with one of the S.S. men appeared, all murmuring stopped, and we paid strict attention to the counting. We stood for a while after the counting had been completed. Ober Capo Michael walked directly over to me and said, "I need eight men for a special work assignment and make sure they all speak German." My friends and I walked with him to the other side of the kitchen to receive our ration of coffee and then marched out of the camp where one S.S. guard joined us.

Ober Capo Michael said to us, "You are going to help build Camp Number Eleven." We assumed that this was a better job than the others got. We walked through woods and fields, always under the watchful eyes of the S.S. guard and Ober Capo Michael. We arrived in Camp Number Eleven, and the camp looked finished to me, with the exception of some finishing touches. I asked Ober Capo Michael, "How do they build these half underground barracks?" He pointed to a group of prisoners who were digging a hole in the ground, which was about three feet deep and five feet wide and between forty and fifty feet long. It was just as though you ripped out a hole in a straight line. The earth from the dug hole was thrown onto a mound about twenty feet from the hole. Beams were installed and connected the entire length of the future barrack. Onto the cross beams they nailed a wooden roof that slanted to the ground about nine feet from the edge of the hole. The front wall had a door, and the back wall had a window. The bottom of this hole was actually the floor we walked on, solid raw earth. The rest was covered with wood and straw, and that is where we slept. Our heads almost reached the ceiling. On the outside, the roof was covered with the dug earth and seeded with grass. It could not be distinguished from the above whether this was a barrack or a field. Inside the barrack they strung one wire for one light bulb, a hole in the roof for a stove pipe and a tiny little stove.

While working in Camp Number Eleven, we nailed some boards or strung barbed wire. It was not hard work, but we worked long hours. We got up around 4:00 a.m. and did not return to Camp Number Seven until eight at night. We did receive our ration of soup in Camp Number Eleven, but that was all we ate the entire day.

When we returned to our camp again, we had to stand appel and be counted. This could last for a short duration, or we could stand for several more hours. Once everything checked out, and everyone was accounted for, we then returned to our barrack, where we received coffee and our ration of bread. Depending on how long we had to stand appel was how long we could sleep, because, come 4:00 a.m., the whistle blew, and we had to return to the spot that we had just vacated. We never slept more than five hours at a time.

The job in Camp Number Eleven lasted only for a short time, then my friends and I were assigned to work for Moll or Holtzman. Ober Capo Michael always made sure that he was in charge of us; that was the only bright spot. He was a kind and talkative person when the S.S. were not around. But once the S.S. guard came near us, he would shout loud and crisp commands. Working for these firms was hard work. They were long hours. The work we had to perform was mostly overseen by the S.S. and by the Organization Todt. They were the engineering and working divisions of the German Army. This organization was headed by a guy named Todt. They wore brown uniforms, similar to the S.A.'s. Our work consisted of laying railroad ties and rails. These heavy components we had to work with were no picnic. We also worked and helped to build an underground airplane factory, so we were told, heavily involved with cement and iron bars.

It was very hard work physically. Many members of the Organization Todt came from the Ukraine, White Russia, Latvia and Rumania. All had volunteered to serve Germany and Adolf Hitler. They hated Jews. They had such resentments toward Jews that they out-Hitlered Hitler. I witnessed several beatings they dished out for no reason other than that we were Jews, and they enjoyed hurting us. Ober Capo Michael knew who they were, and he tried to shield my friends and me from working with them.

It did not take long for all of the prisoners to deteriorate. Bread portions were cut. There were days we did not receive soup. The weather changed from tolerable to cold and wet. What started with a few lice, became an infestation, and all of us had dysentery. I could not move for days. I sat in the latrine whether I had to go or not. Although there was a big bucket in our barrack to be used when you were sick, Hugo put a lid on it and made us go to the latrine. It would be hard to explain what the latrine looked like after a few days of use by men who came running with their pants down. You had to tiptoe, and to find an open, clean spot. We rapidly started to lose weight, and we became very weak. The German command had no mercy. We had to report for work every day, sick or not. Ober Capo Michael kept me on camp duty for two days to perform menial work supervised by Hugo who allowed me to overcome my first episode of sickness.

Marching to and from work occasionally took us through potato fields. Some of us picked up a few potatoes to bring back to our barracks. It was prohibited to do so, but when the German Wehrmacht guarded us, not the S.S.; they were more lenient with the enforcement. One day I picked up a few potatoes and stuffed them into my shirt, hoping to be able to press some of them against the stove in our barrack and eat them. Just before we entered our camp, I noticed that the men in front of me were being physically searched. I immediately dropped my potatoes to the ground and kept on marching. One of the thirteen or fourteen-year-old punks who were kept by capos for personal pleasures, saw what I did, and clubbed me several times over my head with a wooden club. Under different circumstances, I would have taken this little shit and hung him from the wall, but you could not touch these privileged youngsters – not in front of the capos or the S.S. I often hoped that I would catch one of them alone, but I had no such luck. Once I was inside my barrack, I took off my cap. My head was all bloody, swollen and sore. Hugo looked at my head and jokingly said, "This will only hurt for the next fifty years." (He was right. It still hurts, especially when I think about it.) I went to the washroom and soaked my head in cold water, and the pulsating pain subsided a little bit.

Earlier, I mentioned the stove in our barracks, which was lit very seldom and had multiple purposes. One, it gave us a little warmth; two, when we had potatoes or potato peels, we browned them on top or pressed them against the side; and three, we pressed our lice-infested clothing against the hot stove and burned the lice for a few hours of relief. The smell was awful, but it did help. The blockalteste or capos would tolerate occasional burning in our stove. Once the S.S. commander saw smoke escaping from one of the chimney pipes, and we were punished. The entire camp had to stand outside for over twelve hours. It was freezing and sleeting. An icy rain soaked our meager clothing through to our skin. From that day on, we never wore dry clothing. We never had a chance to completely dry out. The next day, it would either rain or snow again, and many of us got very sick.

Day by day our bodies shrank from lack of food and the so-called labor force diminished rapidly. There were no replacements for torn clothing or shoes. Hardie Fleischman, a strong, stocky fellow, became the first Muscleman who walked around without shoes, and with deep, dark, glazed eyes. Little by little, we all joined his ranks, especially when it got freezing cold and rations of bread were cut to sixteen men per loaf.

There were other hard days to overcome in Camp Number Seven. Heinz Stengel, a friend, had escaped. Two days later, he was captured and returned to our camp. He was kept in solitary confinement and occasionally was left unguarded. On the way to the latrine, we would exchange a few words. Herbert, who knew him best, and I conveyed to him that we thought he should try to escape again because we knew what his fate would be if he didn't, but he told Herbert that the S.S. would transfer him to another camp. He had to promise that he would not run away again. A couple of days later when we entered the camp returning from work, Heinzie Stengel was hanging with a rope around his neck as a warning for everyone to see. Another time, it was a father and son whom I did not know. All prisoners had to assemble on the Appelplatz. As a matter of fact, they gave us some soup, and we had to watch the hanging as we ate. There was a wooden crossbeam with two ropes hanging down with a bench under the ropes. The S.S. commander came with a group of high-ranking S.S. men. One was rumored to have been Eichmann. I had never seen him before, not even a picture. The S.S. commander stood near the two men to be hanged and made a speech. "If you try to escape, that is what will happen to you," he said, pointing to the two, "But if you work hard and obey our orders, not one hair on your head will be harmed." (Of course, we were all bald.) "Should another of you try to escape, ten, twenty, or maybe a hundred of you will be hanged." With that speech, he and Peter stepped over to the bench, put the rope around the necks of the prisoners there and kicked the bench out from under them. The younger one reached his hands up to his throat, but Peter pulled his hands down. I had seen people being shot, beaten, tortured and, earlier, bombed, but I will never forget their gasping and tortured faces. The son kept moving his hands for at least one minute, while his father must have died instantly. It was terrible.

There were different kinds of torture. Ober Capo Michael and the five of us had to pull and push a wagon that looked like a hay wagon with sides, which normally would be pulled by oxen. We had to go into the town of Landsberg, guarded by two S.S. men and one army solider with rifles and bayonets to pick up fresh bread for the S.S. and Wehrmacht guards. We rolled the wagon to the side door of the bakery. People were passing us without a glance of recognition. We stood flush against the wall while two women and an old man loaded the wagon to the hilt with freshly baked bread. Even the cover thrown over it could not conceal the aroma. I had convulsing pain in my stomach and a headache from hunger. I was so near the fresh bread I almost did not care what the S.S. guards would do to me. If only I could get hold of one piece of bread. Then I looked at the guards, the rifles and bayonets, and my thoughts turned to pushing that damn wagon, making believe that I could not smell anything. I just pushed the wagon with tears in my eyes. Herbert motioned with his face that he could devour the entire load of bread. But he also put his head down and pushed and pushed. I had this assignment three or four times. It was more than torture and one of the hardest things to overcome.

Several times, a bunch of us were loaded onto trucks and driven to Munich's main railroad station. We jumped off and walked along the tracks, passing prisoners of war and prisoners from other camps. We came to a large crater and two of us had to climb down. I had a pick with a flat side on the opposite side and the other guy had a shovel. By then my strength was sapped from not eating, hard work, lice and freezing cold. I was so numb I did not even know what I was doing, until Ober Capo Michael came to my rescue. We picked and shoveled to expose unexploded bombs. Other prisoners were working in several other craters. I crawled out of mine and followed Ober Capo Michael. He told me what I was doing, and I panicked, after the fact. He assigned me to other work, laying new ties on rebuilt railroad beds. It was much harder work, but not dangerous. A big lorry rolled up and dumped a ton of little stones that I had to hammer under the ties with a pick. As the stones disappeared, the lorry came again and dumped another load. I did this work for days and with each passing day it became harder for me to perform the task.

We always heard distant sirens but this one day, the sirens blasted right near us. Whistles blew and they shouted orders from everywhere. We dropped what we were doing and had to enter a sewer-like crawlspace that had several pipes running along the wall. We had to enter one by one, always moving deeper and deeper into this narrow shaft that seemed miles long. All the workers from above had to enter this below-surface shelter. We heard either bombs explode or anti-aircraft or maybe both. The sounds were muffled; it was crowded with all of us crouched down. As I looked at these pipes of undetermined content, one of the prisoners created a panic by shouting, "We all will be killed. These are gas pipes. A bomb could explode and rupture the pipes or the Germans could turn on the gas valve." His shouting convinced us that this was the end. There was very little air to breathe, and all of us were scared. Waves of pushing and shoving started with nowhere to go. When we finally were allowed to leave this place, it was like emerging from a tomb.

The early harsh winter season began with a tremendous snowstorm. The clothing we had to wear day after day was again soaking wet. The temperature was way below freezing. Going to work and walking on icy tracks became difficult. Before standing appel, I put on my frozen, stiff pair of pants and jacket and only my body's warmth melted the stiffness of my clothing into wetness instead. The entire camp was so loaded with lice that the S.S. minimized their entering our camp. Many prisoners had died by then from dysentery and pneumonia. Some had committed suicide by touching the electric barbed wires. Some had been shot or hanged, and many died of starvation.

My friends and I were again assigned to work in the so-called underground airplane factory under construction. We had the night shift, and they usually gave us coffee around midnight. Walter Wolfgang, Maxie Witrofsky, Herbert Heimerling and I looked for a place to rest and drink our coffee. It was freezing cold, but a clear night. To the left of us were huge cement pipes. A person could easily crawl through them. Well, we did just that and landed in front of a gigantic crane. We climbed up and the door to the crane was unlocked. The guys thought we should warm up a little bit before returning to our station. It was very dark. I sat down on the crane operator's seat when I felt something under my buttocks. I picked the object up and learned that I had just sat on a fresh loaf of bread. We quickly divided the bread four ways, as best we could, ate it and then crawled back through the pipes to our job. No one saw us, no one looked for us, and no one missed us.

Then we had a special detail. Ober Capo Michael took five of us, Herbert, Maxie, Walter, Peter and me, to cut down big trees. We became experts in felling trees; we hacked and cut off all the branches, and with a two man saw, we cut up these big trees into small logs for the S.S. It was a very good assignment because we cut the trees into thirds, then lugged them inside into a large room where we were sheltered from the harsh wind, snow and extreme cold. That day Peter was my partner on the two-man saw. No matter how often I told him not to push the saw, just pull it, he still pushed. He pushed once too often. The saw jumped out of the cut and onto my left thumb. The bleeding and the pain were bad enough, but I could not use my left hand.

Ober Capo Michael called Maxie out of the room to do something. Maxie returned within one minute, up-set, and began to tell us what had happened. Ober Capo Michael asked him to check his underwear for lice by pulling his pants down. Maxie did not need any expla-nations as to what he had in mind. Maxie said to Ober Capo Michael, "Please, don't disappoint us. We believe that you are the best person in camp and that you are a political prisoner, not a homosexual." He swore Maxie to secrecy, especially not to tell us. That was his only attempt, and it went no further.

A few days later we had to return to the underground factory to do iron work. Walter asked us to explore the crane again, but we all refused, saying that it would be dangerous and that we could be caught. But Walter apparently went alone. We returned to camp, standing to be counted. One person was missing. We stood for hours, for everyone had to be accounted for, dead or alive. Finally, we could go to our barracks, but my friend Walter Wolfgang did not return with us.

That very week, a group of prisoners from Camp Number Seven were transferred to Camp Number Eleven. Peter Neuschiller and I were among them. From Hugo Epstein, who arrived in Camp Number Eleven at a later time, I learned that Camp Number Seven was quarantined because of an outbreak of typhus. Both Maxie and Herbert, despite the care Ober Capo Michael gave them by bringing them water and extra food, died of typhus. Ober Capo Michael, with his dedication to helping my friends, also got typhus and died a couple of weeks later. They erect statues for less humane people. I believe that Ober Capo Michael deserves one in memorial.

When I arrived in Camp Number Eleven, I was surprised to see so many people I knew from Theresienstadt (Terezin). There were a whole bunch of guys I played soccer with and against. There was Tausig, a gifted goalie, Goco, who played guitar for the orchestra in Terezin, Lederer, the foremost pianist and accordion player, Dr. Franz Hahn, a physician from Vienna and so many others. Peter was in the barrack next to mine, while in my barrack were prisoners from Czechoslovakia, Austria, Holland, Germany and Lithuania. One of my friends was the blockalteste, and from him I learned that some friends from Terezin were working in the delousing chamber. We had to exchange our clothing there and go through a delousing procedure. The problem was that you never got your own clothing back, but our friends made sure that we at least got clothing that was our size. I now seldom received a little extra soup, because the soup was measured to the last drop.

My work assignment was still the same – the construction site. I had no concept of time; what hour, day or month it was. All I knew was that the weather was freezing with ice and snow and that it was dangerous just walking to work. We had to walk on rail tracks, and beneath the track ties were empty spaces. Most of us slipped on the icy surface with either one leg or both, slipping into the empty space, at times hanging by our crotch and trying to lift ourselves up before the last S.S. guard passed us. That was a piece of work in itself. We had to get up very quickly. If the S.S. guard passed you and you were not within the group, they would interpret it as an attempted escape, and without hesitation, shoot you. I saw two men shot for that reason on two separate occasions. Once I saw a group of 1,000 men were marching to work. They were divided into groups of 100 or at the most 200. Each group had several S.S. guards. For prisoners in the last row it was especially tough. When they slipped, they had to recover much faster than if they were in the front rows. If someone had to go to the bathroom, they ran to the front, dropped their pants, and before the last row caught up with them, they pulled their pants up and ran forward again, and so on, to make sure that they were not outside of the guard's chain. If someone had to pee, they learned to perform that function while they were walking. Toward the end, it was not unusual for 1,000 men to march to work, but for only 800 to return. The rest succumbed to beatings, hunger, sickness, the elements, or their hearts just gave out.

When we were ordered to march, we had to be in a straight line. S.S. guards would run along the sides with bayonets and push you into the formation. Several prisoners were stabbed. I was walking on the left outside when I was pushed by one guard. I did not notice that he had ripped my jacket (I had no coat) and that I was bleeding from my left hip. It did not hurt, but later on, lice got into the wound. It became infected and oozed for a very long time. Once, while marching, I yelled something to Peter in Viennese, when one of the army guards approached me and asked, "Where are you from?" I replied, "Vienna." He said, "So am I." We talked often, mostly about soccer and soccer players like Sindelar, Binder, Plaza, Mock, and Nausch. He used to give me the crust off his bread, which he disliked, but for me was like manna from heaven. I thought that he was a good and humane person, until I saw him beat a Polish Jew into unconsciousness with his rifle butt.

My jobs varied at this underground factory project. Mostly, I had to carry iron bars up a cement dome that covered the entire project. Narrow, wooden strips were supposed to simulate steps. The iron bars came in different sizes. Sometimes two men could carry one up, but with the extra long ones, you needed three men. We had to synchronize and balance ourselves walking up these narrow slats of wood. They extended up no more than an inch and a half. They were always covered with snow and ice, and in order to get some traction, I had to kick my heels to loosen the ice. The iron bars were bouncing up and down with every step. Several men slipped and rolled down to the bottom. Some got hurt, but were able to continue to work, while others were badly injured. I had no gloves, and the ice-cold iron bars stuck to my hands until my skin peeled off to the raw flesh. I tried to carry these iron bars with one hand covered with my jacket sleeves, but it just did not work. Finally, I was able to obtain two pieces of paper to insulate the frozen iron.

Then, my Viennese army guard assigned me to a different detail. We had to unload cement bags from a rail car and stack them in a warehouse. In order to carry that dead weight, we had to walk up a narrow wooden board that reached from the rail car down to a platform. We walked up on one side and down the other board. Under these narrow bouncing wooden boards was a drop of five or six feet. The boards were slippery and dangerous to walk on. The army guard turned me over to an Organization Todt overseer, who made me foreman. We walked up into the car. Two men put this heavy cement gag on my shoulder, and I had to walk down with this load on a bouncing slippery board. Not falling off was a miracle. One older man could not carry these heavy bags so I told him to stay in the warehouse and help the men stack them. Instead of helping or at least making believe that he was helping, he sat down and did not move. The Organization Todt guy caught him sitting and asked him why he was not working. The old guy said that I told him to sit down. He was beaten up, and I had to carry two cement bags all night. God forbid someone dropped one or tore the wrapping. That was considered sabotage and people were shot on the spot for it. Luckily, the Organization Todt man did not tell my army guard of this incident. That was my one and only moment of glory during my time as a foreman.

Another time the guard got me what he thought was an easy job; instead it was the worst nightmare of my incarceration. I had to climb to the highest point of this partially finished cement dome. On it stood a little wooden shack with an Organization Todt engineer in it. I had to stand outside in front of a wooden board that had three switches attached. I was totally exposed to the elements, howling wind, a snowstorm, sub-zero temperatures and dressed only in wet pants and a jacket. I could look down into the cavity where hundreds of prisoners were hooking iron bars. The three switches I was to attend controlled huge cement pumps. As the workers below me finished one section, a tiny window opened in the shack, and the Organization Todt man yelled a number to me. If he called number two I had to shut off switch number one and put the number two switch down in order to start the number two cement pump. My hands and fingers were frozen to the point that they did not respond to the resistance of the switch. I attempted to use my elbow, but the switches were too close to each other. The penetrating icy wind caused pain in my face, ears, inside my nose, hands and fingers, and I could not feel my toes. Wind driven snow and icy pellets were pounding against my body. That was one of the few times that I cried bitter tears all night. No one beat me, no one hurt me, but I was almost totally destroyed by the coldest, wettest, penetrating winter night in my memory. I stood like a frozen snowman to carry out the Organization Todt's barking orders every ten minutes. Other than that, I stood still anticipating his orders, which I had to execute without delay. The point came when I could not feel anything, and it became impossible for me to carry on. I slid over to the little window and asked to be excused to go to the latrine. The Organization Todt man gave me a couple of minutes and ordered me to return before I had to throw the next switch, which was in about five minutes. I half slid down to the bottom, reached the latrine, where adjacent was a large stack of cement bags. As I was all alone I kicked one cement bag open and barely was able to dump the contents into the latrine and then I did the same with a second bag. I attempted to stuff the paper under my shirt but could not unbutton myself. I then dropped my pants and stuffed it from underneath. I then stuffed some paper into the front and back of my pants and some into my shoes without touching my feet for I was afraid that my toes would fall off. I then climbed back upstairs to my post. Luckily no one saw what I did. If I had been caught, I would have been shot. Was it sabotage? Yes, but at that time and under the circumstances and the misery I was feeling, what I did was the only rational thing to do. I was that cold and that desperate.

The very next day I got the worst case of diarrhea, which they called stomach typhus. I had nothing to eat or drink other than water for at least three days. The cramps and constant running to the latrine sapped what little strength I had left. The constant pain and cramps lasted and lasted. I used to double up on my way to the latrine and would sit there among many other guys for a long time. All I passed was a little liquid, and my rear was swollen.

Convulsing with extreme cramps and pain, I got so weak that I could hardly walk, much less work. My blockalteste said to me, "Either you go to work or have the prison doctor proclaim you sick." I walked to the barrack that was staffed with prison doctors. Anyone who was severely sick, but might be able to return to work, was kept in this so-called hospital barrack. They could only keep you for a short duration, then you had to return as healed. I entered this barrack to report myself sick. The attending doctor who barely examined me said, "You are not sick enough not to report for work." He said this, even though I could not walk and had constant cramps that felt as if my intestines would exit through my rear. Dejected and holding my stomach, I was about to walk out when the head doctor came through the door. He stopped me and asked, "Are you Kurt Ladner?" I said, "Yes." He said, "Don't you recognize me? I'm Doctor Frei". I looked at him and I really did not know him, but he went on to tell me that he was always standing behind the goal when I played soccer for Jugend Fuersorge in Terezin. He kept on about what a great soccer player I was. I just nodded and told him that I seemed to remember him, cheering us on. He then asked me what my complaint was. I said, "Doctor, if I have to march to work today I will die." I told him what was wrong with me, while having severe spasms in front of him. He wrote me as sick and put me into the hospital barrack. As I entered I saw several other soccer players, mostly from Czechoslovakia. Everyone had the same sickness, severe diarrhea. Amazingly, Dr. Frei kept me on sick leave for more than two weeks, even though I was much better.

That was during the coldest, iciest winter month, I think, in the history of Germany – at least it was for me. One morning, Dr. Frei came into the barrack and asked if anybody would like to volunteer to leave the hospital barrack to perform light work in camp. The reason for asking was that there were so many sick people in camp, and he needed the room. I was feeling better, not good, just better, so I volunteered to make room, and I think I was the only one. He gave me a job as an orderly in my old barrack. It was lucky that I decided to go because a few days later the hospital barrack was quarantined because of a severe outbreak of typhus or typhoid fever. All but two men died in the hospital barrack, including my soccer playing friends.

My job as an orderly was to sweep the earthen floor in the barrack with a tied-together broom of tree branches, help to distribute food rations and assign two people every day to carry out the wooden toilet bucket to the latrine and dump it. This bucket was huge and heavy. It had a handle on each side. When it was my turn, my friend Franta and I very carefully carried this monster to the latrine and dumped the mostly liquid content and brought it back for the sick people to use. That was the order I was given, and I fulfilled my obligations. Dr. Frei checked with me every day and with the blockalteste as to how I was holding up. I did not realize then why he was so concerned about my wellbeing.

I had several fights in the barrack, and all of them were with the same guy. I did not know his name or where he came from because we never spoke more than two words to each other. When it was his turn to carry out the bucket he always refused. He was not sicker than any one of us. He could work and collect his ration of bread, but he, like a stubborn ox, refused to carry out the bucket. I could have reported him. That would have been easy. Instead, we had fights. Had I reported him to the blockalteste, he would have been severely punished, but, after a few blows from me, he began to cower. I then asked the next guy to take out the bucket. We only asked the able-bodied people to carry out the toilet bucket to the latrine. None refused, except this one brazen bastard. A few days later it was his turn again. This time Franta asked him, and again he refused, so Franta had a fight with him. One day Franta and I asked him why. He did not answer. We learned that he was using the bucket, which was to be used only by very sick people who could not reach the latrine. It was his turn again. He refused, and instead of asking the next guy, Franta and I took the bucket that was filled to the brim with this horrible smelly liquid mess and carried it to the latrine. It was ice-cold outside. Everything was covered with frozen packed snow, and about halfway toward the latrine, Franta slipped, dragging me to the ground and the entire con-tent of the toilet bucket spilled all over me. Franta and I covered the spillage with mountains of snow. I had to get undressed in this freezing weather to rub my cloth-ing the best I could with snow, to clean the smelly sub-stance from them. The water in the washroom was fro-zen. So, to clean my clothing and myself, snow was the only alternative. Franta only got a few spots on himself, while I walked back to the barrack, stinking and almost naked. The little runt who refused to carry the bucket was laughing his head off. That was when I, with my last strength, beat him up and warned him that should he refuse again, I would report him to the blockalteste.

After that experience, we made sure that only the very sick used the bucket. When that jerk wanted to use the bucket, Franta and I did not allow him, and we chased him all the way to the latrine.

In our barrack there were people who came from the Baltic countries, all of them conversed only in Yiddish with me. They spoke frequently about a man, a Jewish policeman, in one of the ghettos. I think it was Riga. They talked about him as a traitor and not much better than the Nazis themselves. I must spell this man's name phonetically. It sounded like "Jarmeitis." One day, prisoners were brought into our barrack and among them was this former policeman. The word spread like wildfire that he was in our barrack. Everyone anticipated a riot or lynching. Prisoners assembled outside, chanting his name, ready to kill him. I sent Franta to get our blockalteste. We had enough to do just to protect him from the guys in the barrack. Many of the prisoners outside could hardly walk, but they seemed to gain strength just knowing that they could get their hands on him. The blockalteste came and took this guy outside, followed by a lot of enraged people. About twenty minutes later, he was dumped back into my barrack, and I could not recognize him. His face was three times the size as before. He was severely beaten, bleeding from his legs and barely breathing. Apparently this policeman was guilty of reporting the whereabouts of hidden women and children to the Nazis, who killed whoever they found, so I was told. Of the many other policemen who were interrogated, none of them betrayed the women and children and consequently paid the price, which was death. This guy was always pursued by men whose wife or child or both had been killed because of him. The last time I saw him he was being transferred to another barrack and was in very bad shape.

Camp Number Eleven was overrun with lice, much more so than Camp Number Seven, if that was possible. The wounds on my body had not healed. Besides the cut on my hip, I had many sores from sleeping on wood and dirt. My lice found it comfortable in my wounds, while I killed them by the hundreds. All I had to do was squeeze the seams in my shirt and a huge blood spot would appear.

One day, hundreds of beautifully dressed people were standing on the lawn outside the camp. They must have arrived during the night. They had packages and suitcases, which they had to leave on the ground when they entered our camp. They went through the washrooms, which they called showers, and the water amazingly was running. The new prisoners received some of the clothing that was probably worn weeks ago by us, went through the delousing and then were integrated into the camp. These prisoners came directly from their homes in Hungary. They came strong and healthy, but after a short stay in the camp, most died of typhus.

A day or two later, I got very sick with a high fever, and Dr. Frei's concern came true. He had Dr. Hahn diagnose me as having typhus. Hugo Epstein, Hardie

Fleischman and a couple survivors from Camp Number Seven came to see me. Hugo said, "I survived typhus in Poland. The most important thing for you to do is to drink a lot of water.' A day later the entire camp was quarantined, and I faded in and out of consciousness. Hugo came every day with water, and I gave him my slice of bread, so I was told. I could not eat and only with help could I drink water. The closer a person was put to the door determined when they expected the person to expire. The next thing I knew I was second to the door. Then it got dark. I don't know how long I was unconscious or how many days I was near death. I heard people say that I was next. Dr. Hahn did come to see me, but I was totally beyond help. Typhus was carried by lice, and I had lice. There was only one thermometer in the entire camp, and the top of it was broken. Dr. Hahn said that it was good that the top was broken because my high fever would have blown it off anyway.

The latter part of my sickness is a total blank. When I slowly started to regain consciousness I could not hear, and I could not see. I had severe headaches but my vision and hearing very slowly came back. I could not walk at all. My body was a skin-covered skeleton. My lice-infested sores were bleeding, and my headaches were getting worse. The word spread that Camp Number Eleven would be closed, and anyone who could not march out with the prisoners would be killed. Hardie, Hugo, Jackie and others dragged me out of the barrack and made me walk. I had no strength at all and to lift my foot only an inch was an insurmountable effort, but somehow I did march out. I finally was able to eat my piece of bread and a little soup. Anything left over I gave to my friends. Later on I saved what I could not eat and, as I recovered and got a little stronger, I ate it all. I still could not walk by myself. I mostly crawled on all fours. Eventually I could pull myself up, holding onto something or someone, and slowly I started to walk in stuttering steps.

The weather had changed from freezing cold, and we had a few warmer sunny days. The accumulated snow had melted, and I again walked around in the mud. I had not seen my friends for a few days so I searched for Hugo, Jackie, Hardie and Dr. Hahn, but was told that they and many other prisoners had been transferred. Orders came that Camp Number Eleven would be closed. Anyone who could walk would be transferred to Camp Number Four, and those who could not walk would remain in camp. Remain in camp? I knew what that meant, so I linked up with the prisoners who could walk, not knowing if I could make it to Camp Number Four. My brother, Hans, was in Camp Number Four. When I used to march to work to Holtzman or Moll, my brother passed me as he was returning from his shift. He held up four fingers to indicate that he was in Camp Number Four.

I did not walk; I was dragged, carried, and supported by friends as I partially walked into Camp Number Four, anxious to be with my brother. Guys were alternating holding me up, even though they were weak also – we all were skin and bones. None of us had any strength left in our bodies, but we managed to help each other and drag ourselves into Camp Number Four.

As we entered the camp, Walter Beyer, a friend of my brother's, waved to me and yelled, "I'll see you later." He also passed the word that I was among the new arrivals. Eugene Deutsch was a blockalteste, who singled me out and took me to his barrack. There were mostly Czech and Viennese people from Terezin. They all knew me, and I knew most of them. I asked Eugene where Walter Beyer was, and he told me that Walter was working as a shoemaker for the S.S. outside the camp. He also said that the S.S. liked Walter's skills and that he could walk in and out of the camp unsupervised.

In the evening, Walter came to see me and brought some bread. He told me that my brother, Hans, had died. Once he had returned from work all bloodied and beaten up, and he never recovered. Walter thought that my brother died of internal injuries. I felt as if someone had thrown a rock on my head. My brother was no weakling, but apparently, he also could not cope with the inhumane treatment of the German S.S. To overcome the bad news he brought me, he also told me that the war would be over very soon. The Germans were almost defeated. He said for me to hold on because he wanted to see me play soccer again. In conversation with Walter I learned that there were many prisoners from Vienna here who were in Terezin. For instance, the cook in the kitchen was from the Twentieth District in Vienna. I asked him if I might know him or if he knew my family. But Walter did not think so. Before Walter left, he said that he would see me tomorrow and that the cook's name was Nussbaum and he came from Poland or France.

The next day I slowly walked to the kitchen, which was guarded by a prisoner. As I got close to the guard I recognized him as the father of a schoolmate in Vienna and as a neighbor who lived across the street from where we lived. I told him who I was, and he was so glad to see me alive. We spoke for a while, and I asked about Mr. Nussbaum, the head cook. He was about to answer when a man came through the kitchen and said, "This is Mr. Nussbaum." I just wanted to tell him that I used to work in the kitchen in Terezin and maybe I could do some light work and maybe get some extra soup. But the way I looked and walked, I knew that I could not perform the slightest manual labor. I then looked at Mr. Nussbaum a bit closer and recognized him as the son-in-law of one of my mother's customers. I had been to their house and factory (they produced lederhosen) to collect money for poultry that they had purchased. When I told him who I was he put his arm around me and asked about his family and if I knew anything about them. I sadly shook my head no and told him about my brother Pepi's death in Belgium and my brother, Hans', right here in Camp Number Four. We talked for a few minutes longer. He could not use me in the kitchen, but he asked who my blockalteste was. I told him it was Eugene Deutsch, and he said, "When Eugene comes to the kitchen for his barrack's rations, I will send extra soup for you," and he did. I received two soups every day, and the extra bread Walter Beyer used to bring, and with Eugene forcing me to walk at least twice a day, I slowly got better.

Then, the great surprise: the International Red Cross came to distribute packages. They could not enter the camp for we were still quarantined. Lice and typhus were still rampant. I received a package that contained some sugar, a can of some kind of fish, a small pack of cigarettes, and chocolates, which were confiscated by the S.S. I ate everything on the spot, and I traded my cigarettes for sugar and bread. I was so happy for the good fortune that I felt that my prayers were heard.

For the first time since my imprisonment, allied planes flew over our camp. As these planes were approaching, a whistle blew, and all prisoners were confined to the barracks. On one occasion, a plane dropped leaflets, and one prisoner ran to retrieve one, but he was shot before he could reach a leaflet. We never learned what the leaflet said, but we felt a stirring among the S.S. guards and even among the prisoners. Maybe Walter was right; maybe the war would end shortly.

It was early April, 1945. The rations started to get smaller and smaller. Some days we did not receive our ration of bread. Prisoners who collected the dead from the barracks, which at one time was also my assignment, got busier and busier. One prisoner always had to check the dead person's mouth in case they had forgotten to pull anything of value. They then swung the corpses onto a wagon for them to be dumped into a mass grave. Some of the guys who worked this detail told us that there was cannibalism in camp. I saw many prisoners eat the early growing grass. The next few days, people died like flies in Camp Number Four.

I then had a relapse. I don't think it had anything to do with typhus. I just had severe diarrhea, and I was heaving. Again, it sapped what little strength I had. Soon thereafter, orders came for all healthy prisoners to line up to march to another destination and for all sick prisoners to remain in the barracks. Walter came running to see me, to persuade me to line up with the marchers, because they were marching to Austria. There was no possible way I could walk all those miles. I could hardly make it to the latrine. Then, the rumor mill started to grind. The rumors were frightening. The word was that the camp would be set on fire with us in it or that we would be shot. I knew that I would collapse after a short distance walking with the marchers, and then I definitely would be shot, so I decided to remain in camp. I found out later that the march to Austria was called the death march. Many of the prisoners could not keep up. They either died on the road or were killed.

Two other fellows from Vienna, Otto Schick and Ferry Scheuer, remained with me. The three of us sat together contemplating what we should do. I recommended that we sleep far from the barracks, somewhere outside in case they did burn the camp. Our dilemma was solved very quickly. A whistle blew, and all were ordered to assemble. Prisoners—walking skeletons—came from every corner of the camp. As usual, we were counted and ordered to move in the direction of railroad tracks. We were being guarded by a few S.S. men, capos, some army and a few civilians. The word spread fast that we were being sent to the main camp, Dachau. That was not good news. Mass killings there were normal. We were now completely at the mercy of the Germans. How much longer we lived was up to them. We all knew that it would not be very long, and a quiet atmosphere of surrender fell over all the prisoners.

We heard a train whistle, and a train arrived with additional guards. We were loaded into cattle cars. It was not easy to climb up onto the train, but two capos helped most of us to hoist ourselves up. Once in the cattle car the doors were only half closed. But guards were on top of the train with their guns, guarding us. Otto, Ferry and I sat next to the open door as the train rode through the spring countryside. We rolled like this for half an hour, when the train stopped just outside of a small station. Other trains were standing alongside ours. Then all hell broke loose. The spring quietness changed into a horrible war zone. Suddenly, planes appeared and started to drop bombs on the station, on the trains and on us. I looked out and saw every German guard running in every direction. Straight ahead of us was a forest. To the left guards were running and shooting at planes. To the right bombs were exploding. I said to Otto and Ferry, "We have to get out of this cattle car or we will be blown to bits." Simultaneously as I spoke, I jumped off the train and rolled down a steep embankment. With all the strength that I could muster, I dragged myself into the woods, with bullets flying all around me. Otto and Ferry were right behind me as we attempted to get deeper into the woods. Germans were shooting at prisoners out of the woods, while the allied planes were flying low and strafing anything that moved. By then, other prisoners had long passed us, running and screaming. Bombs were exploding and bullets were flying all around us. It was a panic. As a plane appeared, I put a tree between myself and the plane and moved around the tree shielding myself from bullets. I really did not know which way to move to protect myself. The Germans were shooting at a low level out of the forest and the planes came at us from above. Then Ferry yelled, "I've been hit," as he stood just inches away from me. Sure enough, he had a German bullet in his knee. He dropped and could not move. Otto suggested that we move away from the tracks as quickly as possible like the other prisoners. We helped Ferry up, and he tried to walk but could not put any weight on the wounded leg,so Otto and I dragged him through the woods. He was much taller than I, and I could not support my own weight, much less his. However, at a very slow speed, we moved deeper into the woods with Ferry holding on to us for every inch.

Then it got very quiet. All the other prisoners had passed us long ago. We had to rest. We rested most of the time, because Ferry's knee had turned a reddish/

blue color. His bullet entrance wound was very small, a bloody dot. We slept in the woods during the night. We could hear the sounds of canons, anti-aircraft, and the sky looked lit in the far distance. We knew then that the allies were very near. We did not know how near, but near. I suggested that we walk in the direction of the anticipated advance of the allies, but it was easier said than done. Ferry's knee started to swell and any movement was agonizing to him. We decided to seek shelter in a barn, hopefully without the farmer's knowledge and hide until the allied army arrived. Should we be discovered by the S.S. we would say we turned ourselves in to the nearest German. Should the farmer see us, we would tell him that we would be of help once the allies arrived.

We kept on walking and came to an opening in the woods at the edge of the trees and field. We saw prisoners who previously passed us shot and very dead. They were either shot by the planes or, more likely, by the German S.S. We crossed this opening carefully and re-entered the forest on the other side. A short distance later we saw farmland. For the last few days we had nothing to eat or drink. Ferry said that he could not drag along any longer. He either had to get to a doctor or keep his leg still until he saw a doctor to minimize his pain. Otto was the strong one, while Ferry and I were completely exhausted. We decided to get to the nearest farmhouse and hide.

As we reached the rear of a barn the farmer came out and ushered us into his barn. The farmer gave us something to drink that tasted like lemonade and, as we entered the barn, we found that other prisoners had found shelter there too. They praised the farmer for his kindness. He fed them and had promised that no one would know of their existence. With this information, I relaxed and fell into a deep sleep. Maybe four or five hours later, the barn door opened, and S.S. men with dogs were standing and yelling, "Everybody out!" We had our story well rehearsed, should we be questioned, but the S.S. did not ask any questions. The farmer was standing there like the S.S. had turned us in, even though it was only a couple of days before the allied forces would have been there.

The S.S. herded us together and took us back to an awaiting train. The walk back seemed much closer than from where we jumped off. Ferry was hobbling on one leg, and Otto and I were very dejected at the turn of events. Within a few minutes' train ride, we entered the main camp, Dachau. We knew that this was the end for us. After all the tortures we had to endure, I could not comply with any order given. I had nothing to eat for a long time. Between the hard labor I had to perform, the typhus among other sickness, and the lice, I had nothing left, and now I entered Dachau, sure that this was the final destination.

Kurt Ladner

The Greenblatts

Ladner's brother Pepi, and sister-in-law, Bertha

Ladner singing with the band at the Flagler Hotel, Catskills, New York

Ladner addressing American Council of Equal Compensation of Nazi Victims from Austria (ACOA)

Ladner with his parents before Nazi occupation

The five friends who survived the camps and later lived together. From left to right: Kurt Ladner, Ernest Sterzer, Walter Fantl, Walter Kormis, Kurt Reich

Ladner's brother, Fritz

Ladner's son John and daughter Fern

Ladner with his wife Betty

Signing the Austria Agreement
From left to right: Gideon Taylor, Rabbi Singer, Kurt Ladner,
Secretray Stuart Eisenstat

World Boxing Champion Gus Lesnevich with Kurt Ladner

Ladner with Mr. Silverman, steward at the Flagler Hotel

(Left) Ariel Muzicant, President of the Jewish Community in Vienna, and (right) Gideon Eckhaus, chairman of the Central Committee of Austrian Jews in Israel

Ladner's friend and president of the organization, Henry Wagner

CHAPTER FIFTEEN
THE LIBERATION

They took us to barrack number four, which was full of sick people. To my surprise, I saw Jackie Hacker and Hardie Fleischman. Looking around and seeing these weak skeletons, not unlike myself, we knew that we could be of no use to the Germans, and my mind was running with thoughts of being killed. Every so often, Germans and capos came to our barracks and took a few prisoners, then a few more and so on. We didn't know what happened to these people, for they were never heard from or seen again.

I was fortunate to receive a bottom bunk because I could not have climbed up a ladder. I spoke to Jackie, my former goalie, who could hardly raise his voice, and to Hardie, who could not shake my hand. The progression in Dachau was that you get sick, you go to barrack number four, and from there you exit the world. I still had not eaten anything. I crawled into my bunk and slept intermittently.

Early the next morning a prisoner came in and told me that the S.S. were no longer in the camp. They had been replaced by Volkssturm. This reserve army was staffed mostly by old men and young boys, but they all had guns. Later that afternoon, I was told that some prisoners took over the guard towers and the allied forces had surrounded the camp. I was in an ambiguous state. I had not left my barrack since I arrived. Rumors are only rumors. I said to Ferry and Hardie, "I'll go out to see what is really going on." Before I could reach the door, it swung wide open, and American soldiers, dirty and crumpled looking, with beards, holding machine guns and rifles, entered my barrack. I was only a couple of feet away from them. This must have been the first time that these soldiers had seen this kind of horror. You could see in their faces that what they saw was unbelievable to them. Prisoners started to crawl and walk toward them, and I could see tears running down the cheeks of these tough, battle-hardened soldiers. Someone in the rear began to sing the Hatikvah. First, just this one lonely voice, then another joined in the singing. It got louder and louder. Everyone was joining in, except me. I was sitting on the floor in front of the American soldiers, crying and sobbing like a little baby, with the realization that I had survived this horrible nightmare. Then, I too joined in the singing. I did not get up from the floor because of my repeated crying jags. But with the doors wide open, the fresh air coming into the barracks, and the stinking air escaping, I felt like a new life was beginning from that moment on.

It got noisy outside my barracks. The original soldiers had withdrawn, but soon others entered. More and more came just to look at this unbelievable sight of mangled skeletons. I was still sitting on the floor when one of the soldiers, who seemed to be an officer, asked, "Who is in charge of this barrack?" Nobody answered. I then answered from the floor, "There is nobody in charge. Nobody." "Do you speak English?" he asked. "I understand, but you should speak slowly." I think he said that the U.S. Army was now in charge. They would see to it that we got food, and he said for us to remain in the barrack. Ferry had dragged himself to the front and told the officer that he had a bullet in his knee, which I translated. He ordered one of the soldiers to take Ferry to a doctor.

There was a lot of commotion inside and outside the barrack. Prisoners tried to get out of their high bunks and fell to the ground. Soldiers lined up to view our grotesque barrack and its inmates. I finally got up from the ground and walked out of the barrack. I saw a soldier with a Red Cross armband. I waddled over to him and said, "Sir, I am very sick. I need a doctor. Please help me." He picked me up, which was not hard to do because when I was put on a scale I only weighed sixty-four pounds. He put me on his little truck, which had benches on both sides and drove off. We arrived at a large tent-like structure, just outside of a building. The soldier helped me to get off the truck and told me to go inside.

Once I was inside, I was stripped naked, and I walked through a fog of white stuff. They then pumped DDT all over my body. This procedure took a few minutes. Then I took a shower. The water was not exactly hot, but it felt so good. I stood under the water for a while, then went directly into the building. They assigned a cot to me; a cot with a sheet, a pillow and a sparkling clean blanket, and this was a makeshift hospital. It was heaven just being there. Later on, a doctor, nurse and a German male nurse came to see me. The doctor examined my head, eyes and ears, and slowly worked down my body to my toes. I was still naked when the nurse took some blood from my finger to test if I was still a carrier of typhus. The test came back negative. They checked the wounds and scabs over my back. The wound on my side, which I got from a bayonet, was still infected and oozing. The biggest wound I had was on my coccyx bone. Not only was it oozing, but it also bled. The doctor ordered me to go upstairs to a ward with bunk beds. Only non-carriers of typhus were allowed upstairs. If you were a carrier, you were quarantined. Still naked, I got a downstairs bunk and an orderly brought me a long shirt that easily covered my body.

That evening all I had to eat was clear soup and shortly thereafter, I went to sleep and I slept until the German male nurse woke me early the next morning. He said, "I have to take care of your wounds and scabs.

There is only one way to take them off and it is radical." He said, "It will hurt, but once it's done you won't have any further problems." With this explanation, he asked me to stand on an elevated platform and removed my shirt. I had to bend over and with a very rough, course rag soaked in alcohol and iodine, he rubbed every scab and sore down to the raw flesh. I screamed with every stroke, and he said, "I understand." I called him every name in the book, including Nazi sadist, but he just kept on rubbing. He tried to get this procedure over with as soon as possible, but for me, it was not soon enough. I had to lie on my stomach for two days. The only time I stood up was to eat. I had no dressing or bandages on my back. I just had to expose my rear to the open air. It did scab slightly later on, but there was no more pain or infection. It healed, and all I was left with were a few scars.

The amount of food I received was not much more than in the concentration camp. I received clear soup, a few peas and carrots and some kind of applesauce, and all of it was served in a sectional dish. I complained bitterly to the nurse, telling her that I had not eaten for three years and was that all she could give me? She patiently explained to me that I must learn to eat all over again and to increase my food intake very slowly. She told me, "Prisoners broke into German warehouses and ate cold meat from cans and other stored food and many died because of this behavior." She again emphasized that I must eat only small portions and introduce new foods little by little. But this was much too slow for me and I said that I would like to leave the hospital, but again she urged me not to rush.

While I was in the hospital, I met a nice older man, a Jew from Belgium, who told me about the transports that left Belgium. Based on his experiences, he was very much afraid that he would be all alone, afraid that he had lost his family. When I told him that I lived in Antwerp, he suggested that I return to Belgium. He would be picked up by the Belgian government and that they would care for us. He was either in the jewelry or diamond business in Antwerp. I thanked him for his offer and told him that I must return to Vienna in case any one in my family was still alive. He agreed that I must return, but if no one was alive, I should come to Belgium.

After a few more days in the hospital, I started to feel better, walked better, and I gained a little weight. I told the doctor that I wanted to leave, and he gave me release papers. I was assigned to the Austrian block in Dachau. This time, though, the Austrian block was where the German S.S. used to live, and the S.S. were in prison where we lived. When I signed in at the Austrian block, I was given a bunk with plenty of extra room. My prison clothing had been cleaned while I was still in the hospital.

Even though we could not leave the camp without permission, it was the first time since Liberation that I actually felt good and free. In the Austrian block were several friends. One was Herman Riegler, the other, Kurt Breitbart. I asked them about Jackie Hacker and Hardie

Fleischman. That is when I received the bad news. Jackie died seven hours after the Liberation. He was too sick and weak, and even his strong will to live was not enough. From others I learned that while Hardie was being transported to a hospital on a laundry truck, a bundle of laundry fell on him, and he did not have the strength to push this bundle off his face, and therefore, was smothered to death. The tragedies did not end with our liberation. Many prisoners were beyond help, and many who did survive were left with physical and mental problems.

I started to explore the goings on in Dachau and the surroundings. My first activity was to find a way to return to Terezin and then Vienna. I had to find out if my parents had survived. Since I had last seen them in Terezin, my search for them began there. Transports to all four corners were being organized, but without any coherent timeframe. I decided to walk over to the American Headquarters to find out if they could get me to Czechoslovakia. I learned that the Americans were trying to get all former prisoners to their desired destinations, but it would take longer than the impatient people expected.

It was late afternoon when I met a guy I knew from Terezin and asked him what he was doing. Ernst Seinfeld seemed to be in a hurry and asked me to wait; he would be right back. He returned and told me that he was working for the American Army, and he invited me to eat with him in the army's mess hall. I joined him, and I had a really good meal. After we ate, he asked me to hang around with him to watch a variety show later. There were singers, comics, and all kinds of entertainment. I understood the English that all the entertainers spoke, except the comics; they spoke too fast. I must have been a pain, asking Ernst, "What did he say?" What stood out from this evening's entertainment was a tall, blond soldier with a very good voice, singing "Always." From then on, I have been singing, humming and whistling "Always" all the time.

Dachau was still closed. No one could leave without permission. I asked Ernst if he could get me a soft job with the Army because I liked eating in the mess hall and the evening's entertainment, but he said, "I do not know if I can." The next evening I attended a compulsory meeting. We were addressed, in perfect German, by a captain of the United States Army's Law Department. He said, "I need to explain to all of you the legal situation as it exists. When you are allowed to leave Dachau, although ragingly in need for revenge against the Germans, you are not allowed to do so. From now on, you fall under the jurisdiction of the American Armed Forces, and under it, freedom, democracy, law and order has returned. Should you know of anyone who has committed any crimes, killed, maimed, beaten or participated in atrocities, you must file a complaint with this department and never take the law into your own hands, for if you do you will be no better than the S.S., and you could be punished for your deeds." He assured us that no guilty German would go unpunished.

After his oratory, I spoke to the captain. He told me that he was from Vienna and that he had been imprisoned in Dachau in 1938, but let go because he had a United States visa. We talked for a long time. He gave me some food and chocolate. I asked him if he could get me any kind of job in the American headquarters, and I explained why. He said yes. The next day I sat at a little desk assigning former prisoners of Dachau as guides for visiting brass. The job was short-lived because transports away from Dachau had started.

I retained my headquarters I.D. card and ate my rations in the Austrian barrack and then in the American mess hall. I rapidly gained weight, and my body and brain started to respond. I even played ping pong against a lieutenant who chased me from corner to corner and easily beat me. He could not have done so before Hitler even though I was never the greatest ping pong player. I felt better. I moved around much like normal, yet I had a weakness that was hard to overcome. I had to take the typhus blood test all over again. They took some blood and dropped it onto a white slab that had three drops of some solution, and once again, I tested negative. I received a stamped piece of paper that allowed me to leave the camp.

That afternoon, Kurt Breitbart, Herman Riegler and I left camp and walked to the nearest farmhouse and asked for food. We still wore our prison uniforms and the farmer, without hesitation, gave us a little sack of flour and about forty or so eggs. We obtained a large bucket to boil water, mixed the flour and made nock-erln (dumplings). Then we threw the eggs over it and ate until we could no longer move. That night we slept in their barn. The farmer's young daughter, who was very pretty, came to the barn and slept next to me. I think the farmer sent her to placate us out of fear. I fell asleep, and in the morning she was gone. We again knocked on the farmer's door and his wife gave us some milk and bread and she said, "Would you believe it? I lived so close to the camp, Dachau, and didn't know what was going on in there." We knew then that this would become the standard answer for all Germans. "We did not know." Herman passed that farmhouse every day, surrounded by armed guards, and yet she claimed that she did not know. "How come," Herman asked, "every German was afraid that he would join us in the concentration camp?" Everyone knew.

We returned to camp where clothing was being distributed. I received a jacket, a coat and a pair of felt boots, the start of my first wardrobe. How sad. We also made a trip into Munich. We stopped at the U.N.R.A. Headquarters for information and were directed to a school building that was set up as a temporary quarters for former prisoners. We were about to leave when three men came toward us. One of them was Dr. Hahn, who could not believe his eyes when he saw me alive and walking. He said, "I left you for dead." As we entered the school building's office and checked the lists of people who perished in Dachau, my brother's name was among them, and, to my surprise, so was mine. I told the clerk to correct this mistake and to put my name among the living. Inside were bunks and in them survivors were either sleeping or resting, when I heard my name called. It was a friend, Heinz Wegner, who had, thankfully, survived. We spoke for a while, and he asked, "If you should return to Vienna before me and should run into my wife, Trude, tell her to wait for me in Vienna."

After spending a few more hours in Munich, we returned to Dachau. The word spread that if anyone wanted to return to Czechoslovakia, a transport would be leaving in a day or two. Surviving Czechs, Poles, Austrians, and others registered for the transport, and two days later I left Dachau.

CHAPTER SIXTEEN
IN SEARCH OF
MY FAMILY

The train ride, although in boxcars, was joyful. We had food and drink. The doors were wide open. It was spring. Everything was blooming, and we felt reborn. The amazing thing was that none of us spoke of the past. Every conversation that took place was about the future. Where will you go? What will you do? All of us looked for surviving members of our families: aunts, uncles, cousins, friends and girlfriends. We had no contact with any surviving females and wondered what their imprisonment was like.

We were riding for some time when the train stopped. Some rail cars were uncoupled, and the rest continued on to Prague. There we changed trains and only a few of us went to Terezin. When I entered the former ghetto, it seemed empty in comparison. As I walked through the streets on my way to the administration building, memories were flashing of my family and friends: Herbert, Maxie, Peter, Hardie, Jackie, and so many others were all gone. All the guys I played soccer with and against – where were they? How many had survived this tragedy? Instead of stopping at the various buildings and places, I just eyeballed them and walked straight to the administration office. The Russian Army was in charge of the ghetto, and when I entered the office some recognized me, but I did not know anyone. I asked about my parents and was told that they had been sent to Auschwitz two weeks after my brother and I had left. I inquired about my girlfriend who was also sent to Auschwitz on the same transport as my parents. I asked if there was any news. Who had and who had not survived? Their answer was, "We don't know." The only information they could assemble was that most of them were gassed. I told them that I wanted to go to Vienna. They assured me that I would be included on the next available train.

My assigned room in Terezin looked like a cheap motel room, but it was clean. I met many people I knew. We were happy to see each other alive. Conversations were mostly about people and friends who did not survive. I learned that my best friend, Ernst Sterzer, and his brother were alive and living in Vienna, as well as Walter Fantl, Kurt Reich and several other friends.

Almost everyone I spoke to in Terezin asked me if I would play soccer for Hakoah Vienna or some other team. I was always confronted with this question, and I always changed the subject. They all assumed I could still play. I just knew that my dream of becoming a soccer star was squashed in Dachau. I still could not walk long distances, and running was completely out of the question.

The next morning, I learned that my girlfriend had survived and was living back in her hometown. The fellow who gave me that information said that he would be back in town that night, and he would bring her the good news that I had returned to Terezin. She arrived in Terezin the next day. We held each other for a long time. She looked well. Her hair was still short because all women prisoners' heads were shaved. We told each other our nightmares. I asked about my parents. She told me that they went to the other side, which meant the gas chamber. I was prepared for her answer, but I still cried and was solemn for the rest of the day, thinking and thinking to myself, questioning myself, "What will I do? What should I do? Why should I go back to Vienna? For what? For whom?" I was holding my girlfriend's hand very tightly to make sure that she would not vanish. I thought of my brother in Russia and my sister in Belgium, hoping that they had lived through the horrible war. Thinking out loud, I said, "I must return to Vienna." I hoped that either my brother or sister would have inquired about our family and would thus be known in Vienna.

My girlfriend tried to persuade me to go with her to her home and start my new life with her and her mother. That was too drastic a decision to make at that time. I promised her that I would come to see her very soon. She stayed with me for three days. When she left, I kissed her goodbye and again promised to see her in the very near future.

The next train to Vienna was canceled, and I was stuck in Terezin. Every day a few survivors returned in hopes of finding some member of their family, and with each new arriving person, I had to repeat the same story of who was alive and who died and no, I would not be playing soccer. The train to Vienna was scheduled for the next day, when I joined a few friends in a cattle car for the uneventful ride to Vienna. I really did not know what I expected to find in Vienna. The fact was that I was all alone at eighteen and a half years old and was still uncertain about my recovery from near death in a concentration camp. But I was free, and hopefully on the road to recovery. If my sister or brother was alive, I would probably live with or near them. One thing I was sure of was that I would stay in Vienna for the time being only. Any further decision I would make as events occurred. The thought that I had to live among people who not only deserted the Jews of Austria, but had participated in the extermination of them, was repugnant to me.

What would I do in Vienna? I had to earn money to live. The only thing I was qualified to do was be a painter or soccer player, and at that time, I could do neither. I was spinning ideas in my head and always came to the conclusion that I had no options. We pulled into Vienna, stopped at the outskirts for a short while, then continued on to our destination. I looked out of the cattle car and saw an awful lot of people waiting for us to arrive. Among them were my friends, Ernie and Walter. I could not figure out how everyone knew when we were arriving, especially since they knew the day and time, despite the many changes and delays. I got off. Ernie and Walter came running toward me. They took my meager sack of belongings and tried to get me out of the station as quickly as possible. I was constantly stopped by people I knew and by people who I did not know but who seemed to know me. The welcome from all of them was wonderful.

Once we were out of the railroad station we took a streetcar, and off we went. I asked Ernie, "Where are we going?" And he said with a grin, "To my apartment." I thought he meant his apartment in the Twentieth District where we grew up. Instead, the streetcar took us across the little Danube and into the First District. Then Ernie explained his new apartment to me. Ernie's father was the first renter of a very, very large apartment in the First District. During the Hitler years, he had to share this apartment with many Jewish families. When Ernie and his family were sent to Terezin, the apartment was taken over by a very important Nazi. Upon Ernie's return, he reclaimed this apartment by proving it with copies of his father's last rental agreement obtained through the

Jewish Community Center and a police registrar document. Supported with this proof, he went to the Russian Headquarters, who had confiscated and held under their jurisdiction all unclaimed apartments. In addition, he showed his identification card, which proved that he was an inmate of a concentration camp, whereupon the Russians then turned this apartment over to Ernie, lock, stock and barrel. When it became obvious that Hitler had lost the war and that Vienna would be liberated by the Russians, this big shot Nazi committed suicide, and his wife and daughter had run away.

When I entered this apartment, my mouth fell open in disbelief. First and foremost, it was huge. Big rooms furnished with the most expensive furniture – Persian carpets, and a Boesendorf piano, among other things. There were windows almost from the floor to the ceiling with mock balconies, parquet floors throughout, and stucco designed ceilings. Every piece of furniture had lights, with beautiful pieces of silver or porcelain displayed. There was a bar with liquor neatly stored. All the accessories were mostly antiques, paintings on the walls and silent butlers in every corner. I don't even know how many rooms there were. Ernie had one room, and his brother, Fritz, had one. I had one room, as did Kurt and Walter. On the other side of the apartment lived an elderly lady. She had two rooms, and I think there were two more. There was a bathroom, tiled with the most beautiful marble and a huge conference room with designed walls and floors, with large palm trees standing against the window. Ernie said that he found papers confirming that the man who lived in the apartment during the war was a high ranking member in the Nazi party and most everything in the apartment was confiscated by him from Jews in Poland and Austria. It was an impressive looking apartment. Since I was the last to return to Vienna, I therefore had the smallest room near the kitchen, but the five of us were like a family and shared almost everything.

That evening we sat in the living room and shared our experiences. We spoke about everyone's family members and friends we had lost. Together, we mourned them all. Ernie, who was a diabetic since childhood, survived the ordeal with very little or no insulin. In Oranienburg, he was struck on his head and began hemorrhaging in his already weakened eyes and had to cope with enormous problems. Walter, who was in Auschwitz with us, remained in the barrack that Herbert, Maxie and I ran away from. He was sent to Gleiwitz and luckily was liberated in January, 1945. We who did not want to remain in Auschwitz were sent to Dachau. Those of us who survived were not liberated until April 30, 1945. January, February, March and April of 1945 were the worst months in the history of the concentration camps. That was when the most prisoners were killed or died of sickness, malnutrition or exposure to the elements. We sat and talked until we were all talked out. I tried to sleep. I could not and was awake for a long time.

The next morning I realized that I would have to adjust to possibly being the sole survivor of my entire family. I walked from my apartment to just across the street where the new Jewish Community Center building was located. I walked up one flight to a room marked "Information." It was half filled with people standing in line, with only two women behind the counter. My purpose for going there was to register as a survivor and to give them my address in case my brother or sister inquired about me at the Jewish Community Center. I also had to register to receive whatever food, clothing or general assistance was available.

I stood in line only a few minutes when people who knew me from Terezin came into the room and clustered around me. They asked me all kinds of questions about friends and from which concentration camp I was liberated. But no matter to whom I spoke, the one question they always repeated was, "Will you play soccer for Hakoah?" My answer was definite. "No." It was not that I did not want to, but that because of my illness in camp, I could not. I was moving slowly to the front, and finally I was next. A very nice lady told me that she received a list of the arriving people from Terezin. All she needed from me was my address and information about my family. This office constantly updated their information roster. I also received vouchers for clothing and a pass to be able to eat in a kitchen that distributed cooked food to all returnees.

I was about to return to my apartment when Walter Kormis, a friend, stopped me. After the greetings and conversations, he told me that a Mr. Blumenfeld, President of Hakoah Vienna Sports Club, would like to see me. I thanked him for the information and we both went back to the apartment. I thought to myself that a lot was happening on my very first day back in Vienna. When we entered the apartment, several of our friends had come over to welcome me back. I was so happy to see everyone that I forgot about everything. Ernie sat at the piano and was playing boogie woogie, and not bad at that. Ernie was an American jazz fanatic, and so was I. He never missed a chance to play or barter for jazz recordings. Soon, some girls came to join us. Some I knew and others I met for the first time. Ernie had opened a bottle wine, and soon we had a party going.

That evening, after everyone had left, I sat down and talked to Ernie, who was always my best friend. I told him about Mr. Blumenfeld and Hakoah, and he said that he knew all about it. They had heard about my playing soccer, and they hoped that I would start playing again as soon as possible. I told Ernie that I could never play again. I still could not walk up one flight of stairs. I had no stamina, and I would have been too embarrassed to put on a pair of soccer shoes. I told Ernie that I did not know Mr. Blumenfeld and asked if he not I should see him to give him my message. But Ernie was a wise old owl and he said, "Why don't you hold this conversation a couple of months from now? Maybe you will feel better." Ernie – the constant optimist. It was his way of saying don't worry now; you'll get better, and wild horses would not be able to stop you from playing soccer again. I also asked what my obligations were, like rent, food and household expenses. He said for the time being, the support of the Jewish Community Center would cover most of the expenses. Later on, we could come to some kind of arrangement. I told Ernie that I would visit the painter I worked for during Hitler. Maybe he had a soft job for me.

Times in Vienna were not good in mid-1945. Food was hard to come by. Most of us were still too weak to do manual labor. Every returnee ate in a kitchen run by the Jewish Community Center in the Second District, but we were able to get extra food through Ernie's connection with the Jewish Hospital. Times were tough even with all the extra help we were getting.

The next day, I took the streetcar to visit my former painting boss. Ernie tagged along with me and asked, "Why would you want to be a painter?" I answered, "I am a very good painter, and I have to start somewhere." I rang the bell and waited a while for someone to open the door. I rang again and my boss' wife came to the door. When she saw me, she started to sob and said, "Thank God you are alive. Thank God you came back." She was still crying, and I could hardly understand what she was saying. "Mr. Ladner, you have to help me. My husband is in prison on some unknown charges made by foreign laborers." I said, "Foreign laborers? They must have worked for him after I was sent to Terezin." She said, "They filed charges, and they never showed up to testify. The hearings are always postponed while my husband lingers in jail." She asked me to be a character witness. "Mr. Ladner," she said, while she grabbed my hands, "You knew him best." She gave me the name of a detective who was stationed at the main police station in the First District. I said to the shaken woman that I would inquire about her husband, and I gave her my address. She thanked me a hundred times, and Ernie and I left her still crying. Ernie had listened to all this and once we were down the steps said, "He probably deserves to be in jail." I told him about my relationship with this man and how he had tried to help me, so I had to find out what he did to be in jail.

Ernie said that the Chief of Police in the First District was the uncle of our friend Maxie Witrofsky, and before I did anything I should speak to him. He could give me all the information I needed. Maxie's mother survived the concentration camp, and I was the one who brought the tragic news about Maxie and his father. The Chief's wife owned one of the most popular cafes in Vienna, Cafe Dobner, which eventually became our second home.

I visited Police Chief Rossen in his office and for the first few minutes we spoke only of his nephew, Maxie. I told him my recollection of Maxie and our friendship. He swallowed hard several times to resist crying. He had no children and Maxie was the nearest thing to having his own child. He quickly changed the subject back to the one I had come to see him about. He then asked me to wait outside. I sat while a man walked into his office, and shortly thereafter I was called in. The Chief introduced me to a detective who did not live up to my vision of a detective. He said that my former boss' wife had called him saying that I would make a statement on behalf of her husband. I wanted to know of what crime he was accused. The answer was unspecific. I told them about my two year association with him and about his offer of protection during my employment. I also said, "I cannot vouch for his behavior before I knew him or after I left Vienna." After about 45 minutes, I was told that he would be released, not because of my testimony only, but that the two accusers had returned to Yugoslavia and would not be returning to Vienna. I called his wife from the Chief's office and told her that her husband would be released. He was a good guy to me. I could have done no less.

After his release, we met. He thanked me for seeing the police, and he also expressed his sadness about my family and offered me a semi-partnership. For every job I obtained and finished, I would receive fifty percent. He would supply all the materials and everything else needed for the job. My labor, his everything else. It was not a bad offer. I accepted and actually worked for a couple of weeks. However, climbing up and down ladders and stroking with a big, loaded brush was too hard a job so soon after my ordeal. I told him that I had to quit;

that it was too much for me to overcome. He said, "I will keep my offer open, and you can decide at a later date."

I went to the Jewish Community Center and applied for a job. They were very happy to employ me, and assigned me to the very busy information office. I immediately started to work. The system for running this department was in place, but I did recommend certain improvements. We received many inquiries for relatives and friends of people who had been deported to various places. Once we investigated, I suggested that we have several copies of this report, for we could receive inquiries for the same person from every corner of the earth. We received requests from people I knew, including a request for my own sister-in-law from her sister in England. Everyone we suspected had died we answered as "Has not returned," accompanied with a police data sheet where he or she was deported to. Every inquiry was answered to the best of our ability. In addition, we had to register every returnee and supply all assistance. Many times people walked in who were rumored to be dead, and every time that happened a celebration of rebirth took place. The work was not hard, but we worked long hours, at least in the beginning, and for very little pay.

A few days later, Kurt and Walter came home and told Ernie and me that Dr. Tuchman informed them that the American Joint Distribution Committee had been sending food for the returning survivors. Carloads of food were piling up at the railroad, and there was no one to receive or distribute it. Dr. Tuchman accepted the responsibility and obligation of storing and then distributing everything received. He also asked Kurt and Walter, and they in turn asked Ernie and me to help him. We were told that some boxcars were broken into and food was disappearing. Ernie, Walter, Kurt and I decided that we must help out and organize the entire situation.

We called the police chief in the Second District, who was with me in Terezin and Dachau, and was a friend of ours. We asked him to secure the shipments at the railroad station, which was in his district. Within minutes, police guards came to protect the shipments day and night. With the help of the Jewish Community Center and Dr. Tuchman, we rented warehouse space to store all that was being sent. Our friend, Walter Kormis, joined us in the effort, plus a few additional employees from the Jewish Community Center.

We inventoried every item. There were canned goods, sugar, and food articles of several varieties with more food arriving daily for the Jews in Vienna. Kurt Reich was and still is the best organizer in the world. That evening, the five of us sat down and planned a course of action. We established that all Jews had to register with the American Joint Distribution Committee (which was us). Also included were non-Jewish spouses and children of mixed marriages. We advertised and made it known through every means possible that people should register. Within a day or two, lines began to form, and the five of us registered everyone who was entitled to share the donated food. Occasionally, we cross-checked persons with the information office to see if people were registered with the Jewish Community Center. Several people applied who divorced their partner with the excuse that Hitler made them do it. We chased such people from the building without mercy because we knew better. Non-Jewish spouses who stuck loyally by their partner suffered almost as much as we did. Hence, they were included in the sharing. As soon as we could judge how many people would be sharing, the food was divided equally into packages and distributed. We worked like this for a couple of months, then politics entered the proceedings. Some people did not like Dr. Tuchman, while others did. People from all directions wanted to get involved, while the five of us were only concerned with the packages being distributed to the right people. By then, everything was running smoothly; as new people registered, they received packages. The five of us did not want to get involved in choosing different factions or supporting one side or the other. We therefore submitted our resignations to Dr. Tuchman. Thank God other friends of ours took over our positions with the Joint Distribution Committee, and it continued to work very well.

I returned to my job in the Information Department, even though the returnees had reduced to a trickle. My life in Vienna began to settle into a routine. Besides working, my friends and I just wanted to have a good time and recapture some of the lost years. We were steady opera-goers, and we saw most of the operas performed in the temporary quarters because the opera building was bombed during the war. We saw almost every operetta being performed, from Franz Lehar to Emerich Kalman, and everything in between. Dancing at the Triumph in the Anna Gasse was a regular activity for us. Horst Winter and his orchestra were not exactly Glen Miller, but they were the best Vienna had to offer. We met many striving jazz musicians who got together and rehearsed in our apartment, taking advantage of our beautiful piano, Ernie's trumpet, and the several other instruments that were stored with us. There was always music in our apartment, and many friends came to see us, invited or not.

We had several political leaders of Austria visiting us. Bundes Kanzler Figel, a former inmate of a concentration camp, and I shared the same barber. An organization was formed of former inmates of concentration camps. In order to become a member you had to prove your imprisonment with documents and eye witnesses. Upon acceptance, you received a green card with a red triangle and the number 369 printed on it. The number, I believe, represented how many weeks Hitler had lasted in Austria. We used this green identification, which was printed in four languages, French, English, Russian and German, on many occasions to our advantage, like when the first American movie was shown in Vienna, "Sun Valley Serenade." I knew of Glen Miller but my love for his music grew each time I saw the film, and I saw it fourteen or fifteen times. The lines for this movie were extremely long, but when my friends and I went there, we flashed our green card and walked right in without having to stand in line. There were rumblings from the people, but I explained that they enjoyed the German propaganda films during the war while we had to miss these glorious films while in concentration camps. My thoughts about the people who were murmuring under their breath were not complimentary. The attendant's explanation to the people was that the policy of the movie establishment was to give privileges to members of the concentration camp organization.

Maxie's aunt, who owned Cafe Dobner, became our guardian mother, and we spent our time in her coffeehouse. Besides the usual café services, they also had variety shows every weekend. If we were not otherwise busy, we always had a table in her cafe.

One evening, I was sitting with friends in the cafe when a man came over to our table and said, while shaking my hand, that he was Mr. Blumenfeld, President of Hakoah Sports Club. He urged me to visit him in his office. He said, "Even if you should decide not to play soccer again, your services to the Hakoah Sports Club could be very important in another capacity." We talked and talked. He was a nice, jolly man, and I liked him instantly so I promised to see him the following week. Over the weekend I inquired about the soccer team, Hakoah. I learned that it was staffed by players of distant Jewish heritage, mixed marriages, and one of two returnees from immigration. The team was headed by a player-coach who was a star player for Hakoah before Hitler.

Also, the team had very good personnel and players. I would be the only returnee from a concentration camp competing against talent who was never near a camp. I also met with my brother's friend, Walter Probst, who said that he also heard that I had developed into a very good soccer player. I told him the facts about my life in a concentration camp, typhus and every other ailment I had. I also told him that I would not ever be able to play again. I told him that I had been invited to play for Hakoah, but how could I? He looked at me and thought, then said, "Look Kurtie, why don't you try? Even if for no other reason than to get into shape." Since my liberation, I had gained 120 artificial pounds. I was bloated, and the weight I gained was mostly flab and fat. I listened very carefully to the advice he gave me. After all, he was my brother's best friend, and my idol. He was an all-star major league Austrian soccer player. During the war he was inducted into the German Army, but he had broken his leg and wore a cast for the longest time. The army then put him in a limited service position, pushing pencils in some office where he remained during the war. Walter knew that I was a good soccer player even when I was a kid, and I said that someday I would be better than Sindelar or even Walter Probst. We talked for a long time, mostly about my family and soccer. I then promised that I would go to see Mr. Blumenfeld and stay in touch with him.

I met with Mr. Blumenfeld in his office; the player-coach was present. When I entered, Mr. Blumenfeld made the introductions. "This is Kurt Ladner, and this is Mr. Platcheck." I not only knew him, but I had seen him play and was impressed with his many abilities on the soccer field. The coach said, "I have heard about you. We could use a good player." I answered, "Whatever you heard, discount ninety percent. I was a very sick guy, and I am in no condition to play ball." Mr. Blumenfeld intervened by saying, "We have good doctors, good trainers, and maybe, just maybe, you could play again." Platcheck said that he was sure. He shook my hand and left. Mr. Blumenfeld and I were alone. He said that he was an up-front guy, and until I was sure that I couldn't or wouldn't play ball again, I should sign a contract with Hakoah before another team made me an offer. I laughed out loud and said to him, "My dream, ever since I was a little boy, was to play for Hakoah," mentioning the players I looked up to like Donnenfeld, Ehrlich, Fischer, Mausner and Lowy, the goalie for the club who lived around the corner from me, and their present player, Coach Platcheck. "If I could play, I would never play for anybody other than Hakoah," I said. I explained again that I was only a shell of my former self. I hoped that he understood, and I continued by saying that I would be interested in being part of Hakoah in any other capacity. "In that case," he said, "sign here." He put a piece of paper in front of me, and I signed. I was to receive the minimum pay while I was not playing and full pay if I should ever play again. When I got back to my apartment, I told Ernie what I had just done. Not only could I not run, but

I also knew I was going to make a total fool of myself. Ernie said, "So what? Work out with the team, and if you can't do it, you'll quit."

I arranged my work schedule so that I could train with the team, and when I joined them and met all the other players, I knew that I did not belong. They all looked fit and well-conditioned, while I looked more like the water boy wanting to hang around. I received my uniform and shoes. I participated in calisthenics and jumping jacks, and when it came to pushups, all I could lift was my head. We then had to run around the soccer field. The coach said to me, "You run at your own speed and only as far as you can." I gratefully looked at him and started to run. I was slow and far behind everyone else. I ran only half around the field and continued to walk the other half. I then sat down, huffing and puffing, while gasping for more air, and watched the rest of the team run several more laps around the field. We then assembled in front of one goal. A few soccer balls were thrown onto the field and we started to kick and pass the ball to each other, not running much. I could surprisingly handle the ball proficiently. I passed where I wanted and, when I kicked the ball into the goal, I seldom missed my intended placement. They started a game, offense against defense. I was not included, but they put me in at the very end. I played offense, and I completely forgot what was ailing me. I thought I was very good. I lasted only a few minutes, then I felt my knees buckling, my heart racing, and I was gasping for air. Mr. Blumenfeld, who had arrived late, called me out as I was sweating and breathing very hard. He said, "You'll be ready to play in a few weeks." All I could do was shake my head and say, "I don't think so," barely audible to his ears.

Yet, I kept coming to practice. When I was running, it felt like I was running against a 100-mile per hour wind. Speed, combined with my technical skills, used to be my strength. Now, I had neither. As time passed I started to run a little faster and longer distance. I was losing weight, and I kept on with the training discipline. The day actually came when I was installed into the first team as inside right. Imagine that! The first game I played, we lost. I even remember the score: three to two. My teammates were very nice to me. I was nervous and made mistakes. I only played one half, and I surely did not play like I played before the concentration camp. Many of my friends came to watch me play, and I knew that I disappointed them. They were kind and told me how good I was. After the game, I said to Mr. Blumenfeld, "Are you convinced now that I stink and can no longer play?" All he did was laugh and say, "It's only your first game." I did not start in the second game, but I did start in the third game, even though I was slow. I kicked my first goal, and I walked on air. I played for Hakoah, off and on, for over one year. Every so often I had to take off because I was suffering from severe headaches, just like in the concentration camp. When I took the prescribed pills, I slept for more than half a day. Hakoah was very good to me, especially Mr. Blumenfeld. I was good enough to play in the first team, but I felt that I was not motivated. Motivation was my biggest problem. Even when I physically felt good and played well, it was not like it used to be. Mr. Blumenfeld did not give up on me. He said, "Just lose a couple more pounds, and you can be the best player on the field, in the city, the country, and everywhere else." He was the nicest guy. He wanted me to make good because I was the only returnee from camp who could even come close to competing. Ernie said, "You are not there yet, but you will be."

Ernie, by profession, was a baker, and he did all the cooking for us. At that time in Vienna, the only food that was available in abundance was peas. Ernie cooked pea soup, pea puree, pea cakes, pea soufflé and just plain peas. The food supplements we had were packages from the American Joint or packages Ernie received from his sister in America, my aunt in Santo Domingo, and my cousin in England. When Ernie spoke to our friends' mothers, his question was, "What are you ladies cooking today?" The answer always was peas something. None of us were complaining about food, but when Ernie spoke of having peas for dessert, we clobbered him.

My girlfriend in Czechoslovakia and I wrote to each other every week, but the longer we were apart, the less chance we had for a future together. I decided to travel to Czechoslovakia to determine what her thinking was about us and to find out if there was a future for us together. I traveled to Prague and stayed with my Czech friends and pre-arranged to meet her there. I arrived a few days earlier and was able to explore the magnificent city of Prague. My friends took me sightseeing during the day and night-clubbing at night. I got reacquainted with several former soccer-playing friends who all felt the way I did. It was tough to get back in condition to play top-notch soccer.

When my girlfriend arrived, we spent a couple of days in Prague. I wanted her to tell me what her plans were. Had her plans changed? Did she still want me? In her letters she sounded as if she would like to remain in Czechoslovakia, while my plans were to leave and settle some place other than Europe. We traveled to her hometown, and she introduced me to her mother. She was nice enough, but I was taken aback when she said that I could share the bedroom with her daughter. She explained further that she could not protect her daughter in Terezin and that it would make no sense to separate us now. So we shared the bedroom, but knowing that her mother was in the next room made me feel uneasy.

That evening, my girlfriend and I had our first serious discussion. I expressed to her how I felt. I did not know what my future was going to be. I wanted to find out was the reason I was there; were we to map out a future together? I said that none of my family was alive and to live among the people who killed them was definitely not possible. I wanted to leave Vienna and try to get to the United States. When she asked me how, I said, "I don't know as yet, but America is my preferred choice." I also said that we could go to Palestine and live among our people, but when I mentioned the word "Palestine," she stiffened and, lifting her arm, said, "Oh no, oh no, not there." I repeated that my first choice was the United States, and I got no response. After a long pause she asked what she had in mind all the time: "Why not move here? We could live here." I said, "My moving here is not the solution. Your city, my city – it is still Europe. Why can't we get away from it all and start a new life somewhere without having to look into the faces of our persecutors?" After I turned down her suggestion, there was again a long pause. I started to feel like a wall was slowly creeping up, but then she finally said, "Okay. I'll come to live in Vienna." At that point, she either could not or did not want to understand me, so I dropped the whole subject for the time being. I believed that she wanted to be with or near her mother, which I could understand, but staying in Vienna or moving to Czechoslovakia was not in my future.

The following day was the last day before I was to return to Vienna. My girlfriend took me sightseeing, and as a last attempt to persuade me, she took me to a beautiful church. As we entered, she went to one side, kneeled down, and crossed herself, while I looked at her in amazement. She had just survived a concentration camp as a Jew, mind you. Now she was kneeling and crossing herself in a church. I realized that her mother was not Jewish; had she persuaded her to change her religion? I then remembered her reaction when I said that we could live in Palestine. Her definite, "Oh no," made me wonder even more. We walked silently through the church and before we left, she repeated the religious ceremony. It probably meant a great deal to her, and so I did not say one word to her about what I observed. At that time, so soon after my ordeal, I was not too fond of the Catholic Church. The betrayal of Cardinal Innizer of Vienna, when he urged the Austrian population to embrace Hitler and not even once intervened on behalf of Jews or preached to his flock to stop the slaughter of Jews, was, in my opinion, participation of the clergy in the crime of the century. The Jews of Vienna looked up to the Cardinal, hoping for some expression of compassion, but to no avail. So, to see my girlfriend, with whom I was planning our future, converted so soon after the Liberation was not what I expected. I was sad and disillusioned. I should have sat down with her, right then, to discuss how I felt. However, I never did, and that is something I regret. When I left the next day she must have sensed that something was wrong because all I said was, "I'll write to you." I made no promises. I wrote to her once or twice after that day, but our correspondence stopped, and our paths never crossed again.

When I returned to Vienna, I told Ernie what had happened; that it was over. He said, "It was not meant to be." It took a while to get over our breakup. Until Ernie said, "Cheer up, you are not even twenty years old. Live!" Every possible girlfriend in Vienna knew that I had a girlfriend in Czechoslovakia; therefore, we were nothing more than good friends. However, after my breakup, things started to change. I sensed that some girls were interested in having a closer relationship with me, but I was not about to get involved so soon. I started to have a good time with everyone.

My workload decreased at the Jewish Community Information Office, and Ernie and I began work in the American Headquarter in Vienna. This offer came just at the right time, and I liked my job description. We had to register all foreign residents who lived in the American sector of Vienna, legally or illegally. They had to prove whether they were stateless or citizens of a foreign country. If they could not obtain permission to stay in Austria, they had to leave to return to their respective country. Most did not want to return to their country, and my primary interest was why they did not want to return. My questions were slightly different from the norm because I wanted to know if they were Nazi collaborators. Sometimes, if we did not believe the stories they told us, we would refer them to our superiors with our suspicions. They, in turn, handled this person. I was told that they would be sent to Germany for further investigation.

While I continued working for the American Headquarter, Ernie changed jobs and became a cook for the American Officers' Club, and our food problems were solved. He not only brought cooked food home, but he collected all fat drippings from bacon, which we, in turn, sold or traded for things we needed. Fat was a rare commodity and could be bartered for almost anything.

We had a large circle of friends and were very close. We visited each other, attended sponsored parties, went dancing to various nightspots, went to sports events, and attended masked balls and Mardi Gras. Once, at an artists' ball, a friend and I won a dance contest. She received flowers while I got a handshake. By having a good time I overcame, however slowly, my reservations about mingling with the Austrian public. I still preferred to relate to my friends, who had similar backgrounds. I remained friends with the two sisters I had met in Belgium as a young kid. We were friends when in Terezin and after the Liberation. The older sister always urged me to take her younger sister dancing and she grew up to be very good looking. Occasionally, we did go out, but it never went beyond friendship.

We planned a big party in our apartment. As always, the two were invited, and only the younger one planned to attend. I invited another girl as my date for the evening, who was a knockout. I met her at the American Officers' Club where Ernie worked. He told me that she was the girlfriend of an American officer who had since returned to the Untied States. Ernie had tried to date her several times, without success, so Ernie dated her friend and asked me to meet this gorgeous blond on a blind date. Ernie swore that she was beautiful, so I agreed to meet her, but Ernie could say that someone was beautiful and she could look like Frankenstein. I met her the day beforehand, and she actually was the vision of beauty Ernie had described, so I brought her to the party as my date.

Our place started to fill up with friends, and friends of friends. A three-piece jazz band was just about to start playing when a couple from Prague arrived to stay with us for one week. We had the usual hugging and greetings all around, when he asked me, "What's going on here?" I said, "We knew you were coming, so we are throwing you a party." We served wine and hors d'oeuvres, and pretty soon the party was in full swing. Dance, talking, friends came as couples, some came alone, some stayed a while and left, some who had left came back and some did not want to leave at all. The party had pretty much thinned out. I retreated with my blond date to my room for some private time, and all of a sudden the door opened, and my girlfriend from Belgium walked into my room. Maybe she was a little tipsy. She took her lipstick and scribbled graffiti all over my shirt and in an angry voice said, "I'm leaving. Hope you have a good time." I was still looking at my shirt in disbelief while she ran out of the apartment. She must have gotten on the streetcar, which was only one block from our house, because I was trying to run after her. When I returned, I said to Ernie, "She is crazy – look what she did." Ernie answered, "No, she is not crazy; she is jealous." I looked at him and said, "Whaaat? Nah, that's impossible. I wish it was true." Secretly I loved her, but I had never made a move.

Shorty after the party, I made my way to my girl-friend's house. I had to find out if Ernie was right. I hoped that he was. When I arrived at her apartment, only her mother and sister were at home. I sat down with her sister and told her what had happened. I also told her Ernie's interpretation of what took place and she told me outright that Ernie was correct. Her sister was a good friend and ally, and she often ran interference for me.

I sat and waited until she came home. I took her aside, sat down and had a very serious talk with her. We found out that we loved each other, under the camouflage of friendship. I told her that the blond was just a date. We hugged and kissed, but I had to run to catch the last streetcar, so we made a date for the next day.

From that evening on I took my new relationship very seriously. We both were working, but on evenings, weekends and holidays we were together. Her mother insisted that she come home every night. Therefore, we spent a lot of time on streetcars. She lived in the portion of Vienna that was the Russian Zone, while I lived in the International Sector. Late one night as I was taking her home, we sat on the streetcar in front of a very drunk American soldier. As we neared the Russian Sector, I kept wondering when he would get off the streetcar. It was almost midnight, and to be a drunken American soldier in the Russian Zone was not very smart. There were only two more stops left before we crossed over, so I turned around to ask him where he was going. This GI looked at me with glazed-over eyes, then hauled off and hit me in my face with his fist, burying his knuckles deep into my cheek. He was saying something, but rambled total nonsense. All the Viennese men on the streetcar jumped up, ready to defend me and beat this poor guy up. I had enough sense to pull the conductor's cord to stop the streetcar and, with some help, took the drunkard off and planted him safely on a bench, still in the International Zone. At that time, jeeps were always cruising with four Allied representatives in them, and I am sure that they picked his slumped body up and had him sleep it off. When this guy woke up the next day he probably did not remember anything, or that I saved him from harm. I was black and blue for the next few days, and had to explain to my friends how I got my shiner.

In mid-1946, a sports gathering of Jewish athletes from around the world was supposed to be held in Paris. Every sport was to be represented, and how I was selected to represent Hakoah soccer I do not remember. Earlier, from the French military authorities I had obtained a "Permit Militair" that entitled me to visit France and use the railroads. I intended to visit my cousins who lived in Lyon. This delegation to Paris served my purpose because Hakoah was paying the bill and sometime after the meetings I could take off and go to Lyon. Hakoah handled the travel arrangements, and a former swimmer a bit older than I led the delegation. We were to take the train through Switzerland and continue on to Paris. When we crossed the Austrian-Swiss border, we were taken off the train because we did not have permission or a "through visa" to enter and exit Switzerland. Whoever arranged this trip either did not know or forgot to obtain this permit.

The Swiss border guard searched our luggage, confiscated our money and returned us to the Austrian side of the border where we were again searched and asked if we had made any purchases in Switzerland. We told the Austrian guards that we only spent an hour across the border, all of it in the border patrol guard house. We complained that they took our money and asked the chief guard if they could do that. He answered, "Yes, if you are entering Switzerland illegally." He then directed us to another platform and told us that we should take the next train to Paris through Germany. What was to be a simple trip turned into an odyssey. The train we boarded said "Strassburg-Paris." We made ourselves comfortable in one of the compartments, when the door re-opened, and a magnificent looking woman joined us. The rail porter stored her little suitcase above my seat while she conversed with the porter only in French. He did not seem to understand her and had no idea what she was talking about, but he constantly bowed his head. We assumed that she did not speak German, so we explained to the porter that she wanted her suitcase to be next to her. He then took the suitcase down and put it next to her seat. The train started to move, and I immediately started a one-sided conversation with her in the poorest of poor French. She did not even look at me, but she did smile. Her head and eyes were fixed on a book she was reading. I continued with my conversation while the other guys were telling me in German that it was of no use. We spoke in German and Viennese about this beauty. We told clean stories, dirty stories and talked about imaginative sexual situations. The girl just kept on reading and ignored all of us. When we arrived in Strassburg, she took her little suitcase and got off, and in perfect German said, "I enjoyed the train ride and wish you well with your infatuations." I looked for her through the window when an old French officer embraced and kissed her, and off they went. I hoped it was her father because how could she turn me down for this old man, especially when I told her that I was a movie star? Well, we had fun after all.

When we arrived in Paris, we learned that we were at least one week too late for the sports meeting. Now we were in Paris, with no money, no hotel and no railroad tickets to return to Vienna. Our fearless leader said, "Let's visit Donnenfeld, the former Hakoah soccer star, who owned a bar on Rue LaFayette. I know him well." We marched to this establishment and introduced ourselves one by one. When I saw him play as a kid, he was tall, strong, and fast, the foremost Jewish soccer all-star player. But when I stood next to him up close he was not tall. He was almost demure looking. Either he shrunk or I grew up. I told him that I had seen him play and how I admired him. To my surprise, he told me that he had heard about me. He kept in touch with the goings on of Hakoah Vienna and said that Mr. Blumenfeld was very happy with my rapid progress. I looked at him and told him that I had no stamina and that I had not sufficiently recovered from typhus and the concentration camp. He put his hand on my shoulder, walked with me to the side and forcefully said, "Training, conditioning, training and more conditioning. Stick to it, and you'll be just great." I thanked him and thought, "Easier said than done." He then gave us money, made reservations for us in a hotel and said if we should need anything else to let him know. Our fearless leader promised that the Hakoah would reimburse him. But he just laughed and waived his hand to forget it.

I shared my hotel room with one of the guys. It was a huge room with mirrors on the ceiling and around the room. It had several wash basins. One, I didn't understand until it was explained to me later. My roommate and the others went out in the evening while I went to sleep. Imagine that – my first night in Paris, and I was too tired to go out. Explain that to Mr. Donnenfeld.

The next morning I sent a telegram to my cousins in Lyon. They answered that they would pick me up in three days. I had a terrific time in Paris. We ate in good restaurants, saw French Revue, and an interpretation by two semi-nude girls of how men made love from the four corners of the earth. When it came to the United States, one girl stood against the wall, the other pretending to be an American said, "One, two, three, finished, goodbye." The audience laughed. I also thought it was funny, but I also thought of the French retreat during the war that was even faster than that.

The absolute best meal I had there was in a Hungarian restaurant. We entered a building and had to walk through the yard and down into a cellar. The ambiance and the service were great, and the food tasted terrific. Our fearless leader was a marvelous guide. He showed us famous buildings, sculptures, and paintings, including the obvious ones that were available at that time. The days went fast and were much too short for what Paris had to offer.

My three cousins, two brothers and one sister, survived the war in Switzerland. One of the guys was recently married, while his sister, the oldest, had been married for a long time. She had two sons and one was my age. In addition, she had adopted her niece, a very young girl, who had survived the war in England while her parents were killed in Poland. I was looking forward to spending some time with them, for they were the closest thing to a family that I had. At noon, I met my cousin at the railroad station, and we took the train to Lyon. On the way we caught up on each other's lives. We talked about our families and learned how many aunts, uncles and cousins had been killed by the Germans. Everyone lost loved ones, and only the few who escaped to countries not occupied by the Germans survived. When we arrived in Lyon, we went to his house, which he shared with his brother and new bride. After we greeted each other I planted my suitcase, and all of us walked to their sister's place. She was happy to see me, and I was happy to see the kids, my second cousins.

From the beginning, my cousin acted as the new matriarch of all of us. She told me all kinds of stories about my mother and father, my brothers and sister. Some of the stories would have been better left untold. She told me about arguments between my father and mother, my mother and her sister. It was real gossip, whether true or untrue. I resented it and took an immediate disliking to her. Being their guest, I just nodded and changed the subject as often as I could. I further disliked my cousins when they asked me to paint their apartment, but I quietly accepted this request. Everything was makeshift: for a brush they gave me the bottom of a broom and instead of a ladder I had to climb on a table, and then from the table onto a chair in order to reach the ceiling. It was very difficult work and physically hard for me to do. I thought it was an outrageous demand for them to make. So I disliked them for this also, but I did the best I could, and that was that. My cousins tried to talk me into settling in Lyon, but I could not warm up to them, even though I loved my second cousins, with whom I should have stayed in touch, but regrettably I did not. I cut my stay in Lyon short, and my cousins financed my return trip to Vienna, thankfully.

Back in Vienna, I was about to walk up to our apartment when Walter Fantl and Kurt Reich walked up behind me. After we greeted each other, they became very silent. As I entered, Ernie said, "Hi," and that was all. The three of them followed me to my room like puppy dogs. I stopped, turned and asked, "What's going on?" They just kept pushing me into my room. As I walked in I looked toward my bed and I saw the outline of a figure lying in it. I stopped, pointing to my bed and asked, "Who is the guy in my bed?" The three of them stood very quiet in anticipation, then the guy in bed turned around and faced me. I stared at him in disbelief. "You are supposed to be dead! I told everybody you got killed." It was Walter Wolfgang. After the severe beating he received, he was left lying half frozen, half dead, but, somehow, I am sure with divine intervention, he survived and was liberated. He spent a long time in hospitals, and two days before I returned from France, Walter returned to Vienna. I hugged Walter so tightly. I could not believe that I was looking at him, alive. Even weeks later, I stared at him and shook my head. When we all sat around and talked about our horrible experiences and the awful void left by the loss of our families, we were glad we had each other as friends. We were much more than a support group. We were sad, but we urged each other on, to go on with our lives.

While I was in France, Ernie and his brother, Fritz, received affidavits from their sister in the United States for them to immigrate to the United States. Other friends had also received affidavits. The handwriting was on the wall. The old gang would break up within a year, at the most two years. The way it looked, I would be left in Vienna with very few friends. It was still too early to worry, and my friends' departures were not yet in sight.

I continued working for the American Headquarters and I continued playing soccer. I could not train as often as others did and my progress did not improve in leaps and bounds. It only improved in inches. To be honest, I had lost my enthusiasm, if I ever had it, for the strenuous conditioning routine, but Mr. Blumenfeld kept after me and forgave my infrequent training schedule although I played in fewer games.

A few days later was New Year's Eve. Ernie usually got tickets for all of us for the opera's traditional performances of "Die Fledermaus," or "Wiener Blut" and to go dancing afterward. My girlfriend came to my apartment all dressed up because I told her what we usually did on New Year's Eve. This time Ernie did not buy the tickets. Another friend did, and he did not include my girlfriend and me. I yelled at Ernie, at all the other guys and especially the friend who bought the tickets. He wanted to crawl under the carpet. I said, "How stupid can you get?" Ernie just assumed that we would be included and offered us his tickets, but I said in anger, "No, thank you." I would have said more, but my girlfriend pulled me into another room and repeatedly said, "It's not important, it's not important." She tried to calm me down, but I was really angry. I took her by the hand and walked out and we wound up in Cafe Dobner. We ate, drank, and danced, but we left before midnight and went back to my apartment. I believed that the oversight of not including us was purposeful, and no one could convince me otherwise. Fifteen minutes before midnight, I walked to the bar and poured two glasses of sweet red wine for my girlfriend and myself. I sat next to her, slowly sipping, awaiting the stroke of midnight. I opened the door of the huge, white tiled oven and watched the flickering wood. The sweet red wine took my thoughts back to Dachau. The prisoners always talked about food, as if it could still the pain of hunger. Everyone expressed his wishful dream of eating their favorite food. One prisoner always talked about Wiener schnitzel with dumplings. Another spoke of roast chicken or beef. When I spoke of my wish, I always thought of sweet red wine. One glass of sweet red wine could cure everything that ailed me. I often wondered why I had this one and only urge. In Dachau, while the others talked about foods they loved, the only thing I could think off was how much I liked to drink wine as a kid during the Passover holidays. Even on New Year's Eve, long after the Liberation, these thoughts kept flashing by me.

The room was warm and comfortable, and we still had a couple of minutes to wait until midnight. I was still upset with my buddies, but my girlfriend calmly pulled me to her side. We kissed and at the right moment wished each other a Happy New Year. We fell asleep after midnight, and later I heard the guys come home with a bunch of giggling girls. I did hear a faint knock on my door, but I did not answer.

Shortly after New Years, I received a letter from friends of my family in the United States. The letter read,

> *Dear Kurt,*
> *If you are the son of Fani and Isacher Lad-*
> *ner and brother of Pepi, Fritz, Hans and Greta, then*
> *please let us know if you wish to immigrate to the*

United States. If yes, we will sponsor you and send
you an affidavit as soon as possible.
    Signed,
    The Greenblatts

I immediately answered positively, and within two weeks I had my affidavit. I moved to the Ninth District, which was in the American Zone, to expedite the consideration for departure. Other zones were either not eligible at all or had to wait for a much later date. The consulate conducted a background check, health, political, criminal, etc. Since I was already cleared previously to be able to work for the American authorities, I therefore received my American visa in record time, way before Ernie and my other friends. I notified the Greenblatts and my cousins Lina and Sol in New York that I was ready to leave, but must wait until the next transport left Vienna.

With my departure to America one month away, I had long discussions with my girlfriend about the future. I promised her that I would sponsor her to come to the United States as my fiancée as soon as possible and maybe get married in America. If she agreed with my plan she must move out of the Russian Zone, otherwise she would never leave Vienna. Every time I urged her to move into the American Zone she always hedged by saying, "What about my family?" I answered, "We will take care of them at a later date." What she was saying to me was, "Take me, take my whole family." I wished I could.

But how could I? "First, I have to get you," I said. "You will be my first effort, and I am sure we will be able to solve the rest at a later date." But as long as I remained in Vienna, she made no effort to move, and that told me she would never leave her family, not even for a short period of time. It did not make me feel good, but there was nothing I could do, except go on with my life.

As soon as I had received my visa I went to the Jewish Community Center and asked them to be included with the next transport to the United States. The HIAS (Hebrew Immigrant Aid Society) would pay for my transportation. A projected date for departure was around March/April. I asked and received letters of recommendation from the American Headquarters and my former painting boss/partner. When Mr. Blumenfeld heard that I was leaving, he gave me the address of Hakoah New York and urged me to play for them. Even if I did not want to play soccer for them, they might be able to give me a good job.

The next several weeks were happy ones in expectation of my departure, but, it was also sad to leave my girlfriend and so many friends, old and new. Even though I continued to work, it was idle work with the exception of Ernie's and my involvement helping people immigrate to Palestine. Most of them were Jewish soldiers from the Russian Armed Forces or Partisan fighters from Poland and other Eastern countries. It had started with one Russian officer, and it snowballed into a major effort. My small part in the scheme of things was to find them shelter and clothing, while Ernie got them identification passes to cross from the Russian Zone into the American Zone. How they then reached Palestine was someone else's problem. We had several safe houses for them in Vienna, and I obtained clothing, mostly from the Jewish Community Center and from some private sources. One former Russian officer, getting rid of his uniform, gave Ernie a beautiful pair of Russian boots and in return the officer begged for a winter coat. It seemed the only coat that fit him was mine. So, Ernie, without giving it a second thought, gave him my coat. I said to Ernie, "How could you give my one and only coat away?" But Ernie, looking at his boots, said, "You'll get a new and better coat in America."

Later on, a displaced persons center was opened and housed in the old Rothchild Hospital, where thousands of Eastern Jews passed through to their destination. During this waiting period, I played my last game for Hakoah Vienna. Mr. Blumenfeld said, "If you don't like America, come back. There will always be room for you in the Hakoah." I thought to myself, come back to Vienna to live? Never. I couldn't wait to leave the city of my birth, to leave all the bad memories behind. The Jewish Community Center notified me that the next transport to the port of Bremen would be leaving in twelve days, and I needed to have all my papers in order. I was well prepared. My passport with the American visa stamped, my physical papers, a release that I had no tax liabilities in Austria, and my personal belongings were all ready to jump into a suitcase. I again notified the Greeblatts and my cousins of my departure date and hoped that they could obtain my arrival date in New York.

The next twelve days were very hectic, saying goodbye to everyone and a attending lot of farewell parties. During the last few days I did wander through Vienna. The picnics with my parents – now they were gone. Swimming in the Danube with my brothers, also gone. The many times my sister threw sandwiches out of the window for me to eat so that I would waste no time playing soccer. Now she was gone. The summers I spent with my aunts and uncles, gone too. And all the things I planned to do with my friends after the liberation – now they were no longer alive. I came to the realization a long time ago that there was nothing in Vienna for me to cherish except a few memories. Presently, my friends felt the same way as I did. Therefore, I had nothing but good things to look forward to.

The last farewell party I had was in Cafe Dobner. Maxie's aunt cried because she was losing one of her adopted sons. Old and new friends came to enjoy my last evening in Vienna. My girlfriend was with me all day and decided to stay the last night before my departure in the morning.

I gathered my belongings and an entire entourage joined us on the way to the railroad station. On my arrival, I was summoned to an office, in which representatives of the Jewish Community Center, the HIAS, and the American Joint Distribution Committee were present. I was introduced to an American Army sergeant who was going to be the military liaison at the Russian-American Border Zone. I was appointed transport leader, and I had no idea how many people I was supposed to lead. There were several boxcars and regular rail cars with people. As soon as we crossed into the American Zone, the Army sergeant's journey would end, and I would have to lead my people into the Promised Land, Bremer Hafen! The whole thing was silly, until I learned that the boxcar I shared with the sergeant was loaded with food – bread, canned goods, you name it, and I had to distribute it during our train ride.

I had said my farewells to almost everyone, yet so many of my friends came to the station. Everyone brought something: cookies, candy, and various other edible things, including apple strudel from a good friend and distant relative of my parents. We had to board. I gave a last hug to my girlfriend. To Ernie I said, "I'll see you over there," and I left Vienna to start a new life in America.

CHAPTER SEVENTEEN
MY NEW HOME

T he train pulled out of the station as I was standing in the wide open door of the boxcar waving to my friends who became smaller and smaller as the train picked up speed. I then turned to the sergeant, who was a stocky, broad-shouldered redhead, and started a conversation. I wanted to know in detail what his and my role were to be. He repeated that once he cleared the transport with the Russians, and we reached Linz, his assignment was over. After that, everything would become my responsibility until we boarded ship in Bremen.

It was a sunny day. The sergeant was dangling his feet out of the open door, when he pulled out his revolver and started to shoot at birds sitting on telephone wires. I was startled by the first shot, and I looked to see what he was shooting. The train was going at a pretty good pace, so fortunately, he could not hit his targets. My conversation with him was sparse, and my complaint was that shooting a gun in the Russian Zone was, at best, an unwise thing to do. The sergeant started to laugh and said, "Have no fear." He reminded me of the GI who hit me in the streetcar, but I was glad it was not him because this guy looked stronger than an ox.

I was happy to learn that another friend, Bert, was on the same transport, and after my conversations with the sergeant had been exhausted, I asked him if he would mind if I were to bring a couple of friends to join us in our boxcar. The sergeant was an extremely nice guy and answered, "Of course not. Come have them join us – the more the better." At the next stop I asked Bert to join us, who also brought a young girlfriend. From then on, it became an enjoyable ride. We talked, we laughed, and the sergeant said that he was going to take a nap and to wake him when we reached the border.

Not much time had passed when we arrived at the border of the American and Russian Zone. The sergeant jumped off the train, carrying these huge envelopes stuffed with documents, which he presented to the Russian guards. In the meantime, Bert and I had jumped off and stood a discreet distance from the sergeant. The Russian guards rummaged through the papers looking for something that they could not find. They wanted to inspect the train, but the sergeant prevented them by saying, "No, this is a closed transport," pointing to all the papers for them to examine. They did not understand each other, and in frustration the sergeant then turned to us and said, "Can one of you talk to them? Maybe they understand your language." Bert talked to them in broken Czech and some Russian, explaining that we were a transport of former prisoners of concentration camps on the way to America. He showed them a concentration camp identification, which had, after all, a Russian translation that meant nothing. They were searching for some kind of paper. I was lost, and I left it up to the sergeant and Bert to handle. Finally, after going through the papers piece by piece, they found the missing paper, which was left in the envelope. Apologetic and smiling, they waved us on to pass the border. The three of us climbed back onto the train and within a few minutes were in the American Zone, where we stopped for an extended time. The sergeant turned the documents over to me, said goodbye and wished us well. I distributed the rations of food. Everybody supplied themselves with water and drinks, and then we proceeded with our journey.

It soon was nighttime, and the next day we arrived in Bremen. We checked into a holding camp to wait for the next boat to take us to the United States. The predicted waiting period was a few days. We could leave the compound during the day, but had to be back by midnight.

I had little German money, but I fortified myself with several packages of American cigarettes that could easily be bartered or exchanged for money. Being a soccer player, I never smoked, so cigarettes meant nothing to me. Every pack I acquired I usually exchanged for something I needed. Bert and I asked a young German attendant in the compound what we could do in Bremen, what to see and where to go dancing and meet girls. He gave us some names and addresses of dance halls and variety theaters, and he also mentioned that we should visit Helenen Strasse.

The next day Bert and I took the streetcar, and sitting in front of us were two young, good-looking women. We asked them to tell us where we should get off for Helenen Strasse. The girls started to giggle and smile and they shyly said, "Four stations." We could not understand why they were laughing into their hands, but we found out later. Asking about Helenen Strasse was like asking where the nearest whorehouse was. We shook our heads and took the streetcar back to our compound.

The next day I was called into the transportation office, where they advised me that there would be a final medical checkup. I handed in all our papers and I.D.s and was told that it would not be long before we could embark, and at that point, my obligation as transport leader ended. That evening, Bert and I went to a nightclub. It was really a nightclub / dance hall combination. We sat at a table, watched a few acts, and then the dancing started. The band was so-so and Bert said to me, "Look at that gorgeous girl." She was just a couple of tables away. I said, "Go and ask her to dance." Bert slowly got up, walked over to her table and asked her to dance. She looked at him for the longest time. She then got up, and got up and up and up. She was the tallest of the tallest. Bert, who was rather short, followed her up with his eyes and tilted his head. Then she took him to the dance floor. Bert held what seemed to be her thigh and proceeded to dance. I was holding my stomach, bent over the table trying not to burst out laughing. The dance ended, and Bert returned to our table and, without hesitation, without blinking, and in all seriousness, said, "She is a very good dancer." Well, that was it. I could not longer refrain from laughing, and I keeled over.

The day before our departure, we received our last medical checkup and from then on we were confined to our quarters. I sat on my bed, leafing through a newspaper, when my mind wandered back into my past. I thought of everything. It was like seeing flash cards. How close my brother, Fritz, had come to going to the United States. I saw faces of my family and friends who were no longer alive. I thought of the plane in France that had almost plunged straight at us. I thought of Walter Wolfgang who, from infancy, had been brought up in the Catholic faith, and yet was ripped from his family who had adopted him and was persecuted because he was born to a Jewish mother. I thought, what crime had I committed as an eleven-year-old that I had to suffer such cruelties and face a future without my family? Only because we were of the Jewish religion, and I did not even have anything to do with that fact. The renewed faith that I found in God in a ditch in France in 1940 helped to keep me alive, and I would face my future, wherever, as a proud Jew. Bert interrupted my thoughts by saying, "We are leaving tomorrow morning. They just announced it." I could not imagine what an ocean voyage would be like. The largest body of water that I had to contend with was the surf in Ostende in Belgium and the Danube in Vienna.

The next day we boarded a rather small ship called "Marine Marlin," a liberty ship. A little sign on the ship read that this ship was built in either three days or three weeks. I don't remember which. In either case, it did not take long to build this vessel. My assigned bunk was below deck – way below deck, near the engine room. Our quarters were small and narrow, and every bunk was taken. It did not take me long to settle in. I had an upper bunk and a small space for my belongings. I immediately started to explore the ship. As I exited my cabin, to the right was a larger area that had a ping pong table. A few steps up and to the left was a larger room with a piano and chairs around the walls. A bit further was the cafeteria and kitchen, and climbing up to the top deck, I was surprised to see that so many other people had joined this voyage. The majority were young girls from Germany and other European countries known as "war brides." They either were married to GIs or were going to be married. They also had to wait for permission to join their husbands or soon-to-be husbands. I met several of the young women who had left their families to start an unknown new life in America. They were too young to have participated in the German Reich's criminal activities. They learned from us that most of the people on the ship were survivors of concentration camps and that most of us were alone and without any doubt would have a better future in America than in the countries that persecuted us. They, like us, had to start a new life. Some of the young women were very nervous about their unknown situation, other than having a husband. They also learned from us about our miseries in camp and how many of our family and friends were killed. Their reaction was always honest shock and repulsion. They, in turn, told us about bombings and how they had to live in fear, mostly underground, and how many of their families had died and fallen in the war. Fathers, brothers, uncles and cousins had either not returned or were prisoners of war almost two years after the war had ended. These were bad times all around, and the only blame must be placed with Adolf Hitler and his supporters.

We left Bremen, and for the next couple of days we had beautiful weather. I sat mostly on the top deck, and the fresh ocean air, the gliding motion of the ship, and the gentle waves were like a wonderful vacation. At our departure we received ten dollars, of which a portion was deducted for tips to be given to the staff of the ship. I basically hung out with Bert, two nice girls, (war brides), and maybe one or two others from my transport.

After couple of days on the ocean, a storm was brewing. It started slowly during the night. The ship started to rock and roll, going up and down and from side to side, and never in the same rhythm. The guy in my quarters got sick, and on the way to the toilet, left a trail of his supper. It was very early in the morning. I got up, climbing gently out of my bunk, avoiding everything my bunk mate had left on the floor, and like a ballet dancer, tiptoed up to the lounge. I had hoped to see someone familiar, but all I saw was people running to the side of the ship or to the toilets, throwing up all over the place. In the lounge, two sailors with heavy ropes were tying the piano to the wall and stacking and securing furniture. They also had ropes along the side walls strung throughout the entire ship for passengers to hold on to. I asked the sailors if I could sit in the lounge and why were they roping and tying everything down? They told me that a small storm was approaching, and they tied down objects to make sure that no one got hurt. I asked again, "The storm is not here yet? Everyone on the ship is throwing up already." They started to laugh, and one advised me to be sure that I ate and drank. Otherwise, I would pay the consequences. I thanked him, and I did go down to the cafeteria. Either I was the first in line or I was the only one to have breakfast. The cooks were smiling when I received my food. I asked, "How bad of a storm are we going to have?" One answered, "Not bad, not bad – just bad enough to have a lot of food left over." I finished my breakfast and went up to the upper deck. Bert had secured a couple of cots and stated very firmly that he was not going to move, not even one inch. I sat down next to him, and he said, "I can't go back to the quarters because everyone is throwing up." I looked at him just as his face was getting a greenish tint and asked him if he had breakfast. That question did it. He jumped up and ran to the bathroom, barely making it.

To me, the weather was not that bad. I even had a date with a guy to play ping pong. Surprisingly, he showed up, but had to cancel the game. It was more of a challenge to stay on our feet than to return a serve. A few minutes later Bert returned to his bunk, not to be seen again until we disembarked. An hour or so later, the weather got much worse. The wind started to howl, and it rained like no other rain. People were hanging over the rails, unloading. The washrooms and toilets were standing room only, and the stench was intolerable. Where could I go to get away from these people?

By then, I had a giant-size headache, but I could not throw up. I almost did once, when one woman was retching right in front of me. I walked to the only place I hoped to be alone. Hand over hand, holding on to the ropes, I went to the cafeteria. By now, the wind was really blowing, and the ship's motions were not easy to tolerate, up and down, left and right. When I reached the cafeteria the room was empty. I sat in one corner, my headache had gotten worse and throwing up would have been a relief. One of the workers came over to me and asked if he could do anything. I answered, "Yes. A couple of aspirins would be just great." He brought me two pills and a cup of water. He also advised me to eat something because throwing up on an empty stomach was awful. The pills did not help. I could not throw up. So I just sat in the corner lamenting to myself. The cooks opened the counter for lunch. A few stragglers did come to eat. I also ate my lunch and returned to my safe corner. After a couple of hours, it stopped raining. I dragged myself to my quarters, took my blanket, and went to the very top of the ship's deck. I wrapped myself in the blanket and lay down on a chaise with the wind blowing all around me. The sky was still dark and menacing, but the rain had stopped for good. I got used to the ship's motions. There were only a few people on the deck. I was looking for a friendly face, but all I saw were drawn, haggard, white faces, not interested in idle conversation. I closed my eyes and I actually fell asleep. When I woke up it was near suppertime. The clouds had moved on and the sky looked much friendlier. The stormy winds had subsided to a brisk breeze; the waves were still choppy but the short-lived storm was over. I walked down to my quarters and was pleasantly surprised to find everything cleaned up from the stairs to the very corner of my room. They had sprayed a deodorizing spray that reminded me of the refreshing smell of a movie house that was sprayed during intermission.

That evening, I ate my supper with more gusto and spent more than an hour strolling around the ship, visiting the casualties of the storm. The following days we had very good weather conditions, but being on this vast ocean with only water and sky as your horizon, it seemed as if the ship made no progress. The sunrise and the sunsets were beautiful, and the rest of the voyage was wonderful.

CHAPTER EIGHTEEN
DOCKING IN
NEW YORK CITY

Finally, on the morning of May 7th, the ship's captain announced that we would be docking in New York City in the late afternoon, ten days after we embarked from Bremen. People started to scurry. Everyone tried to occupy a preferred spot along the railing on the upper deck. I was more than ready to get off the ship. The last few hours were the longest of the voyage. Old and new friends exchanged addresses. The two war brides were going to far away states, but most of my friends were remaining in New York City. In the far distance a bluish-gray stripe appeared on the horizon, and one of the stewards confirmed that it was land. Even though we were getting close to the United States, there were no other ships in sight. As we approached land and turned into the harbor, the ship's crew pointed to all the landmarks that I had seen in films and photographs and had been told stories about. I promised myself that I would visit all of them.

We docked. A few minutes later, men from the Immigration Department came aboard to check our passports and visas and to confirm that everyone had their shots. Everything went smoothly, and I disembarked to set foot on American soil somewhere in Manhattan. Stepping onto the dock I was directed to Section L where suitcases and all kinds of luggage were lined up. I secured my two suitcases and backpack and waited for further instructions. We then were told that all HIAS-sponsored passengers had to assemble outside the doors on the left side. Many people were waiting in this reception area, standing behind chains. Mrs. Greenblatt, her son and daughter were waiting for me, and when the chains were finally dropped, people, like a huge wave, rushed toward us. The Greenblatts came to me and we greeted each other with repeated hugging, and I had a chance to thank them for sponsoring my visa to the United States. Mrs. Greenblatt said that night I had to stay in the HIAS provided quarters, and they would pick me up tomorrow morning. She also added, looking at me with a smile, "Provided that you have changed from the hellion you were as a kid." Visitors were asked to leave. Mrs. Greenblatt slipped me five dollars for emergencies, which I promptly lost. HIAS representatives brought us to a building in Manhattan where we ate and spent the night.

Early the next day I was picked up and driven to Mr. and Mrs. Greenblatt's apartment. We crossed from Manhattan into the borough of Brooklyn, passing several interesting sights, which I further stored in my memory for a later visit. The Greenblatt's apartment house was adjacent to Prospect Park, and as I entered the apartment, almost simultaneously, the telephone rang and my cousins, Lina and Sol, were eagerly expecting to hear my voice. There were cross greetings all around me while I was talking to my cousin. She told me that I would be living with them and either they would pick me up or the Greenblatts would bring me to them. My cousins and the Greenblatts made arrangements over the phone, which gave me a chance to thank Mr. Greenblatt for sponsoring me. The entire Greenblatt family was in this apartment, including their son and daughter with their spouses.

We sat around a large table for lunch, and we talked and talked. Mrs. Greenblatt's mother and sisters were our neighbors in Vienna. Mrs. Greenblatt's first question was, "Have you any news about my family?" Regrettably, they were sent to Poland and did not return. They asked me about my family, about my experiences in the concentration camp. They told me how they learned about my survival. Then the conversation turned to when I was a little boy. They told me things I did that I did not remember. When I fell into the Danube, when my parents searched for me late at night finding me on a soccer field squeezing out the last drop of daylight, reminding me of all the childish pranks I had committed.

Then, Nellie, the Greenblatts daughter, said to me, "We are taking you out tonight. Where would you like to go and what would you like to see?" Without hesitation, I answered, "Times Square." Nellie looked through a paper and asked, "Would you like to see a movie and a show?" I asked, "What do you mean by a show?" She answered, "Well, these are acts performing or an orchestra is playing before the movie starts." I asked, "An orchestra, like maybe a jazz band? I would like that." She kept on looking and searching through the newspaper, then asked, "How would you like to see Duke Ellington?" I said, "What? Duke Ellington in person? Yes, many times yes, thank you." "Okay, the decision is made. Fred and I will take you tonight." It was a long time to wait, but I masked my anticipation by answering and listening to many questions and stories.

I then asked if I could call my friend, Boffi, who also lived in Brooklyn. Boffi and I had been childhood friends. We lived in the same apartment building in Vienna, went to school together. He was the one who watched me jump into the little Danube, which I narrowly survived. He and his entire family were fortunate enough to immigrate to the United States in 1938. I reached his house, but he was not at home. I left a message with his mother for him to call me. She asked me a thousand questions within a minute. I promised her that

I would visit them soon and that I would spend time answering everything she wanted to know.

Just before we were to leave to see Duke Ellington, Boffi called and said that he would come to see me the next morning. Early that evening, I took my first subway ride. We emerged from below on 42nd Street and 7th Avenue and in front of me was Times Square. I said to Nellie, "Now, right now, I know I have arrived in America." The lights, the hordes of people, the hustle, the excitement, the smiles on the faces of Nellie and Fred looking at me standing with my mouth wide open. What an introduction to New York City on my very first full day in the United States.

We walked—well, let's not say walked—we were gently pushed by people in the direction of lights and theaters. We kept on walking, passing movie houses and always surrounded by happy people. We finally turned around, and I think it was the Paramount Theatre where Duke Ellington and his orchestra appeared that evening. While Nellie and I stood in line, Fred bought the tickets. We stood like this for half an hour when the line started to move into the theater. Once we were inside, we still had to wait for people to emerge from inside the movie house. We then walked down darkened isles and found three very good seats. I was amazed to see how many people remained in their seats although the show was over. Nellie explained that you could stay here all day and most of the night for one paid ticket. I really don't remember what movie I saw that evening. I was just waiting for Duke Ellington. The movie was over, and in the dark, Duke Ellington's Orchestra started to play their theme. The lights went on, and the entire orchestra appeared. I stood up and applauded. I stood up after every number or solo and clapped like crazy. People around me, I am sure, thought that I was nuts. The only problem was that the performance was too short. I had such a good time that I did not want to leave the theater, but Nellie persuaded me to leave. On the way out I thanked them many times for taking me. Just before we took the subway back to Brooklyn, we stopped at a restaurant called Grants, on the corner of 42nd and 7th, and had the best frankfurter on a roll and a coke. Nellie said that this place was open twenty-four hours a day. I logged that in my memory file.

The next day Boffi came over. We had not seen each other for almost ten years. We wanted to talk, so we took a long walk through the Prospect Park and caught up with each other's lives. Boffi then asked me, "How would you like to see a ball game?" I naturally thought he meant a soccer game, but he laughed and said, "No, we are going to see a baseball game." I knew all about baseball from the G.I.s I met, and I said, "Okay, that would be nice." Late that afternoon, I watched the Brooklyn Dodgers play against Philadelphia at Ebbets Field. Watching the game played with such skill and having Boffi explain it to me let me begin to see baseball in an entirely different light. Before that game, if someone had wanted to talk to me about sports, they had better have been talking about soccer and nothing else, but I liked baseball from the beginning, and I became a Dodgers fan. Watching the Dodgers play was not a bad second introduction to the United States. Two historic events in my life: the Duke and the Bums.

The following day I said goodbye to the Greenblatts, promised to visit them often, and I moved my belongings to my cousins', Sol and Lina. They lived with their little son, who is now Dr. John Gottman, on Park Avenue, Williamsburg, Brooklyn. Theirs was a ground floor railroad apartment with three rooms and a kitchen. The front room was bright and cheery. The rest were rather dark. They let me share their place until I could find a better situation. Lina's mother, my Aunt Emma, was about to arrive in the United States from Santo Domingo.

My cousins and I sat for hours and talked about our families. I learned things about my family that I never knew. Everyone loved and respected my mother. She was the equilibrium; a thoughtful, steady person of the aggregated family. She solved my cousins' unsolvable problems, and they all looked to her for guidance. Aunt Emma and my mother had a very close sisterly relationship; therefore, their children were more than cousins to each other. My cousin, Sol, became my mentor, guide, brother and close advisor. He said, "The first thing you have to do is register with the Joint Distribution Committee." This organization would temporarily assist me financially until I could support myself. They would also help me find a job and in general steer me in the right direction.

The next day I registered, and my caseworker was an exceptional lady. She gave me good advice. She suggested that I continue going to school, try to obtain all my credits from all over Europe and then apply to attend college. I explained to her that going to school was not possible at this time, not with the few dollars in my pocket. Her next suggestion was to at least attend night school, to which I agreed. But first, I had to get a job and earn money. She recommended several job opportunities, and I started to go on interviews. I received financial help for personal necessities, and I had to return to her office every two weeks. The few interviews I went on were jobs of no consequence. I then went to the painters' union and applied for a union card and a job. The man behind the desk said that I could only join as an apprentice, and the cost to become a member of the union, I think, was over $300. I said, "What? That is a lot of money." I further protested stating that, one, I was not an apprentice, and two, I thought that this was an international union. I told him that I was a partner in a painting business, for however short a time period, and that I had a painting certificate and union membership from Vienna. He then said to me, in a snippy way, "Go home and bring proof of what you have been telling me." I returned the next day armed with a handful of papers, confirming what I had told him. He took the painting agreement with my former boss and my painting certificate from Vienna, and he walked into another office, had a conference with another man, then both approached me with their findings. They told me that I could receive an American union card at once. Not only that – they gave me a job as a finisher, which I was to start the next day. A finisher paints the last coat of paint, does all touch-ups and adheres to the requests of customers. I started to make good money and worked lots of overtime. Some weeks, I would make between $100 and $150. I called my caseworker at the Joint Distribution Committee to let her know that I was working. She thanked me for calling and told me to stay in touch.

My job as a painter did not last long. One day I checked if a job was completed and found that a painter had forgotten to paint the inside of a closet. So, I carried a bucket of paint inside this cubbyhole and finished the job. When I emerged from the closet, my eyes were tearing. They swelled up as if I had been in a boxing match. My skin was turning blue, even under my fingernails. I cleaned up in a hurry and went home. My cousin took me at once to the doctor, who just looked at me and asked what kind of work I was doing. I told him and he said right away, "You must look for another kind of job." His explanation was that the paints in this country contained lead, among other ingredients, and that I was severely allergic to the paint. I asked, "Lead poisoning?" The doctor answered, "Possibly. It's not serious, but in any case find a different profession." I went to the union with my medical report and asked to be replaced. I also resigned from the union. They generously returned the few dollars I had paid, and the hunt for a new job began.

I decided to call the Hakoah Soccer Club and ask for an appointment. My interview was scheduled on Monday at 7:00 p.m. with the president of Hakoah, New York, in his office on 72nd Street. When I arrived promptly at 7:00 p.m., a young woman was sitting behind the desk, and I told her that I had an appointment to meet the president of Hakoah. She asked me to take a seat and said that he would be there shortly. Forty-five minutes later a man walked in, passed me and the young woman, and into his office he went, without saying good evening. He then called the girl into his office. This meeting lasted another few minutes. She finally came out, gave me a card to fill out my name, address, age and the last soccer team I had played for. I was still sitting in the outer office when the president came out and had a rather long conversation with the girl. He then asked me to join him in his office. I entered with the card in my hand. He asked me to sit down, and I realized that I had come on the wrong day. He started to lecture me in a raised voice, "Everybody who comes from Europe thinks he is a soccer player. I waste my time, waste money, trying everyone out, then I waste more money and more time. For what?" He kept on ranting without even looking at me. He then started to scribble something on a piece of paper, which he handed to me and said, "You come to this soccer field early Sunday and you'll try out with our second team. We'll leave shoes for you and a uniform, and don't be late." I meekly asked if I could try out with the first team. I figured among better players I would look better. I should not have asked this question. He started to raise his voice again and adamantly said, "You'll try out with the second team and be early." I thanked him and asked, "If I am accepted and pass my tryout, how much money will you pay me?" "We don't pay much, if you play for the second team. The best we can do is pay your expenses." I again thanked him and said, "I'll have to think it over if I want to come Sunday." As I got up and walked toward the door, he stopped me and asked me for the card that I still had in my hand. I walked back and gave my card to him and said goodbye. He read my name on the card and jumped up before I could reach the door and said, "You are Kurt Ladner? I've been waiting for you for over six weeks! Where were you?" He had received a telegram from Hakoah Vienna that I would arrive in New York sometime around May 1, and to make sure to sign me for Hakoah New York. He had been trying to find me since then. His tone of voice changed instantly. He made me sit down again and said, "You don't have to try out." He said that I would be playing with the first team that coming Sunday, should I sign with the Hakoah. I again asked, "How much will you be paying me?" He said, "The maximum we pay our best player is around $40." He offered me $35 plus some expense money. My net total was under $50. Expenses consisted of going to and from the soccer field and buying my own shoes and equipment. He also got me a job in a watch factory, which was an experience. I had to assemble tiny pieces with the tiniest screws, hour after hour. At first I was clumsy, but I got better. The job paid under $40 per week, but I could work overtime.

That Sunday, when I got to the soccer field, I met the former Hakoah Vienna soccer player, Mausner, and a fellow by the name of Wantman, a player from Argentina. When the game started, I felt awful – almost depressed. There were more people playing the match than people watching it. I was installed in an unfamiliar position at inside left, but I was pretty good and lucky. I kicked two goals. One I had to work for, but the other I kicked on a rebound. We won my first game four to one. I played a few Sundays with less and less people watching. The caliber of soccer players, with few exceptions, was very poor. They had no technical skills, and they played the man, not the ball. Getting kicked in the legs was common. They rushed and shoved. They played football, not soccer. They committed so many fouls that in the few weeks I played, I had more injuries than in all the time I played in Europe. The condition of the soccer field was the poorest of the poor, especially the home field on Teller Avenue in the Bronx. One of my teammates was seriously injured and had to be carried off the field. I decided that playing soccer in America under these conditions was not for me. It was not worth the risk to continue. I came home after a game depressed rather than uplifted, even when we were victorious. In short, I hated to play on fields with rocks with no soccer patrons to support us. I resigned. There went my job in the watch factory, and I also lost my income from playing soccer.

The following Sunday I visited the Greenblatts and told them about my trials and tribulations—the jobs I had and the need for another job. Just as Mrs. Greenblatt was serving coffee, her daughter and son-in-law arrived. They were listening to our conversation. The son-in-law came up with a suggestion. "I think I can get a job for Kurt in the Catskill Mountains. He could make good money. He'll have room and board. It's hard work, but at the same time he can have fun." The conversation and suggestion was discussed completely over my head. Everyone was very excited with the idea and Mrs. Greenblatt said, "Go ahead and call." Mr. Greenblatt intervened saying, "Hold on, hold it. Let's explain to Kurt first what the Catskill Mountains are all about. He has no idea." They then explained that it was a resort area with large and small hotels, cottages, and bungalow colonies. The large hotels had everything: good food, golf, tennis, pools, boating and entertainment day and night. In the smaller hotels and bungalows, families stayed for the entire summer while in larger hotels vacationers would come and stay for one or two weeks and some for the season. The son-in-law's connection was his cousin, who ran one of the large hotels called The Flagler. If I agreed, he would call him right away, and I asked, "What kind of work is available?" He replied, "Probably waiter or busboy." He explained their work and again emphasized that they made very good money. With the enthusiastic way the entire Greenblatt family talked about the Catskills, I figured I could save a lot of money over the rest of the summer. The whole setup sounded good, and I asked him to call. Mr. Greenblatt warned me to be careful when I met young girls. They all look older than they really are, he said. If I were to fool around with one of them I could go to jail for life. He mentioned lawsuits and troubles of various kinds. Everyone's face became serious and they nodded their heads. Mr. Greenblatt repeated again, "Just stay away from young girls, and be very careful." After agreeing to the warning I received, the son-in-law went to the phone and called. When he returned, he gave me the name of a Mr. Silverman and the address, Hotel Flagler, South Fallsburg, New York. I could go any time, but the sooner the better. I thanked all of them and said, "I can leave within a day or two. I'll stay in touch." Then I left to take the subway to Williamsburg.

Mr. Greenblatt's warning made an impression. Every time I saw a young girl walking, I stepped off the sidewalk. He had scared the heck out of me. The next day I went to Ripley's and bought one suit, two leisure jackets and pants, had them fixed the same day and, with a few items I still had from Europe and a couple of pairs of new shoes, I was ready to leave. I packed all my belongings in two suitcases, said goodbye to my cousins, and according to instructions, I took the subway to Manhattan and a bus to South Fallsburg.

CHAPTER NINETEEN
THE FLAGLER

I was about to leave when my cousin's land-lord told me that the apartment in the rear was available for rent. I looked at the apartment, one large living/bedroom, kitchen and bathroom for $18 a month. I said, "I'll take it." I authorized my cousin to handle everything on my behalf. According to the Greenblatts, the hotel closed after Labor Day, so when I returned, I would have my own apartment.

The bus ride to S. Fallsburg took almost four hours. Upon arrival, I asked where the Hotel Flagler was located and was told that it was just up the road. Well, I walked this busy, two-lane highway from the village, expecting the hotel to be only a short distance away. Instead, I walked and walked, carrying two suitcases for quite a distance. When I finally arrived at the front gate of the hotel, a guard stopped me and inquired as to where I was going. I told him that I was there to see Mr. Silverman. Still looking at me and my suitcases, he directed me to walk behind the main building to a door from which I could reach Mr. Silverman in the kitchen. I walked around, up a few steps and entered into a large room with tables, benches and chairs, which turned out to be the helps' dining room. An elderly man asked me, "Who do you wish to see?" I said, "Mr. Silverman." He asked me to sit down and he would get him for me. He entered the kitchen and yelled, "Izzy, somebody to see you!" Soon thereafter, a short, paunchy man wearing a white chef's jacket approached me and asked me in Yiddish who I was. I told him in Yiddish that I was Kurt Ladner and that his cousin had called him about a job for me. I could not understand why he only spoke Yiddish to me. He proceeded to tell me that all waiter and busboy jobs were filled, as were all positions for dishwashers and kitchen help. He then asked me to leave my suitcases and to follow him. We walked across to another building and into a laundry. Steam was coming through the door, water had accumulated in front, and Mr. Silverman yelled for a Mr. Goldstein. A hard-of-hearing, toothless man in a sleeveless shirt, pants over his belly, rubber boots past his knees, with a cap that was too small on his head, appeared. Mr. Silverman asked him in Yiddish if he could use a man. He said, "Sure, they quit on me every day." Also in Yiddish, Mr. Silverman turned to me and asked me if I would want to work in the laundry. Looking at the man's condition, the laundry in the basement, the heat emerging through the door, I slowly walked back up and thankfully declined, but somehow, instead of speaking to him in Yiddish, I spoke to him in English and said, "I have to make money and hopefully get a job with a future." He stared at me, surprised that I spoke English. Apparently he must have dealt with immigrants who could not speak English. He asked me where I learned to speak English as well as I did, and I explained that I had to study English since I was a little kid in public school and that I also had private tutoring. His attitude toward me changed, and he asked me to join him in the kitchen. He then inquired about my past, where I came from, and how I survived the concentration camps.

We sat for a while at his desk talking, when he asked me, almost in a fatherly fashion, what I would like to do, what I would like to learn. I said the people in New York spoke of becoming a waiter. He then persuaded and advised me to become a salad man and to learn the works of the pantry. He offered to pay me $40 per week with room and board, and I would be able to learn from a master by the name of Mr. Kennedy. I gratefully accepted his offer. He assigned me sleeping quarters, a room which I had to share with the hotel engineer, in other words, the fireman who worked the boiler room.

After I placed my belongings in my room, Mr. Silverman took me around and showed me the workings of the pantry. He introduced me to Mr. Kennedy, the other workers in the pantry, the various chefs, the kitchen personnel, and whoever was present at the time.

Mr. Silverman was not only the head steward, but he also managed the hotel for an ailing owner.

I was free to explore the hotel grounds for the rest of the day. There was a golf course, a large pool, tennis courts, a lake with rowboats, and clusters of houses for guests and the hotel staff. It was one of the larger hotels in the Catskill Mountains, and it was usually filled to capacity.

That evening I met my roommate, a scruffy looking guy; even dressed up he looked as if he had just returned from a work detail. He seemed to be a nice guy, but was not very talkative. I don't think that he was pleased about sharing his room, but neither was I. I told myself to make the best of it. I just had to sleep there.

The next morning I reported to the pantry before 7:00 a.m. Mr. Kennedy was already working, portioning a huge smoked whitefish. He told me to take care of the orange juice. I had to cut crates of oranges in half, then squeeze them for fresh orange juice. I had to put each half of the orange onto an electric, rotating, grooved blade that extracted every ounce of juice. I alternated my left and right hand, each containing half an orange, pressing down on the squeezer, which made the sound of a motor with each application. Left hand, right hand, and soon a big bowl was filled with fresh orange juice. I transferred the juice into several pitchers, ready to be poured into juice glasses. I also prepared grapefruit juice and the ever-popular prune juice. We prepared dishes of two kinds of herring, lox, whitefish, fruits and morning salads. Waiters, waitresses, and busboys were flying by all the time, scooping up the prepared dishes. Anything that was not ready on the countertop, they ordered, and we had to give it to them on the double. Anything a guest requested was furnished. Even though they had a coffee man, coffee was Mr. Silverman's domain. Even if he let the coffee man make the brew, Mr. Silverman would taste it several times during the meal. He had one saying, "Give the guest the best meals, made of the finest ingredients, then give them a lousy cup of coffee and you have lost the ball game." He prescribed the formula, how to prepare and make coffee and how often the urns had to be cleaned.

While the breakfast was dragging on and on, we were already preparing for lunch. Mr. Kennedy was a genius in utilizing time. He always had two guys and himself working on the next meal. Certain things could only be done at mealtime. He never allowed lettuce, vegetables or other perishables to be prepared in advance. We served six or seven different kinds of salads every day, and every plate was served picture-perfect. Every kind of canned fish, from sardines to anchovies to tuna and salmon, could only be opened when requested and not before. Mr. Kennedy was also a master sculptor. He could sculpt anything and everything out of chopped liver and especially out of blocks of ice. He was just fantastic at his craft.

In the huge kitchen, we had three long tables. On these tables, we would spread dishes from end to end. Certain appetizers had to be prepared before the dining room opened, such as hors d'oervres, gefilte fish, grape-fruit halves, and juices. Once the dining room opened, these special dishes were swept up by waiters and wait-resses within a few minutes. The work was relentless, from early in the morning until late at night, with only a couple of hours off in the afternoon. Day after day, seven days a week. I just could not believe I was surrounded by that much food, and a lot of it was often wasted. I could have saved many of my people who died of hunger dur-ing my imprisonment in the concentration camps with the wasted food. Every day we served over 1,200 people, sometimes more, between guests and employees.

Just as I started to like my job, Mr. Silverman got sick and did not come to work. Harry, an old time waiter who served the hotel help, came to me and handed me a bunch of keys that opened and locked the hotel's store-rooms, freezers, refrigerators, kitchen, bakery, butcher shop and many other things. A few minutes later, I re-ceived a phone call from Mr. Silverman, who said, "If anyone needs anything from the storerooms or other departments, give it to them. If you cannot find it, call me at home, and I will tell you where you can find it or order it." That day I was pulling double duty. Every few minutes the chef needed something – ten cans of this or two cans of that, cases of tomato sauce or two cases of something else. I kept running up and down, up and down, until I said to myself, "This is stupid. Why not prepare the daily kitchen needs in advance and avoid the constant running up and down?"

In between working in the pantry and running and getting things, deliveries came. Usually Mr. Silverman checked all truck loads for content, quality, amount, if it was ordered, or if someone wished to sell on a freelance basis. People were starting to yell my name from all directions. "Kurt, I need this; Kurt, please see the butcher; Kurt, you have a delivery." I had a delivery? I ran down to the side door and there was a dairy truck delivering eight tremendous cans of milk, two cans of sweet cream, four cans of sour cream, butter, cream cheese and on and on. I checked and counted everything and then signed for it. Now, this array of dairy products stood on the platform. Not knowing what to do with it, I phoned Mr. Silverman and told him what had arrived. He patiently told me to go to the kitchen help and ask two guys to help me to store everything in the big walk-in refrigerators. We had several walk-ins – one for dairy, one for fruits and vegetables, and one for beef products. In addition, we had walk-in freezers. I walked up and asked the chef which two kitchen workers could help me. He said, "I don't care – any two." Then I said, "Look, I am new to this duty. I would appreciate your sending them down." A few minutes later, one showed up, and by the time the second came down, everything had been stored.

I pulled double duty for several days. Mr. Kennedy needed my help, and three chefs constantly needed ingredients, while I stood at the platform checking in all kinds of deliveries. I spent more time talking to Mr. Silverman on the phone arranging for special orders than I did helping Mr. Kennedy in the pantry. I was constantly being paged to accept deliveries, to answer a call from Mr. Silverman, or being told that someone else needed something from me. The name "Kurt" became known throughout the hotel. Not only the employees knew who I was, but guests started to inquire as to who Kurt was.

The next time I spoke to Mr. Silverman to inquire as to how he felt, I told him that the people were running me ragged; working with Mr. Kennedy, answering the constant requests from the chefs, tending to the constant flow of deliveries. I did not know what ailed Mr. Silverman, but when he said that he would come back to work in a few days I felt relieved.

I was also having recurring headaches, which I had to overcome by taking strong pills and having a couple of hours of sleep. These were terrible hours because it reminded me of my bout with typhus in the concentration camp. It was not always easy to wait until I had a couple of hours off in the afternoon. Mostly, I worked feeling as if my head was going to burst. I visited a local doctor who also came from Vienna. He suggested that as soon as I got back to New York City I should visit one of the hospitals that specialized in head injuries. I had been to two already; one in Vienna and one in New York. The only thing they gave me were pills.

The Flagler's kitchen help consisted of Mr. Silverman, the head steward, the head chef, the second chef, a breakfast chef, and eight in-kitchen help, who mostly prepared the side dishes and did things such as peeling and cleaning potatoes, washing and cutting up vegetables and keeping all pots and pans sparkling clean. We had several dishwashers who cleaned plates, stacked them into boxes and pushed them through a huge washing machine. Two different kinds of dishes had to be used – one set for dairy meals, and the other for meat meals. Inspectors constantly checked to make sure that dairy and meat products, dishes and pots were kept separate, to be certified as Kosher. There were two glass washers, five of whom worked in the pantry, three in the bakery, and two in the butcher shop. Every department head always complained that his department was understaffed. Mr. Silverman hired all of them and kept each department very lean.

When Mr. Silverman returned to work, he pulled me out of the pantry and announced that from now on I would be the newly created assistant steward, which was great. My salary was raised to $50 per week, but from then on I had to be the first in the kitchen in the morning and the last to leave at night. Mr. Silverman had me participate in meetings with the chef, baker, butcher and the head waiter when planning the meals for the following week. I participated so that I could prepare all ingredients needed and because I had to take care of most of the steward's work while Mr. Silverman took care of the running of the entire hotel while he was recuperating from his illness. I made my work easier by having a list of the chefs' needs well prepared in advance. That kept my running up and down to a minimum.

I will never forget what took place after I received my first pay envelope, which we received every two weeks. After we had finished serving lunch, I went to my room to rest, putting my pay into the inside pocket of my jacket, which was hanging in the closet with the rest of my clothing. I returned to work for the evening meal and rushed back to my room after I had secured everything in the kitchen. I was anticipating a hotly contested basketball game between the staff of the Flagler and the Concord hotels. I showered, changed and went to the closet to get my money, which, unfortunately, was paid in cash, only to find that my envelope with the money was gone. The only people who had entrance to my room were the chambermaid, who had made up my room before lunch, and my fireman roommate who did not return to the room before 3:00 a.m. the next day. He was drunk and smelled either of beer or whiskey or both. I questioned him about my money, but he denied seeing or taking it. He had told me that he was broke, and he had not gotten paid, yet all of a sudden he had money to go out and get drunk. I was positive that he took my money, but I could not accuse him without positive proof. I told Mr. Silverman what had happened and asked him if he could move me into a different room. I not only thought he took my money, but he always reeked of liquor. I was very upset when I spoke to Mr. Silverman and a small gathering of waiters and kitchen workers were listening to my sad story.

Mr. Silverman's home was in town but he also had a room in the hotel in case he wanted to rest, which was very seldom. He suggested that I move into his room. I happily accepted his offer, for it meant that from then on I had my own room. I moved my belongings right away. It was a larger room with two beds, ample closet space and a toilet and shower room across the hall. When I got back down to the kitchen, a waiter, who we called Little Sam, a very nice guy, came over to me and said, "Listen, kid, we took up a collection among the waiters, busboys and kitchen personnel." He handed me a whole bunch of money, which almost replaced my lost money. I was so choked up, I could hardly thank everyone. I hugged Sam, who dismissed his deed with a wave of his hand and walked off as though nothing had happened. A few days later, the fireman was fired for not showing up for work and for drunkenness. From that day on I kept my money with me at all times, until I could deposit it in the bank. I had very few expenses. I tipped the chambermaid every week and spent money for the barber and laundry. That was all. The rest I could save.

Menus were adopted for each day of the week and usually repeated for the entire season. Occasionally the chef made changes and informed us in advance so that we could order and prepare for it. Mr. Silverman gave me two master lists – one for perishables like dairy, vegetables and fruit products, the other for non-perishables, like groceries, can goods and cereals. Eggs were delivered every second day. We had standing orders for beef, dairy products and fruit, while we bought specialty products daily. Mr. Silverman taught me everything he could in the shortest possible time. The Flagler also had a chicken farm on the premises that supplied us daily with fresh chickens. The chicken farm was later closed, and the property was incorporated into the grounds of the hotel and converted into a baseball field.

As Mr. Silverman's assistant, I had to be able to substitute for a salad man or a cook who did not show up on time or at all. I had a busy job and I loved it. All that happened took only a few weeks: a good job, with good pay, and good food. I met nice people; many of them young girls who gave me their phone numbers and invited me to call them when I returned to the city. I got free golf lessons, swam every day, participated in sports and was royally entertained in the evenings. The only thing I did not have was enough time off. A Catskills vacation was an experience. Guests were pampered and catered to. They were well fed with the choicest of foods. The service was five star. People returned year after year with reservations well in advance.

I received occasional mail from my girlfriend in Vienna, who even at this late date had not moved out of the Russian Zone. Even though we had made no promises to each other, I sent her an affidavit. Armed with a co-signed letter from the hotel, I went to the city, and with the help of the Joint Distribution Committee, I was able to send her this affidavit as my fiancée. After she had received it, she wrote that she inquired at the American Consulate in Vienna about her chances of joining me. She was told that the co-signed affidavit was very good, but because she lived in the Russian Zone it could take several years for her quota, unless I returned to Vienna and we got married. As I was not about to return, our letter writing became less frequent, and eventually we broke our engagement. Our relationship cooled and eventually we stopped writing to each other.

After a hard day's work I usually went up to my room, shaved and showered, got dressed and went to the Playhouse or the Fiesta Room. Guests were entertained daily, but the big stars appeared on weekends. The first few times when singers were introduced as the star from Oklahoma, I thought that the state produced a lot of good singers, until I learned that they were referring to the musical, "Oklahoma," on Broadway. Many, many comedians appeared at the Flagler, from stars like Danny Kaye and Red Buttons, to the new and less known comedians. Phil Foster and Henny Youngman appeared often. Famous singers, dancers from ballet to the jitterbug, and many stars from the Jewish stage, Menasha Skulnik, Jenny Goldstein, to a later newcomer, Sam Levenson, all performed at The Flagler. There were two dance bands, Gary Rich and his All American Band, and Emilio Ray's Latin Rhythms. I especially recall one night when Phil Foster was on the stage in the Fiesta Room. The audience would not let him off the stage. They kept him performing for almost four hours. Phil just went on and on. It did not make any difference what he said. The people laughed themselves sick. It got to the point where straight-faced Phil could not stop laughing himself. It was just one of those nights where everything was funny.

There were competitive sports nights, baseball or basketball. The Flagler's athletic staff played against other hotel staffs. These games were hotly contested. We had excellent athletes on our staff. Most played for major colleges, and I was their number one fan.

Other nights, theater groups performed plays. I enjoyed these evenings the most. I sat in the audience, leisurely dressed, sometimes with a girl. It was just a quiet evening without the hustle and noise. I also enjoyed dancing since my days dancing in the Triumph in Vienna. I became a pretty good ballroom dancer. Most girls, guests or employees were nice looking and dancing with most of them was a joy, but I always kept Mr. Greenblatt's warning in mind.

By coincidence, the hotel's dance teacher was a former soccer player who played for Hakoah Vienna a few years before I did. We used to meet in the afternoon on an open field and kick a soccer ball around, and you could tell that neither he nor I were amateurs. One afternoon, a couple of guys walked by, and one of them joined us, kicking and passing the ball. He was very good. He then introduced himself to us and said, "My names is Marcel Cerdan," the one and only boxing champion of the world from France. He was training in the Catskills for his next fight. He just came over to the Flagler to watch Gus Lesnevich, the light heavy-weight champion of the world, who trained in our hotel. Marcel joined us a few afternoons to play soccer, while Gus Lesnevich was another story. He was always hungry. He used to seek me out in the afternoons and good-naturedly threaten me if I did not give him something to eat. He and I went to the empty kitchen and sat at a table. I gave him whatever he wanted to eat. His favorite was cold roast chicken and fruit. I asked him, "Does your trainer know that you eat here every afternoon?" His answer was, "To fight Jersey Joe Walcott, I need more weight." The fight never took place, and all the training and eating was for nothing.

Every so often, they had amateur night when talented guests and staff performed. Mac, the master of ceremonies, always asked me to sing with the band. I was still a very good singer. It was the band that was lousy. I always used to say that to Gary Rich, and he would say, "We have to rehearse harder." Another night was champagne night. Guests would dance their favorite dances with the teachers and then were judged by the audiences as to who would win a bottle of champagne. Before this took place, the dance teachers from our hotel and other hotels performed their expert routines, but waltzes were reserved for my friend's partner and me. She was a terrific dancer and probably the best teacher in the Catskills. Every so often I used to visit her in the studio and danced all the latest Latin dances with her without charge.

Very often a comedy team, whose names I cannot remember, performed at the Playhouse. They had one routine that, no matter how often I heard it, I laughed my head off. They came onto the stage and one would ask, "Ready Rudy?" The other would answer, "Rudy, ready." One was in an insane asylum and went before a panel of doctors to ascertain whether he could be released. They asked him, "What would you do if we let you go?" His answer was, "I would go out, buy a slingshot, go to the Flagler and knock out all the windows." He was rejected. One year later, they would ask him the same question. He would answer, "I would go home, have a good meal, rest, and then I would get a slingshot, go to the Flagler, and knock out all the windows." He was rejected. Two years later, the doctors would ask him again what he would do if they released him. He finally answered, "I would dress in my best suit and pick up my girlfriend. We would go out to dinner and dancing." The doctors were listening and smiling because finally he had reached the point of sanity to be released from the asylum. He then continued with his answer, "After dancing we would go to a movie, then I'll take her home and take off her dress, then her slip and her bra and last I'll take off her girdle and from the girdle I'd make a slingshot, come back to the Flagler and knock out all the windows." These two guys were very funny, and the only place I saw them perform was the Flagler.

These were good times. I used to work very hard. Even though I got very little sleep and felt tired and all, I enjoyed it. The summer went fast; Labor Day was around the corner. Then Mr. Silverman asked me to stay on until after the Jewish holidays. I was happy to stay on because that was when I caught up with my rest. I went to bed early and my work load was next to nothing until the holidays. Then it got hectic again, but not as bad as during the summer season.

In the meantime, I wrote to my buddy, Ernie, who had arrived in New York City with his brother. We had planned to see each other at season's end, but had to plan our getting together until after the holidays. A cantor and his family choir performed the holiday services, and I did have a chance to listen to them. I met the whole family—really nice people—and I did hang out with one of their daughters for the next ten days.

A vice-president of the HIAS (I think his name was Osofsky) arrived at the hotel to solicit donations for the HIAS. When I heard him speak on behalf of the needy survivors of the Holocaust, I introduced myself and told him that the HIAS had sponsored my travel costs when I came to the United States. I offered my services to help him any way I could. He wanted to know everything. He could learn firsthand from me how best the HIAS could help Jews remaining in Europe. After we spoke about my past and my suggestions, he said that the HIAS did not have enough money to do what was needed. I did go with him when he spoke to various groups in several hotels, and I told them about the virtues of giving to the HIAS. I served as an example for the HIAS. That was the only way I could repay what they had done for me, and I felt good about my small contribution.

The day came for me to pack up and go back to the city. Mr. Silverman asked me if I could come back for Christmas and New Year's Eve. I said, "At this moment I say yes." He also planned to re-hire me for next year's season and said that he would be in touch with me. I said my goodbye and went back to Brooklyn, this time to my own apartment.

CHAPTER TWENTY
BUMMING WITH ERNIE

I had saved most of my money but not enough to furnish my apartment. The place was freshly painted, and the landlord gave me a good-sized refrigerator. The day I returned I called the lady from the Joint Distribution Committee and asked if she could get me a job. I told her that I had to buy some furniture and that would wipe out my meager savings. She advised me to apply for unemployment, to tell them that I was laid off. In that way, I could collect some money until she could place me in some kind of employment. She also said they could contribute a little money until then.

With this knowledge, I bought a convertible couch and chair, new linoleum throughout the apartment, a kitchen set with four chairs, a new shower curtain, shades and curtains for the windows, and a radio. I also purchased a few pots and pans and a coffee maker. My cousin gave me dishes, and I stocked my cabinets with canned goods and a lot of Lipton noodle soup. Eggs, bread and dairy products I bought as I needed. Everything was so much different here in America, after the war. All of the difficulties I faced in Vienna and in the concentration camps did not exist here. It was so easy to just buy what I needed or wanted, and now my household was all set up. I could concentrate on other things, like meeting Ernie every day.

Ernie took the subway from the Bronx and I from Brooklyn, and we met in midtown Manhattan. We bummed around New York City for a couple of weeks, from one movie house to another, watching famous bands and entertainers. Later on, Ernie loved to play ping pong, especially against me. The loser had to pay, and Ernie came close to winning, but never did. It became an obsession with him, to beat me just once. I had certainly come a long way with my ping pong skills.

I called several girls who I had met in the Flagler for dates, always asking if they had a girlfriend for Ernie. Some of the girlfriends for Ernie turned out better than my date. We usually took our dates to 52nd Street, which was where Ernie and I hung out. It was not unusual to see Billy Eckstein in one spot and Sarah Vaughn in another, or Charlie Parker and Charlie Ventura, and so on. 52nd Street was an ever-changing jazz Mecca. We got to know the security men in the various jazz spots, and for the price of a Coke, we could stand at the bar and enjoy the performances. Ernie came to see me in Brooklyn with a German language newspaper called The Aufbau to show me that there would be a dance on Saturday night on 86th Street. I suggested that we go and see what this dance was all about, but I also told him that the vacation time was over because I had been called to go on interviews for jobs. Ernie looked a little sad then said, "I guess I have to look for a bakery that will hire me."

My interview was with the Custom Shop, a shirt manufacturer in lower Manhattan. I was hired to start to work as a spreader. I had to spread layers of fabric from one end of a long cutting table to the other, nice and smooth. On top of the fabric, a pattern was applied, then cut into sections that eventually would be sewn together into a shirt. The other spreader worked piecework and therefore made a lot more money. I asked the foreman if I could go on piecework. His answer was, "Sure." I was fast, very fast, but I did not check for blemishes in the fabric like the other spreader, so I caused a lot of damage. This position did not last. Even though the foreman taught me cutting by hand, mostly shirt collars and cuffs, there was little work and the last hired were the first fired. It made me angry because only a couple of days before, I walked to work during a tremendous snow storm. The snow had piled up on Canal Street to a height that reached above my thighs.

I had two choices for job interviews. One was the Custom Shop, and the other was Schwartz and Lieberman, a children's headwear firm. I went there to speak to a Mr. Schwartz, and after a very short discussion, I was hired as a shipper and charger. I told him that I could start after New Year's for I had a commitment to work at the Flagler. He suggested that I start right away and then return after New Year's, and he very generously offered to pay me minimum wage.

That Saturday was the scheduled dance on 86th Street. I met Ernie in the Bronx, went to an afternoon movie, had dinner in Manhattan in Hector's Cafeteria, then took a bus to 86th Street, which was a mini Germany. From German restaurants to German bakeries, all stores had a German ambiance. We entered a large ballroom after paying a small entrance fee. The dance was already in progress. They had a surprisingly good band. We sat down at the side of the room to have a better overview. I spotted a girl I liked, and Ernie saw another. After a few dances, my partner and I sat down at a table, and Ernie and his girl followed shortly. The four of us had a very pleasant evening. My date was from Germany, but, like so many Jewish kids, came to the United States from Sweden. Ernie's date came from Vienna and came to America in 1938. Ernie's date lasted only for that evening, while my date became my girlfriend. We went together for over one year. I told her that evening that I would not be in the city for New Year's, but I would be in touch with her right after.

When I got back to the Flagler, preparations for the holidays had started. My job by then was routine, and I handled everything with ease. Although the hotel was filled with guests, the weather was not favorable. The two weeks went by very fast and New Year's Eve was a noisy affair. A lot of food was being served, including a midnight dinner, and drinks were available in the dining room. The band was playing while people were eating and dancing at the same time. That day, I worked sixteen hours and then collapsed in my room. Mr. Silverman asked me to return for Passover and the 1948 summer season. I asked him, "For the same money?" He asked me how much I was getting. I said, "$50 a week." He though for a second and said, "Okay, we'll pay you $60." I wished him a happy New Year, and while leaving I said, "I'll see you at Passover."

Back in New York City, I told Mr. Schwartz that I would be leaving again for Passover and the summer season. At the same time, I asked him if he could use another worker who was very good and reliable. It took Mr. Schwartz, who had a stutter, a while to answer in the affirmative. My cousin, Sol, came to see Mr. Schwartz and was hired. That made it a lot easier for me to leave for the Catskills and still have a job when I came back.

While working for Schwartz and Lieberman, I looked with envy into the showroom, watching the salesmen work with various buyers. They were always very well dressed, drove big cars, and were always spoken to nicely. In general, they looked prosperous. I often lingered around the showroom, watching how they sold children's headwear. I thought that selling would be a perfect lifelong vocation for me. Unfortunately, I was hired to do my work in the back storerooms that contained boxes upon boxes of children's bonnets and hats.

Ernie had gotten a very good job with a leading bakery in New York City, and we could see each other only on weekends and occasionally after work. Ernie told me that the bakery was being sold and that he would be out of a job. As I was about to leave for the Catskills, I asked Ernie if I should call Mr. Silverman to ask him if he had a job for Ernie. Ernie thought, then said yes. When I called Mr. Silverman to ask if he could hire Ernie because I sure could use some help, Mr. Silverman agreed, and Ernie and I left together for the Flagler.

Passover in the hotel was a completely different experience. The guests were mostly elderly and the food we served was commensurate with the holiday. Matzos were ordered by the cartons, wine was tasted then selected, and all other religious symbols were observed. Ernie thought that the job was not only too physical, but that the long working hours were impossible.

In the meantime, the owner of the hotel had died, and his niece and her family took over the hotel. They retained most of the key staff, including Mr. Silverman and me. When I came back for the summer season, I found a new team of cooks and a new head for the pantry; the butcher remained but there were new bakers. The new chef and I hit it off from the beginning, but sadly, I learned that he was staying for only a few weeks and then would leave to work for a competing hotel. The chef was of Hungarian-Czech descent, and I came from neighboring Austria. We therefore had similar likes and dislikes in food. He always used to ask me, "What would you like to eat, Kurt?" Knowing what a terrific cook he was and that he knew how to prepare every European dish from our area, I asked for the craziest dishes, which he gladly cooked for us. From basic Hungarian goulash with special dumplings to the best schnitzel, he cooked it all.

In the kitchen was a large round table known as the chef's table, and as soon as the chef and I sat down to eat, Mr. Silverman came over to check what we were eating. Most of the stuff was not Kosher, but he always hoped to find new entrees for the hotel's menu. When the chef told him that he added dairy products to the meat dishes, it turned Mr. Silverman off. The chef always assured Mr. Silverman that he cooked these special dishes for us in a special pot and served it on special dishes in order not to betray the Kosher status of the hotel. The few weeks passed quickly, and the chef, Mr. Kaiser, left and was replaced with a new person.

The summer of 1948 went fast. I was more selective in what shows and entertainment I attended. I had more rest, was less sleepy and was much more organized doing my job. I established delivery times for vendors, so that I was not disturbed during my free time. It became too frequent that the operator paged me to receive deliveries. Many times I ran in my wet bathing suit to check in some goods or had to get up from a nap. I put a sign up for everyone to see that no deliveries would be accepted between 2 and 4 p.m. However, there were always a few who did not adhere to the sign. Once I let a repeater wait until 4:30, but it never happened again. Mr. Silverman, somewhat softer, would accept the delivery if he was around.

My girlfriend came to visit me several weekends. As the summer progressed, she began visiting me less frequently and we sort of drifted apart. That year, I dated girls who I met the year before, and I always took the phone numbers of new ones. Among these new girls I met my future wife. When I met her we spent her entire vacation together. The entire vacation meant one week. I met her parents, and they were the first parents who did not ask me if I was ready to get married. I could not understand the need for parents to come up here to look for husbands for their daughters. I would have understood it if their daughters were older, but these girls were sixteen to nineteen years old.

The one valuable experience I obtained working in the Flagler was my work ethic. I also learned from Mr. Silverman how to get along with all kinds of people – business people, suppliers, and everyone who worked in the hotel. In the meantime, my cousin and his wife came to the United States from England and had no place to stay. My cousin, Lina, called me to ask if they could stay in my apartment until they could find their own. Of course I said yes, but I told her that I would be coming home on Labor Day. The time came for me to return to the city, but my apartment was still occupied.

Since my cousin had no phone, I had to call the corner candy store and they, in turn, called my cousin to the phone. When she told me that my cousin had found an apartment, but it would take a couple more days to move, I remained a few more days at the hotel and did absolutely nothing. I took walks and read everything in sight. It was quiet and beautiful, really. Mr. Silverman said it was time we left, and my cousins moved the day I returned to the city. The beautiful part was that my cousins left my apartment spic and span, much nicer than I left it. I was very happy to see my cousin for I had not seen him since he returned from Dachau in 1938 and subsequently left Vienna.

I then made my calls to Ernie, the Greenblatts, Boffi and my German girlfriend to let them know that I was back. I spoke to my girlfriend to find out if we had a further relationship or if it was over for good. She could not see me that weekend. We talked on the phone for a while and, when I hung up, we had agreed to call it a day. I asked my cousin Sol not to tell Mr. Schwartz that I was back in town as I decided to take off a week. Ernie had also returned. He and I visited newly arrived friends and kept in touch with old ones. He wanted to make plans for the weekend, but I told him that I called a girl I met at the Flagler and that I was invited to Friday night's dinner.

As I entered her apartment that Friday evening, a homey family feeling was in the air, much like Friday nights with my own parents and family. The aroma of cooking was very different than the kitchen in the hotel. There were no airs, no one had to put up a front, and I was who I was. The conversation around the table was not solely about me, my background and what I had to live through, though it did enter the conversation. Her parents were very nice people who made me feel welcome. Since it was getting late, and I had a long subway ride from the Bronx to Williamsburg, Brooklyn, I said my thank you and made a date with her for the next day to go to a movie.

We dated for a few months. We seemed to get along very well. I was twenty-two years old and she was eighteen. As we got even closer and had long conversations, we decided to get engaged. In the following weeks all the planning and preparation for an engagement party was exciting. Luckily, my future wife's father was a jeweler, who had a jewelry store in Manhattan. He brought home a selection of diamonds for an engagement ring, and my fiancée carefully selected the one she liked. Even at cost, the stone was expensive. I gave a down payment of less than half and the rest I paid in monthly installments. I received as an engagement present a solid gold Hamilton wristwatch. We planned an engagement party and invited mostly her friends and classmates. I had only Ernie and Boffi in attendance. Ernie made a gigantic cake, beautifully decorated. Because Ernie took such a long time decorating the cake until it was perfect, the cake itself got a little stale, but no one cared. The party was a lot of fun. There was lots of food, drinks and music, and we scheduled our wedding day for July 10, 1949. I wanted Ernie to be my best man, but he had to return to the Mountain View House in New Hampshire, so Boffi was gracious enough to accept.

At work I told Mr. Schwartz that I was getting married in a few months and that I would need a raise. At the same time, I told him that I was not going back to the Catskills, so he had me for the entire year.

Our next effort was to look for an apartment. My apartment was great for a guy who was seldom home, but not for a married couple. It was impossible to find an apartment anywhere. The best we could find was one room in an apartment we had to share with an old lady in the same building where my future aunt and uncle lived. The next few months I worked long hours to save some money. With the exception of an occasional movie or jazz concert, we spent most of our time at home or visiting friends.

As the wedding day approached, I gave up my apartment in Brooklyn and moved my belongings to Astoria, Long Island, into the one room. We had a formal wedding with all the trimmings. The guests were mostly from my wife's side for I had very few relatives and friends. How proud my parents would have been to see their youngest child get married. I swallowed hard more than once because my parents could not be with me.

After the ceremony and reception we took off for our honeymoon back to the Catskills to the Nevele Hotel, which was considered the honeymoon hotel. We met other honeymooners and became friends with some of them. We swam, rowed, played volleyball and tennis, and rode horseback at the Nevele. As I was mostly shirtless, I got the worst case of sunburn.

When we got back to our furnished, one-room rental, our pursuit for our own apartment intensified. Fortunately for us, but not for my wife's aunt and uncle who lived next door, we had another place to go to visit. They had one of the better television sets, and we took unfair advantage by watching it at all hours. But how could we not watch Milton Berle or Broadway Open House with Jerry Lester and Dagmar, and on alternate days, Morey Amsterdam? Wrestling became a passion. Antonino Rocca was my favorite, while Mr. America kept it interesting. But keeping my wife's aunt and uncle up at late hours, even if they were nice to us and did not say anything, was cruel punishment for being related.

We lived there for a little over one year when a building agent, who was a friend of my in-laws, got us an apartment in the Bronx on 166th Street and Grand Concourse. It was a very nice apartment with a living room, bedroom, very large kitchen and a huge foyer. For the first time, we could stretch out and attempt to furnish the place to our liking. My in-laws bought us our bedroom and some living room furniture, while we slowly furnished the rest. The first piece of furniture we bought was a huge cabinet with a Dumont television in it. We sat on the floor, but we had a TV. Slowly but surely, we fixed the place to completion and started to invite our friends.

At my place of work it got very, very busy. I worked hard and long hours. I packed and checked orders for children's headwear. Different styles were accumulated for various customers and stored in several sections. When the customer's shipping date arrived, we picked the stored boxes, checked the styles and quantities against the order, and packed and shipped them off. My job was to gather the boxes, check the merchandise and do the billing. Of course, I asked Mr. Schwartz for a raise, which was like pulling teeth. Begrudgingly, he gave me small raises, and with the overtime, I started to make a living. At Christmas, everyone got a small bonus, which the bookkeeper handed out during the Christmas party.

I also took on a part-time job for the Christmas season working for the main post office in Manhattan. I used to leave my job at 5:00 p.m., have a bite to eat and began work from 6:00 p.m. until 2:00 a.m. At the post office, I had to sort mail and place it into little pigeon-holes. They dumped a mountain of letters in front of me, and before I could finish sorting them, they dumped another load of letters. There was no chair to sit down on. They only had a slanted board to lean against. I am sure the post office managers thought it was comfortable, but after eight hours of standing, my legs were under my armpits. I must have done a good job, because I was promoted to sweeper. This meant that my responsibility was to sweep Brooklyn. I had to go from one sorter to another, collecting all the letters destined for Brooklyn, put them into a huge canvas bag and deliver these bags to a truck downstairs at a designated time. Almost all the time I had to run the last ten yards at full speed, or I would have missed the prompt departure of the truck. By midnight, I was so tired that I contemplated quitting several times. A few days before my job was to end, the supervisor offered me a permanent position with the post office. I said thanks, but no thanks. After Christmas I said so long. Not only did I not like this job, but, tired as I was, I used to fall asleep going home on the subway at 2:00 a.m. I would wake up way past my station. I then crossed over to the other side to take the train to either 167th Street Station or even the 161st Street station. I no sooner sat down and would fall asleep again, and wake up somewhere in Brooklyn. It was just too many hours to be working. I could not wait for the job to end.

I had remained in touch with Mr. Silverman who said that he would be in the city at an employment agency hiring next year's staff and asked for me to come to see him. When I got to the agency, I saw Mr. Silverman and the owner of the Flagler sitting at a table, interviewing several people. I sat on a bench waiting for the interviews to end, leafing through the New York Times, when I heard a voice near me say, "I hoped you'd come back." I looked up and it was the voice of the owner of the hotel. I stood up and shook his hand, when Mr. Silverman joined us saying, "I'll talk to him." He then asked me to return to work at the Flagler starting on Passover. I explained to him that I was married and that both of us had jobs. He said instead of $60 per week, he would pay me $75 per week, but still I moaned and groaned about my wife. That is when the owner interrupted and said, "We'll give her a job as a hostess in the dining room that pays $25 plus tips." All I saw was $100 plus our own room and ample food. I thought that we could save a lot of money. I said, "I'll have to speak to my wife, but I am sure she will agree to go with me." Mr. Silverman said, "Please let me know by tomorrow." He gave me the phone number of the agency. I called the next day and confirmed our coming to the Flagler.

The entire 1950 summer season was a difficult one. My wife was pregnant, and we were eagerly expecting the baby. The position as hostess in the dining room did not work out too well. The smell of food made her sick and occasionally she would not show up for work. That made the job much harder for the head waiter. The owner asked me if he could give my wife a different job because she was not doing very well, especially in the early morning. We negotiated back and forth and, at one point, I even said that we might go home. He then offered my wife the afternoon shift at the switchboard. That was a better situation for her – one that she could easily handle.

A few days later, my wife developed pains, and we rushed her to the Monticello Hospital. Upon her and my urging, the doctors tried to save the pregnancy, but she felt lousy and the staining did not stop. I called her doctor in New York City, and he suggested that she miscarry. The doctors in the hospital thought that she would be alright, but the doctor in the city had her transferred to New York City and within two days she lost the baby. She was past her fifth month.

It was a sad time and, after recuperating at her parents' house for a couple of weeks, she returned to the Flagler. The hotel gave her a courtesy job, checking and making sure that no outsiders were using the hotel's pool. She sat near the entrance to the pool with lady guests joining her to play mahjong all morning and afternoon. That was a soft job, and it made it easier for her to gain her strength back. It was a trying season for both of us. Even though I was asked to stay on for the Jewish holidays, we decided to leave Labor Day. I had a disagreement with the chef. The owner and Mr. Silverman took my side in this confrontation to the point that they were willing to fire the chef. I asked them, "Who would do the cooking?" That late in the season, who could they hire? They still argued, and they wanted me to stay, but my wife and I had had enough problems.

As I was loading my car, the lady owner of an employment agency who I knew offered me an even better position for more money at the Concord Hotel. I thanked her but declined; my wife and I agreed that we should go home.

I took a few days off then called my cousin Sol to see if he thought Mr. Schwartz would still be interested in me working for him. My cousin did ask, and Mr. Schwartz said to see him on the following Monday or Tuesday. When I sat down to speak to Mr. Schwartz, I explained to him that I was married and hoped to have a family, that for me to make out bills and pack and check orders was really not a job for the future. He asked me, "What would you like to do?" Before he could continue, I said, "I would like to sell – become a salesman on commission and possibly take over a territory, and if you cannot offer that, I might as well try with another company." He said, "Look, I know you. At the moment there is no opening." But he promised me that I would be the first in line to be promoted from within. He urged me to stay with the provision that I would not always run away for the summer to work for someone else. I took him at his word and agreed to stay, with an ever so small raise.

That very same year he broke his word. Mr. Schwartz's son, who took care of portions of the New York City's metropolitan area, was transferred to California to represent the company. When I asked, "Why did I not get the chance?" Mr. Schwartz said, "You will take care of the position my son vacated." It really was no advancement at all. At best, it was a small one, without him having to pay me extra money.

I became a member of the Knickerbocker showcase, a salesmen's organization in the children's clothing field. Their purpose was to hold organized exhibitions or what we called "shows" for the wholesale trade only at the New Yorker Hotel on 8th Avenue. I was about to attend my first showing.

I checked into the hotel with cases upon cases of children's headwear. I organized my room with tables and risers all around the walls and displayed kids hats for spring and summer use, from the tiniest infant baby bonnets, to the most beautiful straw hats for teenagers and everything in between for boys and girls. The salesman next to my room was a former buyer who I knew. He was helpful in explaining how best to arrange my room and still have room for buyers to sit down.

My first customer was an old lady who wore a man's coat, wrongly buttoned. Her shoes, hair and entire demeanor were disheveled. She carried a torn folder under her arm. I asked her to sit down and she answered, "No, I only work standing up." I saw two or three salesmen looking in to my room, smiling. As she picked out styles and ordered two, three, and sometimes four dozen of a style, I played along and said, "Is that all you need?" She again answered, "You are right, make this one five and this one six dozen." It took about twenty minutes, and I had a really substantial order. I yelled after her a loud thank you. With the order under my arm I walked next door and told my friend, "Thank you for sending me a good customer. I played along once, but from now on, cut out the funny stuff because to me this is serious business." He stared at me with a blank look and said, "I don't know what you are talking about." Another salesman joined us in the room. Just as I was about to tear up the order, this guy said, "I saw you working with Mrs. So-and-So." That is when my friend started to laugh and began to understand my gibberish. He said, "Kurt, this is one of our best accounts in Long Island; she is not the usual buyer, in buying or appearances." I could not believe it. I could have sold her more with a little effort. It was also a new account for the firm. That was a valuable lesson I learned; I learned not to prejudge anyone, but to go on in a professional manner, presenting your commodity, and to sell with integrity. I did very well at that show. I surpassed the volume of Mr. Schwartz's son's previous showing in dollars and new accounts.

Soon thereafter, I was called into the firm's showroom to work with buyers from all over the country. Our salesmen knew their customers and showed only the styles they usually bought. I did not know anyone or what a customer bought previously. I just showed our product from soup to nuts and consequently wrote bigger orders. When we compared my orders against the previous years' orders, my bosses were impressed with the increases. Everything increased except my salary. In order to make more money, I had to work overtime in the back, packing orders and billing.

I took all kinds of part-time jobs. Once I worked for Dale Dance Studio. After I finished my regular hours, I would buy a sandwich and eat it walking to Times Square where Dale had a studio and worked until 11:00 p.m., and sometimes even a little later. It was funny how I got this part-time job. When I applied, I said that

I worked in the Catskills, but I never mentioned that I was an assistant steward. A young woman interviewed me and directed me to a private room and said that she would join me shortly to dance with her. Another tryout ensued, which reminded me of my first encounter with the president of Hakoah New York Soccer Club. I was wondering whether she was the first or the second team. As it turned out, she was the manager of the studio. Once she entered the room she pushed some buttons and music came from everywhere. First I had to dance the most popular Latin dances of the time with her, like the rumba, samba, tango and the newly arrived mambo. Then came the fox trot, the waltz, and even the seldom danced or taught, like the peabody and carioca. I was accepted to attend classes to learn the system of teaching. I sat through classes for a couple of weeks, after which a talented girl and I started to teach beginner group lessons. Working all day and dancing in the evening was hard enough. In addition to that, on Thursday afternoons, teachers and students went to the Tavern on the Green in Central Park for social dancing and mingling, which I very seldom could attend. Hence, my job with Dale Dance Studio did not last long.

It was the summer of 1952 that I learned my wife was pregnant again. Since this was our second effort to have a child, the doctor suggested that my wife be careful in her pregnancy. She could not lift heavy objects and had to rest more often in the hope of having a healthy baby. The building we lived in had a congenial bunch of tenants. Mostly, it was full of young couples. Some had children, and some, like us, were about to have children. The women got together to play mahjong, while the men played penny poker at least once a week. We also got together for an occasional softball game, while the women and kids cheered us on. I had joined a soccer team called Blue Star as a right halfback. I played for that team for my own enjoyment, and so that I could keep playing the game I loved, until I was thirty-three. I was asked to continue to participate in the sport as a referee or management, but after I stopped playing I no longer had any interest.

My wife's pregnancy was not easy, especially considering her past experience. She was under an excellent doctor's care who guided her through the nine months. My in-laws were in my house when my wife got mild labor pains. They waited until past 11:00 p.m. for further developments, but the pains stopped, and they went home. No sooner had they left when the pains returned, and I knew that was it. I called the doctor, who lived in Connecticut, who said, "Don't wait. Bring her right to the hospital, and I will leave now." I called my in-laws, who had just gotten into their apartment, saying that I was taking off and to meet us at the hospital. My destination was Flower Fifth Avenue Hospital in Manhattan. It was past midnight. There was almost no traffic, and I passed under every light, red or green. I drove carefully, but at an accelerated speed. On arrival, a nurse wheeled my wife upstairs while I had to wait in a room just outside the labor room. I don't know if my wife did the yelling or if it was the wives of the other two men also waiting. I sat for only a few minutes when our doctor arrived and told me that it would not be long. A very short time later the doctor reappeared and told me that I had a little girl and that mother and child were doing just fine. After we shook hands, he said, "You can see the baby in a couple of minutes, but your wife will not be ready for visitors for at least an hour." I sat down on a chair that stood in the corner of the waiting room and my eyes filled with tears of joy and jubilation. A few years ago, the German-Austria Axis destroyed my family and was killing babies. Today, I became a father, and this was the start of a new family.

Our daughter was born in April of 1953, and our lives changed. For the first couple of months, she was nothing but joy. Then a change took place. She kept us up most of the night; she could not keep her formula down, throwing up and having diarrhea daily. The doctor suspected that she was a celiac baby, meaning that her mother's milk was totally disagreeable to her system. She was very uncomfortable and cried most of the time. All the many tests she took showed negative; then our pediatrician said to us, "I would like to keep the baby in the hospital for further tests. I want to make sure that she will be alright." She was admitted to the hospital and was kept there for eight or nine days. When we came to see her, she was crying, and when we left her she was crying. I felt that more than one week was enough testing, and I told the doctor it was time that I took my little girl home. She was discharged the next day. The doctor said that even though the tests were inconclusive, he would treat her for celiac. As soon as her formula and choices of food were changed, the baby started to rebound, gained weight and finally slept through the night.

That summer my in-laws and I rented a cottage for the season in Spring Valley. I commuted daily to New York City. Even then the traffic was heavy. I drove an old car – a 1941 Buick that I purchased for $100. After a few repairs, it drove like a tank. This car could drive through hurricanes. The following summer while we rented a room in Far Rockaway, my newly acquired friends in their brand new cars got stuck during the heavy downpour and very strong winds, but my 1941 Buick kept running.

In late fall, my selling job got another boost. My other boss, Mr. Lieberman, returned from his Midwest business trip almost without any orders. Snow, cold and icy conditions for an extended period kept most of the store owners and buyers from attending the scheduled shows, and it carried over to other cities where shows were planned. I was called into Mr. Schwartz's office. He gave me an account list that covered the states of Indiana, Michigan, Illinois, Missouri and Kansas. He said, "We want you to leave as soon as possible, go to the Midwest and try to save as many orders as you can." Mr. Schwartz further told me that he would send my salary check to my home and my expense check to key hotels in the Midwest territory. First, I had to argue with Mr. Schwartz because he did not include the overtime in my average weekly salary. We argued back and forth, and he finally agreed to include my overtime and a tiny bit more for me to make this long business trip.

Luckily, my father-in-law had bought a new car, and he gave me his old 1948 Plymouth. This car had low mileage and was in top condition. For the first time I was driving a really good car. My salary at that time averaged $125 a week and $125 for travel expenses. I told my wife of our arrangement, that she would receive my weekly check, which would take care of our expenses and some savings. Whatever I could save on my expense check, which I was sure Mr. Schwartz had carefully figured, would be added to my salary.

A few days later, I took out my back seat in the car, replaced it with stacks of sample cases and left for the road. I started in Indiana, then on to Michigan and Illinois. Missouri and Kansas were to be my last two states, and then back home. I not only saved every order from established customers, but I opened quite a few new ones. My expense money was sent in advance to either the Statler Hotel in Detroit or St. Louis, the Palmer House in Chicago, the Muhlbach in Kansas City or the Claypool in Indianapolis. I used to call our bookkeeper a few days in advance to inform her where I was going to be. I had to schedule my route so that on weekends I would be in one of these hotels.

My first trip lasted thirteen weeks, and the amount of orders I mailed to my company far surpassed, if on commission, my salary and expenses. When I called my company, Mr. Schwartz got on the phone, and he suggested that he would send me next week's check to— That is when I interrupted him and said, "No more checks on the road. No more next week. Thirteen weeks away from home is enough. I am coming back. I'll see you in a few days." And I hung up.

When I got home I reacquainted myself with my wife and child and decided to take an extra day of rest because driving from Kansas to New York was not an easy task. When I walked into our showroom I was praised and scolded at the same time. I was praised because I did a good job and scolded because I came home. But what I proved was that if given a chance, I could sell.

Mr. Lieberman's son and I traveled the Midwest the following year. While I was working with Palais Royal in Kansas City, I received a phone call from Mr. Schwartz to pack up my samples immediately and drive to Buffalo, New York. Mr. Wesson, the New England and upstate New York representative took ill, and I had to substitute for him until he could return to work. I had appointments made for the following week, which Mr. Schwartz canceled, claiming an emergency. That was on a Friday afternoon, and the Buffalo show opened Sunday morning.

I left Kansas City a round 3:00 p.m., drove all night Friday, all day Saturday, and I arrived at the Statler

Hotel in Buffalo Sunday morning at 4:00 a.m. Most of my driving was done in rainstorms that traveled from west to east at the same speed I drove. When I finally landed in my room, I displayed my entire line of children's headwear, slept for three and a half hours, then opened for business, waiting to serve a new set of wholesale customers. In addition to Buffalo, the show traveled to Syracuse and Albany, and we spent an average of three days in each city. My room at the Statler in Buffalo was huge, while at the Onandaga Hotel in Syracuse and the Ten Eyck in Albany, the rooms were somewhat smaller. Show hours were from 9:00 a.m. until 9:00 p.m., which got gradually reduced to 7:00 p.m.

Right after the upstate New York shows, I had to attend the big show at the Statler in Boston, which lasted five days. From then on, I only traveled the New England and upstate New York territory, subbing for the ailing Mr. Wesson, who was in his mid-eighties. He tried one comeback, traveling with me in mid-winter when the temperature was twenty-six below zero, and he returned home. The following season I thought that I was still subbing for him when the president of the Boston show informed me that Mr. Wesson had resigned almost one year ago, and the time had come for me or someone else to become the new member of the Eastern Travelers Association. I was very upset to learn this fact, which Mr. Schwartz conveniently kept from me so that he could pocket the difference of money earned between my salary and Mr. Wesson's previously earned commission.

When I returned to the city and told Mr. Schwartz what I had learned and asked him what he was going to do about it, he said, "When the season is over. We'll talk and make arrangements starting next season." I said, "I'll go on straight commission and will pay my own expenses, like all other salesmen." But he walked away without acknowledging my request. I became the member of all the shows; the company replaced my old car, which I had driven over 110,000 miles, with a new 1957 Plymouth in September 1956. It was a very good looking car, fully automatic and had fins just like a Caddie.

The following season was more than half over, and Mr. Schwartz still had not talked to me. When I returned after several weeks of traveling, the first words Mr. Schwartz uttered were for me to go to the back to help pack orders and do the billing. I was tired, and I surely did not expect this kind of request. I said to Mr. Schwartz that I wanted to speak to him right away. He saw that I was very upset, so he told me to wait in his office, and he would be right in. He kept me waiting and waiting, I am sure, hoping that I would cool off. Instead, the longer I waited and the longer he delayed, the more upset I became. I walked out into the showroom several times just to see what he was doing. He just sat around, slouching over a table and doing absolutely nothing, while I sat in his office on hot coals. I repeated my walk several times. I then decided to just sit and wait until he made his entrance. Maybe he was right. I did start to calm down by rehearsing in my mind what I would say to him. I would say, "Mr. Schwartz, I have been a worker, an apprentice, a journeyman, a salesman subbing for another salesman for the company. I have performed my duties beyond what was expected of a man for almost ten years. Since Mr. Wesson has been retired for more than a year, I have earned the right to replace him in the New England-upstate New York territory and on straight commission." I was willing to work in the showroom and even do the billing when I was not traveling. Everything entered my mind. I rehearsed my responses to anything he might say. I felt very comfortable with my reasonable request because it was just. I sat in the chair a while longer when the door opened, and Mr. Schwartz entered.

First, let me explain that Mr. Schwartz had a stutter and his thoughts were far ahead before he could express them. He, therefore, spoke in half sentences, especially when it could cost him money. The door had not closed and already he had taken a battle stance and said, "What do you want and make it quick? I have no time to sit here and talk." I tried to speak. I tried to ask him to change my status but he interrupted me after every word I spoke, raising his voice, stuttering more than usual, until he was completely out of control. He yelled at me, "You are not a salesman! You are not selling Schwartz-Lieberman! Schwartz and Lieberman is selling you! What nerve you have to ask me to go on straight commission!" Before I could answer, he had walked out of the office, slamming the door. One minute later he reentered, still yelling. "You will have to work many more years before

I will consider such a move. Did we not buy you a car?" That is when I raised my voice. "You replaced a car. You replaced a car." Hearing me say that, he ran out of the office again, slamming the door. I remained sitting and thought that he was fighting for money, commission money that rightfully belonged to the salesman, and I felt that the compensation I received for the work I did just was not enough. He let me sweat another few minutes before he returned. This time I started the conversation before he could and said, "Mr. Schwartz, make me a reasonable offer or I can no longer work for you," and out of the office he went. I opened the door slightly and watched him march through the showroom. I heard one of the senior salesmen ask him, "What's going on, Leo?" Instead of answering him, he returned to the office. I quickly closed the door and sat down again. He entered and in a loud voice started to scold me again and repeated everything from the beginning. I stood up and walked up to him and looked him straight in the eyes, even though he was much shorter than I, and calmly said, "Mr. Schwartz, either you make me an offer that I can live with and talk to me in a calm voice, or", then I took a deep breath and heard myself say, "the next time you walk out of this office, I'll walk with you, and I'll walk straight home, which will mean goodbye Schwartz and Lieberman." He sat down and got very quiet. He did not even utter one word. He just looked at me, deciding what he should do. He then called my bluff, got up and walked out. I was right behind him. I walked over to the closet, took my coat and rang the bell for the freight elevator. Mr. Schwartz came running, yelling at me, "I want you to bring the samples and the car back by tomorrow." He instructed the elevator man never again to bring me to that floor. As the elevator was moving down I still could hear his loud voice, yelling something.

I walked to the subway to go home, and during the subway ride, I realized that I had just quit my job and for the remaining stations. Panic set in. What was I going to do now? As I entered my apartment, my wife immediately asked, "What's the matter?" I answered, "I am stupid. I just walked out of my job, and I don't know what I am going to do next." She asked, "Why?" I told her the whole story. She thought that I acted in haste and that maybe when I brought back the samples I would have another chance to talk to Mr. Schwartz. I thought and said, "No way will I ever go back to work for Mr. Schwartz under the old arrangement." I felt that I had stood up for my rights. It would be Mr. Schwartz's loss. Had he given me a reasonable counter-offer, I probably would have accepted, but now, I could not and would not go back.

My wife, who was expecting again, had to go out, and I said I would stay home with our little girl. I sat down on the couch in our living room, and my daughter crawled up and sat next to me. I held her close and spoke to her. "Well, honey, you helped me out once before – how about helping me now?" She looked at me, and she did not understand what I was talking about.

My daughter helped me earlier while the Korean War was raging. I had to register for the draft and was ordered to report to White Hall Street for my physical. I sat among naked men waiting to go through the various examinations. I was and have always suffered from severe headaches since my imprisonment in concentration camp. I went to see many specialists and had about ten different tests. I had wires dangling from my head. They performed x-rays and examined my eyes over and over. While I was working at the Flagler Hotel, I met an ear, nose and throat doctor by the name of Dr. Dlugash, who had an office on 36th Street in New York City. In conversation, I mentioned to him that I suffered from severe headaches. Doctors were giving me strong morphine pills, which rendered me incapacitated. I slept for hours, only to get up with the same pain. He looked into my eyes and throat. He said that I had very bad tonsils and that this could be the cause of my headaches. He suggested that I come to see him when I returned to the city.

When I went to see him he confirmed that my tonsils had to be removed, headaches or not. He also diagnosed that my sinuses were infected. He removed my tonsils in his office. I also received continued treatments for my sinuses, and I started to feel much better until I got another headache attack. The next time I saw him I told him that I had to report for military service and asked if my headaches could keep me out of the army. He then told me that he was one of the head doctors in White Hall Street. He would give me a letter stating his opinion of my lament, and I just had to make sure to present it to another doctor to make the decision of my fate. As I passed from doctor to doctor, I reached a neurologist. He asked me questions about my health, my headaches, how long I had had them. I said, "Since I had typhus in concentration camp." He inquired a bit more about my past physical history and wrote me 4F. I had to return to him every few months to be re-evaluated, and I was always rejected. The last time I had to see him, he said the standards for induction had been lowered. He said, "I will pass you with the recommendation for limited service." Five doctors later, I was classified 1A and was told to be ready for induction within four weeks. One week later, President Eisenhower proclaimed that fathers would no longer be drafted. Since my wife was expecting a child, I submitted a certificate from my wife's doctor of this fact and I was reclassified 3A. When my daughter was born, I presented her birth certificate to White Hall Street and received a permanent 5A classification that excused me from military service. Therefore, my daughter saved me from going to Korea. That is why I asked my little girl, "What can you do for me now?" She looked at me with her dark eyes. Then I kissed her nose and walked over to the telephone.

I called a newly formed children's headwear firm whose owner and salesman I knew and asked him if he could use a new New England / New York State sales rep, even though he, himself, was covering this area. He was gracious and asked me to come and see him the next day. I called another firm, and the owner also said to come and see him the following day in his factory. After I hung up the phone I had two interviews, hoping that one would work out.

The next morning, I loaded my samples in my car to return them to Schwartz and Lieberman. I pulled up near the building on 36th Street, loaded the sample cases into the freight elevator and said to the operator, "Hold it. I will go up with you unless you want to unload and get me a receipt." He answered, "No, I'll take you up. I don't care what the old man said." Once I was upstairs, I called for the foreman to accept my samples, when the senior salesman of the firm came over to me and said, "You should have talked to me first. I could have straightened everything out. By the way, you are absolutely right – Mr. Schwartz is a pig. He wants to have his cake and eat it too, and I told him so." He continued, "Just stay here. Maybe I can talk to him." I interrupted and said, "Thank you for your kind offer, but I don't think that either he or I can recover from what took place." I thanked him again, said goodbye to my cousin and everyone who was near, and I left.

I parked my car in a parking lot and walked over to my first appointment. The principals were very nice to me. They did offer me the territory, but they wanted to exempt several major accounts. The rest would be on 10% commission. Even this offer was worth more in dollars and cents than what I had been earning. I thanked them and asked them to let me think about it. I would let them know shortly.

I then walked to my second appointment with Mr. Fish of Greenberg and Fish. Our discussion lasted less than ten minutes. He offered me the position, and I accepted. I was to receive $200 per week plus expenses and 3% commission in advance, against 10% on my volume to be adjusted at the end of the year. I ran back to my car. I was so happy. To land a job with the best children's headwear manufacturer in the country after the way I had quit my previous job was unbelievable. I promptly called my cousin Sol and told him the good news and to spread it at Schwartz and Lieberman.

Now it was up to me to perform, to increase the established volume in my territory of Greenberg and Fish and to convert Schwartz and Lieberman accounts to the product of my new company. The best part of representing Greenberg and Fish was that they were manufacturers, while most of the competitors were jobbers and carried mostly the same things. We also coordinated hats with the largest and best coat manufacturers. Among them were Fischer, Coatcraft, Gastwirth and many others. This alone represented a large portion of my income. Customers came to us with their purchases of outerwear, and we matched preferred hats in the color, fabric and styles of their choice. In addition, we had a substantial selection of hats in many versions and fabrications like felt, beaver, velvet, velour and cloth. These fabrics we used for fall and winter, while for spring we sold Easter hats produced out of straws such as milan, leghorn and straw braids in several colors, in addition to natural and white.

The only thing I did not have to complete the commodities I sold were infant bonnets, knitted headwear, gloves and mittens. I held many conversations with Mr. Fish to add these to our line. When he finally asked me if I knew enough about it to purchase knitted hats and bonnets, I assured him that I did. I then contacted the best knit and bonnet makers in the country to inquire if they would manufacture individual styles for us to complement our standard and fashion. They understood my request and promised to serve us, provided we order 120 dozen per style. Mr. Fish agreed, and he and I selected the styles. By the time we repeated this with several knitters, we had a substantial assortment of exclusive knitted hats, gloves, mittens and scarves from infant to preteen. Mr. Fish also selected several solid and basic styles. I said, "These are dumb basic styles. Everybody and his uncle are selling these. We don't need them." But Mr. Fish said, "Let's just order a few hundred dozen different silhouettes, and let's see what we can do with them." We repeated the same thing with bonnet manufacturers, and within a short time, samples started to trickle in. The factory prepared to inventory all ordered merchandise, while I set up a simple system to record orders and prepare the hopefully heavy shipments.

As I was setting up displays in the showroom, I received an urgent call from Mr. Fish to come to the factory. I took a cab, and when I arrived, Mr. Fish was waiting. He said, "I want to show you something, and I need your honest opinion." He showed me the most beautiful appliquéd knitted hats that he had converted from the "dumb basics" that I objected to, into the most exciting styles. He had trimmed them with silhouettes of snowmen, dangling cherries, pom-poms everywhere in an assortment of holiday glitter in ten or twelve different styles. I said, "This is terrific. We'll capture the knitted headwear business in one season." I was very enthusiastic until I asked, "How much will these sell for?" He said, "Between $22.50 and $36 a dozen." I grabbed my throat as if I were choking. I never sold knitted hats for more than $15 a dozen. I then gave it a little more thought and said, "You are at least one or two price ranges above everyone else, but I think they are different enough to warrant the higher prices. I am sure that the consumer will pay for something new." He could see that I liked what I saw. Mr. Fish started to smile and said, "Let's go."

He gave me samples for the showroom, and his son and I started immediately to make appointments. To his son's credit, he had substantial commitments from major stores before the season had started. Locally, he had sold to stores such as Macy's, B. Altman, Best & Company, Saks, Bamberger, and Lord and Taylor. These were just a few that ordered early from us. Shortly thereafter, the orders from outside New York City started to come in, and the new venture was started. It was a huge success from the beginning. Buying offices came in and committed quantities for their clients, and when I went on the road my volume was just shooting up. Everything was working out for me. My sales volume was up. That meant that by the end of the year I would get extra money. My wife was expecting our second child, and I had nothing but good things to look forward to.

Mr. Fish, who was a genius in his profession, was not an easy man to explain. No one, and I mean no one, could produce a better product than Mr. Fish. In addition to his business expertise he was also the last Damon Runyon character and a heavy gambler. His factory was located in the same building as the daily racing paper. Between 11:00 a.m. and 4:00 p.m. he ran up and down, figuring out on which horse, on which track and on which jockey to bet. When he was in action he was somewhat secluded. When he had tips on horses he shared the information with everyone. I could never tell whether he was winning or losing, until he volunteered to tell us. His family spent the entire summer at the Windsor Hotel in the Catskills, while my family was not far away in a rented bungalow near the hotel. During the summer months, Mr. Fish used to call me in the showroom and ask, "How about leaving early for the country?" Friday was the usual day for us to leave, but many times we used to leave on Thursday or Wednesday. I always took my car to work beginning on Wednesday. I was always prepared for an unexpected call for us to leave. He was a very generous man. He always invited me to join him for dinner in his most favorite restaurant, The Hickory House. The company was making money, and I was making money, but Mr. Fish's love for gambling kept the company from exploding.

In the meantime, Schwartz and Lieberman's partnership dissolved, and Mr. Lieberman died shortly thereafter. Mr. Lieberman's son joined our company, and since he was much more experienced than I was, he took over the purchasing of knitted headwear and bonnets, in addition to his selling in the Midwest. I could then totally concentrate on working on my territory and in the showroom.

One day I was working with a very important account when I received a phone call from Mr. Fish to drop everything and come at once to the factory. I excused myself to the buyer and turned her over to another salesman, when she said to me, "What's the matter? Max has a hot tip?" To defend him, I said, "No, not this time. It has something to do with a shipment." As I entered the factory Mr. Fish stood waiting. He handed me an envelope while pushing me out of the door and said, "You got to get to Aqueduct Racetrack in a hurry and bet the daily double for me." I looked at my watch and said, "I'll never make it on time. It's too late." He just kept pushing me until I firmly said, "I am not going alone." So, he ordered his son-in-law to go with me. I ran downstairs to start my car, and while waiting for his son-in-law to join me, I counted the money in the envelope. It was $1,200. On the envelope the names of the three horses were written. One horse in the first race was the key horse to bet with two in the second race. When his son-in-law came puffing into the car, I handed him the envelope, and I drove in record time from 52nd Street to the Aqueduct Racetrack. We arrived a few minutes before the first race started. His son-in-law jumped out of the car and raced inside to place the bets while I moved up to valet parking. When we met inside, he had a bunch of tickets in his hands, and I asked him for the numbers while standing in line to make my own bet. I bet four dollars on Mr. Fish's selections and two dollars on the horse in the first race, and another two dollars on a third horse in the daily double. All bets were placed with a couple of minutes to spare. The horse in the first race won, but the two choices of Mr. Fish in the second race lost. My third selection won. I told his son-in-law that I had bet on the first horse separately and asked him to wait a couple of minutes for me to collect, but I never, never mentioned that I had won the daily double. We left and drove right back. Mr. Fish already knew the results. Smiling like nothing happened, I gulped and thought, "Twelve hundred bucks – a few losses like that would be enough money for me to buy a house."

Greenberg, Fish and I had a mutually profitable and satisfactory association, but betting on horses permeated throughout the company. The only thing that made it impossible for me to join this excitement was that I was saving money to eventually buy a house and never had enough money left in my pocket.

CHAPTER TWENTY-ONE
JOHN

My wife and I were eagerly awaiting our second child, and in February of 1957, my son was born. As in the case of my daughter, I had to rush to the hospital while our doctor rushed to New York City from Connecticut. He no sooner had arrived than my wife gave birth. When I learned that we had a son, I was so ecstatic I can hardly describe it. I had gone from being the sole survivor of my family, to now having a wife, a daughter and a son – a family. I fortified myself with an ample amount of cigars and offered them to people I knew and did not know. I was just so happy. The circumcision was performed at home, and my son, my father-in-law and I were part of the ceremony. Friends and family had joined us in a little party, and my son was positively a joy. Either we were more experienced with our second child or he was easier than our daughter, except for his nightly rocking. It was not unusual to find him in his crib next to my bed in the morning. It seemed that he had his driving lessons while he was still a baby. Before too long, we moved to a larger apartment in the same building, which doubled our rent.

With the added responsibilities, I traveled my territory more often to add more customers to my account structure. Most of the year, when not working in the showroom, I traveled from Monday to Friday and spent weekends at home. That was my time to be with my wife and kids. On Saturday I took the kids to the park where I usually met Ernie, while my wife took care of her personal needs. In the evening, we hired a babysitter, and we either went to a movie or visited friends. Summers continued to be Catskills time. We stayed in a small hotel or rented a bungalow. While my family was gone for the summer, I worked during the week, either in New York City or on the road. While I was alone in the city I spent evenings with Ernie when he was in town, or after having dinner in a restaurant, went home or to a movie. I was very lonely in the city during the summer months.

One day Ernie was rushed to the hospital. He had difficulty breathing and was diagnosed as having a form of tuberculosis. He was in isolation in a hospital on Long Island, and I was not allowed to visit him for ten days. When I saw him, he told me that they collapsed one side of his lungs by pumping air into his stomach. By doing that, the doctor told him that his lung would heal much faster. I visited him every other day.

Once, he asked me to do him a favor. He told me that he met a wonderful girl and that he wanted me to tell her that he was in the hospital because he did not want to call her himself. He instructed me to call and meet her, to explain his predicament and tell her that I thought he liked her very much. He also said that I should persuade her to visit him.

I did what Ernie asked me to do. I felt like John Alden speaking for his friend. When I met her, she was very nice and understanding, and I almost proposed to her on Ernie's behalf. She promised that she would visit him shortly. Their relationship started, and a few months later they were married. They lived three blocks from us, and our long-time friendship now included our wives. Life moved along with few changes. My daughter was now attending school. My son was getting bigger, and my work load got even busier.

You could not get involved with Mr. Fish and not participate in his activities. One Friday morning in August, we had just returned from a shortened Catskills stay, Mr. Fish called me at home and said, "You have to drive me to Saratoga. I am meeting a friend who has good information for Saturday's race card." I protested and answered that we had something planned for Saturday, but he insisted. He had guaranteed hotel rooms and said that his car was in the repair shop; that his son and son-in-law had to work and that I was the only one available. I said, "My wife and kids will be very upset if I leave them for the weekend." He said, "Let me talk to your wife." I handed her the telephone, but apparently Mr. Fish did all the talking. She only shrugged her shoulders and said, "Okay." At noon, I picked up Mr. Fish from his house and drove to Saratoga. Mr. Fish's friend was the chief clocker for the racing paper and the track, and I was sure that Mr. Fish was looking for some hot tips.

That Friday evening, we had dinner with his friend, and he suggested that we join him for breakfast at the racetrack at 4:00 a.m. Mr. Fish eagerly agreed. The next morning, very, very early the next morning, we drove to the racetrack. The weather was beautiful. Horses were running, men with stopwatches clocked every horse working out. Many times, owners of horses consulted Mr. Fish's friend and asked him how their horses looked and the time he recorded. This man seemed to know a lot about horses because owners, trainers and track people seemed to swarm around him.

We had breakfast in the open air, and Mr. Fish was in his element. He almost looked serene. When we said goodbye to Mr. Fish's friend, he said, "I'll see you in your box during the races," and gave him the names of two horses to bet on in the daily double. Mr. Fish asked him if he was sure about one horse, whose odds were in the stratosphere. His friend's answer was, "As sure as you can get with horses. Who knows?" But, shortly after, he said it had a good chance of winning.

We had an early lunch, and onto the track we sauntered. Mr. Fish had passes. We sat in box seats right at the finish line. After we had further studied the pro-

gram, Mr. Fish got up to bet. It must have been a substantial sum of money, because his stack of tickets had a
rubber band around them and the top ticket was $50.00.
He asked me if I placed my bet. I said, "No, but I am going to now." I bought a two dollar ticket on the daily
double and a two dollar ticket on the horse to win. The
race started, and our horse won easily. When I cashed in,
I bought two tickets to win on the horse in the second
race. By the time the second race was over, I had won
$228. I can imagine what Mr. Fish collected. His friend
came down to see him from the press box after every
race. Sometimes he gave him a horse to bet on and sometimes not. On those occasions, Mr. Fish chose his own
selections and lost every time. On one race alone he lost
$1,000. I knew that for sure because I bought his tickets.
His friend's selections were perfect. He selected horses
that could win, but most of them did not pay much.
Hence, the frustration of Mr. Fish, who always made side
bets on horses with better odds. I was only betting my
couple of dollars on the selections of his friend. Consequently, I was winning, while Mr. Fish was probably
losing.

Behind me sat a young woman. From our conversation, I learned that her husband was a steeple chase
jockey, who would be riding in the next race. I told Mr.
Fish who she was, and he asked her if her husband would
win. She answered, "I don't know, but I hope so." I got
up and told her that I would bet on her husband and
bought a five dollar ticket. When I returned to my seat,

Mr. Fish was not in the box and when he returned, he told me that his friend gave him a horse to bet on, and it was not the woman's husband's horse. The race started. Her husband won. I collected while Mr. Fish dropped a large amount of tickets on the floor.

A salesman friend who owned horses sat in a section behind us and, in passing, I spoke to him and learned that one of his horses that could not lose was running. When Mr. Fish's friend came down, I told him of my friend's horse and that he was sure that it would win. But he said, "No way can this horse win. This horse will stop. It cannot run against the slightest wind," and he gave us another horse to bet on. Mr. Fish and I chose the horse he gave us, and I told my friend what I learned about his horse. But he shrugged his shoulders. Sure enough my friend's horse was leading the race, and when he ran around the bend, it slowly seemed as if it was going backward, while our horse went all around them and won the race. I thought to myself, if I could hang around Mr. Fish's friend, I could make a lot of money. Maybe.

He came down one more time and gave Mr. Fish the last horse in the last race, and said, "I'll see you at suppertime." Mr. Fish asked me how much money I was ahead. I told him around $200. Actually it was way over $400. He then said, "Bet everything on the last horse. Either you go home even or you go home with a lot of money." I put $400 in my pocket and had exactly $26 left over and that is what I bet. It was the largest bet I ever made. I bet $20 to win and $6 to place. In short, the horse came in second and I collected a few dollars before Mr. Fish found out. Mr. Fish said he was even. I said I was even and we drove home early Sunday morning. I am sure he lost money, and if he would know that I came home with over $400, he would have been very upset with me for not telling him.

At home I gave my wife the money and told her to buy something for herself and the kids, and if she had some left, to put it into the bank for our house fund. Every so often, Mr. Fish would tell me that his friend called and gave him some horse to bet on that was racing on some forsaken track. I also learned that a man in the factory building was taking bets from all the workers, and when Mr. Fish called me, I asked him to bet two or four dollars for me. Sometimes I would lose $10 or $20, and sometimes I was owed a few dollars. The good part about this situation was that his friend did not call that often. But this did not stop Mr. Fish. He just bet his own selections and was losing heavily.

Business was very good. I opened more and more new accounts. I wrested almost 200 accounts away from Schwartz and Lieberman, and I persuaded my cousin to ask Mr. Schwartz who was selling to whom. I was told that he was very unhappy with my successor and soon thereafter fired him.

I had to spend a lot of time on the road, but I would call home every night. It was not unusual if I was needed at home to drive back at night and leave early the next morning for my appointment. It became a routine, me calling after supper to speak to my wife and kids. However, what was seldom became more frequent and our babysitter was answering the phone, saying that my wife went out to play mahjong. It went from her sitting for us once a week to sitting for us two, three or four times a week while I was working on the road. It was always the same. My wife was playing mahjong or she went to the movies.

The conversations with our babysitter instead of my wife became very annoying to me. One, it was costing me money and two, why was my wife going out every evening?

When I got home, I said to my wife, "When I call at night, I don't want to talk to the babysitter. I want to talk to you and the kids." I further explained that having a sitter every night was a luxury I could not afford. She interrupted my lecture by saying, "I need time for myself and I am not going to sit home waiting for your phone call." I then said, "You don't have to. Just tell me when you are playing mahjong so I won't call, and if you go out, leave a phone number where you can be reached. Emergencies do happen every so often. Every time I ask the sitter where you went or where you can be reached, she never knows." That was all that was said and all that happened that evening. I had said my piece.

However, she was not very helpful to overcome our spat. For the next few weeks, she stayed home most of the time, and I thought that this episode was over. But one night, I called in the wee hours of the morning, and she was still not at home. I asked the sitter if my wife left a phone number and she said no. I thanked her for staying and told her that I would be home the next day. When I got home that Friday, the babysitter was again in my apartment. My kids came running to greet me but not my wife. Instead a lawyer's letter was waiting for me, stating that he was representing my wife for a divorce. It also said that I was to get in touch with him before he started court proceedings. The added insult was that the lawyer was Mr. Schwartz's brother. After reading the letter, I was floored. I could not believe what I was reading. The babysitter, who was an elderly lady and was very good with my kids, asked me, "What's wrong?" My disbelief must have shown in my face. I answered, "It's nothing." I paid her and she went home.

There was always food the evenings I came home. That night there was nothing on or in the stove. I took the kids out to eat and played with them, but my thoughts were not in a playful mood. I finally said, "It's time for bed." I chased them into their room, and it took a while before it got quiet. I sat down in the living room and waited for my wife to come home. Way after midnight, she entered our apartment all dressed up, which was not her usual uniform for mahjong. I confronted her about the lawyer's letter, about her behavior, and then said, "Okay, if that is what you want, you can leave. I will take care of the kids, and you get your divorce." She started to scream at me, "You'll have to leave. The sooner the better. I will get every nickel we have and every nickel you earn in the future."

Her voice got louder and louder. That is when I told her to shut up. I said, "You are waking up the kids," not realizing that I myself was yelling. I turned to go to check the kids. That is when she picked up a big table lamp and threw it on my head. Fortunately, the heavy base struck me on my shoulder, and only the lamp shade hit me on the side of the head. She then came after me with both her hands swinging, hitting me on my chest and sides, and it wasn't until she attempted to hit me in my face that I stopped her attack. I gave her one punch to the stomach, and she sat down on the couch. In her attack on me, l could smell the liquor on her breath. I walked into the kids' room, and both children were up. It took a while for them to go back to sleep.

I did not go back into the living room until I heard someone knocking on the front door. She had called the police while I was talking to my kids. Two detectives walked in, and my wife started to cry and scream, "He attacked me," showing her arms to the detectives. Her arms were scratched from top to bottom. One detective took her into the bedroom while the other stayed with me. I told him exactly what had taken place. The lamp shade was still dented. She was hysterical, and I told the detective that I punched her once. I did not know who scratched her arms. Certainly it was not me. The other detective had calmed her down, and they returned to the living room and told us that this was a domestic squabble. They said we should behave and handle our difficulties in a grownup way and call the police only in a real emergency. My wife approached the detective who stood with me and said, "Look what he did to me! Look at my arms." He replied, "Your husband looks to me like a pretty husky guy, and I can't believe that he would resort to scratching. His response, in my opinion, would be to hit someone with his fist, but certainly not scratch her." The other detective agreed, and my wife turned, sat down on a chair and looked out the window. The detectives asked us if they could leave or if we would continue to fight. She turned and looked at all of us belligerently. That is when the detective asked me if I had a place where I could spend the weekend. I said, "Yes, but I am not leaving my children with my wife – not in the drunken state she is in." The detective said, "She is not drunk. She's obviously had a few, but she is coherent." The detectives asked me to wait outside my apartment so that they could speak to my wife. Their conclusion was that I had to leave for a day or two until things were calmer and I had a chance to think about how to proceed in the future. The detectives, whose names I took, assured me that the kids would be safe with my wife, who promised not to leave them again. I walked into the kids' room and found them sound asleep. I kissed them and left.

I phoned Ernie, waking him and his wife up, and told him that I would have to stay with him for a day or so. I said that I would explain everything when I got to his house. The two detectives and I went down in the elevator while I repeated the entire story again. I would not have punched her had she not thrown the lamp at me and then literally attacked me with her fists. I did not hurt her in any way, shape or form, and I did not scratch her. The two detectives said, "For us domestic fights are routine. It seems that all women and men get the same instructions from their lawyers: how best to hurt each other. Almost every case behaves similar." I said, "I have no lawyer. I just found out today of my wife's intentions." They answered, "Well, she has one." We parted downstairs and I walked to Ernie's house without taking pajamas or even a toothbrush.

Ernie and his wife were waiting for me to arrive. We sat down and I told them the entire story from beginning to the end, and all Ernie could say was, "Shit." He tried to console me, but at that point everything became magnified. I was worried about my children, and started to hate my wife with a passion. My ego was wounded, but what hurt the most was that I could lose my entire family for the second time. It was past 3:00 a.m. and neither they nor I could continue talking. Everything became a blur, and I could not foresee what I would do next. Saturday and Sunday, I did not leave Ernie's apartment. I spoke to my kids and acted like nothing had happened. I then called my cousin in New Jersey, informing them what took place.

Monday morning, unshaven, teeth brushed with my fingers, I marched into the factory to talk to Mr. Fish, who immediately said, "She is a bitch, and I'll get you a good lawyer. He will tell you what to do, and you will do whatever he says." We took a cab to the showroom and held further conversations. As soon as we arrived, he went to the phone and called a lawyer. To repeat Mr. Fish's conversation was simple. He said, "You've got to do me a favor and take care of one of my salesman. He's got trouble with his wife. Can you see him today? That's great. Two o'clock. Just one more thing. He hasn't got much money. This is a favor to me," and then hung up. He gave me this lawyer's name and address and said, "Be punctual. He is a very busy man. Trust him, and do what he says." It just so happened that this lawyer's name appeared regularly in newspapers. He represented the most elite and notorious people. In legal circles, he was what Einstein was to science. I instantly said to Mr. Fish, "I don't have money for that kind of lawyer." But Mr. Fish repeated, "Don't worry. I told him that you cannot afford him. Now go home and see him promptly at 2:00 p.m." I thanked him and took the subway home.

When I went into my apartment my wife and kids were not at home. I showered, shaved, changed my clothing and walked back to the subway. I realized that I had not eaten. I told Ernie that I would have breakfast downtown. I was engrossed in my troubled thoughts. I stopped for a bite and took my time and I was still twenty minutes early at the lawyer's office.

It was a large and impressive office. A secretary sat at a large desk. I gave her my name and said that I had an appointment. She called to announce my arrival and, after she hung up, she directed me to a door and told me to go right in. I knocked and walked into the office. The lawyer got up from behind his desk, introduced himself and asked me to sit down. I showed him the letter I received from my wife's lawyer. He read it and kept the letter. He then asked me to tell him the whole story, from my being on the road to the frequency of having a babysitter, to her throwing a lamp at me, to the slight scratch on my forehead, to the detectives, to what I was to do next. The first words he uttered were in the form of a question. "Does she fuck around? Does she have a boyfriend?" I was rather stunned by his questions, and I said, "I don't think so." He said, "We'll find out." With this emphatic remark, he took the letter, reached for his phone and called my wife's lawyer. When he had him on the phone, he mentioned his name and that he was representing me. "What kind of cockamamie letter did you send to my client?" He then proceeded to spell his name, as if either the other lawyer did not hear his name or he wanted to make sure he heard his name correct the first time. His conversation was very short. All he said was, "All further contact with my client has to go through this office, and I will make my demands known in a few days. Goodbye," and hung up. Turning to me he said, "I'll handle your case personally," and he asked me for a surprisingly small retainer. He then asked, "Do you know a private detective agency or shall I recommend one? We have to find out if your wife is playing mahjong like she says she is or if she is playing something else." I then made out another check to engage a private detective, which substantially reduced my savings. He then instructed me not to leave my domicile and under no circumstances was I to move out of my apartment, no matter how she acted and what she did. I had to remain calm, and I had to understand that if she did not want to be married to me, that was her choice. My choice was to make up my mind if there was a way to save the marriage or to cut it off the best way we could. My lawyer stood up, shook my hand and said, "Think about it, let me know and stay in touch." I was about to walk out when he said, "A private detective will get in touch with you, either in the showroom or at home, and he will tell you what he needs from you." I said, "Okay. If a divorce is down the road, I would like to get custody of my children." He then asked, "Why? Can you take care of them? You are a salesman and away from home." I replied, "I will adjust my job situation to be able to accommodate my kids." He did not give me any hope, but said, "I'll do my best."

When I got home, my wife must have had a conversation with her lawyer because she angrily shouted as I entered, "I don't care who your lawyer is. I'll get my divorce on my terms." I did not answer. I just walked past her into the bedroom, took a blanket, my pillow and most everything I needed and moved into the living room, where the couch was rather comfortable. A few minutes later, she left the house all dressed up, not saying where she was going or whether she had called the babysitter. At that point, I did not care. I was going to stay home that evening and every evening from then on. There was no supper prepared, either for my kids or myself, so I gathered my team and we went to a Chinese restaurant.

When we returned, the telephone was ringing. I answered and heard the quivering voice of my mother-in-law. She had spoken to her daughter and now she wanted to ask me what was going on. I told her the truth and ended by saying that it was now in the hands of our lawyers. I did tell her that I would do everything in my power to get custody of my kids.

I no sooner had hung up than the phone rang again. A male voice asked me if I was Kurt Ladner. He introduced himself as a private detective, recommended by my lawyer. He wanted to know if I wished to go ahead with the investigation. I told him that I did. He then inquired if I could talk freely. My answer was yes. He proceeded to ask me all kinds of questions about my wife. What kind of clothing and colors did she wear? What times did she usually leave the house? He said for me to meet him early the next day to give him a good photograph of my wife.

The following day I met an elderly man, not at all the image I had of a private detective. He asked me a few more questions and said, "We will start the job today around 4:30 or 5:00 p.m. Any reports and information will go directly to your lawyer, who, in turn, will keep you informed." I gave him the picture of my wife, and he showed me a picture of man and said," Should you see me or this man," pointing to the picture, "just keep on walking and don't even glance at us."

I called my lawyer every day with little or no progress. For the next few days, my lawyer could not be reached because he was involved in another case. When I finally reached him, I informed him that the joint account we had was no longer available and also that my wife has totally abdicated as a mother. I now mostly took care of my kids. He interrupted my complaining and said, "We know now who she is messing around with." He relayed to me in detail her indiscretions in a car and other places with a man witnessed by the private detectives. The only thing they could not obtain as yet were photographs, but he continued, "We have enough on her for a legal separation as of now and probably more in a day." He wanted to see me the following Monday morning, but I told him that I had to go to Boston for a show, and I would not be back until the next Thursday or Friday. He said, "That's okay, we are not in a hurry. The two guys have a couple of days of work left. Inform your wife that you are going away to work and call me when you get back."

The show in Boston took place from Sunday through Thursday. I usually worked Friday on the road, but this time, I drove directly home. I got in around 10:30 p.m. and again found the babysitter in my apartment. After we greeted each other she said, "The kids are sleeping." We spoke a little longer while I was going through the mail. Every envelope was opened except one, the telephone bill. I opened it, looked at the bill and gasped. It said that I owed around $400 for long distance calls to mostly Florida and some other places that neither I nor my wife had ever before placed. Just as the sitter was about to leave, the door opened, and my wife walked in. I asked her about the phone bill, handing it to her. She said, "Yes, I made all these calls." She put her hands on her hips and pushed her chin forward saying, "What are you going to do about it?" I answered, "What am I going to do about it?" I walked over to the one and only phone in the house and ripped it off the wall. Well my wife started to scream at me and tried to come into the kitchen to get me but the sitter blocked her, stepping between her and me and told her in a loud voice to calm down. I was raging mad and yelled over the sitter's head, "You better tell your lawyer to start the divorce actions, because I've had it with you, and if he does not start soon, then we will, and for your information, I will ask for custody of my children based on your whorish behavior. I will get them. There will be no more telephone in this house and from now on, I will do all the shopping and pay the bills, because you have not bought any groceries for weeks and pocketed the money. If you abuse anything of mine, especially the kids, I'll come after you. So, let's cut the shit and get divorced." With that said, I walked into the kids' room. They slept through the entire episode.

My wife was still yelling and crying when I paid the sitter and walked her to the door, asking her not to abandon my kids and me because I would need her. She nodded her head in agreement. I then went into the living room, now my bedroom, turned off all the lights and, without uttering another word, I attempted to go to sleep. In the morning, all upset, I called my lawyer to tell him what had taken place. He listened to me then said, "She is doing this to make your life miserable and all on instructions from her lawyer. They are hoping that you will get so upset that you will leave." He instructed me again not to leave and to re-install the telephone because I had to be able to reach my children and to tell my wife to cut out all this nonsense because we knew what they were up to. "Also tell her that you will get the phone re-installed, and if she ever abuses the privilege, you will put a lock on the phone. Believe me, she needs the phone more than you do." He said, "Now everything is coming to a head. Her boyfriend either works or owns a bagel bakery. While you were gone, she met him two days in a row. We now have everything in a neat package, and I told the private detectives not to continue the surveillance until further notice. When she goes to court, we have enough against her to make her cry uncle."

In the meantime, her parents were very unhappy. Her father became belligerent toward me while her mother was less supportive of her daughter, which made me suspect that she knew something. I did not tell them anything other then that we would be divorced, and I hoped to get custody of my children. I avoided my wife. I could not even look at her without feeling great disgust. I saw her as dirty, and I had to stay in the house, not only to be with my kids but also on my lawyer's orders.

The following week, I returned on Friday from working on the road and no one was home, not my wife, nor our babysitter or my children. I stepped out to have supper in the cafeteria, and afterward I went to Ernie's house. At that time, there were tragic results of Ernie's beatings in the concentration camp. His long illness of diabetes finally caused Ernie to go blind. Yet despite this handicap, Ernie was a very positive guy who had courage and optimism and only looked to the future. He instantly went to Morristown New Jersey's Seeing Eye School, and spent some time there in training with a Seeing Eye dog. He came home with a beautiful black Labrador, and with his trusted dog, he continued to work as an advertising salesman for one of our friends. He walked with his dog through all traffic conditions in mid-Manhattan rush hour traffic, in the subway, and he served and maintained loyal clients.

Ernie and I, as always, talked about the best and the worst alternatives I had in the battle against my wife. He was not only hurt because I was hurt, but he seemed to feel as helpless as I did. All he could say was, "You have to do what your lawyer tells you." His wife tried to give me some input from the woman's point of view.

I still had to wait until either my wife went to court or my lawyer started some action. It was very difficult to get a divorce in New York City. It would have to be a provable offence of adultery or assault and battery, according to my lawyer. I could not get a legal separation. But I could get a divorce if she would start the proceeding. I could not quite understand the legal mumbo jumbo; all I knew was that I had to wait. I looked at my watch. It was getting late, and I said, "I'll see you guys tomorrow."

Instead of taking the subway, I walked home. I could think much better while I was walking, and I came to the conclusion that if this situation took much longer, I would run out of money very soon. I maintained a household; yet, my kids and I ate most of our meals in a cafeteria or restaurant. I spent all my free time with the kids but I had to go to work to pay for all my expenses, my normal expenses plus the ones my wife incurred, like the phone bill. I did not know how things would wind up. What would be the outcome? My biggest fear was losing my children and of being alone again.

I opened the door to my apartment, and my wife and children were still not home. I

called my in-laws, late as it was, and was told that they had not seen or heard from them.

I also called a couple of her girlfriends with the same result. It got to be midnight, one, two, three in the morning, still no wife and kids. I sat up all night, and in the morning I called my lawyer and told him that my wife and kids left town. I must have been rather emotional on the phone because I just blurted out the news to him when he calmly suggested that nothing had happened except she turned the screw one more turn. He further advised me, "Rather than hiring detectives to look for them, we'll wait until Monday, then check with the school if your daughter is attending classes. If she was not, we then would report it to the truant office and let them look for your daughter. One day of not knowing is not enough time passed to report them missing to the police. In the meantime, when you leave the apartment, put an invisible seal on the door to verify that they have not returned. If they are gone more than three or four days, we will file for desertion." I did what I was told. Whenever I left my apartment, I placed a marker on the door, and while at home, no one came or called. The entire weekend passed, and no one broke the seal to enter my apartment.

Monday morning, I went to the school to see if my daughter was attending class. Sure enough, she was there. I asked if I could speak to her for one minute, just long enough to tell her that I would pick her up after school and not to go with anyone else. I hugged her when she said, "Okay, I'll see you after school."

That afternoon, Ernie and I went to the school to pick my kid up, and hopefully she could tell me where her mother and brother were. I parked my car. While I walked toward the school entrance, Ernie remained sitting in the car. As I was passing cars, I heard a little voice yelling, "Daddy, Daddy." I looked into one car and saw a man sitting behind the wheel and my son was in the back seat. Fortunately, the door on the passenger's side was open, and I took my son out of the rear seat, brought him running to my car, and told Ernie to take care of him and lock the door. With Ernie not knowing what was going on, I ran back to the guy in the other car, who was now sitting in the passenger's seat with his feet on the sidewalk. I said to him, "Do you know that I reported my children missing and possibly kidnapped?" He started to utter some words just as my daughter came toward me. I slammed the open door against this guy's feet and advised him that he better just sit there and not move. "We will settle this with the police present." He made a sound of pain with the impact of the car door. I took my daughter and put her into my car, after Ernie made sure that it was me who knocked on the window. He again asked, "What is going on?" I answered, "Later," and I walked back to the guy's car, which he had started and was pulling out of his parking space, gunning his motor, almost knocking me down. I had to jump between two cars just in the nick of time. I did not get to read his license number. I suspected who he must have been, but at that moment did not really care. All I knew was that I had my two kids.

Ashen as I must have looked, I remained sitting in my car for quite awhile, telling

my kids how happy I was to see them. Ernie, my two kids and I were sitting in the front seat with my kids partially on my lap. I asked them where they had been, and in a roundabout way, my daughter told me. "We were in a hotel room all the time. We could not play or do anything." I know that they were as happy to be with me. I told them that we were going to Ernie's house for a little while and then going out to eat Chinese food. It turned out that they were at the Concourse Plaza Hotel only a few blocks from my apartment.

When we got to Ernie's, I called my lawyer. His secretary took my phone number and said that he would call me back because he was in conference. It seemed like hours until he returned my call. I told him what had taken place, and he asked, "Do you have a place where you and your kids could stay for a few days?" I said, "I will check and call you right back." I phoned my cousin Lina in New Jersey and asked her if we could come. She said, "Sure, absolutely." I called my lawyer back, gave him my cousin's phone number, and he gave me the same instructions as before to seal my apartment door in order to see if my wife had returned.

I left my kids with Ernie, got a few things from my apartment including a few toys,

put my invisible seal on the door and left. While riding in the car, I reminded myself to call the school to tell them that my daughter would not be coming to class for a few days. I told my kids that we were all going to Lina's house for a couple of days, and they did not ask me why. They did not ask for their mother, and I did not volunteer any information. I called Mr. Fish and explained what had taken place and that I would not be in for a few days. My lawyer told me to check my apartment every day to see if my wife had returned. He also said that if she was not back by Friday, we would file for desertion. Friday morning, I informed my lawyer that there was no sign of my wife having returned.

My lawyer also suggested that in case she did return for me to sit down with her and recommend that she and her lawyer sit down with me and my lawyer to talk. Maybe, we could come to some kind of understanding for the divorce. I wanted this divorce so badly.

However, I complicated the matter by wanting custody of my kids. My lawyer also said

to tell my wife that I would bring back the children only if she promised never to remove them from their home again. If she agreed, I was to tell her I would bring back the kids Monday morning in time for school and let her sweat over the weekend. He said he would talk to me Monday afternoon because he would be in court all morning.

Friday night, around 8:00 p.m., my cousin Lina and I again drove to New York to check my apartment. First I checked the seal and found it was broken. I said to my cousin,

"She returned just in time to avoid desertion." I put my key into the lock, opened the door and saw my wife and my in-laws sitting in the living room. There must have been some heated discussions going on because my wife and my mother in-law still had tears in their eyes. As we entered, my father in-law stood up, walked toward me and asked, "Where are the children?"

When he saw my cousin, he knew their whereabouts. My wife started to cry. "Where are my kids?" She became frantic and the more she cried and yelled at me, the more belligerent her father became. I calmly said to my wife's parents, "She did not inform me when she took the kids and stayed with her boyfriend in a hotel, so please, all of you keep quiet for a few minutes so that we can discuss the entire sad situation." My wife started to yell again, "Before I talk to you, I demand that you bring the kids back." I answered her, "You are not in a position to demand anything. Please sit and listen to what I have to say." My cousin and my wife's parents sat down while my wife turned her back toward us to look out the window. I said, "It would be nice if she would turn around to participate. If not, I am leaving." Reluctantly, she turned her body halfway toward her father.

Just as I was to begin talking, her father interrupted me saying, "This is stupid. We should make up. Everybody has fights." That prompted me to start from the beginning, from when I received the lawyer's letter, her constant absence from the children, leaving them with a babysitter at a great expense. I told them about her not coming home until the wee hours in the morning, never knowing where she was going or what she was doing, (though I knew now), not taking care of the kids, or the laundry, or the cooking. The point of no return had long past, because now I knew where she was going, what she was doing and with whom. All I was interested at that point was to go on with my life and the kids. I suggested what my lawyer recommended.

To my in-laws I said, "You are most welcome to participate. Let your daughter express the problems I caused, and I will express mine. Let's see if we can come to an amiable divorce. But I will insist on getting custody of my children," and I gave them the reason why. "For one thing, I don't think that she is a good mother and the other is that she would like to be single, free of obligations, so that she can continue to have a good time. And furthermore, she once said that I can have the kids." That was the end of my speech. My mother-in-law asked, "What would you do with the children? How can you take care of them?" My cousin interrupted, "For the time being, they can be with us, and in the future, he will get professional help, until hopefully, some day, he will remarry." My mother in-law volunteered to help her daughter to take care of the kids, but my wife looked at her with dagger eyes and said, "I'll decide who will take care of my kids. I will get them, and he," pointing at me, "will have to pay for all of us." I answered, "The way you took care of them all of last year? Never being home when I return from the road? I cleaned, washed and took care of things in the house while you were running around." Raising my voice, I said, "No more. We can do it without hostility, or we can do it the hard way. Either way, I will prove that you are an unfaithful wife and an unfit mother." I then turned to my cousin and said, "Let's go."

My wife started to cry bitterly and in a meek voice asked me again to bring the children back. With this emotional turn on her part, her father got up and faced me saying, "I'll fight you to my last penny." I answered, "Save your money. It won't help. Just ask your daughter how the bagel business is." He looked at me, then his daughter, not understanding what I was talking about. When my wife was crying so uncontrollably, I must say I was callous and told her that her tears did not move me. She shook and sighed a few times, then begged me to bring the kids back. That is when I sat down next to her and, in a calm voice, tried to persuade her to accept an amiable get together with our lawyers. I said that to show my good faith, I would bring the children home early Monday morning, but only if she promised in front of all of us that she would not take the kids out of the house, ever again, without me knowing and most importantly that she would not use the kids as a ploy to get at me or to continue her selfish behavior. She could not bring herself to say, "I promise." That is when her father yelled at her, "Promise, promise!" She shouted back at him, "I promise!" I then asked, "For when shall I make a date to meet with our lawyers?" Her mother entered the conversation saying, "Let's make that decision next week" and her daughter nodded in agreement. With this conclusion I said, "Goodbye. I'll see you early Monday morning with the children."

On the way back to New Jersey, my cousin and I talked about what had just taken place, and even she sensed my wife's unwillingness to cooperate. Her feelings as well as mine were that she wanted the children primarily for the money she thought I would supply, and not because she was a devoted mother. When we arrived at my cousin's house, my kids were in bed, but not asleep. I sat with them for a while and then told them goodnight and that I would be checking on them from time to time. Before they let me go, we had to play our game of "zapitzeling." I wiggled my finger in the attempt to tickle them. I would get within two feet of them and they started to laugh from their toes. Then, the usual "I have to go to the bathroom. I want a glass of water" and, finally, it was lights out. A short time later, I checked. I didn't know if they were sleeping, but I said, "I am just making sure you are okay." After all, it was a strange environment for them.

The next day my mother-in-law called to ask how the kids were and to say that she was willing to participate in the meetings with our lawyers. She also confessed that she was not in agreement with her husband or her daughter's behavior. On Sunday, my wife called and asked to speak to the kids and to make sure that I would bring them back early Monday morning. We left early on Monday. The traffic was very heavy crossing the George Washington Bridge, but we had ample time before school started. I took my two kids upstairs and put my key into the lock to open my apartment door when I smelled something funny. As I entered, it became obvious that the smell was gas.

I rang my next door neighbor's doorbell. She opened her door, and I asked if she could watch my children for a few minutes, and without getting her answer, I ran back into my apartment. I walked into the kitchen and saw that all the gas jets for the oven were on and the gas was escaping full blast. I shut all the jets, opened all the windows, and as I entered the bedroom, saw my wife lying across the bed, her eyes closed, unmoving. I was scared. I shook her, but she was limp. I called the Emergency Police, who arrived within minutes. Two police officers stood my wife on her feet, holding onto her while her knees buckled. Every so often, they stopped before an open window, dragging her and attempting to make her walk. My front door was wide open when another officer entered and took all the pertinent information from me. After a while, I heard a policeman say, "I think she will be alright," but they still kept on walking with her. I wanted to call her parents when I noticed that the phone was off the hook. The policeman said, "I took the phone off the hook mainly for precaution." He then explained, "Your actions were absolutely correct: to shut all the jets first, then open all the windows and the front door." He also said, "You were lucky that no one rang the doorbell or called on the phone, because this could have caused a severe explosion – the gas accumulation was high, but seldom does anyone die from it. This kind of gas is only very dangerous if one is exposed for a very long time, or if it is ignited by a spark from the doorbell or a phone call." The officer and I joined the others. My wife, though disheveled and pale, looked much better than when I found her. I said to the officers, "I'll call our doctor to make sure that she is alright." But they said, "No. At an emergency call, we must bring the person to the hospital. That is the standard order and in the case of your wife, we will take her to Bellevue Hospital for observation." I said, "I will go with you. I have to call my mother-in-law to take care of my kids until I get back." I walked next door and explained my predicament to my neighbor. She said that she would take care of the kids and told me not to worry about them.

My kids were fine. They did not know what had taken place. I very quietly called my mother-in-law and quickly explained what had happened and that her daughter was okay. She asked me to pick her up and said that she would go to the hospital with me. I told my kids that I had to do some shopping and that I would be back as soon as possible. I returned to my apartment. My wife was dressed to go. I assured her that the kids were fine and that I would follow her to the hospital in my car. The officer repeated, "Bellevue Psychiatric Emergency Department, and take your time." I kept most of the windows open, and all of us went downstairs. My wife entered the police emergency vehicle, and they drove off.

I picked up my mother-in-law, who was anxiously waiting for me in the street, and we went to the hospital. We had a long talk. Again I explained the things that had been happening and how they had changed my opinion of her daughter. I had momentary compassion when I saw her lifeless body lying on the bed and later being taken away by the police. But despite all the sadness, I said, "Under no conditions will I stay married to her." My mother-in-law had joined her husband in protecting their daughter, which I understood. She asked me, "What will I do now?" I said, "I'll have to discuss this new situation with my lawyer."

When we arrived at the hospital, I parked near the Emergency entrance. As we walked in, we saw my wife sitting in a separate room with a nurse watching her. The police had left, and as we entered the room and my wife saw her mother, she became absolutely hysterical. She started to scream at her mother at such a high pitch that I could not understand what she was yelling about. My mother-in-law retreated outside when another nurse and a male orderly entered the room to calm my wife and take her upstairs. When they saw how hysterical she acted, they attempted to put her into a straight jacket. She fought them, flailing her arms, with those people trying to subdue her. That is when I stepped in and said, "She won't need that stupid jacket. She'll go upstairs quietly." My mother-in-law did not know how she caused the outburst. I took my wife by her arm and we walked quietly into the elevator with the three nurses following us. Once we were upstairs, they took my wife into a large room and locked the door behind her. I kept looking through the window but all four of them had disappeared. A few minutes later, one of the nurses came out and said, "Your wife is quiet, and everything is okay.

You can return this evening for a visit or better the next day." I took the elevator down. My mother-in-law was waiting for news about her daughter. Then she asked me, "Why did she get into such a rage when she saw me?" I said, "Probably because she saw you with me, thinking that you are siding with me in this messy affair."

I went to the nearest phone and called my lawyer, who said to come to his office right away. I explained to my mother-in-law that I had to see my lawyer and gave her a choice of either waiting for me at my lawyer's office or being dropped off at the subway. She decided to go with me, hoping to be of some help to her daughter. In the office, after I introduced her to my lawyer, she said, "I cannot explain my daughter's behavior," but she still tried to plead with my lawyer to save our marriage for the children's sake. She also said that I was a good guy and that I did not deserve the trouble her daughter has caused me. My lawyer thanked her and asked her to wait outside because he wanted to talk to me for a few minutes.

As soon as the door closed behind her, my lawyer said, "Your wife is not crazy. She is using all of you." He then gave me the following scenario. Her lover dumped her. She came home to a scene. Now she had no husband, no lover and no children. Her parents probably were reading her the riot act, and the only thing she could do to arouse sympathy is what she did. He said, "If you want to kill yourself, you stick your head into the oven, not go two rooms away and lay down on the bed.

She knew that you would bring the kids back early Monday morning and that this kind of gas was harmless." I asked, "What about the danger of a spark?" "That," he said, "was the only thing she did not know. My advice to you... Or better yet, let me explain what's ahead of you, and what your options are. Do you want her back in your life? If you do, you will have no case against her. Everything she did would mean that you agreed and that you forgave her; you would be condoning what she's done. I am not telling that you should not. This is your decision to make, but if you decide not to reconcile, then go home, pack your stuff, put your furniture into storage, give up your apartment and move with your kids to New Jersey. You will be rid of her, and you will have the children. This decision will hold up in any court." I was about to say something when he stopped me. "This is an important decision for you to make. This could affect the rest of your life. Go home, think about it and let me know." He shook my hand and said, "Good luck. Your children and your future is now in your hands."

I drove my mother-in-law back to her apartment without making any further comments. I then picked up Ernie and my children and drove to my cousin's house. That whole late afternoon and evening, my cousin, Ernie and I discussed what had taken place. I made my first decision early that I would not reconcile with my wife. Even though I repeated the options my lawyer gave me, as soon as my cousin said okay to our moving into her house, the other decisions I made came rapidly. I would close my apartment in the Bronx, enroll my daughter into the school in New Jersey and my son would attend kindergarten. My cousin's son, John, would be in charge of meeting the school bus in the morning, while my cousin Lina, would pick them up and take care of them while I was working.

When all this was worked out and properly planned, I then took Ernie home and told him that he had to help me close my apartment. The next day, I made arrangements with a furniture mover, who was the father of a friend, who very quietly dropped off five large barrels for me to pack dishes, pots, linens and everything that was not furniture. My good buddy, Ernie, and I worked all night packing. Even though Ernie could not see, he was a better packer than I was. He was much more organized, telling me to mark each barrel with its contents. He was just the biggest help to me. By early in the morning, everything was packed, secured and ready for storage. My wife's jewelry was put into a bank safe. By 10:30 a.m. the apartment was empty. I told the building agent that I was giving up my apartment and thanked him for his kindness. After all, he did get the apartment for us. I said so long to some of my neighbors, and I was gone.

I informed my lawyer of what I had done, gave him my new address and he said that there was nothing more for me to do. I just had to wait for my wife's divorce proceedings or support hearing and watch my kids so that no one would take them back to her. With this new fact and the fantastic help from my cousins and their two kids, I began to manage my problems. A week went by. I received a letter and a phone call from a psychiatrist at the Columbia Presbyterian Hospital asking me to get in touch with him. My father-in-law was able to transfer his daughter to this hospital, which had a much nicer psychiatric department than Bellevue and a much more hospital-like atmosphere.

I called the doctor to inquire as to what he wanted. He explained that in order to help my wife's condition, he needed to understand my relationship in our marriage. He would appreciate it if I would see him. It would take less than one hour. At first I said, "I am not interested. My wife and I are now separated, and I do not want any further contact with her." He said, "I understand. My only interest is to help your wife and to make her better, and you could greatly contribute to the outcome." I finally gave in and agreed to meet him in his office. He interviewed me for over an hour. I answered every question, volunteered my side of the story of our breakup and stated as a matter of fact the scenario my lawyer outlined. I was surprised when he nodded his head in agreement. He assured me that I had nothing to do with what ailed my wife. It went back much further than before I entered the picture. Before I left, I told him, "I don't want my wife to be sick, but my kids and I had enough problems and do not need anymore. It would be in the best interest for all of us if we could finalize an amiable divorce." He thanked me for seeing him and wished us the best.

A few days later, I learned that my wife, with the help of her father, had signed herself out of the hospital, promising outpatient visitation. She then climbed up the fire escape stairs, broke a window of the apartment that I had surrendered and re-occupied it. To what end, I could not understand. I am sure it was with the consent of the building agent who, after all, was a friend of her parents. I asked my lawyer if I would be responsible for the rent. He said, "Absolutely not. You have changed your domicile with your children. You legally gave up your apartment and turned in the key. You have no lease. Therefore, you can move whenever you want. What she is trying to maneuver is to get you and the kids to move back. That is her only chance, and you refuse. There is nothing more she can do, except take you to court, and that would be just fine with us."

Weeks then months passed while she lived in an empty apartment, without taking further actions, except calling me at all hours, begging me to forgive her. She called early in the morning, late at night, at work. She called my cousins, Ernie, and my friends Nat and Francis, trying to get them to persuade me to take her back. She called and cried bitterly that she understood what she had done and the pain she had caused. Then she swore nothing like that would ever happen again as long as she lived. She could not continue to live without me and the children. I received calls from her parents, mostly from her mother, pleading on behalf of their daughter, stating that she had gone through outpatient psychiatric treatments and that she was a different person and asking, "Why can't you let us see the children?"

While all these things were going on, I had additional problems at my place of work. Greenberg and Fish were not paying me my commissions. I knew that the company had money problems, and I also knew why. My children were becoming a burden to my cousin. I could not move because I did not know how long my job would last. The walls started to close in on me.

The pressure for reconciliation with my wife came from all sides. It came from my cousins, Ernie, her parents, the assurance from my wife that she was a new person, (which she repeated with every phone call), and from my friends, Nat and Francis, whose opinion I respected, but most of all from my kids, who wanted to be with their mother. I agreed that my wife and her parents could come to visit the children. When they arrived, I felt bad because they brought a little boat for my son, but the night before, he had gotten a huge Texaco tanker from me. Before my wife even looked at the kids, she came running toward me and repeatedly asked me to forgive her. Fortunately my daughter interrupted the scene when she ran to her mother. My mother-in-law was holding my son, and my father-in-law stood like a statue. My cousin asked everyone to sit down for coffee and cake. The conversation between my mother-in-law and my cousin was about me and my wife, and it made me feel very uncomfortable. They concluded that it would be best for everyone concerned if I would take my wife back and try to be a family again. The visit finally came to an end and my wife asked me if she could come again to see the children. I answered, "Yes, but only if I am at home."

She continued to call me several times a day, always with the same refrain: "Please forgive me. I promise it will never happen again." My mother-in-law and my wife kept calling my cousin when I was not at home asking her to talk to me and persuade me to forgive my wife. One evening my cousin did speak to me saying, "You should get together with your wife. I believe she is sincere when she says she is sorry. Why not give her another chance? You would give a dog another chance. Why not her?" She continued, "With me working, it is very hard and a great responsibility to care for your kids, especially when I am not home." I could not tell if she meant what she said, or was only adding more pressure for me to make up with my wife. I answered, "I know how you feel. Ernie, Nat and Francis gave me the same lecture, but nobody has asked me how I feel – I feel sick and betrayed." That is how I felt.

On another day, I received another phone call from my wife, asking me to meet her because she had some very important things to discuss with me. I agreed to meet her in the 167th Street cafeteria in the Bronx for supper. She spoke to me very calmly—that was the reason I chose a public place—about her terrible existence living in an empty apartment and that she missed the children and me very much. But the important thing she wanted to ask me was if I would return her jewelry. I felt that she called this meeting mainly to get her jewelry. I promised that I will get it next week. She then started again with the questioning: Why couldn't I forgive her? Why was I keeping her from her children? I very simply told her that my marriage and children had been much more important to me that they obviously were to her. I also stated that she wanted out of our marriage – now she could have it. I told her that I knew she had a boyfriend. I then patiently asked her for an amiable divorce. I again said, "I know that you want to be single again, without responsibilities, and for that reason, I would like to have custody of the children." I promised that she could see and be with the kids whenever she wanted. She was thinking. I could almost hear her brain clicking, hoping that she might agree. Instead she answered, "That is not what I want. I want us to be a family again." She quietly started to cry. I looked at my watch and said, "I have to go. I am leaving very early tomorrow morning for several trade shows." I paid, and as we walked out, she asked me, "When will you be back?" I answered, "Ten days," and then added, "Please don't call my cousins' late at night. They get very upset when you wake them up."

I walked into my cousins' house, where they were anxiously waiting to hear the new episode. I told them it was the same old stuff, only more of it. Reconciliation, family again, forgive me, I have learned, then bring me my jewelry. My cousins still tried to persuade me to reconcile. I asked them, "How can I erase from my memory what has happened? I don't think I can do that and still be truthful to myself." My cousin said, "Time – in time all this will fade from memory. If she is sincere, and I think she is, it then would be best for the children. They will have a father and a mother together again. I am not the answer to take care of your kids." If there was one way to get to my soul, it was through my kids. I had sleepless nights just trying to figure out what would be best for my kids, and I never came to the conclusion to reunite with my wife.

I went upstairs to see my kids. They told me what they did during the day, and we spent some time talking. I told them I had to work on the road and that I would be back in ten days. "So be good, and I will call you every day," I said. I did speak to them every day. Some days they were happy and some days they complained about one thing or another. They told me also that my wife called them every day and that she would come to see them when I returned from my trip. They always spoke about their mother, and I sensed that they missed her. I assured them that they would see her as soon as I got back. With each conversation, they told me more and more about their mother, and I started to believe that she was telling the kids stories about us getting together and unjustly raising their hopes.

When I returned and entered my cousin's house after having been away so long, she said, "You better go upstairs because your daughter is pouting, and she is not behaving." I ran upstairs. My daughter was sitting on her bed crying, while my son was a little perplexed as to what was going on. My daughter ran into my arms and said, "I am not staying here any longer, and I wrote you a letter." She gave me a note written on a torn piece of paper that said, "I am going to run away. Nobody loves us here. They yell at us. They yelled at my brother, and he did not do anything ." I took her and my son in my arms, hugged them, kissed them and silently cried with them.

A while later, I told them, "Just hang in there for a little while longer. I'm going to look for a place for us and get somebody to take care of us. So please give me little longer and I'll solve everything." My kids calmed down. "Now let's go downstairs and have something to eat." Once downstairs, I told my cousin that I knew how difficult it was for her to take on this additional burden and that I would be looking for an apartment and a housekeeper, and if I did not find one soon, I would look for another solution.

After the kids went to sleep, I drove to New York to see Ernie, who thought that the best thing for all of us would be to get together with my wife. I asked him, "How can you say that? You more than anyone else know how I feel." He said, "Sometimes you have to take a chance that things will work out. I also have my doubts, but you want a perfect solution. That seldom is achieved."

The following day I visited my friends, Nat and Francis, who had to listen to me for ten solid days while we planned and worked on the road and who knew of all my problems from the beginning. Their recommendation was that I reconcile with my wife, not for her or my sake, but for the most important reason – our children. Nat suggested that my wife and I should go away alone for a few days, and fully discuss the past, present and future. He said I should find out what caused this to happen. Was there anything I did that I was not aware of? He said that by being alone with her, I would be able to better judge if she was sincere about having reformed and about really wanting to be with me and me only. The three of us talked for a long time on the ride back, and I decided to do exactly what Nat suggested.

The next day, I received two phone calls from my wife. The first was to ask when she could see the kids and the second was asking when she could talk to me again. The day came to see the kids, and that was when I gave her the jewelry and made the suggestion that she and I go away for a few days and talk. She jumped immediately at the offer and started to cry, asking me how soon this could happen. I replied, "I will have to let you know when I can arrange it." I had to substitute for our salesman in Pennsylvania, and I thought that this would be a good opportunity for our discussions. I told my cousins what I had planned to do, and they were elated. I also received a call from my mother-in-law who said, "You are very wise. If I was not sure that my daughter has changed, I would not have called you."

The day came to leave, and it was very hard for me to think of being alone with her for four days. My wife told me about her mistakes, about her depression, and her sessions with her doctor. She was calm. She did not blame me for anything I did, and she seemed to miss the kids a whole lot. On the way back, we had agreed to reconcile, but not to expect that everything had been solved in the last four days. We still had to work to do in order to heal our relationship. She promised to make our family whole and that I would not have to worry ever again. I told her that my job was not very secure and that the company was broke. I planned to leave after I received my last commission check. Also, I insisted that we move from the Bronx to New Jersey, and she agreed to all my suggestions. I also told her that she could see and be with the children until we found a place to move.

After a little search, we found a very nice garden apartment and were told that we could move within two weeks. My wife gave up the occupation of our old apartment in the Bronx, and for the few days we had to wait to move into our new place, she moved into my cousins' house. I had to travel the following week, and I hoped that when I returned our new apartment would be ready. My kids were happy, my wife was happy, my cousins were happy, but I made this decision not totally convinced that I would be happy.

In the meantime, my company could not even pay my weekly draw. So, I told Mr. Fish that I had to look for another job. He and I parted as friends, and I hoped that his business would turn around. I had opportunities to represent other firms, but I kept all offers open because I had seen an ad in one of the local New Jersey papers suggesting "Self employment" as a distributor within a designated area for "Bardahl," an oil additive company. I had seen their ads on television and in newspapers so I thought it would be a good idea to request an interview. The deal that was presented to me was to buy stock from a nearby warehouse and resell it to gas stations on Route 4 and 46 and everything in between for a profit. I could restock my supplies daily and therefore did not have to carry a large inventory. I thought this opportunity would be good for the family to get adjusted, especially my wife and me. This job would keep me close to home and this would be helpful to the new start. I accepted this offer and started to work the very next day.

I could work as much or as little as I wanted, but I had to meet a certain quota of sales. It was easy work, and the gas station owners and managers were very familiar with the product. Some used larger quantities while others used less. For the few gas station attendants who were not familiar with the product, I had a selling and demonstration job to do and most were very impressed with the results. The first couple of weeks I worked, I did not earn a fortune, but I did get much more than I expected.

Collecting the money owed to me was sometimes a pain, but slow payers were relatively few.

We now lived in our apartment. The kids went to school. I was able to be and play with them every day. I came home for lunch and supper daily, and the relationship between my wife and I improved rapidly. My children made friends and visited each other constantly while my wife and I formed close friendships with our neighbors. With them, we went to movies or dances. The women played mahjong, and the guys played cards.

Everything was going well, and everything was calm. I finally received the balance of my commission that Greenberg and Fish owed me, and I concentrated on selling Bardahl. Three weeks into my new job, a friend from Boston called me who was also a competitor selling children's headwear. He asked me if I would be interested in going back on the road selling. He wanted to leave his company for another job in another field, but he had an employment contract with Cinderella Hat Company. He was sure that they would release him of his obligation if he could be replaced with an experienced headwear representative. He explained the virtues of Cinderella, and after he gave me particulars, he asked me if I would go for an interview. I repeated the conversation to my wife, and she agreed that I should go to be interviewed, for it would mean, if I was hired, instantly more money and probably a better future.

A few days later, I met with the owner of Cinderella Hat Company, and after I explained to him who I had worked for, to whom I sold and all my other experience, he offered me the New England territory only because upstate New York was covered by a salesman who I knew from my travels and who always spoke well of his company. The territory offered had substantial volume and, combined with the customers I served previously, I really could have a substantial income. He offered me a draw against commission, reimbursement for expenses and the company suggested that I rent a car, which would also be reimbursed. All expenses would be added to my draw, and, at the end of the year, I would get a substantial additional check. It was a generous offer. I would have very little outlay of my own money. Because of my depleted financial situation, I signed a contract for employment. The company had a very fine reputation for being fair and honest in the market and with their sales force. I asked for two weeks to settle my accounts with Bahrdal. I did not wait until I got home to tell my wife. I called her from New York City, and she was very happy with my new deal.

Our family life settled in. Everything was going well, in business and at home. We moved to a better upstairs apartment. My children were doing well in school. A few years passed, and by then, I was sure that I had made the right decision to have reconciled with my wife. Then the bottom fell out and my life took a sharp U-turn.

CHAPTER TWENTY-TWO
THE BETRAYAL

I was in Manhattan at my company's head-quarter picking up my samples for the coming season. Several salesmen from other territories were present to do the same. In conversation with them I said, "I will leave Monday for Vermont and work my way across New Hampshire to be in Boston on Saturday for our exhibition show." All of them asked me to purchase New Hampshire Sweepstakes tickets for them. I collected the money and promised to purchase the tickets by the next weekend.

Early Monday morning, Nat and I met. He was driving a big car with a trailer and I was following him in my station wagon. We started working in Bennington, Vermont, then up to Rutland and on to Burlington. Nat went on Friday morning from Burlington direct to

Boston, while I had to spend the entire day in Vermont. Late in the evening, I drove to Salem, New Hampshire, checked into a motel, ate something and then went to the Rockingham Race Track. I arrived before 10:00 p.m.

I anticipated leaving for Boston the next morning around 6:00 a.m. Therefore, the race track was the last chance to purchase Sweepstakes tickets because all liquor stores were closed. I parked my car very near the entrance, since other patrons were leaving. My first order of business was to purchase the tickets for everyone and then stay for the two remaining races. I left the track with the rest of the people, and when I came to the parking spot where I had left my car, I found an empty space. My car, with all my samples, had been stolen. I informed the security police, and they, in turn, informed the state police. Now, all the wheels were turning except the wheels of my car.

Stranded and helpless, I sat for more than an hour in the security office, only to find out that my car could not be found and that I would have to leave the premises. Generously one of the guards drove me to my motel. Not knowing what to do next, I called my wife and found out from the sitter that she had gone out. I asked her to tell my wife to call me as soon as she got in. I was going to tell her to go to my company, pick up another sample line and put it on the next train to Boston. I sat up expecting the call any minute, but no call came. I called again around 1:30 a.m. but the sitter answered the phone. The same message, but no call came. I fell asleep and awoke around 4:00 a. m. I called again, but my wife had not returned home.

At 7:00 a.m., I reached one of the company sales-men who graciously agreed to go to the office and put another sample line on the train, which I was to pick up in Boston at 6:00 p.m. I then called my house again and learned that my wife had not come home. I took the bus to Boston and arrived at the Parker House around 1:00 p.m. When I called my house again, my wife answered. As soon as she heard my voice, she became defensive, because I had the nerve to ask where she had been. No one had to turn on a light bulb for me to know what was going on, because her vocabulary was the same as a few years earlier. My anger was elevated when I heard her say, "You have no right to check up on me. I can do as I please." That was after I explained that my car had been stolen. She continued by replying, "What do you want me to do about your car?" and hung up the phone.

I held the receiver in my hand for a long time before I hung it back on the cradle. Instinctively, I knew my marriage was over because she refused to explain where she had been. I walked into Nat's room and told him what had happened. He got very upset. I was stuck in the Parker House for the next few days, and there was nothing I could do immediately. I worked the show un-der trying conditions. The replacement samples were few and did not correspond with the upcoming season, so I kept them under the table. As my customers came in to buy, I told them that my car was stolen including my samples. They left me money and asked me to write their orders. This was a service I performed for many of my buyers, but I was pleased that so many of them trusted me to spend their money.

That evening, I called my house to speak to the kids, only to find out that my wife had gone out, and the sitter was taking care of them. For the next couple of days, I could not reach her. After the show ended, I hitched a ride home with Nat. I no sooner had entered the apartment when my kids came running, and the babysitter was in the background. My wife, as in the past, had gone out. Nat shook his head and said, "I'll talk to you tomorrow," and left. I said goodbye to the sitter, who was our neighbor, and I was glad that at least she hung around to watch the kids.

I must have been in the house about two hours when the phone rang. It was the New Hampshire State Police, telling me that they found my car, but no samples. I made arrangements to pick up my station wagon and thanked them for their effort. My wife did not return until 2:00 a.m., and I decided to wait for the confrontation until morning. When I got up, she was still sleeping. I took care of the kids before they left for school, making sure there was enough of a racket to wake up anybody, except, evidently, my wife. I told my kids that I would be leaving and that I would call them and be back in two days. I waited a little longer, then I woke my wife. She was not in the best of moods. I did not want an explanation from her. All I wanted to ask was if this was a repetition of a few years ago. She defiantly did not answer, but then said, "You make of it what you want, and you can do what you want." With this explanation, I walked out of the house to catch a bus to Manhattan and on to Salem, New Hampshire.

My car was parked behind an apartment building; the side window was broken but other than that, the car was not damaged. I signed the form the police gave me for my insurance company and then drove back to New Jersey and stopped at my cousins' house.

I told them what was going on and they were aghast. I said, "I need a good lawyer." My cousin's employer recommended the lawyer I retained who was reasonable and accessible. Again we hired detectives who established that my wife frequented a local bar and left with a male companion, but their success was limited. They reported that they lost them in heavy traffic or something like that. Between the lawyer's fee and the detective's work, I was slowly going broke, and there was no end in sight. I told my lawyer to stop every activity for I had to accumulate money before the detectives could continue. My wife, I am sure, understood that our days together would be of a short duration, and she did not care. She continued to go out without thinking of the consequences.

Now, my cousin, Ernie, Nat and Francis felt betrayed for having advised me to reconcile with my wife a few years ago. One evening, I told Nat and Francis that I had to stop the surveillance of my wife. Nat volunteered to take up the watching and following. He started the next evening and he was rather successful up to a point until the car was had made a sharp U-turn and disappeared in front of Nat's eyes. That made Nat really mad, and he became even more determined to succeed. I told Nat to stop for a few days to lull my wife into a false sense of security. I then would pretend that I was going on the road but instead I would spend a few days at his house and join him in the chase.

We spent a few unsuccessful nights in Nat's car, when I told Nat, "If nothing happens tonight, we'll stop the night ventures and wait until I can hire detectives again." That night, we saw my wife leave the house and get picked up on the corner by a car that looked like a Cadillac. It had high fins and the red stop lights were very visible, even from a distance. Nat and I followed them to a restaurant in Fort Lee. The car stopped and parked while Nat drove by and parked a distance away. I sat in the back seat as if I were a passenger, when Nat yelled out that my wife and a man were heading straight toward our car. I dropped to the floor. It was quite dark. They passed our car so close that they could have touched it. They entered the restaurant while Nat and I waited. I was convinced that they knew we were watching, but Nat did not think so. We sat and waited until they finally emerged and walked toward their car and drove off with Nat and I in pursuit within a respectable distance. They drove quite a distance along the little traveled Route 9W. Then suddenly, they made a U-turn and returned toward

Route 4. I told Nat not to turn around for a while and to wait until the stop lights of their car faded almost completely.

We then turned around and saw their red rear lights plainly in sight. We followed them along Route 4 until their car turned into a motel. Nat parked his car outside the entrance, always keeping their car in sight. The man went into the motel's office to register. Nat had by then left the confines of his car to position himself to see which room they would occupy. The man returned to his car, drove a short distance and then both entered a room. Nat recorded the room number while I ran to a phone to call my lawyer, but remembered while dialing that he was on vacation. I called my cousin and asked her to come to the motel to witness what had just taken place. She was at the motel in record time. I then called the detective whose private number I had. Fortunately, he was home and I asked him what my next move should be or even better if he could come to the motel. He said, "It is not necessary for me to come. You have accomplished what you need for a divorce." He explained what I already knew, that circumstantial evidence was permitted in divorce actions in New Jersey and all someone had to prove was that cohabitation did take place. He also told me that it was against the law and this could also be a criminal case. To be sure to have it both ways, I needed to call the police.

I called the police, and before they showed up, Nat and I asked the motel clerk who he had registered in a particular room. The clerk refused to give us this information. I remained standing at his counter to make sure that the clerk did not call the room. When the police arrived, they took my, my cousin's and Nat's names then asked the clerk for the man's name who had registered about forty minutes earlier and further explained that a warrant was expected momentarily. Another officer arrived, and both of them knocked on the door after we identified the room and asked that it be opened.

It took a little while before a man and my wife appeared in the doorway, ready to jump into his car to take off. The officers intercepted the man and said that they were under arrest and told them to follow the police car to the police station. Just as my disheveled wife was about to pass me, I said, "You are through and good riddance." At the police station, I filed my complaint. Everyone was identified, and the entire thing took only a few minutes. We then raced to my apartment and found my daughter standing with a baseball bat in her hands, scared out of her wits for having been left alone with her younger brother. When she saw me, she started to cry. I calmed her down, even to the point of a smile. Then I took both of them to my cousin's house. After I put them to sleep, we sat around the table having coffee when Nat said, "I feel terrible for having given you incorrect advise the first time around," because he, as well as my cousin, felt then that I had to give my wife a second chance to save our marriage. I then asked, "How do I proceed now? I still have to go through divorce proceedings, and getting custody of my kids will not be an easy task. I hope my lawyer gets back soon from his vacation."

On Sunday night, I returned my kids to the apartment because Monday was a school day. My wife was sitting in the living room, rather subdued, and I said to her, "Well kid, you are now on your own. I'll pick up the rest of my stuff next week, and I'll see you in court." My children knew that I would be moving to my cousin's, but I told them that I would see them every day, unless I was traveling for work.

When my lawyer returned, he could not believe what had taken place. He suggested I go through with the criminal case, although the law of cohabitation had not been enforced for years. But in case the judge ruled in favor of the law, I could get my divorce immediately. The case came up in court. My wife and her boyfriend were represented by two lawyers. One of them was the leader of the Democratic party and, as expected, the judge ruled it out of his court without prejudice. After the ruling, the man's lawyer came over to us and said, "You should not have any problems getting a divorce in civil court, but in a criminal action, you have no chance." The three lawyers talked for a while, then one made a comment about the male defendant. "He does not care about one more conquest, for he is in and out of court all the time."

I filed for divorce in civil court, and I had no idea how long this action would take. In the meantime, my wife filed complaints against me for insufficient support, which was being handled by yet another judge. I presented my earning record to him, and he set a temporary payment schedule for me to follow. It was fair, and I did not object to his ruling, but my wife pulled me into court almost monthly with the same complaint, and the same judge ruled every time in my favor. This action became costly to me because I had to take my lawyer with me, and I would lose a day's work. When she called me before the judge again, I presented him with this fact, and he reduced my payments. After another attempt by my wife and another reduction, she finally stopped harassing me. The judge asked my lawyer when my divorce case would be heard. My lawyer answered, "No date has been set." The judge said that he would recommend that my case be heard as soon as possible. A month passed. I was out of money and out of patience. My work had suffered. I finally was asked before a court counselor, who, according to my lawyer, had to recommend further action. She listened to my story, as well as my wife's, and she recommended to the court that a reconciliation was not possible. Shortly thereafter, my case came up in court.

I assembled all my witnesses, my cousin, Nat and the two police officers. We subpoenaed the motel log, and my lawyer was well prepared. All my witnesses when asked to testify supported my claim, and when I was called to the stand, I was able to bring her previous misconduct to the foreground. All this was presented without objections from her lawyer. When the judge said, "Thank you Mr. Ladner," and I returned to my seat, I felt that I had helped my case. When I asked for custody of my children, the judge made no comment one way or the other. Her lawyer called her boyfriend to the stand and when asked, "Why did you take her to the motel?" The only answer he gave was, "She felt girlish." Without further explanation, he was excused.

My wife's testimony was almost nothing. She had nothing to say and nothing to add, except that she objected to my asking for custody of my kids. The judge called a halt to the hearing at that point and asked both lawyers to his chamber. Fifteen minutes later, my lawyer emerged from behind the huge door and called me aside to speak to me in private. He then explained that under no circumstances would the judge give me custody of my children. He said that he argued vigorously with the judge about my wife's behavior and neglect and how she left the children alone, day and night. However, the judge just shook his head and said, "No." He further said, "A thirteen-year-old child could be responsible, and an unfaithful wife can be a good mother." He said he had made a note of my lawyer's objection, but unless I agreed with his finding, he would rule against the divorce.

I gathered my cousin and Nat and told them of the judge's ruling. I then turned to my lawyer and asked, "What if I refuse and see how he judges?" That is when my lawyer emphatically said, "There is no compromise by the judge," and added that I must pay her lawyer. I almost blew my stack. I said, "What nerve." My lawyer said that to pay my wife's lawyer was usual. It took a while for me to calm down. My lawyer said, "Wait one more minute. I'll give it one more try." He returned to the judge's chamber. He came out and said, "The judge will direct your wife not to leave the kids unattended and you will get unlimited visitation rights and have to support your children only. It will be reasonable." My lawyer said that he would be returning in two minutes, and I had to agree or lose the judgment. At that point, I had to give in.

The judge returned, the lawyers walked up to him and said something, then the judge

rendered his ruling. I was divorced and a free man, again. Exiting from the court after the judge's decision was not an easy task for me. All I knew was what I felt at that point in time. I felt that I lost my entire family for the second time in my life. This was the most difficult time of my post-concentration camp life.

I remained living with my cousins because of the proximity to my children and my employment in New York City. Living a bachelor's life at age forty was not to my liking. When Nat and Francis spoke to me and said, "You should go out, buy some new suits," which was something I had I neglected to do for the almost past three years, to establish my professional and personal life.

For the next couple of years I worked and spent time with my growing children. Ernie and Nat were basically my only contact with friends. I spent my vacation with Ernie and his wife and my kids, mostly in the rural part of the Catskill Mountains.

I dated several women. Some were old, some young and some very young but I found none to my liking until I met my present wife, Betty, through mutual friends. The problem was that she lived in Boston and I in New Jersey. For a while, we had a long distance relationship, until I decided it was time to introduce her to my cousins, my aunt and my kids. I invited a few friends to dinner, and I knew then that I would be married in the not-to-distant future. I had to break my exclusive contract with Cinderella Hats because children's hats, especially Easter hats, were no longer obligatory in churches. My volume dropped accordingly, and I told my boss that I needed additional categories to sell. He said that it would set a precedent for others to follow. I told him that I needed additional income in order to fulfill my obligations. I added other commodities from other firms, and Cinderella did not object to the benefit of all other representatives in the firm who followed my lead. I now had substantially more to sell and an increase in income.

After that I popped the question to get married. We had a comfortable relationship, with similar experiences. She had two children and had been divorced almost at the same time as I had. We were the same age and had the same outlook on life. The only thing we had to settle was where we were going to live. The decision was made that I would move to the Boston area near all the highways. We found a place, and we purchased our new home.

Since I was representing a ski apparel firm and attending a show exhibition in New York, I had to excuse myself the last day because the next day I was getting married in Boston. Our ceremony was private, with only my future mother and brother-in-law attending as witnesses. It was short but very meaningful to us. A weekend at the Concord Hotel was all the time we could take for our honeymoon, because we had to return to work on Monday.

My wife, her two children and I moved into our new home. My children stayed in New Jersey and visitations back and forth were constant. Eventually, my kids, upon graduating high school, moved in with us to attend college, which, thankfully, they completed.

We have been married now for forty-two years. Two of our children are married and two divorced, and combined we have five grandchildren. I formed my own sales agency, with my wife always participating as an active partner. Our children, although separated by many miles, have their own families and their own dreams for themselves and their kids. My wife and I watch our grandchildren grow and blossom, without realizing that we are getting older, and, of course, we have the obligatory aches and pains. Our marriage has always been filled with great support and tranquility.

The choice I made as a very young man to come to the United States and to turn my back on the country that actively participated in the demise of my whole family has been rewarding. Not so much in a monetary way, but in a rich and meaningful life, in devotion to my wife, children and grandchildren with a feeling of reciprocation. Early in 1966, I sat with Ernie in his apartment when other friends came for a visit and complained about Austria. They said, "There will be a meeting in one of the known restaurants in response to an article written by a German author called 'The Stepchildren of Restitution: The Nazi Victims from Austria.'" Ernie immediately said, "That I must attend," knowing that I represented only survivors of concentration camps. I had asked for restitution way back in 1945 from the then Chancellor Leopold Figl. He promised that once Austria was in a position, he would enact laws on behalf of the victims. I left Austria in 1947. Therefore I would attend this meeting.

The only person I knew when I arrived was my friend Henry Wegner. He and I were liberated by the American armed forces. He was on the death march and I, too sick to march, was marked for execution in the main camp of Dachau. All other people at the restaurant were emigrants who were able to leave Austria before it got very dangerous for the remaining Jews. Mister Grossman's article, the reason we all were there, opened the meeting. He started by denouncing the behavior of Austria to its victims, unlike his former country, Germany. There would be restitution for all that was taken along with restitution for all the suffering. This was fully agreed to by all. Mr. Harding, a lawyer, was named president and my friend Henry became vice president. I was elected among others to the board of directors. I no longer was representing concentration camp survivors only; now I had to represent all victims. That is how our organization was formed. Mr. Grossman became our valuable advisor. Just by word of mouth in a very short time, we had over 13,000 members. Articles appeared in the local German newspaper, and the government was informed of our existence and our demands. The majority of our members were quite old, and the most important issue was to demand the payment of their earned pension. Dr. Harding appealed to the consulate in New York several times, and after every meeting, he had our board of directors meet. There was no response or action from Austria. We decided that we must picket in order to bring attention to our cause.

We chose the day and time to picket the Austrian consulate, and the old ladies and men stood with signs asking for justice. This very day I came down with fever and could only watch it on television. Shortly thereafter, the Foreign Minister of Austria called and made an appointment with us. We met the following week. Dr. Harding and Mr. Grossman did the negotiating, and when the meeting was almost over, I represented concentration camp survivors again. I said, "It is time for Austria to live up to a promise made long ago by Chancellor Figl. Many victims had to work at forced labor and some worked before and after the war and may not be of age to receive a pension. He seemed to listen to me and was very friendly. He parted with a promise that we would hear from him soon. Well, weeks passed and we thought to have another picket session, when the foreign minister returned, and we met again. The result was that all victims who were entitled to a pension would receive one, including all who had been in concentration camps. I was forty years old then and had to wait until I reached sixty-five. That did not matter. We accomplished what we set out to do. One and a half years later, I moved to Boston. After a while, our organization was almost dormant. In 1995 or 1996, I received a phone call from my friend Henry, and he said, "It is very important for our organization to become active again. All members of the original board had passed away, and only Henry and I were left. On top of everything, the wife of our secretary, after his death, disposed of all our records. It took an appeal in the German newspaper, Der Aufbau, for the victims to write to us. We voted in a brand new board, and all of them were survivors of various concentration camps.

It was during a time when negotiations with Germany and with the Swiss were in full force. During our dormant period, negotiations took place with Austria about unclaimed paintings, and an agreement was reached without the knowledge of our organization. A leading organization in negotiating was the Claims Conference for Germany and Austria, who called us to participate in further negotiations with Austria. Years before, its leader, Nachum Goldman, when we needed help to negotiate for the victims, told us that he had given a signed letter that said his organization will have no further demands on Austria if they would give money for the needy. Then they settled for almost nothing.

This time, under new leadership, they wanted a united approach asking for fair restitution and return of all properties to the victims or their heirs. The Claims Conference formed an international steering committee, consisting of members of the Claims and from Austria's Jewish Community. Representatives from Israel and Henry insisted that I represent our organization, and above us all the United States Government headed by Secretary Stuart Eizenstat. Before we even faced the Austrian Government we had to come to an agreement regarding how, when and what our demands were going to be. It was not easy even among us to come to an understanding, and over forty lawyers, also representing victims, further complicated it. These negotiations took a lot of time from our home life. We traveled to Washington several times, to New York, London, Jerusalem, Vienna and other places. Once we were face to face with the representatives of Austria, Secretary Eizenstat wisely separated the groups, and in fact he did the declining or accepting at various stages. He ran himself ragged. Each group was in a different room and each group had to agree. At the end, Austria had to agree. It was not until January 2001 that we had come to an agreement. It was not the best, but the best the aging victims needed. What was important was that we came to an agreement before the Clinton administration was leaving Washington. We felt we had done something for the victims after more than fifty-five years. I returned home, glad it was over, but unfortunately the last negotiated fund was being held up because of pending class actions suits.

A short time later I complained of having pain in my throat. The doctor's visit did not last long. After several tests, an ambulance brought me to the hospital. The next day I had open heart surgery. A long recovery, and eight month later, I had surgery on my spine that has ached since the concentration camp. All these operations left me with neuropathy, aches and pains, lots of pills, and barely able to walk. Our organization is still working for the benefit of victims.

RETROSPECT

A few years before Ernie died, he and his wife visited Austria. Upon his return, he said that it was a nostalgic trip for him, even though he could not see. It took more than forty years to include Austria on our visit to Europe. My wife and I anticipated staying in Vienna for only three days, just long enough to visit my friends and my grandfather's house, show my wife where I spent my childhood, where I lived, went to school and especially where I used to play soccer. I happily met with several friends who I knew from the concentration camp, and our reunion was memorable. We had to extend our visit to eleven days, just to absorb what I had not seen for such a long time.

Austria's young people, who were generations removed from the days of Adolf Hitler, were no different than the young people in America. My question was,

"What do they know of the Holocaust? Could it happen again?" The election of Kurt Waldheim as president of Austria and the rhetoric I heard on television made me wonder. I have also come to the conclusion that my childhood opinion regarding Zionism was all wrong. The heroic survivors of the worst tragedy were willing to risk their lives to have a Jewish homeland and that will extend Jewish history forever. We, living in other countries, have and must continue to support their effort in order to be able to say that we participated in a small way. As fewer and fewer people remain alive who survived the Holocaust and are who are the only link between the truth and the revisionist movement of Neo-Nazis, it behooves all of the survivors to document in writing and verbal expressions their sad past. If only for one reason, in the hope that future generations can read, see and learn not to resort to past behaviors. "What did America do for me?" It restored my faith in humanity and gave me freedom. I shall never forget the unknown soldiers who saved my life in Dachau and gave me liberty.

I had searched for my brother Fritz for over twenty-six years. I knew that he was in Russia but the iron curtain could not be lifted. I had every Red Cross searching for him, every organization, but to no avail. Then I thought that since my search originated in the United States, it might be harmful to him. It was after the iron curtain was lifted that the American Red Cross started searching for people in Russia. We started our search in 1992, and I believe six years later we heard from the Red

Cross that they found not my brother but had found his two daughters. When I contacted my nieces, I learned from them that my brother had died six months earlier.

Since I was part of the negotiations with Austria, I used to call offices pertaining to victims, when, one day, I received a call from one contact in Austria, asking me if she could give a gentleman who claimed to be my nephew my phone number. I asked for his name and she said, "Willy Ladner." I was so happy to learn that he survived the war. He now lives in Toronto, Canada, and he came for a visit with pictures of his mother and father, my brother, who had lost his life in Belgium.

It took almost five years for the class action suits to be dismissed. The court quoted the reason for dismissal as the intervention of the United States government and our organization. Henry and I are in bad health and hope that we will be able to conclude our negotiations with Austria to the satisfactions of the victims.

I now also must sadly report the passing of my friends Henry Wegner and Walter Kormis. In loving memory of all the victims including my best friend Ernst Sterzer who died some years ago, may all rest in peace.

Liberated: April 30, 1945
Written: April 30, 1995

50 Years Ago
a poem by Kurt Ladner

In Dachau, freezing cold, ice and snow,
Where I suffered . . . 50 Years Ago

Hard labor, sickness, exposed to winds that blow,
I was near death. . . 50 Years Ago

Vicious SS Guards tormenting, grinning from head to toe,
Watching me shiver...50 Years Ago

Dysentery, Typhus and lice that seem to grow,
Drained my blood...50 Years Ago

Nothing to eat, quarantined, lost everyone I know, to the
"Final Solution"...50 Years Ago

The Allied Forces came and beat their foe,
I was liberated... 50 Years Ago

Alone, my family gone, recovery very slow, I started
A new life... 50 Years Ago

These sad memories, thoughts that come and go,
Of terrible years... 50 Years Ago

But all must deal with "Life" however high or low.
With hope, there will be no repetition of
.... 50 Years Ago

About the Author

Kurt Ladner was born in Vienna, Austria. When Hitler entered Austria in March 1938, Kurt was eleven years old. Kurt spent the next few months in and out of schools. He was still in Vienna on November 9 and 10, 1938 during kristallnacht, the night of broken glass. After this frightening day, Kurt's parents sent him to Belgium to be with his sister and brother who had escaped earlier.

Two years later, Germany attacked and thousands of people, including Kurt, walked to France. Kurt walked almost all day and all night but the German army overran all positions and he was again under German control. When Kurt returned to Antwerp, he learned that one of his brothers had died while emigrating. His brother had left a wife and a baby. Kurt's sister sent Kurt back to Vienna where his parents hoped to get him to Sweden. Instead, in 1942, Kurt, his parents and a brother were sent to Terezin. Later Kurt and his brother were then sent to Auschwitz-Birkenau and then on to Dachau. Kurt got very sick from all the hard labor; he had dysentery, thyphus and typhoid fever. His brother died in Dachau.

In April 1945, Kurt was liberated by the American armed forces. After a stay in the hospital, he returned to Terezin and then went to Vienna. He learned that his parents died in the gas chamber and that his sister, brother, sister-in-law also went to Auschwitz and did not return. Kurt lived for a short while in Vienna as the sole survivor of his family. He was lucky to get an affidavit to the United States and on May 7, 1947, he arrived in New York. In the United States he had several jobs and met his first wife. The couple had two children. After a few years, they divorced. Kurt sold children's apparel for a living. A couple of years later, he married for a second time. Kurt and his wife have a happy home. She also had two children. They have five grandchildren. Kurt and his wife have been married for over forty-one years and are looking forward to many more.